W9-CPC-178

Lauren Crow was born in Brighton and lived on the Hove seafront for most of her childhood. She followed a career in travel publishing before becoming a writer. *Bye Bye Baby* is her first crime novel.

LAUREN
CROW

BYE BYE
BABY

HarperCollins*Publishers*

HarperCollinsPublishers

First published in Australia in 2007
by HarperCollinsPublishers Australia Pty Limited
ABN 36 009 913 517
www.harpercollins.com.au

Copyright © Lauren Crow 2007

The right of Lauren Crow to be identified as the
author of this work has been asserted by her in accordance
with the *Copyright Amendment (Moral Rights) Act 2000*.

HarperCollinsPublishers
25 Ryde Road, Pymble, Sydney, NSW 2073, Australia
31 View Road, Glenfield, Auckland 10, New Zealand
77–85 Fulham Palace Road, London W6 8JB, United Kingdom
2 Bloor Street East, 20th floor, Toronto, Ontario M4W 1A8, Canada
10 East 53rd Street, New York NY 10022, USA

National Library of Australia Cataloguing-in-Publication data:

Crow, Lauren.
    Bye, bye baby.
    ISBN 13: 978 0 7322 8445 9 (pbk.).
    ISBN 10: 0 7322 8445 7.
    I. Title.
A823.4

Cover design by Matt Stanton
Cover image of Brighton Pier courtesy of Mike Slocombe, Urban 75, www.urban75.com
Other cover images © Shutterstock
Typeset in Bembo 12pt on 16pt by Helen Beard, ECJ Australia Pty Limited
Printed and bound in Australia by Griffin Press
70gsm Bulky Book Ivory used by HarperCollinsPublishers is a natural, recyclable product made
from wood grown in sustainable forests. The manufacturing processes conform to the
environmental regulations in the country of origin, Finland.

5 4 3 2 1   07 08 09 10

*For Tony — my brilliant guide into
the world of crime*

1

Jean Farmer took the call, and regretted instantly that she'd been the one to pick up the phone. She knew the Sheriffs and hated that she would now have to ruin Mike's night out at the Castle Hotel with the news from Lincoln Hospital.

'How serious is it, Sister?' she asked.

'Not as bad as it first appeared, I'm glad to say,' the nurse from casualty explained. 'We're sending her home, but she was crying for her dad and I promised Mrs Sheriff we'd call him.'

'What exactly should I tell him?'

'Simply that his daughter has been involved in a sporting accident. The wound to her arm is quite deep, but the bleeding has stopped, and it has been stitched and she'll be fine. Just ask him to get home immediately, please. Mrs Sheriff is on her way there with their daughter now, and both of them are quite upset.'

'Okay, will do. Thank you, Sister.'

Jean put the phone down, grabbed one of the staff just going off duty to hold the fort at the front desk for a couple of minutes, and headed to the dining room. Mike, in high spirits, and a group of work companions sat at the long table near the window.

She touched his shoulder.

'I'm so sorry to interrupt your dinner, Mike, but we've just taken a call from the hospital. It's Susan.'

'Su—' Mike Sheriff put his pint glass down clumsily. 'What's happened?'

Jean saw some of the colour drain from his face as alarm overrode the alcohol's effects. 'I don't want you to worry but there's been an accident,' she started. Mike had pushed his chair back and was on his feet before she could say much more. 'Mike, hold on.' Jean grabbed his arm. 'It's alright. Susan's fine, I promise. She's hurt her arm apparently, but she's okay. I've just got off from speaking with the sister on duty in Casualty.'

Mike appeared to be sobering fast. 'I'd better go.'

Jean nodded. 'I said we'd get you on your way immediately — but head home rather than the hospital. Diane's on her way back to Louth now.'

'I'm sorry, everyone,' Mike said to the teachers around the table as he gathered his things together. 'My mobile! Some bastard stole it today.'

'It was probably that toe-rag, Wilkins,' one of the others piped up. It was John Buchanan, a bitter sort. 'He's the school fence, I'm sure of it.'

She gave Buchanan a pained expression because she knew the Wilkins family too. And they were fine — their children were allowed to run a bit wild but they had good hearts and Georgie Wilkins was unlikely a thief. She returned her attention to Sheriff. 'Mike you're most welcome to use a phone here; call on Diane's mobile as they're travelling now,' she said, ushering the bewildered man away from the table and toward the double doors that led past the bar.

'She doesn't have a mobile either,' he said, frowning. 'Never needs one.' Jean stayed quiet. 'Sorry again, I'll settle up tomorrow,' he slurred slightly over his shoulder to his colleagues.

Jean answered for them. 'That's fine. Now listen, I don't think it's a good idea for you to drive,' she said. 'Let me call you a taxi.' She squeezed Mike's arm reassuringly, then called across to the barman, 'Dave, just keep an eye on Mike for me, will you? He's a bit unsteady, just had some bad news. I'm ordering a taxi — he's got to get home urgently.'

The man nodded. 'Righto. I'm just checking through this afternoon's delivery, but that's fine.'

'Thanks. I'll be right back. Two minutes, Mike, okay.'

And that's when I grabbed my chance. I'd been playing it by ear, so couldn't squander this opportunity with the woman now out of sight, the barman preoccupied and, best of all, Mikey intoxicated enough to be compliant. Both of the staff had seen me, but what's one more tourist in the bar of a popular hotel and I'd gone to some lengths to disguise myself by wearing a false beard, a hat and a loose coat. Besides, I was enjoying the musty, gentle fizziness of a pale ale after so many years of living abroad. I sipped at it slowly, letting the familiar flavour sluice away the fear; killing time before the real killing began.

It was hard to believe the moment of redemption had arrived. I'd watched Mikey for weeks, watched the whole Sheriff family going about their business. The first time I'd laid eyes on him I felt as though all the breath had been sucked from my lungs. For the past thirty years he and the others had loomed in my thoughts as monsters, and yet here Mikey was now, middle-aged and so harmless-looking.

I shook myself free of the unexpected sentimentality. I would go through with it — there was no doubt about that. The deep wound that he and the others had inflicted upon me all those years ago had only pretended to heal. Beneath the scab of the new life I'd built, the injury had festered.

Now, with the fresh pain of loss tearing me apart, that old fury had spewed forth in an angry torrent. To lose our perfect child, lying so sweetly in his cot as if gently sleeping, his tiny six-month-old body still achingly warm, had sapped every last reserve of my strength. It was the end of my marriage too, the end of a happy life with Kim which had sustained me over the past couple of decades. I rued the day I'd suggested that starting a family would complete us. Now we had lost two daughters to miscarriage and our precious boy to some inexplicable string of letters. 'SIDS,' the doctor had said gently, although it had explained nothing.

I had done everything to make my life work; to walk in the light rather than dwell in the dark. No one could accuse me of bemoaning my past and yet it seemed the horror of my teenage years was never to leave me. And there he was, one of the perpetrators, about to pay for the events of his own past. I took a final sip of my beer and felt a rush of adrenaline spike through me as I began my performance.

'Thanks, see you later,' I said to the barman, who was busy counting crates and ticking off sheets of paper. He didn't even look around.

I concealed myself in the corridor that led to the toilets and watched through the glass of the door as the receptionist led Mikey out of the restaurant and into the bar. He looked shaken, a bit unsteady on his feet, no doubt helped along by the beer and wine he'd enjoyed during the evening. The woman said something to him, her hand squeezing his arm, then called out to someone — presumably the barman — and left Mikey alone. He swayed slightly in a daze.

I seized my moment and pulled off the coat, hat, beard and stuffed them into the backpack I was carrying, before I re-entered the bar quietly. I pasted an expression of slight bafflement on my face, then grinned. 'Mikey Sheriff?' I called softly, contrived disbelief charging my words.

Sheriff stared at me in confusion. I could understand why. Unlike me, he hadn't changed much at all. Greyer, paunchier, those dark blue eyes even more hooded than I recalled, but there was no mistaking plain, duck-lipped Mikey Sheriff of three decades previous. That he had won the heart of any woman was a surprise.

My luck was in: the barman was nowhere to be seen, Mikey no doubt already forgotten in his need to get on with his work. I slapped the man I was going to kill on the arm. 'You don't recognise me, Mike? Come on, you used to call me Bletch!'

I watched his confused gaze as the nickname from so many years ago registered. 'Bletch?' he repeated dumbly. I nodded, still holding my smile. 'It can't be,' he went on. 'Not A—'

I couldn't risk him naming me publicly. 'Is something wrong?' I interrupted. I knew I had only seconds now before the woman from the front desk returned.

Sheriff didn't even notice the clumsy shift in topic. Instead, he groaned. 'My daughter's been involved in an accident, I have to get home. They're calling a taxi.'

'I wouldn't bother,' I said. 'I've heard there's a delay of about forty-five minutes.'

'In Lincoln?' he said, aghast. 'I can't imagine it.'

I nodded. 'There's some convention going on. You can try, but I was about to head off anyway. I'm happy to take you home. It's probably far quicker.'

I took his arm and guided him to the side door, keen to get him out the building before the receptionist returned. Help came from an unexpected quarter. A youngish woman — the housekeeper, I assumed, from her clipboard and name badge — entered through the same door we were making for.

'Hello, Mr Sheriff,' she said, then sensed the atmosphere and looked to me. 'What's going on?'

'Help me outside with him, please,' I said. 'He needs some air. He's just received some bad news.'

To my relief she didn't ask any more questions, just took Sheriff's other arm and helped me bundle him into the cold November night. The chill air slapped us in the face. Worried it would sober Mikey up, I quickly explained to the girl what had happened. 'So I'll run him back to Louth,' I finished. 'Thanks for your help.' Behind Mike's back I made a gesture to indicate that he'd had too much to drink.

She caught on fast and turned to him eagerly. 'Mr Sheriff, listen. Give me your car keys and I'll move your car — the red Vauxhall, right? — into the staff car park. It'll be safe there. You don't want to be picked up by the police, do you? Why don't you let your friend get you home safely?'

Friend? I had to stifle a smile.

Mike obviously shared an identical thought. 'Bletch?' he repeated and fresh confusion clouded his face. 'My friend?'

I threw a look of sympathetic concern to Emma. 'It's been a while, Mike, I'm not surprised you don't recognise me.' I gave a shrug. 'When Mike knew me, I was as big as a house.'

She didn't seem to know what to say to that; I was clearly the reverse now. I kept talking, kept moving, drawing Mike towards the car park.

'No one's told me how badly my daughter is hurt,' Mike slurred. 'I need to ring home.'

Emma spoke to him firmly. 'Mr Sheriff, get in your friend's car and go home. It sounds as if they need you back there straightaway.'

I could see she was about to ask me my name. 'Whoops!' I said, pretending to catch Mike as if he'd staggered. 'Come on, let's get you home, champ. Your family needs you.' I looked back at her. 'I'm sure Mike will ring to thank you himself.'

She gave a grin. 'No need to worry. This is my last night here and I was just knocking off. I'm headed overseas for a year, doing an exchange.'

The angels were smiling on me tonight.

I hustled Mike quickly into the car park, all the while making the right sympathetic noises.

I bundled him into my van, locked his door, then jumped into the driving seat. I pulled a bottle of water from the glove compartment. 'Here, Mikey, drink this.'

'What is it?' he murmured.

'Just water. You need to sober up. Drink plenty and we'll see if we can't get you a coffee on the way home. That will help wake you up.'

'Where's Jean? I must thank her,' Sheriff mumbled as he unscrewed the cap. 'Is it really you? Fat Bletch?' he continued, a note of awe coming through the alcohol. 'It can't be, you look so different, so thin. Amazing.'

'Everyone looks amazing through slightly pissed eyes, Mike,' I said, pulling out of the car park. 'But I'll take the compliment. I work out, keep myself fit.'

'I can hardly believe it's you. I would never have recognised you.' He yawned.

'You could say I've reinvented myself along with the new body.' I grinned at him.

He paused then; no doubt the memories were crashing back, closing in around us. No amount of alcohol could fully block those horrors.

'I don't know what to say,' he admitted, and I felt a small stab of admiration that he at least said that much. 'What can I say that can —'

'Nothing, Mikey. Nothing you can say will change it.' I held his abashed stare. 'So don't try, eh? It was almost three decades ago.'

'No, but —'

'Please, don't. I never allow myself to think about about it, let alone talk about it. If I can bear it, you can bear not to discuss it, eh?' I gave him a friendly punch, but he looked like a startled deer, ready to flee. 'Keep drinking,' I said. 'We have to sober you up.'

I watched as he tipped almost half of what was left in the water bottle down his throat. It was enough; I could relax now.

'What are you doing here, anyway?' he said. He was concentrating hard on not slurring.

'Work,' I answered brightly. 'It's such a beautiful city and that cathedral at night — wow! I was just having a beer at the hotel and planning to drive around and enjoy all these fabulous old buildings and landmarks in the dark.'

'A long way from Brighton,' he murmured, leaning against the window.

'Too right,' I replied quickly. 'Drink the rest, you'll feel better shortly.'

'I feel worse. I was coming good, now I feel blurry again. I don't want to be here with you. It's embarrassing. I feel awkward and ashamed. Please don't behave so generously towards me. I don't want your pity and I don't deserve it.'

I smiled in the dark and watched him give another big yawn.

Mikey was mine.

When Mikey came to, he found himself slumped in the back of the van with me hovering above him, snapping on thin surgical-like gloves.

Despite the alcohol on his breath, he was sober enough to think clearly. Terror does that to you.

'What's happening? Why have you tied me up? What happened to your hair?' he asked, fear escalating in his voice as he took in the van's interior, the torchlight, the hideous distortion of the face of the person they had once called Bletch.

'Oh, I took my wig off. Do you like my mask?' I said. 'It's not nearly as much fun as your clown masks, but I've heard that a stocking over the head and face is great for preventing DNA drifting down. Same with the gloves. And I'll be burning my clothes later — there are plenty of bonfires around tonight.' I paused. 'Does the fifth of November mean anything to you, Mikey? It's highly significant for me.'

It was as if he'd heard none of what I'd just said. 'Where are we?' he demanded.

'Oh, Mike, this is salubrious compared with the places you chose for me. But don't worry, I'm taking you somewhere else, somewhere that should prompt memories — not that you'll be aware of them.' I smiled, the gesture no doubt terrifying in the torchlight. 'Do you know, I've been afraid of anything tunnel-like for thirty years, ever since you guys grabbed me in the Hove twitten. You can't imagine how something like that impacts on your life.'

I added, 'You remember what you did, don't you, Mike? I can't remember much myself — not that first time. I was so drugged, you see. Just like you'll be again in a moment. But I wanted us to have this chat so you know what is happening and why. Now, I want you to take these. They're stronger than the stuff I gave you before.' I held out two tablets.

He shook his head, understanding dawning as the memories flooded back. He opened his mouth again. 'A —'

'No pleading, Mikey.' I waved a finger at him. 'I tried that too. It doesn't work. So save your pride. Be courageous instead and go to your death bravely.'

'Death? No!'

'Mikey, I suggest you swallow these pills and save yourself the most exquisite pain, because even courage won't get you through what I have in store. What I gave you in the water was just a light dose, which is why you're awake now. But, believe me, you don't want to wake up in the middle of what I have planned for you. Oh, wait, before you take them, help me get your trousers down, will you, mate? Be easier if we did that first.'

I slapped the duct tape across his mouth so there would be no screaming, removed the knife from its sheath and began undoing his belt. It didn't take much imagination for my captive to appreciate what I intended. He made mewling sounds behind the tape, his eyes flicking to the tablets I'd laid beside him.

'Ah, I knew you'd see sense. Okay, I'll help you with those in a moment, but help me here and lift your arse.'

He obliged, clearly terrified of antagonising me any further.

'Oh, Mikey, still got the eczema, I see,' I said, looking at his groin. 'Must be itchy, eh? You poor sod. Now, are you going to yell?' I grabbed the flaccid bundle between his legs. 'Because if you are, I'll cut you immediately and you can feel all the pain as you bleed to death. And then I'll be obliged to punish you properly by killing someone you love. Diane, perhaps? Rob, Susan?'

His eyes became wider still as I named his wife and children, and he shook his head.

'Alright then, Mikey. I'm trusting you not to begin shouting — not that it will help because we're in the middle of nowhere, but I hate noise.'

I helped him to sit up a little straighter before I ripped the tape from his mouth and stuffed half a dozen of the tablets onto his tongue. The knife was frighteningly close to his face as he drank the sedatives down.

'Swallow, Mikey, you want these to work, I promise you.' He obliged, greedily drinking.

'You're a champ,' I said. 'Now, as Pierrot once suggested, let's be friends and have a nice chat.'

'Please … we were kids, it was so long ago.'

'That doesn't excuse it. You're right, we were kids. But then Pierrot came on the scene and it all turned nasty. I kept hoping you'd all come to your senses and rebel against him, but you didn't. You let him do whatever he wanted. Do you remember him jumping on me? Have you any idea what that did?'

He began to blather. 'I'm sorry, I'm so sorry. You began to cry and we got scared. We were cowards, I know. There was so much more we could have done but we were frightened. We were just kids. I'm sorry.'

'I am too, Mikey, but it doesn't change a thing. You see, you lot had a choice. I didn't. You could have got help. You could have dragged him away — there were enough of you. You could have just said no. Twice you could have saved me, but you didn't. Which of you killed my dog, by the way?'

'What?' he said, confused by the sudden change of subject.

'Beano, my dog. One of you stabbed him. Who was it?'

'It was him! Always him.' Mike was sobbing now. 'Phil did his best to save your dog — I think he even got cut quite badly.'

'That makes me feel so much better, Mike, thanks for telling me.' My sarcastic tone was sharp enough to cut through the drug haze that was claiming him.

'I see the R2 is taking effect,' I went on. 'It's called the "date rape" drug — did you know that? Today's version turns blue in liquid, so guys can't slip it into girls' drinks. But I saved these from my mother's medicine cabinet all those years ago. They're just like the ones Pierrot used on me.'

His eyelids were sagging. 'Good, Mikey. Now it's all easy for you. Just go to sleep and don't wake up. It's time for you to pay for your sins. I've been paying for them for decades. Why should I suffer alone?'

'Why now?' he slurred.

'Because, Mikey, I need someone to blame for all the pain in my life. I need to fix it and set things right. I blame the Jesters Club — I still have your funny note somewhere. *Happy Birthday*, it said, and then, *Let's face it, no one else is ever going to fuck you.* Signed: *Pierrot, Coco, Bozo, Cooky and Blinko.* Humorous, eh?' I sighed loudly for his benefit. 'I think I've entered what you'd call a psychotic episode. I can't be sure, but my psychiatrist could probably throw some light on it.'

'You seem so sane,' he slurred, trying to remain awake.

I laughed bitterly. 'So did Pierrot. But he was nuts and you all followed him like dumb sheep. What was his name, Mikey? I'll pay him back for you, I promise.'

He slumped against the side of the van, unable to hold himself upright. 'Flynn,' he mumbled. 'Don't know the rest.'

He slipped into unconsciousness and there was nothing left for me to do but get on with my grim task.

My thoughts began spiralling into the dark of the past. The floodgates I had locked so very tightly these past thirty years opened and the memories gushed back as freshly as if the events had occurred only moments ago. I could even smell the blood, as though it had just been freshly spilled.

And with the memories came a white rage that burned away the terror. Suddenly I was calm and precise; there would be no sympathy for my victim. I knew that killing the members of the mocking Jesters Club was the only way I could kill the suffering of so long.

'This is for Beano,' I said as the knife slid cleanly, easily, into Michael Sheriff's body. Mercifully, there was no spume of blood; his heart must have already stopped due to the drug overdose. I withdrew the knife and wiped the blade clean, then went to work.

The emasculation was easy and I placed the bloody pile in Mikey's hands. It seemed as good a place as any, and would no doubt give the police something to think about.

I sliced through his fleshy lips to reveal his teeth and gums. The debris from his ruined mouth joined the glutinous mass in his hand. He grinned at me now with a horrible leer.

'Now the final touch,' I told him, and pulled a small paint pot from my plastic bag — a tester size with the romantic-sounding name of Santorini.

'I'd like to go to Santorini,' I said to Mike conversationally as I dipped his fingers into the pot and smeared the paint on his cheeks. 'I'd like to ride a donkey up the hillside, and then look at that famous church's blue-domed roof, just like I've seen in the travel brochures, and sip a chilled light red on a balmy night on one of the rooftop tavernas.

'Perhaps I'll go there when this is over,' I said. But Mikey didn't reply.

2

DCI Hawksworth shifted uncomfortably in a chair in his chief's office. The striped shirt that his sister had sent him from one of her favourite stores in Australia felt itchy. He sighed, knew he should have washed it before wearing it, but it had arrived last night, wrapped in tissue paper and boxed. Today was his birthday and he'd felt obliged to wear it, even though it was clearly a summer shirt, and barely a crisp nine degrees outside. Thank goodness for his thick winter overcoat. He squirmed again as his Superintendent, Martin Sharpe, blustered in.

'Sorry, Jack,' he said, waving some files to explain the delay. Then he stopped. 'Er, that's a very . . . colourful shirt.'

'It's my birthday, sir. A present from Amy.'

'Ah, how is she? Still hitched to that bloke down under?' Sharpe said, lowering himself heavily into his chair, the polished buttons on his black uniform straining slightly at his belly.

Jack smiled fondly to himself, appreciating how Sharpe's sweet tooth was taking its toll. 'Robert, sir. Yes, I think we've lost her fully to the Aussies.'

Sharpe groaned. 'Please don't tell me she supports their First Eleven now.'

Jack grinned. 'I'm afraid she paints her face green and gold at the cricket and has now adopted her own football team. Apparently Man United is no longer sexy enough. Have you ever watched one of those Australian Rules games, sir?'

'Bloody rubbish — can't make head nor tale of it. All that bouncing and catching, running with the ball and leaping into the air like fairies.'

'I don't think they're fairies, sir. From what I see, it's quite a rough game.'

'Well, so long as they don't try and introduce it here in the land of real football! Mind you, Sydney looked magnificent on all the Olympics promotions. Must go see it sometime.'

Jack Hawksworth made a sound of regret. 'Amy begged me to go over for it. It's a beautiful city, sir — in fact, she wants me to visit this year.'

'Well, I don't think you can go anywhere for the moment, Jack. We need you here.'

'Something come up?'

Sharpe nodded, but before he could say anything further, his assistant, Helen, knocked at the door. 'Coffee, gents?' She smiled at Jack.

'I love you, Helen, you know that don't you?'

'I'm immune to your charms, Jack.'

'You must be the only woman who is,' the Super chipped in and then winked at his colleague, who'd bristled. 'Settle, Jack. I'd forgotten that it's his birthday, Helen ... we can tease him all we want.'

She smiled at Hawksworth again. 'I'll be back with the coffee. And here's the pathology report you wanted, sir.'

Sharpe nodded his thanks as she closed the door. 'Don't be too touchy, Jack, m'boy. Unless you plan radical plastic surgery, you've got to live with those looks . . . and their consequences.'

'Was that a compliment, sir, or are we back to that old chestnut?'

His superior shrugged. 'I've been telling you that for years, no need to get the hump, m'boy.'

Hawksworth sighed. He didn't think the shadow of Liz Drummond would ever disappear. 'Tell me about this case, sir.'

'We don't really know what we've got here.' Sharpe pushed a file towards the man he'd been grooming for fifteen years to reach this senior role. 'Lincolnshire Police found the body of a man named Michael Sheriff, from Louth, three months ago in the old quarter of Lincoln. No clues as yet to the killer, although he certainly left his calling card.' Sharpe nodded towards the manila folder.

The younger man frowned, opened the file and reacted as Sharpe had anticipated to the series of photos.

'No lips.' He looked up, puzzled. 'What's the significance?'

The Superintendent shrugged. 'We're yet to discover. The genitals, as you can see, were removed and placed in the victim's hands. We don't know what the blue paint on the fingers and face mean, either.'

'How did he die?'

Sharpe held up a finger and opened the pathology file that Helen had just delivered. Hawksworth studied the photos again. The victim was broad, not especially tall, looked to be in his mid-forties perhaps.

Sharpe continued. 'Ah, it seems the more artistic cutting work was done post-mortem. Alcohol and the presence of flunitrazepam suggest he was likely unconscious, if not dead, before being stabbed. It was a huge dose of the drug.'

'So the stabbing was just to make sure,' Jack commented, unable to take his eyes off the hideous lipless grin that left the victim's teeth permanently exposed.

'Don in pathology is suggesting that the killer is left-handed. We know the victim was married with two children; forty-four years of age. A teacher. Nothing out of the ordinary — not into anything known to the police.' Sharpe pushed the pathology report across the desk. 'Here, you can read it all.'

'Sir, presumably the Lincolnshire boys have it all covered. What has this to do with the Yard?'

His superior lifted another file from his desk. 'Because three days ago a forty-five-year-old male — a Clive Farrow — was found dead in the public toilet block of Springfield Park.'

'Hackney Marshes? We shouldn't be surprised.'

'We should when the MO's the same as for our killer from Lincoln. Farrow lived in Hackney just off Lower Clapton Road with his partner, Lisa Hale. They'd been engaged for four years. He was a year older than Sheriff.'

'Identical death, you're saying?'

Sharpe shrugged lightly. 'Certain classic highlights — the lips removed, emasculation, presence of the identical drug.'

'No alcohol this time?'

'Seems not. Everything's in this file.'

'So we have a serial killer? Is that what you think?'

'Who can say yet, but two bodies suffering a similar fate, seemingly at the hands of the same murderer, suggests a serial killing to me.'

The door opened and the smell of roasted coffee beans drifted in with Helen and her tray. She put a tiny pink fondant fancy in front of Jack. In its creamy centre she'd placed a pale green birthday candle. The garish colours echoed his striped shirt. 'Couldn't resist it,' she admitted sheepishly, and squeezed his shoulder.

'I can forgive you, Helen, but only because this is the real stuff,' Jack quipped in response, loudly inhaling the aroma of the coffee.

'Oh well, since Martin got back from Rome he's been unbearable. Not even plunger coffee is good enough any more — I have to boil the stuff.' She pulled a face of mock despair for Jack's benefit before withdrawing.

Martin motioned for his subordinate to enjoy the treat. He sipped, sighed at the taste of properly percolated coffee, and gave his instructions. 'This is now the Yard's case — we're pulling both events under one unit — and you've got the nod to run it. Get a team together, Jack. Obviously we need cooperation from the boys over in Lincoln, so I don't need to tell you to move into their regions with a light tread. Who would you bring under your command?'

Jack frowned in concentration. 'Brodie, he's tough and he's good, I trust him. Swamp — always reliable and adds the maturity an operation needs. I think Kate Carter's as sharp as they come, I like the way her mind works. I also got to know a young constable while she was in detective school at Hendon. She's a whiz on our database, HOLMES, and a qualified indexer, which I need on the team anyway. DS Sarah Jones — she'd be great. A handful of PCs, of course. I'll put together a list.'

The Super nodded.

Jack looked up from the notes he was scribbling. 'Have we done a profile yet?'

'No, but I'm sure John Tandy over at FSS will have a field day with this material. You can have whatever you need.'

Jack approved. Tandy was one of the better profilers out of the Home Office. 'What are we telling people?'

'We'll be making a statement for this evening's news. As little information as possible, of course. I want you there, Jack. Helen will let you know what time.'

Hawksworth nodded unhappily but said nothing. He sat forward to finish his coffee and felt the scratch of the new cotton again.

Sharpe continued, ignoring his protégé's reluctance to appear on TV. 'SCD has formally named your investigation Operation Danube.'

'Another river?' Jack groaned. 'Can't they dream up something more exotic for major operations?'

'Consider yourself lucky it wasn't Yangtze!' Sharpe smiled apologetically.

'Hmmph,' said Jack as he drained his cup, then looked at his chief, waiting for the signal that the meeting was at an end. However, it seemed the Super had more to say and Jack guessed where they were headed.

'This next bit has to be said, Jack.'

The DCI raised his hands, his expression one of pain. 'Please, sir, you don't —'

'I do, though. This is my job, Jack. You get to catch criminals, I get to keep my personnel on the straight and narrow — none more important in my eyes than you. You understand what's at stake here?'

'I do, sir,' Jack said, grimly.

'I hope so, son. This is the test. Most don't get a second high-profile chance. Your work is exceptional — we all agree on that. None more supportive than myself, but I'm biased. Since your mother and father ... well, you know that Cathie and I have felt like parents to you. But we lost a man and everyone wants someone to blame in such circumstances. It was clearly not your fault, but I want you squeaky clean from here on. On the other hand, I'd suggest you don't get too defensive. I know a lesson was learned when you were an up-and-coming detective. Now it's time to let it go.'

'Then why do I feel as though I can't ever be too careful? That inquiry wanted to haul me over the coals, sir.'

'You were exonerated,' the older man said, peering over the rim of his glasses.

'Mud sticks.'

'Well, you just have to learn to be less prickly, DCI Hawksworth, and more slippery. Don't give it anything to stick to.'

'Liz and I,' he began, then shrugged. 'It was a mistake, sir.'

'Don't make it again,' the Super said, his gaze searing, determined to leave an impression on the younger man. 'In light of that, are you sure Kate Carter is the right choice?'

Jack's bowed head snapped up as if he'd been slapped. 'Superintendent Sharpe, I don't —'

'DCI Hawksworth,' the senior man interrupted gently, 'this is not about whether *you* would seduce DI Carter. This is about DI Carter's susceptibility. It's about temptation, an extremely good-looking female detective and a rather too eligible boss. I may be sixty-four, Jack, but I have not forgotten the drive of a young libido. I also have spies everywhere, none more capable than Helen. She keeps her ear to the ground and we know just how much of a talking point you are with the females. Something like this could seriously compromise you. You're the rising star of the Force, Jack.' Sharpe paused before adding emphatically, 'Don't blow it!'

'Sir,' Jack said, through gritted teeth, 'if we followed that theory I'd have to keep women out of this operation altogether, and then we'd be up for a different sort of inquiry! And just for the record, sir, DI Carter is engaged to be married.' He held his temper as the old man chuckled, his mirth suggesting he didn't believe that fact would stop a romance occurring.

'It got ugly last time, Jack, and apart from the death of Paul Conway, the Met lost a very good DS in Liz Drummond. I was able to protect you then, but your profile is too high now. You have jealous colleagues and the desire to constantly cut someone successful down to size is alive and well at the Yard.'

'I understand, sir.'

'Look in the mirror tonight, Jack. Get some sense of the fact that your good looks are what nearly undid you ... and could again. Use them to charm the Met's hierarchy, but save any amorous pursuits for women outside of the Force. Sleep with a schoolteacher, for pity's sake.'

'I hear you,' Jack said, working hard not to show his exasperation. He stood, moved to the door. 'I'll get on, sir.'

'One more thing, Jack.'

'Sir?'

'Try very hard to follow the rules on this one, eh?'

'I was right on Operation Destiny.'

'Yes, you were, but you took one too many chances. At the risk of being tedious, Jack, I'll remind you again that a lot is at stake. This is your return to the big time — you have been given what is arguably the most high-profile criminal case the Yard has had to deal with in a long time. The media will go into a feeding frenzy once they get the first sniff of a possible serial killer. I want you to be hailed as a hero when you get this bastard, and I don't want any dirty linen being aired in the Yard over your handling of it.' His Superintendent gave a final warning. 'And I don't want a third lipless, dickless corpse on our hands, Jack. Move fast because the media will be onto this in moments.'

Jack didn't need to be reminded. He could already see the first shrieking headline in his mind: KILLER GIVES KISS OF DEATH. He grimaced. 'Well, let's keep the details from them as long as we can.'

'Happy birthday, Jack,' Sharpe added, more gently. 'Find this bastard for me.'

What a day! But he'd finally secured the operations rooms, set up the request for phone numbers, spoken to IT regarding all the equipment required — computer terminals with full CAD, NC and MSS capabilities, as well as additional PCs for HOLMES, the database. He had contacted the relevant webmaster to ensure the Danube home address with contact details was already in the public domain and ready to take daily updates. Most importantly, he'd ensured Joan Field was a cert as the operation's receptionist and all-round mother figure. Joan was the best — kind, firm, generous, tough. All qualities that would anchor a team coming under intense pressure and would keep the baying dogs of the media, the public and their own hierarchy at arm's length.

He had also set up a temporary office at Wellington House, where the new team would gather the following afternoon for their first briefing. Finally, he had called around the country and pulled in the team itself. Everyone had leapt at the chance to work on the high-profile case and he was delighted that each of the senior members — the DIs who would drive the investigation — were now attached to Operation Danube. SCD Reserve had been alerted. It was likely that he'd need to pull in officers and-or clerical staff from the 24-hour available roster at short notice. His mind was whirring with all the details as he finally set off from the Yard that evening.

Jack preferred not to take his roadster to work but he'd have given anything to have it to get him home quickly. By the time he'd battled the Victoria Line's late-night shopping crowd and changed at Euston for the four stops northbound to Archway, he was feeling the weight of fatigue of this busy day. Not only had it included setting up one of the Yard's most important investigations, but there'd also been the key press conference.

Jack had rung the Super before he left the Yard that evening with a promise that in another seventy-two hours they would have broken new ground on the two cases and would have something to tell the media at Monday morning's follow-up press conference. It had sounded hollow even to his ears, but Jack knew he had to remain positive. Sharpe had understood, of course. He had been there enough times himself.

But Jack had also grasped that there was pressure from above and the need for the police to be seen to be making headway on this high-profile case. Journos had picked up the trail since this evening's gathering of the media, and Hawksworth had already been forced to put a constable with a friendly but firm approach onto the phones full-time to deflect the media interest.

Normally Jack relished the long walk up the hill past Whittington Hospital to Waterlow Park near where he lived. But by the time he reached Highgate Village this evening he was desperate for a shower, a glass of wine and a couple of hours of moronic TV — anything to take his mind off mutilated bodies and the lack of leads he would be presenting to his new team. Nevertheless, he turned at the top of the hill, as he always did, and admired the view across London. Highgate was a prized address and once again Jack counted his blessings. There were no positives to losing parents so young in such horrific instances. The motorway crash had given him his inheritance early and he had been determined not to squander it on anything but the bricks and mortar his father would have approved.

The parklands that surrounded the suburb, courtesy of the Bishop of London's hunting grounds during the Middle Ages, lent it a genuine countryside air. This sense of the rural was further reinforced by the presence of Highgate Wood and sprawling Hampstead Heath. Residents of Highgate could take picnics in their own suburb, walk their dogs for miles through woodland, and generally enjoy the impression that a great city, and all of its trappings, was not throbbing just minutes away. Jack had lived here for four years and couldn't imagine living anywhere else.

He thought about dropping into The Flask for a pint of Speckled Hen, but the low mood he had held off all day caught up with him and he ignored the pull of the eighteenth-century taproom and moved instead in the direction of Coleridge House, a grand old Georgian pile tastefully divided into four mansion apartments overlooking the park. He checked his postbox and withdrew a motley assortment of bills, junk mail and a late birthday card from an ageing aunt. He glanced at the name of the owner who had acquired apartment four a few months ago — he had meant to offer a welcome and still had the Harrods Christmas pudding in his apartment. He felt a fresh stab of guilt. He'd better change it to a bottle of bubbly now, and if he didn't hurry up it would have to be an Easter egg.

As the lift doors closed he dug into his pocket for his door keys, still thinking about the meeting with his boss. Martin Sharpe had obviously argued long and hard to win Jack the operation. He was determined not to let his Super and long-time supporter down. The truth was, Sharpe was more than that. Sharpe and his wife, Cathie, had tried their damndest to plug the gap that the death of his parents had left. Sharpe and Jack's father had been close friends since their early days working in the Diplomatic Protection Group at Westminster, continuing together to Downing Street. After DPG, it was clear Martin was a career officer, destined for Superintendent, probably higher.

When Mary and Ken Hawksworth had died in the 1985 M6 pile-up, it was Martin Sharpe who had helped to gather up the bits of twenty-two-year-old Jack Hawksworth and reassemble him.

Amy, three years older than Jack, had been working in Bahrain when the accident happened, and although she was permitted compassionate leave, it wasn't long enough for the Hawksworth siblings to find comfort. Amy was hugging her brother a teary farewell almost as soon as she'd arrived and so it was Martin and Cathie who had quietly taken him into their lives and, with the gentlest of touches, brought him back from a dark year during which Martin had feared Jack might give up the Force completely.

Jack entered his apartment, headed straight to his bedroom and changed from his itchy birthday shirt to comfy jeans and sweatshirt before flopping into the leather sofa opposite a TV that he didn't have the desire to turn on. He needed to eat, he needed to sleep, but for now he couldn't move. He spent several minutes staring across Waterlow Park and its manicured flowerbeds through the living room's tall windows. The Flask tempted him again — he could relax over some tapas, perhaps a glass of wine. The watering hole that had once been a hiding place for highwayman Dick Turpin was probably just what he needed to lift his spirits and placate his grinding belly. But at this late hour it would be buzzing with arty types and he wasn't up to the noise and activity. Instead, he opted to try and clear his mind of mutilated corpses with a splendidly crisp riesling from his fridge. He was too tired to think of food but knew he had to eat properly or he'd end up with a paunch like Swamp's or a complexion like Brodie's: both the result of long hours, late nights, beer and fast food. He couldn't blame them, but Jack spent too many precious hours in the Yard's gym in an effort to keep some semblance of fitness to waste it on a lazy attitude to what passed down his gullet. Health and fitness were important to him, and what he saved on not having to pay for a private gym he invested in decent wine.

He looked again at the shopping bag containing streaky bacon, tomato, onion and free-range eggs he'd grabbed at Highgate Village and urged himself to get up and make an omelette.

Before he could move, the landline began jangling next to him. Wearily he reached for it. This had to be personal — no one from work rang him on his home number. 'Hello?'

A voice began singing loudly into his ear. 'Happy birthday, dear Henry, happy birthday to you!' it hollered, dragging out the final word.

Only his sister ever called him by his middle name. 'Thank you, Amy.'

'You're most welcome. How rude of you not to return my call.'

'I know, I know. I'm sorry. If only you knew ...'

'I do,' she said, her sunny voice making him feel warm inside. 'Tell me it arrived in time. Did you wear it?'

'It did. I did. Another thank you.'

'Do you love it?'

'Reminded me of ice-cream.'

'I can hear that you hated it.'

'That's not true. I just need to gear up to wearing mint and pink stripes.'

'Well, someone has to try and break you free of schoolboy blue. I bet you're wearing that now.'

'I'm naked actually. You interrupted something.' She squealed — as he'd hoped she might — and he laughed with delight that he could still do that to her. 'I'm not, I promise. I can't help that I favour old-fashioned colours.'

'Just like Dad. Are you still listening to Roy Orbison?'

'Now and then.'

'Break free, little brother. Come on, come over here for a few weeks. I'm all alone so I can give you one hundred per cent, undivided attention. There's so much we can do. Shopping for shirts, for instance.'

'Soon, I promise.'

'Now!' she urged.

'I can't. We're in the middle of something here.'

'Nasty?'

'Yes.'

'Ooh, what, really gruesome, you mean?'

'I'm afraid so, just like the stuff you love to read but with none of those smart-talking, whip-cracking, brilliant know-all women solving the murder.'

She sighed. 'I miss you.'

'I wish you were closer, too. Why couldn't you have married a Spaniard, or we'd have even coped if he was French.'

'You know me, never do things by halves. Listen, I have something to tell you.' She sounded suddenly serious.

'What's cooking?'

'I am. And I've got a fat little bun in the oven.'

It was his turn for a pause as this sank in. 'A baby?' he asked, incredulous.

'Yes!' she screamed across the thousands of miles that separated them. 'But not just one bun.'

'You're having twins?'

He heard her begin to weep. 'Two beautiful babies, Henry. Can you imagine? I just wish Mum and Dad were around to share this with me . . . and you're so far away, damn it!'

It broke his heart that he couldn't hug her. 'Come home, Amy.'

'I can't,' she said, sniffing. 'Rob needs me here too, and he's so excited I can't shut him up.'

'When am I going to have nieces and nephews?'

'By June, we think.'

'Well.' He blew out his cheeks, overwhelmed by this happy family news. 'My congratulations, old girl. And to Rob. That's it, I was trying to summon the energy to cook but now I'm definitely going to get drunk instead.'

'Well, someone has to! Robert must be the only Australian bloke who doesn't drink.'

'To Pinky and Perky then.'

She laughed and he was glad to hear it. 'And if they don't resemble sweet, chubby pink piglets, to Bleep and Booster,' she said.

'I'll have to insist upon those names as godfather.'

'Godfathers have to be present at the christening, Henry.'

'That's a promise.' He counted off the months in his head until the babies would be six months. 'I've got roughly a year, right?'

'Don't you want to see me enormous?'

'I want to see you with Pinky and Perky in your arms.'

'That's a date. Next April let's say you're coming to Sydney. I'll take you to a game and you can see football played by real men who run straight into each other — none of this rolling around on the pitch in agony because their toe's been trodden on or they've chipped a fingernail.'

It was a familiar dig but he didn't rise to her bait this time.

Instead he laughed, blew her a kiss. 'Love to you both. Now leave me, woman, I have a bottle or two of riesling to consume.'

She kissed him back. 'I'll ring again soon because I know you won't ring me.'

No sooner had they hung up than the phone rang again. Jack assumed it was his sister again. She often did this — thought of something almost immediately after saying goodbye and rang directly back.

'What about Jack and Jill,' he said, 'if it's one of each?'

'Sorry?' It wasn't Amy. 'Is that Mr Hawksworth?'

'Yes, it is. I'm sorry, I thought you were someone else.'

'This is Traute Becker. I'm on the floor below you — apartment two?'

'Ah, yes, of course.' Jack heard the German accent that no amount of living in Britain could eradicate. 'Is everything alright?'

'I'm sorry to disturb you, Mr Hawksworth, but I need some help. My husband is away and it seems there's been some sort of power failure. I've rung the power company and it's not the grid, you see. It's something local they're saying.'

'What does that mean?' Jack might bake but he was no handyman. None of his lights were on to check, he only now realised, but the fridge was humming quietly and the phone worked.

'Something in the basement, I presume. A switch we throw back on.'

He liked the singsong nature of her voice and the way 'something' came out as 'somesing' and 'throw' sounded more like 'srow'.

'Oh, like a trip switch?'

'Ja, ja, that's the word he used.'

'Would you like me to take a look?' Sounded like the right thing to say even though it would be the blind leading the blind.

'Ja, I would. I don't want to go down there alone, if you please.'

'No problem. But I don't think it's the basement, Mrs Becker, more likely your own circuit box, because I can hear my fridge so I've got power. Give me a few moments and I'll be down.'

★ ★ ★

Jack met Mrs Becker outside her door and she let him into her apartment, using a torch to light their way. She made polite apologies, which he tried to wave away. He wondered if the other apartments were still powered. He knew old Mr Claren was staying in Scotland for a few weeks with his daughter because Jack had agreed to clear his postbox. *Damn*, he thought, *I must do that.*

Mrs Becker seemed to read his mind. 'Mr Claren's post needs clearing. He's not back until the end of this week. Here we go, is this what you mean?' She pointed to a box on the wall.

'That's it,' Jack said, hoping that his basic knowledge would bring light back to Mrs Becker's place. 'I think we flick this switch.' He did so and her apartment flickered instantly back to life.

'Ah,' they said together and congratulated one another.

'Oh, thank you, Mr Hawksworth. I don't know what I'd have done without you.'

'Don't mention it,' he said, feeling quite the hero. 'Any time.'

'Can I offer you something?'

He tried not to smile at that word again. 'No, really, Mrs Becker, I've just returned from work and I'm ready to call it a day, if you don't mind. I was just heading into the shower when you rang,' he fibbed, eager to be on his way upstairs.

'Okay, come visit sometime when Mr Becker is back.'

'I'll do that.' Jack walked to the door.

She bustled behind him. 'By the way, have you welcomed our new neighbour yet?'

Jack felt instantly ashamed again. 'I haven't.'

'Ja, you should. Nice lady, shame about the chair.'

'Sorry?'

She shrugged in that European way. 'She has the chair, you know, with the wheels.'

'Oh.' He understood.

'Ja. Should we go and check, do you think?' Mrs Becker wondered aloud. 'Perhaps her lights have gone too. A good chance for you to say your hello's before a welcome feels awkward, no?'

'Er ...' Jack scratched his head. He really didn't want to, neither did he think it was necessary, but Mrs Becker looked determined. She was the building's obligatory busybody and clearly about to use him as her battering ram into the new tenant's property. But without her, Jack wouldn't know much at all about the little bits of cooperative administration he should be involved with from exterior painting to care of their gardens. 'Okay, let's go together. She may not like a strange man knocking on her door in the evening.'

The lift worked perfectly and Jack suspected it was only the first level that had been knocked out for some reason. They ascended to the top floor. Mrs Becker chose the door knocker over the less intrusive and clearly lit bell. She knocked again a few moments later and was answered by a voice calling out that she was coming.

The door opened. 'Yes?' said the new occupant, looking sideways at them because her wheelchair and a door opening inwards was a bad combination. 'Can I help you?'

Mrs Becker smiled but said nothing, so Jack filled the void.

'Hi. I'm Jack Hawksworth. I live in the apartment below you, and the trip switch went off in one of the other apartments. We thought we should do the neighbourly thing and check all was okay with you. This is Mrs Becker, by the way.'

The woman in the wheelchair beamed and Jack felt drawn to the warmth of the smile. 'How kind. Um, all's well here, but thank you.' She reached out her hand. 'I'm Sophie. Sophie Fenton.'

Jack took it, noticing the well-kept nails and the waft of his favourite perfume. Amy wore it sometimes, and although it was an old brand it was a classic. He was going to mention it but bit his tongue. It might come out as though he was flirting. Wheelchair-ridden or not, Sophie Fenton looked terrific with her hair tied carelessly in a ponytail and wearing baggy grey trackies, the hoodie unzipped just enough to reveal that she had smooth skin and, from what he could see, a very nice upper half. Sophie was now shaking Mrs Becker's hand, her golden hair glinting beneath the lights in her hallway.

Jack shifted from one foot to the other, embarrassed that he was staring so long and hard. 'Right,' he said, 'so again forgive the disruption, but at least we all got to say hello. I'm actually truly embarrassed it's taken me so long.'

'Don't apologise,' she said, her eyes sparkling with the smile she still wore. 'It's great to meet you both, and I hope the painters, removalists and all the banging around didn't cause you too much grief as I settled in?'

Jack shrugged. 'I didn't hear a thing. In fact, I didn't even know you had physically moved in until just before Christmas,' he admitted, again reminded of the Christmas pudding.

'I've been here since late November, but to be honest, you're as much a stranger to me. I'm exceptionally good at remembering faces and I've not seen you coming or going.'

Jack felt the familiar surge of shame. 'I don't keep very regular hours.'

Mrs Becker was shaking her head. 'I used to hear the previous owner's loud music. You won't be playing loud music, will you?'

'Not when I can't dance to it, no,' Sophie said, stealing an amused glance at Jack after realising the humour was lost on Mrs Becker. He returned a slightly perplexed grin, captivated and yet somewhat disarmed by her directness.

'Are you settled?' he asked.

'Absolutely, I'm no procrastinator. Would you like to come in for a coffee, or . . .'

He'd have loved to, but it wasn't appropriate under these circumstances and not with present company in tow. He could feel Mrs Becker rocking on her heels, ready to barge in and snoop around the place. 'Another time, perhaps?'

Sophie nodded and he hoped she had picked up that he was doing her a favour.

'Well, hope to see you soon,' he said. 'I'm sure we'll pass in the corridor, and don't hesitate if you ever need sugar. Just bang hard on the floor with a broom or something and I'll come running.'

It was a lame comeback to her kind invitation, the one he was already regretting turning down, but the wryness in her expression told him she appreciated his discretion.

She smiled. 'Use the lift, then you'll be sure to see me, although there's not much room for more than me and my chair. You'll all hate me.'

'He runs up the stairs like a child,' Mrs Becker said, poking a finger towards Jack. 'Me, I walk the one flight. Can't wait for the wretched lift.'

'I promise to use the lift if it means we can meet,' Jack said.

Blimey, I sound desperate, he thought instantly. It was true he hadn't really connected with a woman in a long time. Oh, he'd dated often enough — too much, in fact — but hadn't enjoyed any woman's company enough over the course of an evening to want to see her again. But here was Sophie, face shiny and clear of make-up, daggy tracksuit, hair tied up messily, sitting in a wheelchair and talking to them from an awkward position, and in less than a minute or two he'd decided he seriously wanted to meet her again.

'I'll hold you to that. Nice seeing you — I'm very glad to know who my neighbours are,' she said to Mrs Becker and gave him a final glance.

Jack wanted to watch that smile blaze all night, but instead he turned and guided Mrs Becker away.

'Now there's someone who eats her parsley,' Mrs Becker muttered as the door of the lift closed on herself and Jack.

He didn't know whether to be confused or amused. He opted for poor hearing. 'Pardon me?'

'The teeth — beautiful, no? Lots of calcium. Good skin.'

He gave her a bemused look. 'Goodnight, Mrs Becker, I'm glad we solved the problem,' he said, grateful that his floor arrived swiftly. 'My best to Mr Becker too.'

'Ja, thank you.'

Jack returned to his apartment, took the phone off the hook and turned his mobile on to silent, then felt guilty and returned it to outdoors mode. He poured himself a slug of the riesling that was no longer quite as chilled, banished all thoughts of the case and instead focused his mind on Sophie Fenton and how he might contrive to meet her again.

3

They'd always been early risers, but now they were nearly sixty both of them seemed to need even less sleep. They were usually wide awake by four and got up at first bird's peep, around five. Clare sighed as she felt the warmth of her husband leave the bed to follow his usual ritual of ablutions before heading downstairs for the first cuppa of the day.

She often wondered what their hurry was these days. There was nothing to rush downstairs for since Garvan had retired a year or so ago. His health had forced him to leave work much earlier than he should, but he'd been given a great send-off. Everyone loved Garvan and the company was sad to see one of its most loyal employees leave. She was thrilled though. Unlike many women, who found their husbands got underfoot once they retired, Clare was happy to have more time to enjoy their son and stay busy together. Her parents had left them pretty well set up: they weren't wealthy but they were hardly struggling. Life in retirement was good.

'What time is it?' she mumbled, finally finding the courage to brave the cold, unwrap the quilt from around her legs and move to the bathroom where her husband was just finishing shaving.

She'd always wanted an ensuite bathroom, but it hadn't worked out that way, what with Peter's education, giving him the money for his first flat, and then helping him to buy that silly vintage car he loved so much. Perhaps now they could make some improvements — now they had the time and some savings to play with. Clare sighed with quiet pleasure. Peter was well set up and everything they'd worked so hard to provide for him was paying off. She even sensed an engagement in the air and couldn't imagine she would be any happier once it was made formal.

'It's nearing six, love,' Garvan answered. 'You don't have to be up, though. Stay in bed, I'll bring you a tea.'

'No,' she said, 'I might as well get going. I want to start working on the cake.'

'Is that the one for the McInerneys?'

'Yes. They've ordered a fourth tier now, so I have to adjust all my weights and measurements because the bottom slab of the cake will have to be bigger to hold it all.'

'Blimey, how many are coming to their reception?'

She shrugged. Weddings were such an industry these days and the caterers really ripped off the bridal couple — or their parents, more to the point — especially for the cake. Clare had been a cake decorator all her working life but her specialty was wedding cakes. She'd retired, of course, but now and then took on the odd job that interested her. This was an Irish couple from County Clare — her parents' birthplace — and she felt a kinship and need to help the young couple out. 'I imagine it must be over two hundred by now if the cake is any indication.'

'They're nuts.'

'You'd better get used to the idea. Peter and Pat will ask at least that many,' she said.

'Well, they might ask, but we'll only be sending out invites for a hundred guests tops,' he warned, brandishing his razor.

'Oh, go on with you and your silly threats. No one takes any notice of you, Garvan!'

She could see he knew he was beaten. 'I'll get the heaters turned up for you, then,' he said. 'It's a cold one today.'

'Turn the news on as well,' she said, shooing him out of the bathroom.

'Why?'

'I want to hear about those murders that were on the radio last night,' she called through the door. 'We missed the news on the telly because of your Rotary dinner.'

'What murders? Down here in Sussex?'

Clare began washing her hands. 'No. Two men, one from Lincoln, the other from London somewhere, I think. But the police reckon their deaths are similar — they're saying it could be a serial killer,' she finished as she opened the door.

'This is England, love, not America,' he said, his tone suggesting she must have misheard the report. He kissed the top of her head. 'Hurry up, tea's on its way.'

'I'm just telling you what the news said,' she called to his back as he went downstairs.

Her husband reached the hallway and looked up at her. 'Why are you interested in them anyway?'

'Because who's to say the next one won't be from Brighton, that's why. Hurry up with that tea — I'm going to pull on something warm.'

'Okay, okay. I'm on my way.'

Clare arrived in the sitting room just after the BBC presenter had repeated the unsettling news that the bodies of two men had been discovered in separate locations in Lincoln and North London several weeks apart.

'Both males were brutally murdered and similarities at the crime scenes indicate that the same killer may be responsible for both deaths. There is no indication at this stage that the murders were the result of robberies as personal items were untouched. A full investigation is now under way and a special incident team has been established. Police are following up several leads,' the announcer said 'and have revealed the victims as forty-four-year-old Michael Sheriff of Louth in Lincolnshire and forty-five-year-old Clive Farrow of Hackney Marshes. Both men were —'

'There you are,' Clare said over the presenter's words. 'Believe me now?'

'Sssh!' Garvan hissed, surprising her.

She rounded on him, noticed his gaze intense on the screen, his body leaning forward in anticipation as the BBC ran the footage from the night before showing a grey-haired senior police officer speaking about the murderer they were now hunting.

'We would like to interview anyone who may have come into contact with the men since November last year or who may have any information that might assist with our inquiries and establish the victims' movements in the past week,' Superintendent Sharpe said from the podium. 'If anyone has been in the areas concerned and has seen or heard something that they think may be relevant to the inquiry — no matter how insignificant — please contact us on the numbers on the screen now. All information will be treated in the strictest confidence.'

'Garv—'

Her husband held his hand up to quieten her as Sharpe accepted questions from the reporters. It took all of Clare's composure not to yell at him.

'Do we know what he looks like?' a reporter asked.

Sharpe shook his head. 'No, we have no news of sightings as yet.'

'What about a profile? Have you had one done for him yet?' another asked.

Sharpe's expression did not change. 'We're working with only very limited information at this stage but we'll be using every tool at our disposal. At this point, all we can say is that the killer is mobile and it's highly unlikely that we are dealing with a mindless thug or opportunist.'

'Has he left any clues? Any notes? Taken any trophies?' a blonde reporter asked, no doubt hoping for ghoulish details.

Sharpe cleared his throat. 'There are no notes left behind, no trophies, as you put it, taken from either scene. But evidence at the two sites is being scrutinised by our team. Which brings me to Detective Chief Inspector Jack Hawksworth,' he turned to gesture to a man standing just behind him, 'who is heading up this major investigation at Scotland Yard.'

'Garvan, the tea,' Clare urged, annoyed by her husband's intense interest in something he had mocked her about only moments earlier.

'Just a minute,' he said crossly, his gaze transfixed by the screen as the cameras zoomed in to focus on a tall, dark-haired man.

As much to irritate Garvan as to win his attention, she said, 'Well, that Jack Hawksworth can leave his slippers under my bed any time.'

'Good-looking bastard, isn't he?' her husband growled, shocking her with his language. 'And arrogant too, to be wearing that ridiculous candy-striped shirt.'

Then he muttered under his breath, *So you're the one to look out for.*

4

It was the following day that Jack saw Sophie Fenton again. She was entering the lift as he was exiting it on the ground floor.

'Whoops!' he said, nearly walking straight into her chair.

'In a hurry, Mr Hawksworth?' she asked, her tone filled with good humour. 'I thought you preferred the stairs.'

'But you told me to use the lift! And call me Jack, please.'

'I warned you I'd frustrate you within a very short time,' she said, pointing to her chair.

'Not at all. I'm glad to see you. I kept meaning to bring around a cup of sugar or something.'

She grinned. 'Flowers would be nicer,' she said, wheeling herself into the lift as he held the door open.

He nodded. 'That can be arranged.'

'I'm only joking. My offer for a coffee stands, though. Come and join me sometime.' She shrugged as she spun the wheels to face him. 'Come now, if you like.'

Jack gave her a pained look. 'At the risk of giving you a complex, I have to be somewhere and I'm running late.'

'Another time then,' Sophie said, reaching for the button. 'But three strikes and you're out, Jack.'

'Next time you invite me, I promise we'll have that cuppa.'

'I'll hold you to that promise,' she said and he felt a surge of pleasure as her bright smile broke across her mouth. If the doors weren't closing he might have done something ridiculously impulsive. Mercifully they groaned shut and, with a protesting squeak and rumble, the lift eased Sophie Fenton away from him.

Later, at Wellington House, a short walk from the Yard, he was still thinking about Sophie. He pushed her out of his mind and regarded the people around him — the team he had assembled. Jack was confident that these were the men and women who would help him fulfil the Super's plea.

'Alright, everyone. We all know each other, I think?' Heads nodded. 'Good, because we need to move fast. Today's meeting here at Welly House is for expediency, but rest assured we've been given our own operation rooms on the twelfth floor of the Tower Block. For any of you new to the warren that makes up New Scotland Yard, just make for the library and you'll find your new home next door.'

Bill Marsh gave a low whistle. 'Bit posher than Victoria Block, eh, Jack?'

Jack winked at the older man. 'I do my best for us, Swamp.' He looked back at the main group. 'Now, we'll be moving over to our new premises from this evening, when I'm assuming all our designated phone numbers and home page on the intranet will be up, so grab one of these photocopied maps if you're unsure.'

He looked at PC Patel and PC McGloughlan. 'If you're first-timers here, then expect to get lost because the lifts are a bastard to navigate. Incidentally, apart from the amazing views I can promise from Operation Danube, the library is one of the best spots for Yard gossip.'

Everyone laughed except Sarah Jones, the detective fresh out of Hendon, who nodded rather seriously. Jack made a mental note that he would have to put the young DS at her ease over the next few days.

He got down to business. 'You've all been given the file notes, so you know what we're dealing with.'

'Are we treating this officially as a serial killing?'

It was the obvious question that perhaps most didn't want to ask, but Detective Inspector Kate Carter was never afraid to ask the difficult questions. It was one of the reasons that Jack liked and trusted her. He'd worked with her twice before, once when she too was just a few years out of Hendon, and again five years later, and she'd impressed him both times. Kate was a terrier who couldn't let anything go once she'd latched onto it as a potential clue. She was also an instinctive detective, who, like him, tended not to follow the rule book so much as trust her gut. She'd been his first choice when pulling together the team, especially now that she'd made DI.

Cam Brodie, her counterpart and all too familiar colleague, grunted. 'What else would you call it, Kate, two in a row?'

'Just checking the official line on it, Cam.'

'Yes,' Hawksworth said, over their sarcastic glances, 'we're treating the murders as a serial killing.'

'Thank you,' Kate said, but might as well have added, 'Touché'.

'Okay, I'm going to hand you over briefly to John Tandy from the Forensic Science Service,' Jack went on. 'He's had only the briefest of chances so far to look over all the crime notes and come up with something we can work with. John?'

People shifted on the hard wooden chairs in an attempt to find slightly more comfortable positions as a man in his late fifties with thick dark hair shot through with silver took the floor.

'This is a very loose picture, folks,' he began. 'We'll improve it in coming weeks.'

'When we get more bodies, you mean?' Bill Marsh called out.

'Come on, Bill,' Jack cajoled. 'Poor taste, eh?'

Bill Marsh — known as Swamp, a middle-aged man in a rumpled suit — had ten years on Hawksworth, but had never been material for a DCI, even though he'd dreamed of running his own unit. To Bill's credit, he'd never held it against the young lion roaring up the ladder, nor had he ever voiced what everyone presumably believed: Martin Sharpe had made that ladder a little easier for Hawksworth to climb.

Tandy cleared his throat and continued. 'Alright, so far we have a left-handed killer. This is a cold personality — the actual dispatch of both victims was calm, calculated and handled with minimum fuss. Neither killing was done in a state of uncontrollable anger. If rage was present, I believe the killer had his emotions in check.

'Michael Sheriff was drugged and taken to a quiet place, where, presumably, he was quickly dealt with. The same goes for Clive Farrow in Hackney.'

'Why do you describe the killer as cold, John?' Kate asked.

'No passion,' Tandy replied, pointing to the images blown up and pinned on the board behind him. 'No need for a lot of blood, and he didn't make the victims suffer as much as he could have. He drugged them first.'

'That could have been to make them compliant, though?' Brodie's Scottish brogue cut in.

'That's probably true. But according to Don Larkin in pathology, the killer waited until the tranquilliser had taken full effect — in both instances, the heart had stopped — before going to work with the knife. He could just as easily have waited for the victims to be drowsy, incapable of a struggle, and then really made them suffer. But apparently he didn't.'

'What do we surmise from this?' Jack asked, mainly for the benefit of the younger members on the team, who looked slightly overawed to be working on this case at Scotland Yard.

'At this point, only that our killer doesn't fit the usual profile of a psychopath.' Tandy drew inverted commas in the air with his fingers as he said the last word. 'In serial killings there's usually a level of enjoyment, certainly involvement —' He made the inverted commas gesture again and Jack could see that it irritated Kate. He smiled to himself. '— but in these cases both men were dispatched quickly, efficiently. So this wasn't about revelling in the act of killing as such. The killer did not choose to prolong their death, and clearly had no interest in them suffering, perhaps beyond the original shock of realising they were captives, blah blah.'

The 'blah blah' clearly annoyed Kate. 'So, John,' she interrupted, shaking her head slightly with frustration, 'why is he killing if there's no pleasure to be gained?'

'Oh, there's pleasure alright, Detective . . .'

'DI Carter. Kate.'

'Kate, thank you. Oh yes, the killer is certainly gaining satisfaction, but not from the suffering, the blood, or the act of killing even. He doesn't even take a trophy. Instead, he neatly leaves what is clearly his prize in the dead men's hands.'

'So what does it all mean?' Kate asked impatiently.

Tandy closed his eyes, kept them shut as he spoke. 'It's a means to an end,' he said with satisfaction.

'He just wants these guys dead?' Bill finished.

'Correct,' Tandy said, and blinked slowly. 'The reward is the end of Sheriff's and Farrow's life.'

'Revenge?' Hawksworth offered.

'Quite possibly,' Tandy said, nodding. 'It's certainly the scenario I'm postulating.'

'What else, John?' Jack encouraged.

'Well, so far so good — let's say we have a couple of revenge killings. It doesn't explain the oddity of removing the lips and genitals. That does smack of the psychopath. But again I tread here with caution, because it was done calmly, neatly and having already deliberately minimised suffering to the victims.'

'Age?' Brodie asked.

'I'd say our killer is late thirties, perhaps early forties.'

'Why?' Kate asked.

The profiler raised his chin, stared at the ceiling for a few moments. Jack liked that Tandy was taking Kate's question seriously and not just giving her a rote answer. It was a good question, and it was always with some wonderment that Jack listened to the answers these experts came up with. Despite his irritating mannerisms at times, John Tandy was one of the best in the business. The Met used him frequently and, although profiling was hardly an accurate science, Tandy had reliable instincts.

'Well, this is someone, I believe, who has thought through their kill very precisely,' he said. 'You're dealing with someone who is highly intelligent, who has the ability to remain clear-thinking and utterly in control of their emotions throughout the event. Age and the journey of life teaches you patience, even if you're a naturally impatient person. I just don't think a much younger person would have remained so ...' he searched for the right word, '...committed,' he finally said. 'It takes enormous control to do all that was done and not feel compelled to leave some sort of note behind, or clues to his identity and so on. And if this is revenge, I believe a younger murderer would have wanted his victims to suffer. In my opinion, only an older person would be so single-minded as to never lose sight of what he wants — death for these two men. There was no need to draw out the events leading up to it, and to offer them both an escape from the agony of what was occurring is odd. I really believe this is an older person because everything was a means to an end. No showing off, all clinically done and meticulously planned, it seems.'

Brodie began to speak but Tandy continued, apologising with a nod for cutting across the detective. 'The care taken to immobilise the victims points to maturity, as does the swift kill — although I think it could have been done faster, neater, considering the murderer had them so helpless.'

Kate frowned. 'Can you clarify that notion, please, John?'

He shrugged. 'Just a feeling. It's another reason why I sense this is about payback. The victims were drugged, presumably unconscious. The killer is showing all the signs of not needing them to suffer past the point of their obvious horror at being taken captive and by whom, and, I imagine, realising that they were going to die. At this stage, he could have just put a plastic bag over their heads to ensure death — a much cleaner, easier way to kill. All of this would follow the pattern he's set of the manner of death not being important. But he stabs them, risks blood spurting everywhere. Why?'

He let the question hang.

Bill piped up. 'That's when he got angry perhaps?'

'Unlikely,' Tandy said. 'At this stage of events, his care suggests he has all of his emotions thoroughly under control. It's the early stages — the adrenaline rush of stalking and then successfully capturing and immobolising his prey — that are more likely the time when, if he was going to allow his anger to play a part, it would have occurred. He would have stabbed them at the beginning if he was prone to anger over whatever it is that has forced him to do this.'

'Time constraints?' Brodie offered, pulling a sheepish face to indicate he knew it was a lame guess. His shrug begged his colleagues to give him a break.

Jack was pleased to note that Tandy showed no impatience with the questions and answered each with equally measured care. All notions, worthy or lame, were helpful for the younger members to listen to and learn from.

'No, it can't be a time issue because the killer only now goes to work on his victims. Genitals to emasculate, lips to remove, the scene to be cleared of any props and evidence. He's being thorough, remember.'

'It's something that does give him pleasure then,' Kate offered. 'Or at least satisfaction perhaps.'

Tandy smiled. 'That's what I think. Whatever these two men have in common, I think the stabbing put to right something in their killer's mind.'

'The revenge?' Jack asked.

'Yes, I believe the stabbing is integral to that revenge. Something these men have done in the past perhaps has involved a stabbing, either being part of it or witnessing it, and the killer has taken it personally. Or perhaps it happened to the killer — that I can't tell you. But the stabbing is definitely at odds with the rest of our killer's MO. It's unnecessary, because the victims are most likely already dead, and as I said before, if he wanted to make sure, a plastic bag is much simpler and cleaner. I might add, both stab wounds were in an almost identical spot on the victims' bodies — it has significance.'

Jack let this sink in before adding, 'Even though the trophies seem such a vicious act?'

'That depends on whether these are trophies,' Tandy said. 'I don't think so, to be honest.' He realised his listeners were staring at him in bafflement. 'What I mean is, our killer didn't take anything away from the scene. A genuine trophy from a kill would be kept, treasured. Instead, he left them behind, in the victim's hands, which may also have some significance.

'I'd also pose the idea that the lips and genitals, together with the stabbing and even the quirkiness of the blue paint, are the glue that binds these people. They are meaningful only to the killer and his victims. I don't believe that any of the knifework or the paint is a message to the police or the public at large. I'd suggest it's more likely a private message to the people he's taking revenge on, and I feel all three ways in which the blade was used are connected. That is, they were all meaningful to the act of payback.' He looked around. 'That's all I have.'

There was a moment's silence before Jack spoke. 'Thanks, John, lots there for us to consider.'

The psychologist nodded, smiled sympathetically at his audience and departed, a young PC accompanying him to see him out.

'Right, has anyone got anything to add to the profile?' Jack asked. No one did. 'Okay, then. I want one of you getting final confirmation from pathology that we are indeed looking for a left-handed killer. That will help narrow down the field a little.' He nodded with understanding at the groans that greeted this understatement.

'Bill, as soon as you can, get across to the Lincoln scene and get a full briefing from the boys at Louth. And go lightly. Remember, we need to act as the umbrella guys on this and I don't want complaints that the Yard team are stampeding over local investigations.'

'On my way, Hawk.'

Jack knew Bill would have the right touch. It was Brodie he was more concerned about. 'Cam,' he said, 'you do the same over at Hackney. And remember, don't leave any footprints.'

'You know it's going to be just another day, another body, to them, sir,' Brodie said. 'Lower Clapton Road's not called the Murder Mile for nothing.'

'I realise that. But Clive Farrow is someone's fiance, someone's son, and so we'll treat his death as though it's the first murder we've ever investigated.'

Jack turned to the room at large. 'For all of you newbies out of Hendon, Hackney is considered a poor, relatively deprived borough. It's home to a large Hasidic Jewish community, as well as large Asian and Caribbean populations, and tends to be overrun with Yardie gangs. It's not unusual to find bodies around there, which is why Cam said what he did.' He gave Brodie a brief hard gaze to warn him about the youngsters on the team who needed education and encouragement, not the assumption that their efforts were pointless before they even began.

'Kate,' he said.

'Sir?' Her expression of resignation told him she was anticipating the tiresome task of wading through files, finding out about blue paint suppliers or something equally tedious now that the two plum jobs had gone to the blokes.

'We're going to visit the families of the victims. We'll start in Lincoln.' He didn't wait for her response and flicked his gaze away from her grateful look of surprise. 'The rest of you, I want to know what brand of paint is on the victims' hands, where it can be bought, and ideas on why it might be significant. I want to know what knife was used by the killer, and as soon as you do know, I want the brand, where it can be purchased and someone compiling a list of those stores to visit or contact. Someone else, go back over the scenes of the two crimes — constantly ask yourself, have we missed anything? What questions haven't been asked yet?'

'What about cold cases, sir?' DS Jones asked.

Sarah Jones was a bright young woman, definitely a rising star, and Jack had witnessed her efforts on a previous case. She didn't have Kate's instincts but she possessed an enviable trait of attention to detail and a need to tie off every loose thread — both of which had led to her receiving specific training on the national police indexing system.

'Tell us more,' he said, hoping to encourage her by letting her show the rest of the team her strengths.

She looked nervous, shifted her glasses. 'Well, sir, it occurs to me that if we follow the line of reasoning that these could be revenge killings, then we need to go back over some old crimes. Perhaps something might bob up in London or Lincolnshire, or there may be some similarities with the paint, type of injuries, use of the drugs, stabbings . . .'

Jack had hoped someone would suggest this crucial and tedious legwork, yet none of the senior people had and it should have been one of their first thoughts. He imagined it was because none of them wanted to do that kind of work, which troubled him. He noticed Kate's not very well concealed scowl at the young detective. He made her expression darken further when he said, 'Excellent, DS Jones. Why don't you take that on, run some comparisons through the database?'

'Yes, sir,' Sarah said crisply.

When he had first drawn up his list of people to be involved in Operation Danube Jack had wondered whether these two women would hit it off. Although they were both ambitious, they were opposing poles. Kate had the looks and personality to command attention, while Sarah had neither but made up for it with a shrewd mind. He realised his instincts had been right but couldn't fret on it now.

'So, you all know what you're doing,' he said. 'I'll see you at our new home on the twelfth floor for a debriefing tomorrow morning. Happy hunting, all.'

5

It was one of those freezing, drizzly, depressing days. Kate grabbed her scarf, gloves and leather jacket and hurried down to the car park.

Don't run, she told herself, as she hit the bowels of the building. *Be cool.* She could see Hawksworth now, beside a Vauxhall Zafira, talking to another man. Jack spotted her and gave a wave before turning back to finish his animated conversation.

Oh, this is very dangerous, she thought. Kate had worked with Jack Hawksworth twice before, the most recent occasion being three years ago, and had found her mind clouded with irrational, often ridiculous, daydreams that at times threatened her ability to function lucidly. It was a state of mind she hated and she'd sworn never to allow it to occur again, not at work anyway, and certainly not with a colleague.

Kate didn't believe in love at first sight — she didn't even believe in lust at first sight — and yet she was ashamed to admit that during that March of 2000, whenever Hawksworth stood near her, her hands went clammy. Eye contact with him had been hard because she was convinced he was able to read her mind with that penetrating gaze of his that made whomever he was speaking with feel as though they were the only person that mattered. Everything about him, from his charming manner to his maddening aloofness, even his questionable taste in music, was a turn-on.

But that was three years ago and, when he'd called to ask if she'd join this special team, Kate had convinced herself that she had grown up. She was thirty-two now, after all, and engaged. She'd figured her previous infatuation was simply that. So why was she feeling so jittery now?

'DI Kate Carter,' Jack said with a smile, 'this is DCI Geoff Benson. We've worked a couple of cases together.'

Kate looked at the enormous bear of a man who stood opposite her. She knew of him but they'd never met.

'How are you, Kate?' Geoff said, extending a colossal hand.

She shook it. 'Fine, thank you. So, you guys go back a long way?' They looked like Beauty and the Beast.

The men shared a conspiratorial grin. 'Er, yes, I'm afraid so. Geoff's been responsible for many an untidy weekend in our youth,' Jack admitted.

'We were probationers together,' his friend explained.

'Ah, Hendon,' she said, her tone matching an all-knowing expression. She wasn't really sure what was coming out of her mouth, distracted by the way Jack was looking at her with that soft smile. She couldn't read him at all. His giant friend said something she didn't catch that made Jack laugh and in that moment she was sure she could see the carefree boy he'd probably once been. *Bet that hair flopped right over your eyes too and gave you a wickedly cute look*, she thought.

'We've got to go, Geoff. See you for a pint soon, eh?' Jack said.

Geoff used his hand to mimic a phone. 'It's your turn to call,' he said. 'Nice meeting you, Kate. You're welcome to come for a beer, too.'

Jack opened the front passenger door for Kate, and laughed at Geoff's parting shot. Again, Kate didn't catch it; she was too busy wondering whether any other men still did that opening the door thing. Dan reckoned opening doors these days for women was fraught with danger. *The last time I did that for a female colleague, she snapped some waspish comment at me,* he had moaned. The lines were clearly drawn between him and Kate: equal terms, equal partners in life. With Jack, however, his opening the door for her didn't feel in any way smarmy and it certainly didn't seem to her as though he was using it to reinforce his rank or his maleness. *It's simply good manners*, she thought, and felt instantly feminine for being treated so courteously. An inner voice cut in and urged her to please pull her ragged thoughts together. *It's just the first day*, she replied silently. *I'll be fine by tomorrow.*

Hawksworth threw his jacket across his files in the back seat, got in and was down to business straightaway, reversing out of the parking spot. She inhaled a waft of a spicy citrus cologne she recognised and liked. It suited him. Dan didn't wear cologne, nor did he wear good-looking sports coats. *But let's face it*, she reasoned, *Dan's a software engineer.* A damn good one too, and on a huge salary working as a consultant to some enormous American bank in the city. Dan had no reason to wear suits with sexy shoes, she thought, glancing down at the chunky chocolate suede shoes her boss was wearing. Dan's uniform was jeans and his Doc Martens. He looked great in them, she admitted it, but it would be nice to see him in some chinos occasionally or, heaven forbid, some tailored trousers.

Jack was talking and she forced herself to pay attention, irritated with herself for being so flighty today of all days.

'We're seeing Michael Sheriff's wife in Lincoln — well, Louth actually. Should take us a couple of hours max.'

He rolled his sleeves up as they emerged out of the awkward single entrance-exit into Westminster and the watery sunlight of an icy February morning. 'Freezing in here,' he commented. 'Let's get some heat happening.'

She unwound her scarf as he turned up the heat on the car's dial. It would be steamy and warm in the small car before she knew it.

Victoria Street was teeming with its usual horde of London cabs, now available in maroon, and even white — *perhaps they double as wedding cars*, she thought. An equally famous convoy of red London buses lumbered past. She noticed most were tourist buses, totally incompatible with Britain's propensity for sudden downpours in any season. As expected, the open-air upper deck was crowded with Japanese sightseers. Why was that? Other nations happily sat on the lower deck but the Japanese always rushed upstairs, no matter how inclement the weather.

'I'll take the less obvious tourist route,' Jack said, echoing her thoughts and swinging left past the Army & Navy Store to head towards Westminster Cathedral. 'Any excuse to drive by one of my favourite buildings,' he added, as they glided past the imposing red and cream-coloured stone church that was the home of Catholicism in the UK. 'I love this piazza, don't you?' he said.

'Pity about the McDonald's on the corner,' Kate replied.

'I've taught myself to block it out.'

'Don't you think it looks eastern?' she asked.

'I think it looks like crap,' he replied vehemently.

'I mean the church, sir.' This was the first time Kate had really noticed the cathedral, even though she passed it almost daily. 'That surely looks like a minaret.'

Jack didn't respond to her question, his gaze darting from the road to quickly grab a glimpse of the building he clearly admired. 'The tourists should come here at night when it looks its most heavenly and angelic,' he said.

Kate smiled. 'So, our meeting is with Diane Sheriff, right, sir?'

'Listen, Kate, I don't go in for that "sir" stuff when we're not being watched over by anyone official. You're a DI now, so get comfortable calling me Jack, and at the Yard we'll fall back into the formalities. Okay?'

Kate nodded, and understood yet another reason why the man that people called Hawk was popular.

'Yes, her name's Diane,' he continued, 'she's taking the afternoon off work to see us.' He began negotiating the confusing one-way system around Victoria Station, headed for Grosvenor Place with its line of embassies.

Kate gave a soft sigh. 'And I imagine she's only just coming to terms with her husband's loss. We arrive to re-open the wound like the typically heartless bastards we are.'

'That's why I asked you to come along,' he said gently and glanced at her. She didn't look at him, touched her hair instead. 'I knew you'd handle it the right way. Cam and Bill — well,' he shrugged, 'you're the right person.'

'Thanks.' She cleared her throat, staring at the seemingly endless red brick wall and barbed wire that was the back of Buckingham Palace. 'Look, I haven't really had a chance to thank you for bringing me onto this operation. I appreciate it and I'm glad to be working with you.'

'Bored over at Kingston, were you?'

'Dying,' she admitted and liked how it prompted a chuckle from him. 'Being on the HAT team sounds great, but there aren't many homicides around the Richmond-Twickenham borough.'

'Your talents are wasted over there, Kate.'

'Tell that to management, would you.'

'I did. It's why you're here.'

That was the end of the personal chit-chat. He moved back to the case. 'How did you feel about Tandy's profile?'

'He's right, it's loose,' she answered, definitely on more solid ground now. Work was safe. 'Not much for us to go on. A late thirties, possibly early forties, left-handed killer who's taking revenge.'

'It's more than we had last night,' he replied, boldly entering the notoriously hazardous roundabout of Hyde Park that usually had her flinching. He handled the navigation smoothly though, passing the Hilton and Dorchester hotels slowly to join the thickening traffic. 'I think it's given us a reasonable platform.'

'Yes, but where to start? If we haven't already found a grudge against Sheriff, for instance, you and I both know there probably isn't one, so we're just going through the motions in talking to his wife. That would have been one of the first questions that Lincoln Police asked, surely?'

'I know, but people forget things. When she was interviewed originally, Mrs Sheriff was likely out of her mind with shock and despair. She's probably thinking more clearly now.'

'And you believe no one's bothered to ask since then?' Kate said incredulously.

'All I'm saying is that if anything has occurred to her, she perhaps doesn't think it's important.'

'But Sheriff's death was only three months ago. It would be an active file.'

'Yes, but not everyone's as diligent as you, Kate.'

More praise. She felt her cheeks begin to flush.

'The individual officers who originally interviewed her could have been moved to other cases, different departments, retired, been promoted or just got busy. They might not have revisited the file for a week or more.'

'Bet they do now,' she said, staring out the window as they finally gathered some speed and whizzed left at Speaker's Corner and around Marble Arch.

Jack touched a button on the CD player and Roy Orbison began crooning a sad song, one of his later ones. She smiled. Jack Hawksworth was an enigma.

'Do you like the Big O, Kate?' he asked, apparently reading her thoughts.

'Haven't heard him since I lived at home. My dad liked him.'

'Ouch,' he said and they laughed. 'So did my father. I think it's why I listen to Roy. It keeps the memories of Dad alive. Does that sound corny?'

'No,' she said, secretly delighted that he would mention such an intimate and obviously painful subject. She'd heard about his parents' death and had felt sorry for him, but had never gone in for the doe-eyed sympathy of some of the other women officers. 'And your mother? Perry Como, perhaps? Engelbert Humperdinck?'

'Well, curiously, my mother loved The Police.'

He laughed and she noticed how clean his teeth were. Definitely a flosser and regular visitor to the dentist.

'You're kidding, right?'

'No, really, it was nothing to do with my career. She just loved Sting's music. My father never quite got it.'

'Let me guess, "Every Breath You Take"?'

'Mmm, yes, that's everyone's favourite. She loved it all in truth, and I'm glad that before she died I was able to take her to a Sting concert.'

'Wow, hardly a blogsy mum, then.'

'No,' he said somewhat wistfully, 'she was never that. Oh, here we go, the Edgeware Road for a while until we hit the A1 to Grantham, then towards Lincoln and Louth.'

'Very cocky.'

'I've done this drive many times.'

'Dirty weekends?'

He grinned. 'Well, my grandmother and I did love to bake together and we used to get very grubby with our hands deep in dough.'

'Your grandmother lives in Lincoln?'

'Used to live in Lincoln. She died last year.'

'Oops, sorry.'

'Don't be. She was ninety-two and a great old girl who passed away peacefully in her sleep.'

In an effort to regain some ground from the slippery slide she felt herself permanently on this morning, Kate tried for levity. 'And do you still bake?' she said archly.

Tragically, he answered her seriously. 'Occasionally. She left me her KitchenAid mixer and I can't not use it. Besides, I find that sort of indulgent cooking relaxing.' Then he flushed. 'Quite embarrassing really. If Geoff knew, he'd have me publicly tarred and feathered.'

Was he for real? 'Do you bake for anyone in particular?'

'No.'

Ah, that thread was tied off fairly quickly, she thought.

'Do you wear a pinny when you bake?'

'No, just a mint and pale pink striped shirt.'

Now they both relaxed into genuine mirth. His birthday shirt had been the butt of endless jokes, which even Kate had heard about over at Richmond.

'What do you think the blue paint means?' She asked. It was an odd segue but she noticed he didn't skip a beat in responding.

'No idea. Not even a hunch, other than that it could be some form of humiliation.'

'I agree. It seems like some kind of ritual, so we have to presume it carries significance for both killer and victims.'

'I have a feeling that the paint will be his real message.'

'If it's any help, the colour blue in Feng Shui means relaxing.'

'It's not.'

'Twenty pounds says it is, and you'd lose.'

'No,' he said with a grin, 'I mean, it's not any help.'

'Oh.'

'But you're right, Kate. That's how we have to think. What does blue mean to this killer, rather than what does it mean to us? What is its significance in the scheme of murder?' He sighed. 'It could be anything.'

'The obvious one is woad. You know, the Pict warriors painting themselves. Although real woad is indigo in colour, almost black.'

'Our killer has been very deliberate and organised,' Jack mused. 'Care has been taken in choosing when and where. One would presume he's taken the same care in choosing that paint, especially if it is meant to be meaningful to the victims.'

'So the colour, that brighter blue, is deliberately chosen too,' she finished.

He nodded. 'Yes. I think we should consider painting or tattooing the body as an ancient warrior practice — in fact, it'd be worth putting Sarah on to that — but even so it doesn't fully gel in my mind.'

'Blue means depressed,' Kate said, warming to the task.

'Injury,' he countered, 'as in black and blue.'

'Or sexually explicit.' Kate sat up at this. 'Actually, that's quite intriguing, isn't it? Depressed, sexual, injury — they all relate to our crime scene.'

He nodded, concentrating on the road ahead as he considered this.

'Blue law relates to morality,' he finally said.

Kate ran her hand through her hair, messing up the careful style she'd taken so long to blow dry in order that the highlights she'd paid a fortune for appeared precisely where they were meant to. They were onto something she was sure. 'What else is blue?'

'Sky, sea, swimming pools.'

'Nothing helpful there. Blue, blue, blue ... credit card.'

'An expensive one, gets you into a lot of trouble.'

She smiled but was thinking hard. 'Blue blood?'

'Royalty? I don't think so. But the blue and blood link might mean something. The blue flag in motor racing forces the car in front to give way to faster cars coming up.'

'I'm sure that's relevant,' she said, her tone laced with sarcasm. They passed a snooker hall. 'Is there a blue ball in snooker?' she asked absently.

'Yes, worth five points.'

'Perhaps there'll be five murders then,' she said as a throwaway line.

'I hope not. Blue chip? Blue ribbon, Blue Pages, blue moon, Big Blue?'

She tried not to laugh as she shook her head. 'No, it has to be more visceral than those.'

'Veins. They carry blood. And they're blue. Is that visceral enough?'

'That's not what I meant.'

'Okay then, what about the university blues?'

'What's that?'

'You know, the sporting colours of Oxford and Cambridge. Perhaps our killer and victims were all scholars.'

She groaned. 'I doubt it, but please don't tell me you went to either of those?'

'No, Warwick.'

'Good. Anything else?'

'Chelsea.'

'Right, thank you. Leave it with me, Jack. I do love a puzzle but you're hindering rather than helping now.'

She was already wondering if Jack was right that this paint might be the message. The 'boys in blue' referred to the police after all, and then there were blue collar workers, which might refer to the killer, although that felt entirely wrong.

'What did Farrow and Sheriff do for a crust?' she asked.

'Farrow was a contract glazier who turned permanent casual courier when he arrived in London. And Sheriff was a teacher. Why?'

'Random thoughts. Blue is a political colour, of course.'

'It's also a musical genre.' He pulled a face in apology. 'Information overload, I think.'

She nodded and looked at his watch to work out the time. She liked the shape of his fingers, and the way his thumb crooked and didn't quite grip the steering wheel.

'I'm hungry,' she said. It was the first thing that came into her mind to distract her from his hands.

'We'll get you something. I know a couple of good spots in the old quarter. You can take your pick from the Wig and Mitre pub or the rather famous Brown's Pie Shop. But I warn you — there's an almighty cobbled hill to climb first. Ah, I've just thought of something else. Blue-tongued lizards. They live in Australia, with my sister.'

'What, all of them?'

He grinned at her quip as he overtook a car, narrowly missing it and making her hold her breath.

'And Cashel Blue is delicious,' he added. 'It's the most famous cheese in Ireland, I'm told.'

'Shut up, please, and drive.'

Kate wished he didn't make her feel quite so warm inside. She covered her left hand with her right and twirled the beautiful diamond solitaire that Dan had given her when he'd proposed on a romantic spring weekend in Marlow last year. It had been directly after some 'morning glory', as he liked to call it, and they were both tousled and drowsy in that warm, sticky cocoon of arms and legs that lovemaking provokes. Kate recalled how she'd wept when he pulled a black velvet box from beneath his pillow and, without hesitation or awkwardness, kissed her deeply and asked her to marry him. She hadn't been able to speak for a few moments, and had always believed it was because of the rush of the emotion, the tears, the happiness, but now she was beginning to understand why she'd cried and taken that time to answer Dan. It was because she really wasn't sure that she loved him in the way he loved her, in the way that people who plan to marry, have a family and grow old together should. But she was already into her early thirties, and her two sisters, both younger than her, were married and starting to tease her about still being a spinster.

'Penny for your thoughts,' Jack said into the heavy silence.

'I was just thinking whether to be a thoroughly modern bride and not get married at all. Or whether to go through the whole ceremony thing so my mother won't feel robbed and just opt for white chocolate cake as my act of rebellion.'

'Mmm, that second option is definitely subversive. Very modern.'

'Yes, maybe that's the way to go. And Dan likes white chocolate.'

'And you?'

'Oh, I'm a bitter chocolate kind of a gal, I'm afraid.'

'Milky Bars are for babies, I agree.' He gave her one of those soft smiles, and Kate realised he had sensed her awkwardness about her forthcoming wedding, perhaps even about Dan.

He changed the subject and began regaling her with tall stories of how he and Geoff nearly didn't make it through their cadetship. By the time they caught sight of Lincoln's magnificent cathedral through the drizzly haze that the windscreen wipers did little to improve, she was laughing delightedly, lost in his tales, but she also noticed she hadn't stopped twirling her engagement ring.

Clare felt Garvan's hand squeeze her shoulder. He'd been acting strangely for the past couple of days: distracted and forgetful. After being so close for thirty-five years of marriage, Clare was suddenly feeling left out from her husband's life.

'Want a coffee, love? I could murder one,' he said.

'Who was that on the phone?'

'Nothing important,' he said, moving to put water in the kettle.

'Why so secretive?'

He looked at her, surprised. 'No secret. A doctor's appointment, that's all. I'd forgotten it was today actually.'

'Since when does a doctor's surgery call its patients?' she asked, her tone disbelieving.

He closed the tap. 'When the doctor's not going to be in for some reason and they need to change the appointment.'

She looked at him long and hard. 'What's wrong with you?'

Garvan flicked the switch on the kettle. 'I have to get something for this sore throat.'

Clare moved away, irritated by his manner. She knew this man too well and he was hiding something. 'Don't forget to ring Peter,' she said.

'I plan to call him straight after my coffee. I think I'm going to dig out all my fishing tackle.'

'What? How long's it been?'

'Fifteen years, probably.'

'What's brought this on?'

He shrugged. Busied himself making the coffee. 'Want one, love?'

She shook her head and walked away to the sitting room, inwardly berating herself for overreacting. His mind was probably elsewhere because of this big potential contract Peter was waiting to hear about. Both of them knew it would change their son's life if the deal went ahead. He could afford to buy a house, get on with getting married and starting his own family. Retired, and feeling every one of her fifty-nine years, Clare felt that grandchildren were all she had to look forward to. She regretted being so much like her own mother in this way, and hoped with all her heart that Peter didn't feel the pressure too much, although she suspected she might be kidding herself.

She thought about the dark days of long ago. All Clare had ever wanted in life was to have children, and her mother, Elsie, had desperately wanted to be a grandmother. Elsie was a strong, dominant woman who liked to control her husband and her daughter. Grandchilden had become a burning issue between mother and daughter once Clare had married, and when four years passed with no baby, the relationships between daughter and mother, son-in-law and mother-in-law had suffered intensely.

She could remember the ensuing arguments between herself and Garvan as if they were yesterday. It was the only time in their marriage that they had really fought. Many years later, when she was much older, much wiser, Clare could see that all the aggression was being generated by her mother and being passed on via herself to poor Garvan. Once the tests had confirmed that he was indeed the problem, her mother had had someone specific to blame. 'Slow swimmers,' the hospital specialist had offered with an awkward grin as an interpretation of the sperm test.

She hated to remember those times. Garvan had changed character entirely. It was as though, after four years of marriage, she was suddenly living with a stranger, and by 1975 they were living separately, to give themselves some breathing space from the arguments and the tension of being childless.

She had no idea where Garvan had gone during that time. He'd kept working, and she'd assumed he was staying with a friend, but contact between them was minimal and always filled with pain for both of them. Even in the blur of her own despair she'd understood that he was hurting every bit as much, but Elsie had ensured Garvan had felt it was all his fault, as though he'd betrayed his wife and her family. But then a miracle had occurred and Peter had come along. She had asked no questions, couldn't bear to know the whys and wherefores. All that mattered was that she was to be a mother. She would never forget the moment that newborn Peter was placed in her arms. She had wept uncontrollably, so had Garvan. In fact, the depth of his emotion had surprised her and she had never seen him sob like that before or since.

He had looked so frightened that night. She had been frightened too, but instant love had overcome all fear of any possible repercussions of taking Peter into their lives. All that mattered at that moment was that they were a family and they were together.

Garvan handed her a mug, dragging her thoughts back to the present.

'I made you one anyway,' he said. 'I'm going upstairs to get into some decent clothes for the doctor, and before you remind me, I'll call Peter before I head off. You're meeting Sheila today, aren't you?'

'Yes, you'll be alone most of the day, we're going over to Worthing.'

'Buy yourself something nice.' He kissed the top of her head and pointed at the remote control. 'Could you turn on the news, love, let me know if there are any more bulletins on those murders?'

She watched him go upstairs and wondered why on earth he was so interested in Britain's latest serial killer.

6

I sat in the comfy bucket seat and eyed Dr March with a direct stare. My life had taken a new, dangerous path since the last time I'd sat here and poured out my thoughts. Now it was February and nearing the end of winter, and I had the blood of two men on my hands.

I'd been seeing Dr March for years without my spouse knowing. The psychiatrist thought I was here to talk about depression. About how the unhappy discovery that having children — the simplest, most normal event of all Nature's magic — had been such a problem for us. And then James had been born and had changed our lives forever.

But really I was in therapy for the opportunity to talk about the effects of something that had happened three decades previous. I never referred to it openly, of course — it was my secret. But Dr March helped all the same, without knowing it, for her rooms were the only place I ever felt safe enough to allow my thoughts to go back to that horrific year during the 1970s.

I had spent most of my adult life suppressing the memories, unable to face returning to a time I could recall in such vivid and excruciating detail. But now the time was right for me to recall every nuance of that experience. I needed to remember it, to live through it again, because the rage it invoked gave me the courage to finally seek the vengeance that was long overdue.

The public at large had nothing to fear from me: my next victim was already chosen. There was nothing random about the killings that had the media in a frenzy. But I still had to find my target, and I had to move fast now that Detective Chief Inspector Jack Hawksworth would be closing the gap as quickly as his resources could fill it. Time was surely more on my side than Hawksworth's, though. He had no idea why I had killed two seemingly unrelated blokes from different counties with very different lifestyles. But once he began digging into the past, he would put Sheriff and Farrow in the same place at the same time. I just had to make sure I got to Billy and Phil before Hawksworth joined all the dots and reached them first.

It began for me one Wednesday after school. They were following me. This in itself wasn't so unusual; it happened once or twice a week. I didn't want to look around because that only encouraged them. *Keep walking*, I urged myself.

All I wanted was to be left alone to survive the mire of misery my life had become, make something of myself and build a new life far away from Hangleton and the tragedy that surrounded my family.

But they wouldn't let me. Every group needs a target — someone to ridicule, someone whose life is worse than theirs.

'Bletch' they called me. Some kid from Manchester who'd moved down south said it meant 'oil slick' up north, and the name had stuck, spewing out of my tormentors' mouths like the vomit they mimicked as they said it.

Humiliation — it was my closest companion then. It went perfectly with my poor eyesight, the ugly glasses with their thick lenses, and the hated braces clinging to my teeth. Mother Nature hadn't been terribly kind to me.

But the real darkness had descended when a drunk driver crashed into my father and my baby brother one rainy night. My mother, incapable of coping with her own pain, had sunk into an oblivion aided by a mixture of sedatives and brandy. I needed a mother more than ever during those early teenage years of being goofy, moon-faced and solid all over, but my mother rarely bothered to get out of bed. She knew I'd figure out how to get myself ready for school, organise my own breakfast and pack my own lunchbox — if there was any food in the house.

If school was a minefield, home was a war zone. I was constantly reminded of our loss there, through photos and the way my mother had given up on her own life, and on me. Each Monday after school, I'd force her to stand in the bath — usually in her stained nightie to appease my own modesty — and let the shower bring her back to some semblance of life. Then I'd help her to dress, always averting my gaze to avoid looking upon her bared flesh, and we'd walk slowly to the post office to withdraw our weekly living allowance from the funds my father, a doctor, had left us. Now my mother was so numb, the household budgeting fell to me. Numbers were easy for me, so I took on the financial responsibility as Mum slid fully into the all-consuming abyss of grief. There was one blessing: the house was paid for.

'Bletch!'

That was Billy Fletcher, tall and strong for his age, and good-looking. We were in the same English and Science classes. On top of his handsome appearance, Billy was very smart and I hated that he wasted his gifts simply because of a stutter that brought unwelcome attention from his peers. Instead of rising above it, that simple flaw prompted in him an all-pervading bitterness.

I ignored Billy's call and hurried on, feeling the full weight of my homework in my schoolbag. I clutched it tightly, knowing it would be the first item to be ripped from me and emptied on the street or tossed into someone's garden.

'Hey, Bletch, wait for us.'

That was Michael Sheriff. I could tell by his scratchy voice. Mikey was stocky, permanently rosy-cheeked and cursed with severe eczema behind his knees and thick, forever-cracked lips. I'd been at junior school with Mikey but he was now at a different senior school, although I gathered he had no friends and still relied on his earlier acquaintances for his social interaction.

'What have you got in your schoolbag, Bletch? Anything for us to eat?'

That was Phil Bowles, preoccupied with food as usual. It was Phil who'd begun the routine of following me home from school, doing his stupid Biggles impressions, forming his fingers into goggles around his eyes and pretending to zoom around in an aircraft. He was tiny for his age and I'd known him since primary school, when he used to like pretending to be a dog and would bound alongside the other kids. He was funny then, but something had obviously happened to him since to shape him into something far more sinister than man's best friend. I had no idea what school he went to now for he didn't wear a uniform; just nondescript black trousers and a white shirt without a tie.

Finally, there was Clive Farrow, who solved his problems with his fists. Clive was slow, always in the remedial classes at school, and subjected to a lot of taunting. By secondary school, he'd learned to fight back by picking on people more vulnerable than himself and had become a fully fledged bully. If the foursome of tormentors had an inciter, Clive was probably it, although Billy was quietly accepted as their leader.

It was Clive's coarse voice that answered Phil. 'No, Bletch ate it all. Be careful, Phil, Bletch will eat you too. You're about snack size, aren't you?'

This set off much joshing and I sped up. I didn't want to flat out run because that was an invitation for trouble, giving them the excuse they wanted to chase me down. If only someone would step out of their house or pull up in a car and frighten them off.

No such luck. Billy was on my case now, stammering out the next insult.

'You think you're so clever. I saw that test you did today. Perfect score. Only one in the class. What are you doing in this school anyway if you're so smart?'

Billy Fletcher had hit the bull's-eye, the one taunt that could really injure me. Yes, I was smart, clever enough to have gone to the grammar school and shone. But just before the eleven-plus exam, my mother had been rushed to hospital to get her stomach pumped after an overdose of tranquillisers. I'd been terrified I'd be left alone, and in my trauma I had fluffed the most important test of my life. There was no going back, no resitting it. The brown envelope arrived in due course to announce what I already knew. I remember crying alone at the bottom of the garden in my father's shed, thinking of other kids who received good news in those pristine white envelopes, telling them they were the 'cream' and would attend one of the two county grammar schools and have a better chance in life.

I stopped and turned angrily to answer Billy. 'I don't want to be here.'

Michael licked his flaky lips. 'Go to grammar then! We don't want a fat, ugly, clever bastard around us.'

'What does it matter to you? You're not even at our school, and I'm no more a bastard than you are,' I countered. 'My father may be dead but I know who he was.'

'Oooh,' they crowed, revelling in the high colour creeping up from my neck and the catch in my voice. I was such an idiot to let them do this to me with such ease.

'Yeah, well, bastard or not, you're still fat and ugly,' Phil said and the others laughed.

'Are you alright?'

I realised Dr March was staring at me with a worried frown.

'I'm sorry,' I said and pulled myself back to the present.

'What happened just then?' she asked.

'I just tuned out. Something must have triggered a memory. I was remembering my childhood for some reason.'

'Was it the deaths, do you think?' she prompted.

'Deaths?' I echoed, startled. Mikey's and Clive's death grins were still vivid in my mind.

'You told me, remember? How your father and brother were killed. We've never really discussed that time in your life, have we? You've never felt strong enough to go there.'

'Oh,' I replied, trying not to show my relief. 'Do you mind reminding me what we were talking about before?' I wanted to move her away from the subject of death.

Dr March gave a small smile of sympathy. 'Of course. We were discussing how it feels to be told that you can't be a parent.'

'That's right, I do remember.' I smoothly picked up our previous discussion. 'Well, James solved that issue, I suppose, although we can't have any more children.'

'Any more? You wouldn't consider it at your age, surely?' Dr March allowed her surprise to break through her normally professional facade. It was quite amusing.

'No, of course not,' I said, trying not to laugh.

I didn't need Dr March any more. Perhaps I'd come back for

one more session, so as not to provoke any alarm bells, but right now I wanted to be gone from here and my memories.

'Dr March, I don't feel at all well. I've got the most hideously sore throat and talking is making it worse. I'm so sorry to cut our session short,' I lied.

'Oh, absolutely,' she said, closing her notebook with a light slap. 'We can have a slightly longer talk next time perhaps? Now, when are you back in London?' She consulted her diary.

'Actually, Dr March, I'm not sure of my movements or when I'll next be here. How about I call you later this week?'

'Oh,' she said, frowning at her diary and flicking backwards through the pages. 'I'm actually rather full this week. Um . . .' She tapped her pencil against a page. 'But give Teresa a call — she's a witch, as you know, and capable of magicking up space for all my clients.'

I smiled. I was always impressed at how she referred to us as clients rather than patients. 'That will be fine. Thank you.'

Dr March had been very kind and earnest in her endeavours to help me through the past couple of years. I wondered how calm she'd remain if she knew Britain's latest serial killer was sitting opposite her now, thinking about my next victim.

7

Jack and Kate sat awkwardly in the damp garden at the back of Michael Sheriff's small farmhouse outside Louth. Diane Sheriff had welcomed them warily and was now approaching with a tray holding plunger coffee and a plate of biscuits. Kate didn't want a custard cream. She'd been pounding away at the gym to get into shape for 'the dress', so everything sugary, starchy or even vaguely fatty was best ignored. But she didn't want to appear rude to a woman who looked as though she was barely holding it together. Just as she had the thought, Diane Sheriff dissolved into tears.

In an instant, Jack was on his feet and grabbing the tray. 'We're deeply sorry to resurrect Michael's death, Diane,' he said gently, guiding her to a seat on the bench next to Kate as he balanced the full tray with his free arm. He glanced at Kate and she took up the thread.

'It's just that we now believe that the attack on your husband wasn't random as the police first thought.'

Diane sniffed into a hanky she'd produced. 'I thought it was odd that Scotland Yard phoned,' she said, sniffing. 'But when you think of the horrific injuries inflicted, I don't know why anyone could think it was random. They had to have a purpose, didn't they?' She regarded them both with red-rimmed eyes over plump cheeks.

Jack, now seated, leaned forward. Kate could tell he didn't want to upset Diane further with news of the second murder but it was unavoidable. She watched him take a breath.

'We're beginning to suspect that the person who did this to Michael is taking some sort of revenge.'

'For what?'

'We don't know yet, that's why we've come to see you. We hoped you might know something or remember something about Michael's past that might give us a clue.'

'Revenge,' she repeated, looking between them. 'What makes you think that? Mike had no enemies to my knowledge. Where has such an idea come from?'

An almost imperceptible nod from her boss gave Kate permission to say more.

'There's been a second murder, Diane. It has too many similarities to Michael's death not to be connected.'

Diane stared at Kate, her face tear-stained and bloodless. 'He did the same things?'

Kate nodded. 'Apart from location, the only difference was that the second victim wasn't intoxicated by alcohol at the time of death. But he was drugged, as Mike was,' she said, dropping the formality and falling in line with how the woman referred to her husband. 'Diane, I know this is painful, and again we apologise for raking over Mike's life, but have you ever heard the name Clive Farrow mentioned in any of Mike's conversations?'

She thought for a few moments, dabbing at her eyes as she did so, then she shook her head. 'I don't think so. It doesn't ring any bells.'

'Did Mike ever go out with a group of his own friends?' Kate tried.

'No,' Diane said quickly. 'Not really. Apart from his work colleagues, who he had to socialise with from time to time, he was a loner. We were really each other's best friend. I don't have anyone close either, other than our son and daughter.'

Kate felt a pang of guilt at making Diane confront her pain all over again.

'What about before you two met? Did he ever speak about life before then? Mike was a teacher, wasn't he?'

Diane sipped her coffee. A good sign, Kate thought, that the tears were done with for the moment.

'Yes, he taught general science to the middle school age group.' She smiled sadly. 'They called him Ducky, because of his lips.'

'What about his lips?' Kate asked, her interest piqued. Perhaps this had something to do with why they'd been removed, although she dismissed that thought almost immediately because it wouldn't account for Clive Farrow's lips being taken as well.

'He had thick lips — very smoochy,' Diane replied, smiling sadly, losing herself in her memories momentarily. 'So they called him Ducky, but also because his lips tended to gleam a bit from the special cream he used to keep them smooth.' She noted Kate frowning. 'He had a chapping problem.'

'Ah.'

'Mike enjoyed teaching. He said to me once that school hadn't been very good to him. He wanted to make it different for the kids who passed through his life as a teacher.'

Kate glanced towards Jack. He kept his silence, but his nod urged her to continue.

'School was rough, was it?' she said.

'No, not rough, I just don't think he was popular.' Diane's expression turned sheepish. 'He had eczema, thick chapped lips and he wasn't terribly tall. You know how kids can be.'

'Did he get into any bother?' Jack asked softly in the background.

She shrugged. 'I wouldn't know any details — we met thirteen years ago. I think he might have fallen in with the wrong crowd, though, at one point.'

Jack nodded. 'What makes you say that?'

'Oh, I'm not sure. Let me think.' She bit absently into a biscuit and Kate watched the crumbs fall unheeded onto her lap. 'Um, I think he might have mentioned there was a gang he moved with for a while. But something happened,' she shrugged, 'and they fell out with each other. I really don't know much at all. I only knew Mike from when he moved to Lincoln.'

'Oh, I see,' Kate said. 'Where was Mike from?'

'He transferred to Lincoln from Aylesbury where he'd been teaching, but originally he lived in a place called Hangleton, down south. Couldn't wait to escape it, I gather.'

'Hangleton?' Jack frowned. 'Is that a village somewhere?'

'No idea, never been there. I know it's somewhere close to Brighton.'

'Brighton?' They said it together, startling Diane.

'Yes, why are you looking at me like that?'

'Diane, the second murder,' Jack said gently, 'it happened in London but the victim was originally from Brighton — well, Hove.'

This set off a fresh wave of emotion. Kate put her arm around the woman's bent, sobbing shoulders, but a glance at her boss showed the same gleam in his eye. They'd just had their first breakthrough.

As the tears subsided once again, Kate asked for what was needed. 'Diane, would you have any photos of Mike when he was younger? School photos perhaps, or better still, some teenage shots?'

'I ... er, I don't think so.' Diane shrugged as she sensed their surprise. 'We've only been together since we were thirty. And Mike wasn't terribly sentimental about his childhood.'

'You're quite sure?' Kate urged. 'I can help you look.'

'Why do you need them?'

'Because we might be able to find a link through this gang you mentioned, or perhaps we'll find the other victim in his school photos,' Jack explained. 'All we need is something to link Mike with the second victim — photos can be a great help.'

'Truly, I don't believe we have anything of Mike's from those years. Any number of my childhood photos, and hundreds from when we first met through to today, but nothing from his early years.' She shrugged. 'I'm sorry.'

Jack nodded and stood up. 'This is my card,' he said, pressing it into her hand. 'If anything should occur to you, however small or seemingly inconsequential, phone me or leave a message and I'll call you the moment I can. Kate's put her mobile number on the back too. Feel free to call either of us.'

'Thank you,' she murmured, his card crumpling in her grip.

'Diane, is there anything we can do for you before we leave?' Kate asked. 'When do the children get home?'

She shook her head. 'I'll be fine. I've got to get used to being alone. It's just talking about it makes it seem like yesterday.'

They both nodded sympathetically, and Kate hated herself all over again.

'The school bus should be here in just over an hour. Time to get myself cleaned up,' the woman said, the tremor in her voice clearing as she rallied. 'I don't like Rob and Sally to see me like this. It's hard enough on them without their mum cracking up all the time.'

'You've been very strong, Diane,' Jack said. 'And we can't thank you enough for seeing us today.'

'You catch that bastard,' she said as they left.

Jack was reminded of his Super's similarly charged demand.

Jack recommended Brown's Pie Shop.

'It never gets easier,' Jack sighed, as the waitress placed a freshly squeezed orange juice in front of him.

Kate had opted for a latte, and a steaming pie sat before each of them.

'What, that walk, you mean?' Kate ripped the top from a packet of sweetener and tipped the fine powder into her coffee. She hated the stuff, but if she wanted to fit into her wedding dress, it was a necessary evil. Especially as she was about to tuck into a pie. 'From the bottom it looks easy.'

He grinned. 'I know. It's better to park in the old quarter and walk down. It's not called Steep Hill for nothing.'

'No understatement there. Why didn't we park at the top anyway?'

'I wanted to see how well you'd negotiate the cobbles in those unlikely walking shoes.'

'Bastard!' she murmured, which made his grin widen.

'Actually, I meant it never gets easier dealing with the victims' families,' he said. 'Each time I think I get the bedside manner right, it deserts me or they say something that makes me feel a complete git for asking such painful questions.'

Kate blew on her latte and sipped. 'She'll be hurting for a long time to come, I reckon. I'll call her tomorrow morning; press on the photos just in case there are some lurking. Everyone has photos, right?'

Jack nodded. 'You'll have to press gently but with urgency. Time is not our friend.'

Kate looked up from her coffee. 'I've never been to Lincoln before. It's lovely.'

'Mmm, it is. Just up from here,' he said, taking a gulp from his glass, 'is the area known as Bailgate, which includes the cathedral. And in the Norman castle just above us, they've got one of the four original copies of the Magna Carta.'

She cocked her head to one side. 'Bakes, likes old churches and seems to enjoy history.'

He put his hands up in mock defeat. 'These Brown's pies are famous. You'll never want any other sort of pie after this one.'

'Dan loves pies.' She stopped, embarrassed that Dan's name was now flashing like a huge neon sign between them. She had no reason to feel awkward and yet she did.

Jack didn't seem to feel the awkwardness, however, asking without hesitation, 'So Dan is your fiance?'

She nodded. 'We're getting married later this year.'

He raised his glass. 'Congratulations to both of you.'

She clinked her latte against his orange juice.

'What does he do?'

She really didn't want to get into the Dan thing now. She cut deeper into her pie. 'Computers,' she replied, the all-encompassing answer that didn't explain anything but was unlikey to prompt further queries.

'All Greek to me. I just want them to work.'

'Dan ensures they do.'

There was a small, fragile pause that Jack filled almost the second it arrived. 'So, Kate, you'll phone Mrs Sheriff, right?'

She nodded, realising he had once again picked up on her wariness regarding Dan. 'It's a long shot but somewhere to start.'

He finished his food in five neat gulps while Kate was still only a quarter through hers.

'Will you excuse me?' he said. 'I'm just going to check how

Bill and Cam are faring. Enjoy your pie whilst it's still hot.' And he went outside.

Kate poked at her pie, suddenly losing all interest in its decadent deliciousness. She turned instead to her cooling latte and focused on the case. She agreed with Jack: the blue paint had obvious significance for the killer, and perhaps his victims. Why else would he have dipped Sheriff's and Farrow's fingers into the paint? Something else was niggling at her too. The more she considered the mutilations, the more it nagged at her that something wasn't quite right about the profile. She just wasn't sure what. She ate another couple of mouthfuls, just to make her plate look less full.

Jack returned. She could see frustration flitting across his normally carefully controlled expression.

'I can't raise either of them,' he said. 'I've left a message. Let's go take a look at where Sheriff's body was found.'

'Okay.' She reached for her bag. 'Have we —'

'All paid. Let's go,' he said, holding her jacket out to her. 'You might need this, it's cooled off out there. I'll walk you past the cathedral.'

She smiled thinly, hating him momentarily for being so considerate. Why couldn't he be boorish, and then she could go home to Dan tonight and complain about her new boss.

'We're not doing the hill again, are we?' she asked, wondering how her heels would hold up on the cobbles.

'We're almost at the top anyway.'

He guided her towards the peak of the hill. She couldn't help but be awestruck by the magnificent structure once they crested the rise.

'Oh, it's brilliant!' she exclaimed. And it was. Her bleak mood vanished at the sight of one of the most glorious medieval buildings in all of Europe.

'We can get a closer look on our way down. They say nothing stands between its spires and the Urals of Russia,' Jack said. 'It was begun nearly one thousand years ago.'

'Have you swallowed a textbook?'

'Sorry. I admit I find history comforting.'

'Like baking.' She leapt back to the safe ground of work. 'Listen, I've been thinking.'

'Mmmm?' he murmured distractedly, staring at the northern transept where work was being done.

'Can I run a notion past you?'

He didn't reply, still gazing at the cathedral.

'Are you listening, DCI Hawksworth?'

'I'm waiting for your notion, DI Carter,' he replied.

'Ah, right. Well, our murderer . . .'

'Yes?' He turned back to her, the wind that Lincoln was famous for pulling at his jacket and tousling his hair.

'Er . . .' Kate felt her thoughts disintegrate. This wasn't the right time. In fact, not only did she need to take more time to think through such a crazy notion but she also needed to get a better grip on herself. Wedding or not, doubts or otherwise, this was her boss and they were working on the highest-profile criminal case in the UK right now. And while the rest of the team was applying all of its available hours to hunting the killer, she was admiring the colour of Jack Hawksworth's hair and wondering what it might feel like if she touched it!

'Perhaps I'll save it for now,' she said. 'I need to think it through a bit.'

'Okay, I'm all ears whenever you're ready.' He glanced her way quizzically. 'Let's go see the alleyway where Sheriff's body was dumped.'

She nodded, hiding her embarrassment by wrapping her scarf around her nose and mouth to protect her face from the wind.

'So, have you any theories on how these two guys are connected?'

'Well,' he said, pointing towards the path that led down into the new quarter of the city, 'I guess we may learn a lot more about Sheriff and Farrow if we can establish the link in Brighton.'

'You're thinking about the gang that Sheriff's wife mentioned, aren't you?'

'It's logical, because she made it sound as though her husband had fallen in with the wrong sort. Maybe Farrow was one of them and they got up to some mischief that got out of hand, led to some crime that someone's now trying to hide.'

'Like what?'

'No idea yet,' he said, frowning as they descended a short flight of stairs. 'Incidentally, a ghost apparently lives near these steps.'

Kate looked up, distracted. 'What?'

'People believe a ghost lives here and grabs you by the ankle as you walk up the steps. He sometimes appears in photos taken at this spot. People only realise when they have their films developed.'

She couldn't resist. 'Doesn't he choose to appear in digital photos?'

'Apparently not,' Jack said, and went on before she could respond. 'He usually turns on the light over the staircase for those.'

'Anyone can do that,' she replied, appreciating his helping hand on the slippery stonework.

'Not really. They've never been able to make this light work.'

'Ever?' she asked with a shiver.

He grinned mischievously and shook his head. 'So the story goes.'

She didn't know whether to believe him or not, but it was a good tale; definitely made the hairs stand up on the back of her neck.

They'd arrived back at the Guild Hall and the traffic swirling around them and people swarming across the Mall meant all talk stopped in favour of negotiating their way through the lively activity and down towards the city's canal where they were parked.

'Do you know where you're going?' Kate asked as Jack negotiated Lincoln's busy streets.

'Only sort of,' he admitted, but eventually they found the silent alleyway where Michael Sheriff's body had been found. It was still technically in the old quarter, away from the usual tourist areas.

'Why here?' Hawksworth asked aloud, as if expecting the black, damp walls to answer him.

Kate shrugged. It was even colder in this alleyway. 'Deserted, dark.'

'Don't you get the impression that our killer is more calculating than opportunist? I don't think he or she did anything without thinking it through carefully. No clues were left and Sheriff didn't die here,' Jack reminded her, 'he was brought here. Now I agree this is a deserted area, but there have to be less difficult places in the city to dump a body than this.'

'So an intentional drop.'

Kate looked around. There was nothing to suggest this place was in any way special. She glanced at the broken police tape flapping at the entrance they'd just come through.

'Perhaps,' Jack began, 'this is like the blue paint — meaningful only to the killer and victims.'

'So where was Farrow found again?'

'Some public toilets in a park.'

'A more probable spot then — easier access, quiet and dark.'

'But there are still easier places to leave a corpse. Farrow could have simply been dumped on Hackney Marshes. No, Kate, I think our killer is choosing these locations. They have meaning.'

'We'd better tell John Tandy.'

'Immediately,' Jack agreed. 'It may help in working up his profile for us. Come on, it's getting late, let's get going. I'm heading back to the Yard, but can I drop you somewhere?'

'You're going back to work?'

'I've got to check on a few things in our new operations room. We start tomorrow on the twelfth floor, remember, don't go to Welly House.'

'Ah, of course. The twelfth floor — they must be very sexy offices.'

'Trust me, they'll blow you away. So, back to the Yard?'

'If you can drop me at Angel tube station, that would be great.'

'Done. I might even get a gym session in.'

Kate groaned. 'Oh, make me feel guilty why don't you.'

Jack grinned at her. 'More than anything the exercise gives me a chance to clear my thoughts. Doesn't it do the same for you?'

'Nothing more than my comfy sofa, a glass of wine and a DVD couldn't achieve.'

Or another row with Dan, she thought and turned away from her boss's smiling face to stare sadly out of the car window.

8

Jack had ignored the cross-trainer and opted for a forty-minute random run to nowhere on the treadmill, the 'Big O' singing to him through his miniature headphones. Jack preferred to use New Scotland Yard's gym late, when only the shift workers drifted in and out and he didn't have to queue for machines or deal with conversations and other people's noise and sweat. The downside was that the showers took a century to warm up and, more often than not, he had to grit his teeth and have a tepid shower, as he was now.

He dried off and dressed in the tracksuit he habitually carried in his training bag. He didn't bother with his hair, just legged it back up to the new operations offices to grab his gear and get home for a few hours' sleep.

He strode past reception and Joan's home-made sign — a piece of A4 paper declaring in bold red letters that he had entered the Operation Danube Office — and down to the end of the long, narrow chamber where an attempt at separate offices had been achieved with partitions.

Joan had left various notes on his desk: the *Daily Express* wanted to interview him; the BBC was enquiring as to the possibility of doing a fly-on-the-wall documentary; a magazine was keen to learn just how much an operation such as Danube cost taxpayers and could it have a photograph of the Danube team, please? He screwed that one up and lofted it so he could kick it into a bin. 'Goal!' he said and glanced at the final message. It was from DCI Deegan of the Ghost Squad, and was simply a number, nothing else.

'Ghost Squad?' he murmured, frowning. 'What the hell does he want?'

The arrival of someone at the entry to his office startled him and he tossed the note onto his desk. 'Sarah, what are you doing here?'

She frowned. 'I hope you don't mind that I've started in our new offices a little earlier than you planned, sir. I had some research to do and everything was shut down at Welly House. I've still got my coat on from three hours ago, sir, I did mean to leave.'

He softened his expression. 'No, of course I don't mind. Do you like it?' he asked, turning to look out of the window.

'I lost the first fifteen minutes just ogling, sir. It's so beautiful — I've never seen Westminster from this angle, or at night.'

He smiled. 'Go home, get some sleep.'

'What's your excuse, sir?'

He saw the twitch of a smile at the corners of her mouth and wondered how much more open her face might look if she let rip with a laugh and ditched the heavy-rimmed glasses.

'I hit the gym in an effort to blow the cobwebs from my mind.'

'Did it work?'

'No, but I'm exhausted.'

'Well, I might have something to send you off with a smile on your face ... er, no pun intended.'

He gave her a quizzical look. 'You've got me ... go on.'

'It's about the blue paint, sir.'

Now she had his attention. 'Oh yes?'

Sarah glanced at the notes in her hand. 'Blue paint is a superstitious colour, particularly in the theatre.'

'Sit down, Sarah, please.' He gestured to a chair and reached for his half-drunk bottle of water and gulped some down. 'How on earth did you get to that point?'

She shrugged, her expression one of slight embarrassment. 'I got onto the net, sir, and started typing in all sorts of things, hoping to stumble across something that might give us a connection with the paint.'

'And you have, obviously. Explain it to me and how the theatre links in.'

'Not the theatre precisely, but it's what led to me to what came next. As I said, blue is a highly superstitious colour. They say if you paint it on your doors it can keep bad things away from the house, and if you wear a blue bead no witches will approach you. Theatre actors don't like to wear blue on stage, particularly on opening night —'

'Why's that?'

'Something to do with blue being a difficult colour to achieve in medieval times and thus expensive. If theatre companies were extravagant enough to spend their money on blue costumes, people believed the show would close fairly soon due to lack of funding. Unless, of course, they wore it with silver.'

'With silver?'

'Meant the company must have had a very wealthy patron and so the show was less likely to close. The silver negated the blue.'

'Ah, interesting, go on.'

'Well, I thought so too, and to tell you the truth I got a bit lost in my fascination and kept clicking on all the various sites about blue and its uses and superstitions. I ended up at one site that talked about clowns. Apparently it's considered intensely bad luck for a clown to use any blue face paint. None of the famous ones ever have or do.'

Jack had been rocking back on his chair legs, but now he slammed forward. 'They avoid it on their face?' He felt the thrum of excitement hit his belly.

'Always. Goes back a long way in history and is now part of the clown mythology. Something bad happens if you wear blue on your face.'

He was staring past her shoulder, thinking as he spoke. 'How does this work with our victims? Any ideas?'

'I have a theory, sir.'

His gaze snapped back to her bespectacled eyes. 'I can't wait.'

She pushed back strands of hair that had come loose from her ponytail. 'Well, the blue paint on Sheriff's and Farrow's faces was put there deliberately, and because it occurred at both scenes we have to assume that the killer is making an important statement. My gut agrees with John Tandy — that this isn't a message to the police or public but something far more intimate between these three people.'

She paused to let him say something, but he was staring at her intently, silently. She cleared her throat.

'I couldn't make any major links to the woad you asked me to look into, and my gut tells me that if the killer was thinking woad, he or she would have scarred the victim's flesh somehow, maybe applied makeshift tattoos. Or they might have used indigo ink — it would have looked far more like woad, if that was the intention.'

Jack nodded. He was sure Sarah was right.

She continued. 'Regarding blue paint, the only genuine link that came out of all the sites I surfed today is that clowns don't want blue on their faces. Otherwise there's no other mention of blue on the face.'

'The killer's laughing at them?'

Sarah shook her head. 'More than that. I think he could be accusing them of being clowns. Clowns to whom bad things would happen.'

'Well, how does that hurt them?'

'I don't know, sir, although I'd suggest the killer's mocking them. Clowns don't want blue on their faces, so he's forcing them to paint that colour on their cheeks.'

Jack looked up to the ceiling. 'It's a clever connection, but I can't see how it ties in with the victims. They're bound, drugged, frightened. How do they make the link between themselves and clowns — why is our killer making them put blue paint on their own faces?'

Sarah took a deep breath and explained what had been on her mind ever since linking the blue paint with clown lore. 'Sir, I might be way off here, but I think that by cutting off the lips of the victims, our guy is leaving them with a permanent smile. It could have been painted on, but this is where I'm sure the killer is taking full revenge. That and the emasculation.'

Jack's gaze came back to rest on hers. The room felt suddenly warm and there was a curious frisson that both felt between them. They knew she was more right than wrong in her notion.

'The killer's making them permanent clowns in death,' Jack murmured, settling it in his mind.

'That's what I think, although the actual why of it is something between him and the victims.'

Jack's face creased into a grin of wonderment. 'We've got to talk to Tandy. Damn good work, DS Jones!'

Sarah couldn't successfully stifle a yawn and he frowned. 'Time to get you home.'

She glanced up at the clock. 'If I leave right now I can probably catch the last train.'

'Where's home?'

'Strawberry Hill on the embankment in Twickenham.'

'Well, tonight, DS Jones, the Yard pays for a cab. Come on, let me walk you down to Victoria. There'll be plenty of taxis there.'

Jack parked his car out the front of his building. As he was getting out, he noticed Sophie Fenton wheeling herself inside. He couldn't believe his luck. Considering they hadn't crossed each others' paths in weeks, it was a pleasant surprise to have this sudden social opportunity. Jack was glad of it, keen to get to know his neighbour better.

'Hey, Sophie,' he called and then dropped his voice, remembering the hour. 'Wait for me!'

She turned and waved, waiting at the entrance for him.

He was still wearing his tracksuit, his work clothes in his gym bag. 'You're up late.'

'Wheelies have a social life too, you know.'

Jack's expression turned to one of mortification. 'I'm sorry, I —'

'You're too easy to tease. Relax. My problem is that I can't resist the theatre.'

'And that would explain the fancy clothes. You look very lovely.'

'Thank you, and you don't look fancy at all,' she said, her smile bright beneath the streetlights.

He looked down at his dishevelled tracksuit. 'It's a sham. I just wear these to feel fit! How were you going to get up those steps on your own?'

She stared at him, bemused. 'There you go again. I'm not helpless, Jack Hawksworth.'

It was only his pleasure that she'd recalled his name that overcame the cringing realisation that he was inadvertently patronising her.

'It's only two shallow steps, and after this long in a chair I've learned how to negotiate all manner of obstacles. This new-fangled model makes it all easy. Watch.'

And he did, impressed with the way she hauled herself with great dexterity onto the top stair.

'Bravo!' he said.

'Oh, I can do plenty. You should come and watch me steeplechase.'

She was delicious. 'Do you do any sports?'

'Yes, now and then — I'm no Olympian, I might add. I used to do a lot more, but I'm so busy at the moment that just going out tonight felt like a rare treat.'

'It's sad that you go alone.' That came out wrong. He wished he could take it back and realised he must be tired.

She gave him a look of puzzlement. 'I don't think so. Are you a chauvinist, Jack?'

'I didn't mean it like that.'

'How did you mean it?'

He felt himself treading water. 'Just that I've always believed the theatre — like travel, sightseeing, other sorts of escapes — is best shared.'

'Reading is an escape. Do you read aloud to your friends?'

'Sophie, I —'

She rescued him. 'It's alright, I'm having fun goading you. I do get what you mean. The thing is, I don't have anyone to share it with, and before you rush in to tell me it shouldn't be that way, I'm not complaining — it's just how it is.'

'Let's right that. I'll come and share the theatre with you, if it suits, next time you get the urge.'

She smiled. 'Alright. I can tell you now that the urge never leaves.' Then she glanced at her wristwatch and added, 'Although I fail to see how your working hours would ever suit something so normal as a seven-thirty curtain call.'

'I would make a huge effort. You can choose.'

'*Les Miserables*. Definitely one to see more than once or twice.' She smiled; his face must have told her he'd already seen it. 'Still want to go?'

'You can't see it too many times. Yes, I'd love to go. Towards the end of the week is easier.'

'I'll organise the tickets. My treat.'

'Then let me take you to dinner. My treat.'

'I don't eat seafood.'

'Pity. But that's fine. I know a great place in Chinatown, and just a stroll — or wheel in your case — to the Prince of Wales.' He paused, realising they'd just made an offer to each other to go on a date. 'Shall we go in? It's freezing out here; you must be shivering because I am.'

She nodded and permitted him to push her inside and also squeeze himself into the cosy but elegant lift of their mansion apartments.

'Don't you have to carry a briefcase home?' she asked.

'Not tonight. I'm going to force myself to go to sleep.'

'Force?'

'Oh, my mind's whirring. I'll probably struggle to close my eyes.'

The door opened on his floor and he began sidling around her to exit.

'I have just the thing for that complaint,' Sophie said conspiratorially.

'Oh?'

'Milo.'

'The Australian drink?' He pressed his finger on the button to keep the door open.

'You know it?'

'I do. My sister lives over there. She sent me a tin once. I don't know where it is. Never tried it.'

'Well, there's a first time for everything. Come on — I'm going to have one. And remember, Jack, this is my third invitation.'

He grinned. 'Okay.' He let the door close and the lift jerked upwards to the top level. 'If you're sure.'

'I won't have any trouble sleeping, to be honest,' she said, yawning, 'but I do like my Milo before I go to bed. For some reason, unlike Ovaltine or Horlicks, it stops me dreaming.'

He smiled, stepping out first to keep the lift door from closing as she wheeled herself out and dug in her bag for her key. 'Don't you like dreaming?'

'No, I often have scary ones. Always have. That's why I keep myself up late, and always ensure I go to bed tired.'

'You'd make a fine police officer.'

She pushed open the door. 'Come on in.'

The entrance lobby, he remembered, with its gallery of watercolours of cottages, opened up into a cavernous room.

'Wow! It's big.'

'Top floors always are. It was perfect for me and my chair to get around.'

'What a great view!' He moved to stand before her huge windows — similar to his but more of them — with a fabulously comprehensive view across Waterlow Park to Hampstead Heath, which was currently a dark blotch in the distance. He turned back. 'And I really like this cream colour you've chosen. I can smell how fresh it is.'

He liked a great deal about this room but felt it would sound too gushing to praise her taste in furniture or decor.

'Thank you. I prefer it all light and neutral. It's the perfect background for artwork.' Sophie began to clatter around in the kitchen behind him. 'I think the previous owner must have knocked through a couple of rooms to achieve this.'

'Yes, I have a sitting room and study as separate rooms that would make up this space. The study is a third bedroom, actually. But I see your working area is all in one. I definitely prefer it this way.'

He looked at the smart white, huge-screened computer that sat atop a beautiful old desk he would kill for. 'Do you use it much?'

'What?' She looked up from the stove. 'Oh, the G5? Yes, it's everything to me. My link to the outside world. I'm an email junkie and a tragic surfer of the net.'

'You know, I never do. Computers just aren't my thing.'

'So, what, you handwrite everything?' she said, pouring milk into a saucepan.

He snorted. 'No. But I do think we've lost the gentle art of handwriting and letter-writing, and the even more diplomatic art of face-to-face communication. If we can send an email, we do. We even have hideously tedious abbreviated conversations by text to mobiles, even if the other person is just down the corridor. People are losing touch with each other. I fight that every day. I like our people to work as a team and the only way to do that is to ensure everyone's communicating, meeting regularly, even socialising now and then. Ah, remind me before I go about dinner.'

'We just made those plans. You won't forget, surely?'

'No, sorry, I definitely won't forget our date. I meant work. A staff dinner. Good chance for everyone to get to know each other.'

'What do you do for a living, Jack?' She was heaping teaspoons of chocolate-coloured granules from a green tin into two white china mugs.

'Oh, I thought I'd told you when we met last. I'm with the police.' That was how he always described himself. 'It's why I said you'd be good in the Force.'

Her face wore a look of incredulity. 'I'd never have picked it.'

'Why?'

'Oh, I don't know,' she said, suddenly reticent. 'Don't policemen smoke, drink, use bad language, have egg yolk or gravy spilt on their ties, dress badly?'

'Only on TV. But my sister would argue I do dress badly.'

She cocked her head to one side and observed him. 'I don't agree. Judging by the two occasions we've met, I think I would ask the fashion industry to set up a new pigeonhole for you — conservatively trendy. I thought the ice cream-striped shirt very daring.'

He groaned. 'Don't start, that was my sister's gift.'

She laughed and changed the subject. 'Put some music on, Jack. You can choose.'

He did as he was asked, enjoying browsing her CD collection and learning a little bit more about her.

'So, you moved in towards the end of November, was it?' he asked.

'Er, let's see — it was about the twenty-third.'

'Well, it looks like you've been here forever.' He pressed the button, watched the disc spin on the expensive Bang & Olufsen system and instantly Marvin Gaye began singing about the ecology.

She raised an eyebrow at his choice of music. 'Ah, the picture becomes clearer. Conservatively groovy and just a hint of soul.'

'Yes,' he shrugged. 'Very boring.' His mobile rang. 'Excuse me.'

'Not at all,' Sophie assured as he answered the call. 'I adore Marvin.'

'Hawksworth,' Jack said into the phone. He took the mug that Sophie handed him and watched her wheel herself back to the kitchen counter to fetch her own. 'That's okay, you've got me in the flesh instead,' he said. 'Good. Look, I've got to go, I'll speak to you in the morning.' He rang off, shrugged. 'Sorry.'

She gave him a soft look of sympathy. 'Don't be. I can't imagine yours is the kind of work you can leave on the desk at five each evening.'

Jack blew on the steaming drink and sipped. 'This is good. So, how about you, Sophie, what do you do?'

'I'm in property. Buying, selling, renovating, renting.'

'How did you get into that?'

'What you mean is, how can I afford to live here when I'm wheelchair-ridden and should be living on a pension?' He began to protest but she spoke over him. 'You'll get used to me, Jack. My grandmother left me everything in her will. She was my father's mother and because Dad was her only child and died quite young, I was the recipient. I used it wisely you could say, but then I also had very good advice. And I started young.'

'What about family?'

'No brothers or sisters but my mother lives in Devon, in a picture-postcard cottage by the river in a place called South Molton that I helped her buy. It's not especially old but it feels it because it's built in stone, if you get my drift?' He nodded. 'She's happy.'

'Do you see each other often?'

'Mum's a bit fragile so she doesn't travel, but I get down there as often as I can, which probably isn't enough for her. I suppose I could easily do what I do from Devon but I'm a bit of a city girl. As you can see, I like London, the theatre, its restaurants. I'm selfish; I don't want to live with my mother all of my life, and even though she doesn't want to accept it, I'm really very independent. I like working out of here and it's very central to where the properties are.'

'So you buy in London?'

'No, the prices are crazy, although I do restrict myself to investing only in the south.' She noticed his look of query and shrugged. 'I like to see what I'm getting.'

'Well, congratulations, looks like you're doing well on it.'

'It's lucrative, I'd be lying if I said it wasn't, but I think I've done alright because I started so early. I've inched into my forties now, so I've had plenty of time to make my money.'

He did a double-take. 'You definitely don't look it, if you don't mind me saying so, Sophie.'

'You can say it as much as you like!'

'Do you eat a lot of parsley?'

She had a wonderfully infectious laugh. 'Why do you ask?'

'Mrs Becker is convinced it's what makes you sit so straight and gives you that brilliant white smile.'

'Hasn't Mrs Becker heard of good dentistry?'

He grinned, looked around. 'I see you buy art. And they're originals?'

'Yeah,' she said dreamily, following his gaze around the walls. 'I'm investing in emerging artists, so you could say I'm speculating with art as I do with property, but I buy only what I like. I couldn't possibly hang something on my walls that I didn't enjoy looking at.'

'For a girl who likes the city, you buy a lot of rural scenes.'

'Well, I like vineyards.'

'Oh, sorry, that's a vineyard?' he said, staring at one very bright, mesmerising painting.

'Yes, done by a wonderful artist called Murray Edwards whom I can probably no longer afford, but I bought that when he was struggling so it came to me for a song. He sees colours that no one else sees.'

'It's magnificent,' he said, staring at her sparkling dark eyes. Much as he liked it, he was referring to more than the painting.

'Thank you.'

'But I think I like these photographs best of all,' he said, turning back to a series of monochromes. 'All of the same place, obviously.'

'Why do you like them?'

Jack shook his head as if to say he wasn't sure. 'They're awfully lonely, very bleak. Despite that, I like the defiance of the place — probably because it's a ruin rather than its once-proud self.'

She nodded, clearly impressed. 'I love it that you see that. It's exactly what makes them so poignant, and defiance is definitely the right word. You're good — you could be an art critic!' He smiled at her, disbelieving. Sophie continued. 'Do you know that in its heyday it was the finest Victorian structure of its kind in Britain?'

'Well, its pedigree and its loneliness aside, I think it's beautiful because of its strength. It's been battered by weather but it's still standing, still trying to rear itself up out of the sea — to remain alive in a way.'

'Yes,' she said, sadly now. 'That's how I view it.'

Their eyes met in one of those moments that potential lovers sense. He felt it pass through him like an electrical current but this was not the time to act on that impulse. He should go, before his fatigue lowered his guard completely.

'Well, you're right. The Milo is working its own magic,' he said. 'Suddenly I feel knackered.'

He watched the spell break in Sophie's gaze too. She smiled brightly. 'Good. Off you go then. Don't waste a moment — just climb into bed and fall asleep straightaway. Then you'll be ready to save the world tomorrow.'

He stood from where he'd been seated on a stool near the fireplace, a newfangled gas thing that looked like a log fire and was very stylish. 'Was this in here when you came?'

'Yes. The previous owner shows good taste, don't you think? One of the reasons I bought the apartment.'

'It's great. You make me feel as though I need to begin renovations downstairs tonight, and as for my singularly sorry, framed still life, I'm now planning on rushing out this weekend and finding it some company.'

She smiled. 'You must never rush art, Jack.'

He stretched, put his cup in the sink to distract both of them from his sudden desire to kiss her. 'Thanks for the bedtime drink. So, shall we try for Friday?'

'Yes, but I can't be certain tickets will be available. Friday night and all that.'

'Good point. Let me write down my home number — can I use this pad?' She nodded and Jack scribbled down the details. 'I've given you my mobile as well as a number you can reach me on at work. That's a direct line — not necessarily to me, but into the ops room where I'm based.' He grinned. 'Let me know which day you can get them for, but I'll warn you that earlier in the week is useless for me.'

'Okay.' She raised her cup, still almost full. 'Night-night, Jack.'

'I'll see myself out,' he said.

Jack slept the sleep of the dead that night, his final thoughts of Sophie and how much he was looking forward to seeing her again.

9

She got home to their flat by six and spent half an hour, while she prepared some food, poring over a list of teachers from Hove Park Comprehensive that Dermot, one of the eager young staff attached to Danube, had compiled and emailed to her laptop. She began phoning people on the list after eight, when she thought they might have finished dinner.

The conversations all went much the same way: she explained who she was, and that their team was trying to track down old scholars who might have been friends with Sheriff. As she'd imagined, most teachers scoffed at the notion that anyone who had attended Hove Park Comprehensive was a scholar but Kate had used the word for courtesy and in the hope of playing to their individual vanity to encourage them to open up. She drew a blank on Sheriff. Two of the four teachers who did remember him couldn't recall him having any particular friends. He was variously described as shy, a loner, punctual and neat, but she gathered that although they used the word 'loner', he wasn't necessarily someone without people to 'play with' as they put it. Michael Sheriff had been no high flyer academically, although one teacher who remembered him quite well from his fourth form of senior school — because of his eczema — said he was a capable student, particularly at science, but didn't apply himself with any vigour to his studies. All expressed similar pleasure at hearing he had become a teacher, and sadness at his death — they'd already heard from news reports; it seemed teachers never forgot a pupil. No one remembered anyone called Clive Farrow.

Kate moved glumly to the list of teachers who had taught at the secondary school Clive Farrow had attended, now called Blatchington Mill. She went through the same spiel, not getting much until the third call.

'...and I was wondering if you'd be able to help me, Miss —'

'Mrs.'

'Er, Mrs Truro ... if you could help with any recollection you have of who Clive Farrow might have knocked around with. Do you remember him?'

'Very clearly. Knocked around with?'

'Well, hung with ... played with?'

'Oh, I see. He didn't have anyone I'd consider a real friend. Clive Farrow was a big lumbering chap with a retarded mind.'

Mrs Truro clearly hadn't taught in the era when political correctness was insisted upon. 'That's a rather severe description,' Kate said.

'It's precisely how I remember him,' Eva Truro replied, her clipped, precise tone giving Kate a mental picture of a straight-backed old lady with grey hair pulled back tightly into a bun and pursed lips. 'He was a difficult boy, bigger than most of the teachers and certainly intimidating. Clive was not clever but he was cunning. That got him by.'

'You have a good memory, Mrs Truro.'

'Thank you. I can recall all the children I taught English Literature to, Miss Carter, and Clive Farrow was not one to embrace the finer points of Wordsworth or Hardy, Keats or Shakespeare. But I'm very sorry to hear that he is dead. I always felt that given the right encouragement and the right people around him, Clive could have done so much better. I think we all let him down.'

'Do you?' Kate was surprised at the sudden tenderness.

'Yes, but what do you do with classes that are so big? I had thirty-six children a class during the early seventies and it was impossible to do much more than teach to the average mind. There was no scope to offer remedial help — even though I seem to recall that Clive received this assistance in his junior school.'

'And what do you mean by if he'd had "the right people" around him?'

'Oh, Clive was a problem waiting to happen. He was frustrated, you see.'

'I'm not sure I do, Mrs Truro.'

She heard the former teacher sigh. 'Well, Miss Carter —'

'It's Detective Inspector Carter, actually,' Kate said, annoyed with herself for being petty.

Mrs Truro carried on as if uninterrupted. 'Clive's appearance and his slowness tended to mark him as a potential victim. He came to us as an angry young lad who'd seen a lot of the cane at his junior school, and thus learned to use his size and his fists to ensure he didn't become a victim at secondary school too.'

'He became a bully, you mean?'

'Yes, that's exactly what I mean, and people with similar chips on their shoulders seem to find one another, don't they?'

Kate sat up from the slouched position she'd fallen into at the kitchen table. Dan strolled by, rubbed her neck, but she held her hand up to tell him to stop, she was listening.

'Go on, I don't follow, Mrs Truro.'

She watched Dan open the fridge, spring the top on a can of soft drink and sip. He picked up the toasted chicken and salad foccacia she'd prepared and left silently, not even looking her way. She felt a pang of regret at her behaviour, and the fact he'd be eating alone again.

'Clive Farrow and William — Billy — Fletcher became inseparable for a while,' Mrs Truro was saying.

'Billy Fletcher?'

'A very good-looking boy with a stammer. An unfortunate affliction, for he was very bright, very capable, but we couldn't police our playgrounds every minute of the day in a school of that size, Detective Inspector Carter, and Billy didn't fare well with his stammer. This was the early seventies, after all. Children didn't go running to the teachers as they do now; they tended to fend for themselves.'

'Or become bullies,' Kate said, tiring of the teacher's high-handed tone.

'I'm afraid so. Billy wasn't so bad. He fell in with Clive, most likely as a fellow sufferer, but you wouldn't necessarily put them together as friends. They just didn't have anyone else at the time. Billy, I imagine — I hope — has made something of himself. He had brains. He took his O levels and three A levels, one of them English, which I taught. I can't imagine he and Clive stayed in touch with one another, Detective Inspector, if that's what you're hoping? If my memory serves me right, Clive made it through to his exams and left at sixteen with a couple of CSEs under his belt. By the time Billy Fletcher was taking his A levels, Clive was long gone, and I don't think I'd be steering you wrong if I said that even before Clive left school, they weren't moving together as they had before. I can't tell you anything else though, I'm afraid.'

'Did Billy pass his A levels?'

'I don't know about his other subjects but he did well in English — got a solid pass. When the under-achievers leave at sixteen or younger, most of the wayward influence goes with them. Those left behind, who want to study, fare much better, and Billy was one of them. All the former bad behaviour we associated with him — including bullying — stopped, and I could be wrong but I think he might have finally got some help with the stammer, which would also have helped.'

'It was gone?'

'No, no, not at all, but he was certainly beginning to wrestle it under some control. Whether he succeeded, I can't tell you. And I have no idea, before you ask, whether Billy Fletcher went on to college or university. I wasn't the most popular person in his life.'

'I wonder why?' Kate covered her sarcasm with a charming tone filled with disbelief.

Mrs Truro obviously took it to be genuine. 'Because I pushed him too hard. Billy liked to do only enough to pass. I wanted all my students to go to university and prove those silly examiners wrong who think a comprehension test at the age of eleven can tell us accurately how intelligent or capable the adult may be. Billy was clever, he'd just allowed himself to believe that he was stupid because of his stammer and the company he kept. I tried to make him see otherwise and that made me an ogre in his life.'

'So you'd have no clue as to where Billy might be now?'

'Are you mad? No, none at all, Detective Inspector Carter.'

Kate reined in her increasing irritation. 'Well, thank you, Mrs Truro, you've been most helpful.'

'I can't see how.'

'Because we didn't know about the link between Billy and Clive until now. Um, look, I'm hoping we might get a photo from either the Farrows or the Sheriffs. If we do, may I contact you again? We may get lucky and link Clive Farrow with Michael Sheriff. It would be helpful if you could take a look to see if you can identify Billy Fletcher as well.'

'I'm happy to help the police if I can, but please give me plenty of warning if you're coming to my home. I lead quite a busy life, you know.'

'I'll be sure to do that, Mrs Truro. Thank you so much.'

'Please bring identification if you do come.'

Kate looked at the receiver with dislike. No wonder Billy Fletcher hadn't kept in touch with the old battle-axe. Probably all the students had hated her. Mind you, Mrs Truro had obviously cared enough about Billy Fletcher to push him. Perhaps Kate was reading the old teacher all wrong.

More hours passed as she wrote up her findings on her laptop and emailed them through to her address at New Scotland Yard. Her dinner sat untouched on the kitchen bench. Instead she made herself a cup of tea, knowing there was no point in offering Dan one — he hated tea. She was tired, but too alert to sleep, so she sifted back through some other notes on the case, still chasing after the significance of the paint, then decided to do some research on the net.

Finally, delighted to have turned up some information that she felt might help, Kate got up and stretched and went to find Dan. He was slouched behind his computer in the room they called the study but which also served as the second bedroom. His eyes were fixed on the screen where a lone figure stood, its back to her, twisting and looking. Suddenly the weapon the figure was holding exploded into action and it was off and running after whatever it hunted, Dan controlling all its movements with frantic clicks on his keyboard.

'Sorry about earlier,' Kate said. 'I was on the phone to

someone who was just beginning to tell me something interesting.'

'It's cool,' he replied, not turning. 'Your good-looking boss, I suppose.'

She yawned. 'Come on, it's late. Shall we go to bed?' She smoothed his hair.

'I'm not tired any more.'

'I didn't mean to sleep.'

He snorted a soft, mirthless laugh. 'Your timing's always so off these days, Kate. Save the amorous stuff for the office and lover boy.'

'What's that supposed to mean?'

'Have you even noticed me since you started this Operation River thing?'

'Operation Danube.'

'Whatever.'

She felt her hackles rise — something that was happening too often these days where Dan was concerned.

'That's unfair, Dan. You know how important this case is — it's the biggest one in Britain for years. We're trying to catch the bad guy, remember?'

'Yeah, yeah. I've heard it before. I don't mean to be insensitive but I could die too and, let's be honest now, I'm not sure you'd notice.' He spoke without shifting his gaze from the screen, his fingers moving incessantly over the keys.

'Well, this is a great way to lead up to a wedding, I must say.' Kate's tone was filled with injury now, readying itself for the inevitable argument.

But Dan's voice was uncharacteristically cool. 'I agree, Kate. Whenever I need you, you're too busy, too preoccupied, too uninterested. But whenever Hawksworth says jump, you ask how high.' He loaded Jack's name with derision.

She looked at the back of his head, aghast. 'Dan, that's not true. Please remember that he's my DCI and it's my job to jump when he asks. Anyway, I could throw exactly the same back at you. If you're not working overtime for your demanding boss, you're playing childish games with your friends over the net. They're probably all spotty teenagers!'

Dan pulled a weary expression to suggest he'd heard this many times before. 'Well, at least they're loyal and always there. I can't say the same for you.'

Kate made a sound of disgust and turned to leave but Dan grabbed at her hand. His voice was softer, a little shame creeping into his tone. 'Look, give me half an hour. I'm moving with a pack at the moment.'

'I'll be asleep in minutes,' she lied, hiding her disappointment. There would be no lovemaking tonight then, as there hadn't been in quite a long while. Almost two weeks, surely, since Dan had last initiated anything so intimate, and he had been very merry that night, she recalled, after a truckload of sparkling something or other at a party. She ignored the nagging voice at the back of her mind that told her that she too hadn't initiated anything remotely sexual in a long time either. The blame was hers as well. She cursed her luck again that Dan had chosen to show affection just when she was making some headway with Eva Truro.

She went back to the kitchen, angry that Dan was dragging Jack into the frame. Typical Dan, possessive of her when any other male, however innocent, came into her life and yet so willing to take her for granted. She gave a soft growl of frustration.

It really was quite late, past midnight. She picked up the phone from the kitchen table and was about to return it to its cradle on the bench when her traitorous fingers punched in the numbers of Hawksworth's mobile. She really didn't have an excuse for calling. She'd have to rely on details of the conversation with Mrs Truro to pull her through.

She was anticipating that she'd get his voicemail because it was so late. The truth was, she just wanted to hear his voice. She jumped when she heard him answer abruptly. She also heard music and recognised the song instantly. She too loved Marvin, as the woman's voice in the background was saying. Kate froze.

'Hawksworth,' Jack repeated, more loudly.

'Er, sorry, chief — I thought I'd get your voicemail.'

'You've got me in the flesh instead.'

He didn't sound annoyed, he was simply businesslike. No pleasantries, not even a 'hello Kate'. Who could blame him — she'd become a night stalker on the telephone. She felt the tea churn in her belly, along with her crippling embarrassment. In the background she could hear someone moving crockery.

'Um, I just wanted to let you know we may have had a small breakthrough,' she said. 'I've found a teacher who knew Farrow and a boy he knocked around with at school rather well. I'm hoping she'll be able to help us find someone who might give us that link to Sheriff.'

'Good. Look, I've got to go, I'll speak to you in the morning.'

And a dull click, followed by silence, told her he was gone. She glumly replaced the phone on its cradle. He was with a woman. Her cheeks began to burn, she wasn't sure why. Probably because of how awkward she now felt, and also how unimportant in his life she was. Somehow, it was even worse that although he was clearly occupied, he remained a gentleman and gave her thirty seconds of his time. *But only thirty seconds*, a cruel voice whispered in her mind.

Why wouldn't he be with a woman? Did she honestly believe he went home each night, climbed into his pyjamas and watched cooking shows with Jamie or Nigella? She closed her eyes, not totally convinced that the groan she heard herself give was entirely one of humiliation. It was more like intense regret that Jack had someone in his life. It was alright for her to be sleeping with Dan but she hated the notion that Jack Hawksworth might be sleeping with the woman who loved Marvin Gaye.

Kate took herself off to her lonely bed and dreamt of smearing blue paint over the nameless woman's face, while Marvin Gaye crooned sexily in the background.

10

Kate woke sluggishly to an insistent alarm — the type that would keep shrieking until she physically pressed buttons and answered questions and told it her vital measurements. It was 6.29 a.m. Dan was already gone, she gathered. This was confirmed by the note she found in the kitchen when she staggered out to put the kettle on. It read: *Said goodbye — not that you noticed. Will be late tonight. Don't cook or wait up.*

She did notice that he didn't sign his name or a little kiss after his notes any longer, and tried not to dwell on it. She turned her attention instead to another lonely night in the making — she could work late, perhaps visit the Yard's gym.

Kate turned a sigh into a yawn and realised she was freezing. Dan might have kissed her and left behind the dregs of his breakfast for her to clean up but he hadn't turned on a heater. 'Bastard,' she muttered aloud, 'just because you don't feel the cold.' She flipped on the gas fire and flames erupted. She knew she didn't have time to wait for the whole room to warm but she could hug the fire over a mug of tea. If there was one thing she was going to give them as a wedding gift, it would be proper central heating … if they stayed here in Stoke Newington, of course. If they decided to sell and move, then wherever they ended up she'd insist it already had heating throughout the house, preferably underground heating, she decided, as she poured water into the mug.

She'd opted for coffee somewhere amongst thoughts of heating because tea took too long to brew, and she wanted to be first into the office after Jack — no one beat him — as it would mean some time alone, a chance to apologise for last night's disruption. She felt sick all over again as she tried to imagine who the mystery woman was, and whether he'd mentioned to her that his ditsy DI was stalking him.

Only half-finishing her now sour-tasting coffee by the fire, Kate threw most of it into the sink and quickly stacked the dishwasher with Dan's dirty plates and cups — *why does he need so many?* she wondered. It was full to the brim and unpacking it would be a nice chore for her this evening, especially as she had nothing else to look forward to.

Her mobile shrieked into action. 'DI Carter,' she answered.

'Oh, er, it's Diane Sheriff here,' came a shaky voice.

'Hello, Diane. Please, call me Kate,' she said, instantly softening. 'How are you today?'

'Each day is hard,' the woman admitted. 'But I'm calling because I think I've found some old photos of Mike, as you asked. I don't know how much help they'll be, but they're here for what they're worth.'

'That's great. Is it alright if I drive up this morning?' She looked at the microwave clock. 'I can be there by around eleven-thirty?'

'I'm home all day, Sally's not well.'

'See you soon then, Diane. And thanks for all you've done.'

Kate hurried into the shower and, for expediency, cheated with her hair, pulling it into a ponytail while it was still damp.

She dressed and made up swiftly, all of it on and looking back at her in the mirror within five minutes. Kate knew DS Jones envied her clothes — and why not, they were all lovely and chosen with great care to suit her figure. She wasn't deliberately trying to show up the ambitious young detective sergeant, particularly as they were required to work as a close team under Hawksworth, but she was feeling a bit miserable today and had to take it out on someone, even if it was by means of a fashion attack.

She opted not to take Dan's car in today; parking in the city was such a nightmare. She could use a pool car from work to get to Louth. Because there was no tube station at Stoke Newington, it meant a bus ride to Angel where she could pick up the tube. All good reading and thinking time, she decided, hunting down the chick lit novel her sister had insisted she'd read. 'You'll laugh your head off,' Suzy had said. Well, so far her head was still stubbornly attached. Kate preferred movies for her escape from real life.

All the same, she found the book, threw it into her leather satchel and delved for Dan's car keys in one of its pockets. She left the keys next to his pointed note, unsure as to whether it was symbolic of something.

The longest escalators in Europe swallowed Kate into the Angel tube station, and she didn't have to wait long for a train to Monument, where she picked up the Circle line to St James's Park. As she jogged up the steps of the station, hoping she didn't trip on the hem of her long skirt, she reassured herself that the creamy latte she was going to buy at the top would be offset by the exercise she was getting because there wasn't an escalator. She scanned the row of coffee shops, finding with surprise that all were relatively empty and that, thanks to the early hour, her favourite bar, Giorgio's, had the shortest queue.

'Thanks, Joe,' she called over her shoulder to the barista as she left with her takeaway coffee and hurried through the cold drizzle across the road to New Scotland Yard. By mid-morning the place would be base camp for any number of TV crews getting stock footage of the revolving sign, or tourists having their photos snapped below it. It wasn't just Kate who was trying to get to work early; dozens of other police and support staff were piling in through the staff entrance. *May the Force be with you*, she thought, as one not so chivalrous fellow let the door fall back on her, threatening to spill her finely balanced coffee.

Finally, after clearing security and battling the lifts, Kate stepped out at the top floor and moved down the corridor to where Operation Danube was based. Joan hadn't yet arrived but wouldn't be long, Kate suspected. The telltale glow of lights from the back office told her DCI Hawksworth was present. Good.

The view of the city took her breath away.

'This is amazing. Did you arrive during the night?' she asked at his office door, aiming for a breezy start to the conversation.

He looked up and she felt impaled by his cool grey gaze. 'Glad you approve. I do sleep, I promise.'

Nothing breezy about that response; she might as well be direct then. 'Er, sir, I'm sorry again about disturbing you last night.'

He shrugged. 'It's really no problem. I'm just wondering why you feel it's important to check in with me on small things.' Now his tone turned earnest. 'I trust you, Kate; I have since the moment I met you. Perhaps you don't realise that you were the first person who came to mind when I was thinking about the team for this operation.'

Among the waves of remorse, she felt a thrill of pleasure pulse through her. 'I don't know either, sir. It won't happen again.'

His voice came softly now, and once again Kate was reminded of why this man was moving ahead in the Force with such speed. He knew precisely how to interact with people — when to be firm, when to be gentle, when to play, when to be serious. 'It's not a complaint, Kate, I just want you to feel confident to make your own decisions. You know the pressure we're under. Going up to Sussex is fine with me if you think it's relevant to the case.'

'I do, but better news since. Diane Sheriff has found some photos. It's Lincoln for me today.'

He looked instantly cheered. 'That's great. But first a cup of tea. Want one?'

She nodded, chuffed that he'd offer. 'Why not. I swallowed the latte I bought in one gulp in the lift.'

'Give me a moment then. Take your coat off and warm up. Have a snooze. It's far too cold and early for you to be in.'

His grin reassured Kate that the awkward moment of last night had passed and she began digging in her satchel for her notes. She looked out of the window for a minute or two longer as the sounds of a working day in Westminster began to seep up to the highest regions of New Scotland Yard. She wondered how much of Jack's day might be spent looking out to Westminster and Big Ben in the distance; she imagined he loved this view of all the old buildings.

'Sugar?' Jack said, making her jump. 'Sorry.'

'None, thank you.'

He disappeared again and Kate's gaze drifted back to his desk. It wasn't a file he had been reading she now realised. He had the *Yellow Pages* open; she leaned forward. Restaurants.

He caught her peeking as he returned. 'I'm trying to find a Chinese restaurant I went to a year ago but can't remember its name.'

115

Guiltily, Kate sat back and reached, embarrassed, for one of the mugs he was holding. It said: *Here I am ... now what are your other two wishes?* 'Thank you,' she murmured, wondering whether he'd deliberately picked that one out for her. She decided it was unlikely after last night's cool reception to her call. 'Perhaps I can help?'

'It's in Chinatown.'

She flicked a hand, more confident now. 'I know Chinatown really well. Fire away.'

'I remember it had many levels — you know, the higher you go the more expensive it is. I think the ground floor is mainly students tucking into won ton soup. It's not far from Gerrard Street, or probably on it. It has a clock, I think.'

Kate frowned for a moment and then smiled. 'Really busy, reasonable prices and always serving loads of free weak jasmine tea?'

His eyes lit up. 'That's right.'

'I think you're talking about Wan Kei. I've got as high as the fourth floor.'

'That's it, that's the one! Wan Kei. Great, thanks for that. How was the fourth, anyway?'

'Scrumptious but slow, and the tea is served stronger.'

'Good, I'll book it.'

She couldn't help herself. 'Off to the theatre?'

He smiled, although his tone became ever so slightly guarded as he busied himself with writing down the phone number of the restaurant. 'I am, yes.'

'Dan and I took my parents there when we treated them to *Les Mis*.'

'Yes, that's what we're going to see,' he replied, distracted, and then looked up at her, clearly aware of his slip.

She regretted how her eyebrows arched involuntarily at his admission because a shadow definitely passed over his expression.

She was saved by the arrival of various other members of the team. The cold they brought in with them attacked the warmth in Jack's office.

'Morning. Freezing out there,' Sarah said, smiling.

'Morning, Sarah. You got home okay?'

'Whizzed there, sir, thank you.'

'Sarah worked back past eleven on the blue paint. She's formed a worthy idea for us to work with,' Jack explained to Kate, who felt a pang of jealousy towards the stocky DS.

'Can't wait to hear it,' she commented tartly.

They were still here after eleven? Kate's mind raced. She'd phoned Jack just past midnight, so he hadn't been long with the Marvin Gaye fan when she'd interrupted them — probably having a late cuppa by the sounds of things. She hoped dearly it wasn't a drink before bedtime, although she knew she had absolutely no right to think that way.

'Er, actually, sir, that's something I wanted to talk to you about,' she said brightly.

'The paint or late nights?' he asked briskly and she knew he hadn't missed her scowl towards the young detective sergeant. She would have to watch herself.

Before long, all the staff attached to Jack's unit had found their way to their new home. Everyone gave whistles or cheers of approval as Jack welcomed his team to their new headquarters.

'Fuck me,' Cam said, 'and I paid to go on that thing.' He pointed to the London Eye that reared up ahead of them. 'This is better!'

Jack grinned. 'What do you think, Swamp?'

'I think I'm going to get a nosebleed, we're so high. How did you swing this, Hawk?'

'Operation Danube is considered top priority, so we get the best offices.'

Kate was turning on the spot — now that the day had lightened, she was incredulous at the sight of the city sprawling before her, with magnificent bird's eye views of Westminster Abbey, the Houses of Parliament and Big Ben. 'How will we ever work? It's beautiful.'

'Yes, it is,' Jack said, moving next to her. Kate could feel the warmth of his arm close to her own.

'Pity you can't see your beloved cathedral,' she said.

Jack adopted an injured tone. 'No, but life is never perfect.'

He turned to the rest of his team. 'Okay, everyone, close your mouths, you'll get used to it. Let's get down to some work. Our enemy is time. Fetch yourselves a cuppa. There's real coffee brewing in our own kitchenette just outside,' he took a bow to acknowledge further catcalls, 'or the usual tasteless crap that most of you favour. Meeting in five minutes.'

Once they'd all settled, DIs Brodie and Marsh assured their chief that they'd trodden so lightly in their respective inquiries that no one had heard them arrive or leave at either Lincoln or Hackney.

'So, let's start with London first. What do we know, Cam, that we didn't know previously?' Jack asked, twirling a whiteboard marker in his broad hands.

Cam took the floor. 'Okay, we've already got all the pathology and forensics — there's nothing new there that we didn't already know, and what we do know is in the file you each now have. The killer's being extremely careful. There's no CCTV footage for Springfield Park unfortunately, although the records show that a —' he consulted his notes, '— Mr Don Haven did see a council worker wheeling a bin through the park. He thought it was odd because it was late.' He raised a hand to quell the rush of questions. 'And there's a white Toyota transit van — not council issue — but the guy pushing the wheelie bin was in uniform and had a beanie pulled low on his face. The local boys have left no stone unturned but there's nothing on the bin — which was new, and common to hundreds of hardware stores around the country — or the van. No fingerprints, no incriminating DNA — although plenty for the victim, of course, who was carried to the toilet block in the bin.' He let that sink in and looked towards his boss.

Jack nodded at one of the PCs. 'Con, get on to Hackney Council. Find out if anyone's lost a uniform, or there's been a break-in to stores. Get us a lead on where the killer's been.'

'Sir.'

'Carry on, Cam,'

'Clive Farrow had been drinking at a pub called The Grenadier, not far from where he lived with his thirty-three-year-old fiancee, Lisa Hale. I'm leaving her to you, right, boss?'

Jack nodded. 'I'll see her this afternoon.'

'Well, she could give the police very little last week. I should tell you, sir, that the boys at Hackney said she's a few sheep short of a flock. I gather Farrow might have been a bit short of a bob as well. So Ms Hale's information was spartan. Farrow was taking her out that night as she understood it, and she waited for hours. She went down to The Grenadier and learned that he'd left just before dinnertime, but it was the publican who raised the alarm, called the police. She was incapable, I gather.'

'Thanks for the warning. Go on.'

'I spoke with the publican and a few people who knew Farrow and were there on that Thursday evening. They've all been interviewed thoroughly by the police and everything was apparently normal. Farrow was on his way home after work, stopped by for a sherbet or two — as he did a couple of times a week and always on a Thursday. He had a game of darts with someone the folks there knew, a friendly match, which Farrow lost. The guy — he's a regular — left almost immediately but Farrow stayed for about another hour, by which time it must've been around six forty-five. All stories seem to match.'

'And he was going straight home?'

Cam shrugged. 'No one said any different. It was payday and he was talking about taking Lisa out to the cinema for a late-night double bill.'

'But never got there,' Kate muttered.

'Anything else you can give us?' Hawksworth asked, a soft plea in his voice.

Cam grinned mischievously. 'Yes, chief. Like you, I couldn't understand why he didn't just go home. I began to think that if he was going to take his girlfriend out and it was already nearing seven, he'd want to have got a move on, right?' Everyone watched Cam expectantly and it was obvious he enjoyed the attention. 'I went back through his phone records, which Hackney had already done. Farrow made a mobile phone call to his girlfriend at five past seven that evening. The police who interviewed her much later that night said she was obviously distraught and told them he didn't say anything in that conversation other than normal stuff like he was on his way home.' He shrugged. 'But then she's not quite the full quid and, well . . .'

Jack's eyes narrowed. 'So where are you taking us with this?'

'To a fish and chip shop in a tiny parade of shops at Hackney Marshes.'

'Oh, so he bought Lisa a takeaway dinner, his idea of a big night out,' Kate said, a hint of disdain in her tone.

Jack gave her a sideways glance that told her to stop the snide remarks.

'Yeah, but here's the thing,' Cam said, his eyes glittering with excitement now, 'there's a chippie next door to The Grenadier.

So why go to one that's miles away when there's a shop right in front of you?'

A momentary silence followed his question.

'Better food?' Jack offered.

'He's on foot, chief. Farrow didn't drive and didn't have his bike that day, according to his fiancee, because it had been stolen. And from what I'm gathering, Farrow wasn't exactly discerning when it came to food, so I imagine fish and chips was fish and chips to him.'

'You think he went to meet someone? The killer?'

'I don't know, but it begs the question. Listen to this. I've spoken with the fish and chip shop and they remember Farrow coming —'

'Why?' Kate asked.

Brodie looked irritated at being interrupted. 'What?'

'Why would a chippie remember a punter who isn't a regular?'

'Good question,' Brodie said smugly, 'and exactly the same thing I asked the guy — Ritchie Brown, he runs the place with his wife and dad.'

Jack was tiring of the long lead-up to whatever ace Cam planned to pull out of his cuff. 'Come, on, Cam, finish this.'

'Sorry, Hawk. Look, I was cynical too, but they remembered him because as they got talking while the food cooked, they learned he was originally from Brighton. Their family's from Portslade. That's like Kensington and Chelsea — next door. Anyway, Russell Secondary, where Farrow went, is now called Blatchington Mill School and the guy who runs the chippie has a sister whose kids still go there.'

'I can fill in the details on his school life,' Kate offered.

Everyone sat forward and Cam couldn't help but bask in the renewed interest. 'I haven't got much more to go,' he said to Jack, who nodded.

'Ritchie Brown remembers Farrow coming in that evening because he was a bit thick, as he put it. Apparently, Farrow told Brown a joke that took ages to get out and then he forgot the punchline. They got chatting about the school and Farrow told Brown that his best friend in those schooldays was someone who stammered. Ritchie can't remember the name, unfortunately.'

Kate sighed. 'I know it. Sorry to interrupt again, sir, but this is relevant. The stammerer's name is Billy Fletcher. They must have been like a circus act.'

No one laughed. Instead, Jack held his hand up to stop Brodie.

'Alright, Kate, what have you discovered?'

'Right, sir.' Kate nodded towards a PC. 'Thanks to Dermot, who got together a very good list in just a few hours, I spoke to a couple of the teachers in Brighton and essentially learned nothing we hadn't already worked out from our conversation with Diane Sheriff. Her husband, Michael, was shy, bit of a loner, but not an outcast, if you get my drift. He had people around him, but none you'd call friends and no one that anyone I spoke to could say he was in any way close to.'

Jack nodded. 'Okay, that's all disappointing and inconclusive.'

She put a finger in the air. 'But I did better with Farrow. I got on to a Mrs Eva Truro, who took him for English Lit. She obviously has a memory like a vice because she could recall in detail various things about Farrow. As a teenager he was slow — as in not academic at all — but cunning, so hardly a complete dunce. He came to the school as a bully and fell in with a boy called Billy Fletcher.'

Jack watched Kate intently as he sipped his coffee and listened to her report. She found his attention disconcerting and self-consciously tugged at the top of her camisole to ensure no cleavage was accidentally showing. She'd forgotten all the others in the room who were giving her their equally undivided attention.

'Fletcher, I gather, was intelligent, charming and good-looking, but he also had a stammer,' she finished.

Jack put his cup down. 'Bingo!'

Kate felt the glow of his praise infuse her as she sat back. Swamp clapped. Dermot, the youngest in their group, blushed brightly as various team members congratulated him.

'This stammer won Billy Fletcher some unwanted attention from various students,' Kate added, 'and according to Mrs Truro, he and Farrow became thick as thieves for a while.'

'Why only a while?'

'She says it was because Clive left school at sixteen with a couple of CSEs, while Billy went on to take his A levels. That caused a natural separation, but there was a hint that she thought they'd fallen out anyway before Clive left.'

Jack sat forward. 'Did she say anything concrete along those lines?'

'No, sir, just a vague feeling I got when talking to her.'

He drummed his fingers against his mug. 'So if we can find Billy Fletcher, he might be able to help us with our inquiries.'

Kate nodded, noticing how her boss's long, neat fingers didn't have chewed fingernails, unlike Dan's, which seemed faintly ironic considering their two careers.

'We have nothing yet that formally links Sheriff and Farrow,' she said. 'We do know they were both originally from Brighton, but they went to different schools, although the schools weren't far from each other. I'm hoping these photos Diane Sheriff has found might put the two boys together. Either that or Fletcher might throw some light on it. It's odd, isn't it, that Diane Sheriff said her husband fell out with that gang of boys he moved with and then Mrs Truro tells me that this Fletcher fell out of favour with Farrow?'

'Maybe Fletcher was part of the same gang and something happened between them all?' Cam said.

Jack agreed. 'Could be. But we're talking … what? Nearly thirty years ago?'

Joan interrupted him. 'Super wants to talk with you, Jack.'

He nodded. 'I'll call him straight back. Go on, Cam, you'd better finish your info.'

'Well, as I say, Ritchie Brown got chatting with Farrow about old times in Brighton. He ordered enough food for two apparently. When the meals were ready, Brown was still reminiscing — I must admit, I found it hard to get away from him so I understand why Farrow said he had to go. When Brown asked why he was in such a hurry, Farrow apparently pointed to a car outside and said he had a lift and didn't want to keep his ride waiting.'

The ops room erupted into sudden chatter as the new pathway opened up.

'Settle down,' Jack called. 'Did your guy get a fix on that car?' he asked Brodie.

The DI grimaced. 'All he could tell me was that it was red and fast. Presumably he means a two-seater.'

'And the driver?'

'Well, curiously, it's a woman.' Brodie consulted his notes. 'The best he can do for us is she's got longish dark hair. He didn't see her face.'

'Age?'

'No idea. Brown said he made some farewell remark about hoping the lady enjoyed her dinner and Farrow protested that it wasn't for her, she was just giving him a lift. Brown, of course, laughed — a bit suggestively, I gather — and Farrow got stirred up, said she was just someone he knew from the old days and he would never hurt a woman. Odd thing to say, right, chief?'

'Yes, although maybe it's something that goes back a while.'

'Mrs Truro described him as a big lug and very threatening,' Kate offered. 'The other kids were scared of him, so perhaps he's spent his life with women scared of him.'

Jack nodded. 'Swamp, anything new for us?'

The older man shook his head. 'The Lincoln boys did a good job. As we know, the last anyone saw of Sheriff was at a teachers' get-together on fifth November at the Castle Hotel. It was a weekday night and threatening snow so very few people were out and about other than those at organised Guy Fawkes' nights. The receptionist, a Mrs Jean Farmer, took a call from the hospital, apparently around nine, to say one of the Sheriff kids had been brought in bleeding from a fall and asked her to tell Michael Sheriff to get straight home and that his wife would meet him there. He left around nine-fifteen after farewelling everyone in good spirits . . . er, that's very good spirits — the man was apparently on his way to being smashed. According to his colleagues, he was taking a taxi. According to Jean Farmer, he never climbed into the taxi she'd ordered. In fact, he seemed to disappear from the bar. The barman was told to keep an eye on him but he got occupied with checking off a delivery and when he looked again, Sheriff had gone, presumably out the back or side doors — we don't know. Jean Farmer thought nothing more about it, although she did ring the Sheriffs the following night to find out how the kid was. She learned then that the call from the hospital was a hoax and that Sheriff's body had been found in the old quarter later that night.'

'What do we know about the hotel?'

'It's at the top of Lincoln in the old quarter, place called Westgate. Very dark, opposite a park. Our boys up north reckon

Sheriff must have died in a car before being transferred to where he was found in the alley. Nothing was found near the body. The killer was careful.'

'What about the call?'

'No one has any idea.'

'And the bar — anyone else there?'

'No witnesses at all, Hawk. From police notes, I gather there was only one tourist having a beer in the bar, which is separate to the dining room and reception area, who the barman recalls and Jean Farmer corroborated. But the barman — John Harris — says the bloke left before Sheriff came through from the dining room. Again, Jean Farmer concurs that there was no one else in the bar when she left Sheriff with Harris to go call a taxi.'

'No other staff saw anything?'

Swamp shook his head. 'Not according to Lincoln. One girl, er,' he consulted his notes, 'Emma Lansdowne, a housekeeper who was on that night, left for overseas the next day. They haven't been able to reach her — she's on some sort of trek in Nepal, no phone signal, and then on some batty retreat where there're no personal phones permitted — but her parents believe she'll be available any time now. It's a long shot but I'll stay on it.'

'Okay. What about the call from the hospital?'

'Casualty has no record of that call and obviously Susan Sheriff wasn't hurt. That was how the killer got the victim moving alone. The taxi came but no sign of Sheriff.'

Jack blew out his cheeks, feeling momentarily defeated. 'So Sheriff was abducted somewere beyond the bar, or he left the hotel by some back exit and was picked up outside. There has to be a witness somewhere who saw something. Keep hunting. Right, thanks, Swamp. Con?'

PC Constanides looked up eagerly.

126

'I want you to ring the publican at the Castle and find out as much as he —'

'She, sir,' Swamp said.

'Find out as much as she knows about who was in the pub that night. We want to know if anyone else outside of the teachers' party talked to Sheriff. We know the call from the hospital wasn't legitimate — whoever made it is presumably that same someone who met Sheriff either inside or just outside the hotel. Get a list of all the teachers who were present at the dinner and start working through it. And talk again to all the staff who were on that night, especially that housekeeper, Emma. Swamp, we've got to go over everything about Sheriff's movements that evening. I'll say it again: someone must have seen something.'

Swamp nodded and said to the young PC, 'See me after for the publican's direct number. Her name's Debra Hanson.'

Jack stood up. 'Right. It sounds as though I have to go pay my dues with the Super. Kate, you get over to Lincoln and report back here soonest. You've got four and a half hours to turn it around — take a squad car. We meet back here at two this afternoon everyone.'

11

Garvan Flynn heard Clare returning from her day's shopping in Worthing. 'No need to cook tonight,' he told her, pointing at the empty Tesco bags. 'Their heat-and-serve chicken kiev looked irresistible.' He smiled.

'I'm not very hungry anyway,' she said. 'Sheila and I grabbed some lunch. How did the doctor go?'

'Oh, the usual.'

He returned to the sitting room. She followed him.

'What's the usual?'

He could see she was irritated but he couldn't help it. He had far more important things on his mind.

'I've got a prescription for some antibiotics but it's not going to my chest. I'll just do the saltwater gargle. Stop worrying.'

'Seemed rather pointless to go, then,' Clare said and he heard the bite of suspicion in her tone. 'Did you speak with Peter?'

'Yes, he's coming over on Friday. Sounds excited about something but wouldn't say what.'

Clare was instantly diverted, looked at him wide-eyed. 'Has he popped the question to Pat?'

It was Garvan's turn to feel exasperated. 'I don't know. I'm hoping this is about the new contract.'

She nodded and looked out at the garden. 'I see you've been digging through the shed then.'

'I told you, I wanted to find all my fishing stuff. I was just having a breather and I'm about to head back.' He couldn't tell her the truth.

'Make sure you leave my back garden tidy,' she warned, but there was no heat in it. 'And don't strain yourself if you're not too well.'

He needed to behave normally, no matter what the police reports were saying. They knew nothing.

'I'm fine, love. The pot's still warm — plenty left,' he said and headed out to his shed, finally allowing himself to suck in the air he needed to calm down.

The news reports on the murders were intensifying. He'd only just got the television off in time as Clare had arrived home. She would hear it all soon enough; he couldn't protect her from it. The police were either saying little or knew even less. So far they had two bodies that had been murdered in a similar way. The reporters were sensationalising it, of course: Britain's new serial killer would strike again, they warned. They were right. If Farrow and Sheriff were dead, murdered, in different parts of the country, then it was certainly no coincidence. But who was doing the killing? Was it Fletcher or Bowles? He couldn't imagine either of them doing it, or why. Was the murderer suddenly feeling guilty thirty years on? It was ridiculous.

That left only one other person . . .

Garvan felt tendrils of fear creep up his spine. He'd been shocked by the double murder because he'd known both victims, but now he started to feel nervous for himself. If Bletch was picking them off one by one, three decades after the event, then he wasn't immune. In fact, he would be the prime target.

Peter!

He lost his breath all over again. Felt a twinge of pain ripple through his chest. He scrabbled in his pocket for his angina tablets, swallowed one and tried his best to breathe through the pain as he'd been taught. It was panic bringing this on. And he mustn't panic. None of the boys had known anything about him. No one could lead Bletch to him. Peter would be safe, Clare would be safe. He just had to hold his nerve.

As he sat in the shed, trying to calm himself, steady his breathing, his mind wandered back to that time of madness when he was barely twenty-seven.

He had watched them for a few weeks now, smirking at their taunts. 'Bletch': it was a word he didn't know but it suited their target. He wasn't sure why but he kept wishing they'd do more than just throw the stupid schoolbag around. They had no idea of what power they held, especially in a gang. He understood powerlessness — knew how it felt to be the Bletch, quietly taking an unjust punishment. He would love to strike back at the source of the punishment he was going through, but he couldn't; instead, he sat here outside a school, taking sad pleasure in watching someone else being bullied.

Recently, his thoughts had turned darker. He had begun to fantasise about Bletch being at their mercy — his mercy. The fantasy made him feel in control. He could banish the reality of his own messed-up life; the constant disappointment in himself; the accusation in his wife's eyes.

How Elsie had heralded him when Clare had first brought him home! He was young, healthy and in a good, steady job as a legal clerk in a bank. He was definitely marriage material — he could see it reflected in Elsie's welcoming smile and eager gaze. He'd had several girlfriends, but Clare was the first one who'd mothered him, made him feel as though he was some sort of hero in her life. She used to sit and knit jumpers for him, watch him from the freezing stands as he played football for the Blatchington Strikers. And afterwards she'd sit quietly, contentedly, in the pub, listening to him and the rest of the team dissect the game. She loved to cook it was obvious from the little flat she shared with two girlfriends that she was a good housekeeper and although they never went all the way before they married, the sex was enthusiastic and Clare was eager to please him in every way. Loving her was easy. She wasn't especially pretty — but then neither was he — and Clare made up for that shortfall by adoring him. And so they had married after only seven months of courting. She worked in a clerical position at Caffyns Car Company and he got a small promotion. Life was good, especially when Elsie announced that she and her husband were giving Clare their savings early. They wanted their only daughter to have a roof over her head that she owned.

It was incredibly generous but it came at a price. Elsie now owned Garvan, or so it felt to him. Within a year of their wedding day, Clare had become clucky, talking about children constantly. Although he too yearned for a solid family life — his own had been rocky, with estranged parents and no siblings — he'd soon started to hate the way the desire for a child changed their relationship. He and Clare were genuinely the closest of friends and the affection between them was strong, but as the need to nest turned urgent, and nothing he did produced a baby for that nest, Clare became withdrawn. Garvan started to feel like an outcast in his own home. Arguments increased, and Clare's parents got drawn into the fray, with Elsie quick to point the finger and demand tests. Tests that showed he was the problem.

Now he couldn't even get a hard-on in front of Clare, let alone get her pregnant. Their lives had essentially unravelled to the point where a separation was considered the only option.

The loneliness hurt. He was sick of staying with friends, and had even slept rough in his car a couple of times. He had no idea how to kill the time between work and sleep, and had taken to driving aimlessly around Brighton and Hove to pass a few hours. It was parked in Hangleton, staring vacantly out of the car window, that he'd first seen the gang tormenting Bletch. He discovered how watching their bullying tactics made him rock hard. He would stroke himself in the car, safe in the knowledge that no one could see what he was doing. His fantasy escalated. He wanted that power.

He filled his mind with visions of Bletch begging through tears as he straddled that pale wobbling flesh and felt his hard prick entering —

A yellow car stopped and a woman yelled at the teenagers. He heard the sounds of the boys' laughter as they raced off. He started the ignition of his own car, a Ford Cortina, and cruised past Bletch, watching the sad-looking kid in his rear-vision mirror.

Imagining the fat kid under him helped banish Clare's sorrow and her mother's accusing stares. How much stronger would he feel if he could turn fantasy into reality?

Kate left London immediately Jack had ended the meeting and reached Diane Sheriff's house by eleven. She sat at the kitchen table waiting for Diane to return with the photos. A sullen-looking girl was watching television, her eyes red. Kate could tell that this was from tears rather than a cold or any illness.

'Our Susan's not well today,' Diane Sheriff said, bustling back into the kitchen with some dusty photo albums. 'She's having a bad day over her dad,' she added in a whisper. Kate nodded and Diane continued more loudly, 'These are all I could find in the loft. Mike tended to want to take the photos rather than be in them.'

Kate smiled sympathetically. 'Thank you. Can I take a flick through them here?'

'Of course. How about a cuppa?'

'Am I holding you up?'

Diane shook her head as she filled the kettle, talking over the noise of the tap. 'This is my day off. I'm glad of the company to tell the truth.'

Kate opened the first book and saw pictures of the Sheriffs' courting days, which morphed into what must have been an engagement party and then a few wedding pictures, before being turned over entirely to them as smiling parents. The second book was older, mainly of Diane and her family. Mike Sheriff appeared in a few lonely shots.

'How old was Mike here?' Kate asked.

Diane walked to stand beside her, the jar of cheap coffee powder and spoon in her hand. 'Um, well, I was about twenty-two, I think. I didn't know him then, of course, but I tried to integrate some of his photos from his twenties into mine of around the same time, so I imagine Mike would have been about twenty-six.'

Kate kept flipping but found nothing of interest. She wanted earlier photos. The next book was entirely devoted to pictures of the Sheriff children. She put it aside almost immediately. A black photo album came next, almost all the shots of Diane but also a few photos of Mike as an infant with his parents.

'These are very sweet,' Kate commented, more for something to say as Diane placed the mug of coffee in front of her. 'Thank you.'

'Oh yes, that's the only book he's ever had. I think his mother put that together. She did one for each of the children.'

'How many of them were there?'

Kate reached for the coffee she really didn't want and shook her head when Diane pointed to the sugar bowl.

'There were four of them. He had three sisters.'

'Oh, so the spoilt little prince, eh?' She aimed for levity but it didn't work.

Diane grimaced. 'Not really. I think Mike felt he was a bit of a disappointment to his parents from what I can gather. He never talked much about his childhood, but I think he felt a bit ...' She searched for the word and then shrugged, her eyes misting.

'Unfulfilled?' Kate offered, desperate to stop the woman from breaking down.

Diane nodded, gathered her composure. 'I think that's why he worked so hard to be a good father and good teacher. He really was such a decent man. He did far more for the kids in his classes than most would.'

Kate sipped the tasteless coffee. Too much water, not enough milk. But sipping crap coffee was the diversion she needed because she didn't really know what to say to comfort Diane Sheriff. She could see the woman would be a long time in coming to terms with her husband's death, and Kate knew herself to be useless at empty platitudes.

'Lucky last,' she said, reaching for a cheaper-looking album that had a sunset on the cover. The first page was filled with a series of school pictures.

'That's Mike aged eight,' Diane said, pointing a bitten nail at one old-fashioned square photo. Beneath it someone had written '1967'. He was standing with three other children, all of them grinning heartily, save Mike. 'He wasn't one for posing,' Diane said, ruefully. 'I'd completely forgotten we had these few old photos of him at school.'

Kate felt the first spike of adrenaline hit her system. She was tapping into the right era of Michael Sheriff's life and she all but held her breath as she turned the next page. Mike was older here, wearing long pants with a dark blazer, no jumper and a white shirt with a tie properly knotted. This was it. This was what she'd come for.

'This is Mike at his comprehensive school in Brighton somewhere,' Diane said.

Kate had memorised the photograph of Clive Farrow's dead face and her eyes ranged across the pages now, desperately searching for similarities.

'Are you looking for that other man?' Diane wasn't quite as dim as Kate had her down for.

'I was hoping we might make a connection between Mike and him at school, yes.'

Diane shook her head. 'I can't help you there. As I said, Mike didn't really talk about childhood days. He once said he wanted to forget his years of senior school. He said 1974 to '75 was the worst year of his life. Funny,' she smiled as she stared out of the window, 'that was one of my best.'

'Did he say why?'

'No.' She shrugged. 'The odd thing is, he still put his name and photo up on that internet thing.'

'What thing?'

'You know, where they bring you together with your old school pals.'

'Yes, I do. There are a couple of those operating now, aren't there?'

Diane nodded. 'It was my fault, really. I registered and felt so elated to suddenly start hearing from people I'd forgotten about that I kept encouraging Mike to do the same.' Her eyes became misty. 'I think he only did it to prove to all those people from his past that he had a great job and a family who loved him — you know ...'

'That he was successful,' Kate finished for her.

'Yes.' Diane sniffed. 'And that he was happy.'

'Mum?' Susan's voice came from the sitting room.

'Oh, excuse me a moment, Kate.'

Diane left the table and Kate used the time to course through the rest of the book, eager to find any pictures dated 1975. The photos were either of Michael or of the whole school, neither of which were helpful to her as Clive Farrow didn't go to this school. She got to the end of the book and disappointment knifed through her. Nothing here that she could use.

Diane came back in. 'Any luck?'

Kate shook her head and sighed. 'No, I'm afraid not. And this is all you have, you say?'

'Yes. I gave the loft a good long search too, so I don't believe there are any other photos knocking about. Mike was such a squirrel. Never able to throw anything out, you see, but he was a neat squirrel and kept that loft in very tight order. He had a box marked "photograph albums," and you've seen everything that was in there.'

Kate felt a little lost. She knew a lot was riding on this and her thoughts were already reaching towards Brodie and his forthcoming meeting with Farrow's family. Perhaps he would have more luck. Something needed to break to give them a lead. She stared at the back cover of the book helplessly, then noticed a brown piece of paper sticking out of the lining. She tugged at it absently just as Diane said, 'Finished here?'

'What? Oh, sorry, yes, thank you for the coffee. I never seem to finish a cup. Drives my partner nuts.'

The mug was removed but Kate's attention was on the small brown envelope she'd fished out of the lining. 'Look at this,' she said, pulling it clear. 'What's in here?'

'I'm not sure,' Diane replied, wiping her hands on a tea towel as she approached. 'Look inside.'

Kate did, her heart hammering as she pulled out a single snapshot of four boys, all grinning this time. She saw Mike Sheriff immediately.

'Oh yes, I remember that one,' Diane said. 'Mike hated it, so he put it out of sight. I can't imagine this will interest you though. You wanted school photos, right?'

'Why did Mike hate this shot?' Kate said, her pulse surging as she stared at one of the figures, a huge teenager, unmistakeably Clive Farrow.

'Out of sight, out of mind, probably. I think those are the lads he fell in with when he was about fifteen. They weren't good for him, I gather, although they look harmless enough there.'

Kate had to swallow to ensure her voice came out evenly. How she wished for a sip of the ordinary coffee now to moisten her dry mouth. 'Mrs Sheriff — Diane — can I keep this photo?'

Mike's widow gave a soft shrug of acquiescence. 'Yes, if you want to. Is that what you came for?'

The Yard's training, years of reinforcement that their people must always proceed with caution, kicked in. As much as Kate wanted to scream 'Bingo!' to the rafters, she composed herself.

'I think this might help us a lot, Diane. You see, Clive Farrow is this fellow here.' She pointed to the photo, and her thoughts flew to Jack and how pleased he was going to be with her. She missed Diane Sheriff's response. 'Sorry?'

'I said you can keep it. We don't want it. We don't even know who those boys are or what they meant to Mike. If it helps find his killer, be my guest.' Her voice had taken on a hard, emotional edge.

Kate reached out a hand and placed it on the older woman's arm. 'You've done really well here, Diane, and everyone working on this is going to be most grateful for your help. We're going to find him for you, I promise.'

It was the wrong thing to say professionally, but Kate felt it was exactly the right thing to say to this widow, who needed to hear that the police were going to help her get justice.

12

Kate could hardly stop herself grinning as she hit the motorway for London, and she'd be back at the Yard in time for a late lunch, too. She wished she'd brought Dan's car after all — it was so much nippier than the squad car. It could have used the run too; Dan so rarely drove it. He preferred public transport, or taxis, depending on where he had to be. He hated the boredom of sitting in traffic, unable to bury his head in one of the sci-fi books he seemed to consume. He shared his passion for speculative fiction with many others in the nerdy IT community, who did everything from dressing up as Trekkies and attending conventions around the world to taking part in mammoth gaming sessions at each other's homes or even bigger events arranged at halls. Dan was a little more conservative, confining his gaming to sitting alone at his computer screen and plugging into an international community, or perhaps lying on the sofa playing on his gaming console. Nevertheless, he gave over great chunks of his weekend to lose himself in other worlds. In truth, it hadn't really bothered Kate until recently, although she found it rather boyish. But since he'd proposed and their relationship had taken on that new, more serious lustre, she'd begun to feel a nagging concern that this was all that was ahead for her. When would Dan grow up?

She knew another woman who'd married an IT consultant — a supremely intelligent man, like Dan, who also became childlike and a fraction obsessive when given the opportunity to stalk otherworldly people on some extraterrestrial plane. Kate had asked the woman how she'd coped with two years of marriage under those circumstances and the woman had laughed and said, 'I play with him. It's actually great fun and extremely cathartic to go on a killing rampage after a long day in the bank.'

Kate gave a rueful smile now as she considered this sage advice, which turned into a softer smile as she dialled Jack Hawksworth's mobile and heard his voice telling her that he couldn't take the call right now but to please leave a message. Somehow Jack managed to say even that well-worn phrase with charm.

'Jack, it's Kate. I know you don't want me to say this, but bingo! Call me, I'm in the car hurtling back to London.'

It was no more than a few minutes before the phone began playing the opening to *Mission Impossible*, the tune she'd accorded to DCI Hawksworth for whenever he rang her mobile. She loved the tune — always had, long before Tom Cruise made it famous again — and it suited Jack. She grinned and hit the button that hung from her hands-free earphones. 'DI Carter.'

'What was the lucky number then?' he asked and she could hear the catch in his voice. He too was excited.

'What do you mean?'

'You said bingo — what was the lucky number?'

'Number four, sir. Four boys. I've got Michael Sheriff and Clive Farrow in the same photograph, their arms slung around a couple of other youngsters about the same age, although one looks small. They're all smiling, they obviously feel pretty cosy together.'

'The wrong gang he fell in with,' Jack murmured, echoing Diane Sheriff's earlier conversation. 'Tell me more,' he encouraged.

'Mrs Sheriff recognised the picture but no one in it, other than her husband. She did say that Michael didn't like that photo. I found it tucked away in an envelope inside the lining of a photo album. Her theory was that he hated throwing anything away — I'm gathering he was a bit of a hoarder — but by the same token didn't want to see it. Ever.'

'Didn't want to be reminded, you think? Ashamed?'

'Well, that's the inference I'm drawing,' Kate said, surging past another slowcoach. 'I should be there by one-thirty at the latest.'

'Take it easy, Kate. Get back safely, and well done.'

It was so good to hear his praise that she felt suddenly reckless. 'Er, Jack!' She strained to listen, hoping he hadn't put the phone down.

'Yes?'

She felt a fluttering of fear in her throat. 'I need to talk to you about something.'

'Okay. It can't wait?'

'No. I need to speak with you alone and I know that will be impossible in the office today.'

'Alright. Have you got your headset on?'

'Yes, I can't be booked by police, I promise,' she said, desperately trying to lighten the tension she was feeling. Was she really going to do this? He'd probably think she'd really gone off the rails, perhaps regret trusting her.

'I'm all ears. What's up?'

Kate took a deep breath. 'Last night —'

She heard him sigh. 'Kate, look, I don't want us —'

'No, wait, Jack. I meant I wanted to mention this last night but you were in a hurry. I'm just a bit embarrassed actually. It feels crazy but I need to say it aloud.'

She didn't need to see him to know he must be frowning at her dithering.

'You're usually pretty forthright. Just tell me. It's obviously on your mind.'

'Well, our murderer — the left-handed, late thirties/early forties bloke with his liking for lips and dicks . . .'

'Yes?'

'Er . . .' She gathered her thoughts, let the niggling notion that had been roaming her mind since Lincoln crystallise, and knew it felt right. She had to air this whether he laughed at her or not. 'Jack, I'd like us to consider that our killer isn't a man.'

She imagined that if they were in the same space right now, Jack would have turned and stared at her in that intense way of his, making her feel that no one else was in the ops room, even if all twenty-five of them were sitting in a circle. She cleared her throat.

'Go on,' he urged.

'Why are we assuming this is a man? Something's nagging at me that we could be dealing with a female killer.'

'Why do you sense that?'

Her thoughts tumbled out. 'It's the mutilation. The lips and the genitalia — they're both sexual. It's been bothering me why a man would do this to another man. Neither of the victims are gay to our knowledge, right?'

'Not that we know of.'

'And if this was a homosexual man taking his revenge . . .' She shook her head, not quite sure how to say what she felt. 'Well, I think he'd have made them suffer. I could be wrong; I'm just throwing up an idea here,' she added defensively, but when he didn't dismiss it, she continued. 'Straight men can be cold, cruel, brutal in a situation such as murder, but as we're working on the proviso of retribution, then a straight man would probably have made the two victims suffer a whole lot more.'

'Keep talking,' he said and she felt his encouragement like a gentle touch. She managed to keep her voice steady and her thoughts moving forward. 'A gay man, scorned in some way, would be pretty nasty as well, I'd imagine. Again, suffering would surely be inflicted if the opportunity was there.'

'Why wouldn't a scorned woman behave the same way?'

'Well, she might, but I'm hazarding that a woman who's pushed into a very dark place in her mind and prepared to mutilate seems more likely to want to get on with the job — get to the end result, you could say, rather than linger on the suffering.'

She let her notion hang between them momentarily, imagining his silence meant he was reluctant to accept it.

'Well, hear me out,' she went on. 'Let's go on the assumption that this could be a woman ...'

'Alright.'

'And let's say these two men have done something truly awful to her — essentially, pushed her over the edge — and she's decided to take her revenge.'

'Why do the lips and genitals mean more to a woman than to a man, though, Kate?'

'Well, my theory, which I'll admit I haven't fully thought through, is working on the basis that the killer was raped by these men.'

'Hence the lips and —'

'Dicks, yes, exactly! And let's face it, if you did a survey of women and asked how they would physically damage a man who'd raped them or their child even, the overwhelming response would be: cut off his knackers. That's his manhood, his whole claim to fame, it's what he boasts about in the pub with his mates and —'

'Yes, I get the picture,' he cut in. 'It's certainly possible.'

'It's plausible, Jack. Listen, Diane Sheriff clearly said her husband had fallen in with the wrong sort. We now know he was friends with Farrow. Maybe they, or even this foursome, got up to some mischief that got out of hand … like rape. Diane told me that Mike described the twelve months between 1974 and 1975 as the worst of his life. Eva Truro, Farrow's and Fletcher's teacher, said the boys were once friends but it soured. Perhaps it soured in that same year.' She did a quick sum in her head. 'Farrow left school in June 1976. Fletcher and Sheriff seemingly kept out of trouble after that.'

'It might explain why Sheriff hid the photo,' Jack mused. 'It's a solid theory, Kate, I'm impressed. May even fit with the woman in the sports car. Although, it actually makes things harder for us now — means we'll need to cast our net wider.'

'Yes, sorry.'

'Don't be. Be more sorry that, if you're right, our killer hasn't finished. There may be two more deaths to come.'

Kate felt sick at the thought. 'We have to find Fletcher and whoever this fourth boy is.'

'Okay, get back to the Yard. I'm calling a briefing for two-thirty.'

'I'll be there,' she said grimly.

'And Kate?'

'Yes?'

'I'm proud of you. Good work.'

13

The operations room was buzzing — no longer did anyone lose time gawping at the panorama of London. The hunt for Farrow's and Sheriff's killer had taken on a fresh sense of urgency since Kate had presented the photo from Michael Sheriff's album. It had caused the kind of stir that could only be upstaged by the cream buns Jack brought in for their late afternoon meeting. As he called the meeting to order, everyone was consuming buns and hot drinks, muttering gratitude to their chief for the afternoon tea.

Jack sat against a desk, his long legs stretched out and crossed at the ankles, his arms folded loosely. Behind him were the whiteboards and pinboards that his minions had done their best to fill with facts and details pertaining to the case. The photos of the ruined men, stark and sobering amongst the scribblings.

'Alright, if everyone's ready, let's begin,' he said. 'Tomorrow Kate will take this photo to Eva Truro, Farrow's old teacher, and we're hopeful she might identify at least one of the others as being Billy Fletcher, our stammerer. It doesn't mean Billy is the murderer, nor does it mean he is the next victim. Potentially, however, he could be either, as could the fourth boy in that picture. We must identify who these remaining boys are. Did you rearrange that appointment with Lisa Hale?' He directed the question to Brodie.

Cam nodded. 'You're seeing her first thing.'

'Alright, get back to her and ask her what photos she may have, if any. As Kate suggests, it's a very long shot but it might lead us back to an original wrong — something that has provoked our killer to start taking revenge.'

'Who thinks about revenge thirty years later?' Cam asked incredulously.

Jack shrugged. 'We're working on a new hypothesis.'

He saw Cam throw a glance at his running mate, Bill Marsh, and Jack knew what they were both thinking. The Super had warned him often enough about his propensity for working on gut instinct.

'I'm going to let Kate lay out that hypothesis from a hunch that has been niggling at her,' Jack went on. 'Her idea sounds wild to begin with but let her finish. It has real merit. I certainly consider it plausible, especially in light of Cam's work. It's a lead I want us to follow hard now. Go on, Kate.'

Kate smoothed down her skirt in a nervous gesture and shared her idea with her colleagues that the killer was a woman. Jack was impressed that she kept her brief precise, devoid of emotion and open to scrutiny. It prompted a wave of questions, most of which remained unanswered. Gradually, everyone fell silent.

Jack took the floor again. 'It's a notion I'm simply asking you to hold in your minds as we hunt this killer. But the woman in the car has to be found. Cam?'

'I'm reluctant to go with this woman theory because she'd have to be fucking strong to move these bodies around — excuse my language,' he added at his chief's stern look. 'But I'm thinking there may be more to it, considering that call to the hotel for Sheriff obviously came from a woman pretending to be a nurse from the Lincoln hospital.'

Jack nodded, a fresh spike of adrenaline coursing through him. Cam was right. 'As I say, Kate's idea has genuine merit, and whether we're right about the why of it is irrelevant at this point. Our job is to find the killer. We'll worry about what motivated the murders as we go.'

'Perhaps we should call John Tandy back in light of this?' Kate asked.

'Yes, do it now,' Jack replied. 'See if he can come over straightaway.' He turned back to Brodie. 'Cam, get back to Ritchie Brown and try and get more on that car and its driver. Get on to Brighton and Hove car registrations —'

Brodie looked aghast. 'Chief, do you know how many red sports cars there'll be in the East Sussex region alone?' He sounded exasperated to be given this plod work after his seemingly scintillating breakthrough that morning. 'The car could be from anywhere anyway.'

'I know what I'm suggesting is daunting but this is where the hard yards are done.' Jack addressed the last to everyone, so Brodie didn't feel singled out for censure. 'This is where we hunt our killer — in the detail that he or she has overlooked.'

He turned back to Brodie. 'If you can whittle it down to a make and-or model, Cam, it gives us a platform. Do your best. I'm working on the notion that the killer could also originally hail from Brighton — may still live there. Print out some colour lasers of various cars and show them to Brown. It will be more meaningful.'

He watched Brodie's eyelids lower and heard the sigh. He added, 'And, Cam, I think it should be you who visits Farrow's fiancee, Lisa. You're more acquainted with Farrow's history and his movements on the evening of his death. Find out about his mates at school, especially any photos from school, but don't ask about another woman openly. His girlfriend's going to be hurting enough without that kind of pain.'

Brodie's expression instantly lightened at being given the senior task and Jack noticed he flicked a sharp look at Kate, back from her call to the profiler. Kate kept her own face impassive.

'I want you lot to gather the facts so we can start working with something concrete,' Jack went on. He turned to Bill, who still looked cynical that someone could maintain their rage for thirty years. 'Swamp, set up interviews with each of the teachers who were present at the meal and also any of those close to Sheriff at work.' Marsh nodded. 'And I want you to grab a couple of people here and get on to the car rental firms. Let's get a listing of all the cars rented in Lincoln two days prior and up to the day of the Sheriff murder.'

He didn't miss Swamp's glazed expression. None of his DIs were happy it seemed, but at least Swamp would know from years of experience that if the spadework was done well and the digging went deep enough, then clues would be discovered. It might also remind him not to question his boss, however discreetly.

He turned to Kate. 'Go back to Sheriff's old teachers again, or try to find his peers from school.'

To an untrained eye, Kate's expression did not appear to change, but Jack saw the flicker of annoyance in her eyes and the ever so slight tightening of the mouth with its carefully applied, almost not there lip gloss. Kate, like her peers, was not happy with this job, which she probably figured should be done by one of the many PCs they had on the team.

'Find out everything you can about Sheriff as a teenager,' he finished. 'I realise his old schoolmates could be anywhere these days, but they may remember who the other two in the photo are.'

When John Tandy arrived, Jack briefed him quickly on Kate's new theory, then asked Kate to take the floor.

'Run us through what we know so far, would you?'

Kate flicked her head to clear the dark fringe from her eyes. 'We now have a genuine link between the two victims,' she began. 'Michael Sheriff, who died first in Lincoln, and Clive Farrow, who died in London.' She pointed to an enlarged photo of the four boys from Sheriff's album. 'This tells us they were friends. Farrow, the bigger lad, has his arm slung around Sheriff as they mug for the camera.' She looked to Jack and his glance told her to continue. 'We've since discovered from Sheriff's wife that he once admitted to her that he didn't enjoy his school days much — in fact, it's why he took up teaching: he wanted to make school life more enjoyable for the kids who came through his classes. She said he'd also admitted to falling in with the wrong crowd briefly during his teenage years. That sounded like a throwaway line initially, but it took on a more sinister significance after we discovered this photo. Diane also told us that her husband once said that 1975 was his worst year. He would have been fifteen in '75, and this photo is dated 1975 on the back. Sheriff was, so we're told, a neat and methodical man. There was nothing accidental about the fact that we found this photo carefully tucked away in the lining of an old photo album. He didn't want to look at it — it reminded him too much of that year.'

'Then why keep it?' Brodie asked.

'Yes, it's a bit of a mystery, but from what Diane said we can surmise that Sheriff was a hoarder. It went against his nature to throw it out.'

Bill frowned. 'So what are we saying here, Hawk? This gang committed some wrong and thirty years later someone's taking revenge?'

Jack sipped his tea. 'It's a relevant question, Bill. We have no idea that these two other lads were involved in anything, and I agree that near enough thirty years is a long time to stew on an old injury, which is why John Tandy's been invited back, to tackle that very question. Kate, thank you. Let's hear John's take on this now.'

Bill's mobile rang. He excused himself to take the call. No one minded, because every call was a potential break in the case.

Tandy brushed his jacket free of crumbs from the cream bun he'd been offered on his arrival. 'Firstly, I want to acknowledge DI Carter's suggestion that we aren't necessarily dealing with a male perpetrator here. I agree wholeheartedly that each of these victims could have suffered at the hands of a female killer, although she'd need to be a strong woman, strong enough to wrestle with men.'

'No wrestling involved,' Kate said. 'There isn't a man alive who can't help but respond to a flirtatious woman. I'm guessing — if our killer is a woman — that she's using her femininity to lure her victims into a situation they can't get out of.'

Tandy looked at her quizzically over his glasses. 'Are you saying then that DCI Hawksworth here, for instance, is a dead set rollover to your charm, DI Carter, simply because you have breasts?'

She flushed scarlet but held her ground. 'Not at all. What I'm saying is that most men wouldn't be openly rude to a woman acting in a friendly manner. I'm not saying either of these men expected to fuck her, Mr Tandy,' she said pointedly, hoping to sting him straight back, but instead prompting a round of tut-tuts from her colleagues, pursed lips from Joan and a frown of disappointment from her boss, 'but I am saying that any good-looking woman could certainly win your attention if she asked you to help her with street directions or to carry something into her car and the like.'

'What about an ugly one?' Cam asked. Kate ignored him.

Tandy looked appropriately chagrined. 'I'm sorry, DI Carter, I didn't mean to embarrass you. I was simply using you and DCI Hawksworth as a blatant example of how stereotyping is unwise, sometimes downright dangerous, in this job.'

She bristled at the condescending tone. 'I'm not stereotyping, Mr Tandy. We could go out on any Saturday night and watch just how easily led men can be by an attractive woman determined to win their attention,' she said, not attempting to soften her own acerbic tone. 'And in this instance, with Sheriff and Farrow, I'm putting forward a far less erotic situation.'

'But how does a woman tackle someone like the second victim — what's his name?' Tandy looked through his bifocals to the victim photos. 'Ah, Farrow. He's around six feet in my old language.'

Kate was ready for this. It was a scenario she too had chewed over. 'From what Cam found out, the woman who was with Farrow on the night he died was giving him a ride home. She had already persuaded Farrow to get into the car and feel comfortable alongside her. It's not a big leap to think that, if she's the perpetrator, drugging him is likely the easiest scenario, and then if he's not out cold, he's surely dazed, compliant and at her mercy. No wrestling involved, although I do agree she'd need to be strong enough to shift his dead weight later. But with some effort, someone as slight as me could drag DCI Hawksworth or DI Marsh around if they had the time and the upper body strength. Maybe she even used a trolley.'

'But how, Kate?' Cam said, exasperated. 'What do you think she could say that would persuade this big dumb bloke to obediently drug himself for her?' He tried not to notice his chief's glance of censure at his choice of words.

Kate shook her head, equally frustrated. 'I don't know, Cam. Perhaps she had some sort of hold over him already. He wasn't a particularly attractive guy, was he? So to have a hot gal in a red sports car offering him a lift must have been flattering.'

'As if,' Cam replied.

'No, DI Carter's right,' DS Jones piped up, and squirmed to have all eyes turned on her suddenly. 'Farrow was slow, remember, so he probably wasn't thinking as you might, DI Brodie — "this girl wouldn't normally give me a second look".' She paused, realising that she'd possibly just insulted one of the senior members of her team, but a grin from her boss urged her on. 'Clive Farrow's comment to the fish and chips guy tells you that. Remember how he objected to Ritchie Brown calling the woman his girlfriend?' Everyone nodded. 'Well, Kate's theory isn't that unlikely. Perhaps he knew her, so there was nothing intimidating about her.'

Cam shrugged. 'So I'm guessing we're now headed down the path that these four boys in our picture all knew the killer — this woman that we're suggesting.'

'It's not implausible,' Jack offered, keen to let his team do the brainstorming. 'But it's merely a hypothesis at this stage. All we know at this point is that two of the boys in this photo are dead. The other two may be irrelevant to the case. And the female killer scenario is also speculation, but not as farfetched as it may first sound. Kate, you obviously want to say something?'

'Yes, sir,' she said, and turned to Cam. 'So why wouldn't Farrow, after thirty years, be interested in talking to this woman, especially if she's being very friendly? Perhaps she offered him a drink in the car and it already had the drugs in it. Michael Sheriff was already well gone before that hoax call came in, which would have made it easy to administer the drugs to him.' She stopped, stared around her.

Tandy took up his previous thread. 'This is all valid but if this is a she, then she still had to move two big bodies around.'

Kate shrugged. 'She's strong, works out. Hell, there are enough women at the Yard's gym who could lift all of us in this room! Okay, I exaggerate, but it's not an impossibility.' She looked to her chief for support and won it.

'What do we know about Springfield Park?' Jack asked.

'Part of a deprived area,' Swamp answered. 'The River Lee runs through it. Hackney Marshes has playing fields surrounded by council housing blocks and the roads run downhill to the river where it's not all that unusual to find a body, if those dumping it can get past the shopping trolleys and old mattresses.' He glanced at his chief and got quickly back to the point. 'There are various public toilets in the parklands that run alongside the river — known as Springfield Park. What else can I tell you? There's a rowing club, small row of shops, couple of pubs.'

Jack frowned. 'Our witness says he saw a council worker going into Springfield Park in the early hours. We know the body had been in that wheelie bin, which, following the theory of our killer being a woman, would make it relatively easy to move around.'

'Not so easy to get it into the bin though,' Tandy reminded him.

'Well, who said murder is easy?' Jack replied. He wasn't looking at Kate, but if he had he would have seen the glint of triumph in her eyes. 'Sheriff's body could have been pulled by a woman from a car or a van. Yes, a van,' he said, thinking aloud, 'the killer, male or female, could do their ugly deeds in a van. Malek?'

'Sir?'

'Can you check with our witness and both the police teams who originally worked on the cases to see what vehicles might have been noticed around the time of the killings? I'm particularly interested in the red car, of course, but also Toyota vans.'

The young sergeant made a note. 'Yes, sir.'

Jack looked back to Tandy. 'Alright, can everyone hold the thought that John is concerned that if we're working on the presumption of a female killer, then we have to work out how she's moving the bodies around, bearing in mind that she would have to be quite strong to do so. Why don't you continue, John?'

'Thanks. So, just reiterating that I agree in the first instance with DI Carter's proposition that the killer could be a female. The injuries do fit with her theory that this is a woman who has been deeply wronged, and if that is the case then I would suggest that part of this wrong is sexual in nature.'

'Rape?' Cam said.

'Yes,' Tandy replied. 'Perhaps a gang rape, as there's more than one victim.' He looked again at the pimply, grinning youths in the grainy photo.

'Sarah,' Jack interrupted, 'any gang rapes reported through 1974–75 in our region in question?'

'No, sir, none in the Brighton or Hove areas. Of course, amongst the ones that weren't reported is probably where we'll find our killer, if we're on the right track with this.'

'Why don't you follow up directly with Lewes? They cover the Brighton region. See if they have any unsolved attacks on women during the mid-seventies that didn't specify rape but could have involved it if we scratched the surface?'

He knew it was a vague brief but it could lead to something, and he sensed that if anyone could sniff out that something, it was Sarah.

'Right,' she said, and glanced towards Kate.

Interested, Jack followed her gaze, but Kate hadn't seemed to notice the DS's look. Instead, she was staring at Jack, probably feeling awkward that she was still standing in the middle of the room, a bit like a shag on a rock, he thought. That was one of his sister's Aussie sayings and he liked it. It could mean so much.

'Back to you, John,' he said, noticing Kate's irritation with the profiler.

'As to the question of whether a person would suddenly decide to seek vengeance over something that occurred almost three decades previous,' Tandy went on, 'it does sound unlikely, but I have to tell you that deep emotional trauma doesn't go away. Very strong-minded people can build happy lives after a traumatic event, pushing away the past and living the kind of everyday existence that most of us do. They are, however, always dealing with internal demons and it takes strength of character to silence those demons. But if another trauma occurs, especially one similar to the past event, all that emotion can come flooding back. Sometimes so powerfully that it can cause a psychotic episode — which, of course, is what we're talking about with a serial killer.'

'So we're not pissing into the wind then?'

Tandy smiled fleetingly. 'No, Bill. It's not impossible that something can trigger a person to slipp into the past.'

'What sort of trigger?' Kate asked.

Tandy shook his head as he thought. 'Anything from losing a loved one to some kind of major shock. Let's use the scenario of the gang rape and this now forty-something woman. She's built a life over three decades that's kept her safe from the memories. She's strong in her mind, keeps those demons I spoke of silent. Then something unexpected happens. Something that hurts her emotionally. Her mind will almost certainly equate that pain with the old pain, and if the shock is of sufficient magnitude, or is ongoing, then she's instantly back to that terrifying time in the past.' He looked at the photo of the grinning teenagers. 'In this case, when a gang of youths raped her.'

'The woman in your car is crucial, Cam,' he said. 'Dermot, Clem …' PCs McGloughlan and Constanides looked up. 'Help Kate. We need to find the teachers of these boys, and I want the other two lads in the photograph identified. Then we find them. These two could be our next victims. Where's Joan?'

'She had to leave, the phones are going,' Kate said, pointing back to the reception.

Jack nodded. 'Okay, paint — what do we have?'

Patel raised a hand. 'It's a colour called Santorini, made by Dulux, stocked by almost every hardware and paint store up and down the country. I also did some work on the knife. Again, common or garden carver — a home brand from British Home Stores.'

Jack didn't show the disappointment he was feeling. 'Any further clues on what the paint might mean?'

Patel shook his head.

'I need us to get a lead on that paint,' Jack said to the whole team. 'There's got to be a reason the killer forced the victims to dip their fingers in it and smear it on their faces.'

Everyone stared at him blankly. Joan returned, breaking the awkward moment.

'The Super wants to see you, Jack,' she said. 'Oh, and here's another message from that DCI Deegan.'

Jack nodded, but didn't take the note she held out.

He straightened his tie. 'Okay, I want information by this evening. Sorry, Kate, I meant to come back to you. Was there anything else?'

Kate shook her head. She wanted to tell him the knot of his tie was crooked but somehow she didn't think it would matter to Jack.

Jack turned to Sarah, who was waiting silently for a word.

'Anything for me yet?'

Her expression crinkled in thought. 'Well, now that we're talking about rape —'

'The idea of a rape leading to these murders is highly speculative so we shouldn't let that pull our attention too far away from other options.'

'No problem, sir, I understand,' she said, still frowning. 'but I agree with DI Carter's theory and I'd like to give that priority.'

'Go ahead.'

'Yes, sir.'

As Hawksworth turned to leave, he caught Sarah glancing at a scowling Kate before calling to him. 'Er, DCI Hawksworth?'

'Mmm?' He looked back and saw Sarah swallow.

'Did you want me?' he asked.

'Sir, I ... er, I was wondering whether I might make a few phone calls to retired police?'

'What do you have in mind?' His tone indicated neither censure nor approval.

Sarah was relieved her words came out fluidly. 'It just makes it easier to talk through some of the cases with the sergeants who handled them at the time, sir. I've got a handful of names — they could lead nowhere of course, and I'd understand if you didn't want to give up the time to it, but —'

'If you think it's worth it, do it.'

'I do, sir,' she replied, her brow crinkling. 'I know I don't have as many years' experience as the others but I've learned that a case such as this one doesn't happen in isolation. I trust the revenge theory, and DI Carter's notion that the killer could be a woman is inspired and feels right. My gut says to dig deeper into some older events.'

Hawksworth moved closer to her and spoke quietly. She could smell the spicy fragrance of his cologne. 'Sarah. Instincts are truly the most important factor in this game. Learn to trust them. If you feel it's worth following up, then go ahead. Find me the link you think is there and I'll buy the whole team cream cakes from the French patisserie at the House of Fraser for an entire week.'

He stared at her and she felt herself give an involuntary slow blink. And then his attention had moved on. Sarah could still feel DI Carter's rapier look, though. Sarah wished she could assure her that she didn't crave the DCI's attention or praise. No, what she got off on was teasing out the truth from the complexity of information and misinformation. Getting to the core of any puzzle was Sarah's drug, and this unexpected attention from Hawksworth was unnerving. She was also hugely relieved he'd agreed to let her run with it, because she'd already done some prep work.

'Sarah?' It was Joan. 'Sorry to interrupt, Jack.'

'That's okay, we were just finishing.'

Joan handed Sarah a note. 'A Mr Colin Moss is expecting a call back. I gather you were chasing him yesterday.'

Speak of the devil, Sarah thought, her face colouring as she glanced towards her boss. It was obvious he had guessed her polite request for permission had been academic.

'Er, former Sergeant Moss, yes, thank you, Joan,' she said and took the note with its neatly scribed Sussex number.

Jack grinned at her. 'You're fitting right into this team, DS Jones,' he said.

14

I was back in Dr March's rooms for one last session. I hadn't
intended to return, but the past was a huge dark wave threatening
to break over me. I needed to be in a safe place.

'Well, you look so toned and fit,' Dr March was saying. 'It's
hard to believe what you describe.'

'I was near enough obese, Dr March. And that will always
make someone a target. People can't help themselves. Just a stare
can undermine you.'

'I understand. But you've changed all that yourself. That
shows amazing resilience and strength of character. I imagine it
took hard work.'

'It did. I turned my life around when I moved to France.
Over there I was a different person. I hired a personal trainer —
he was tough on me, but it worked. It took nearly two years to
lose the fat and surgery to fix the rest. I was young, my body
responded well.' I shrugged.

'And you said you had poor eyesight.'

'Shocking. So short-sighted. Glasses weren't at all flattering in
the sixties and seventies you may recall. And as a child I wasn't

given much choice anyway. Those terrible heavy dark-rimmed glasses and the braces made for a very plain picture.'

Dr March smiled at me. 'It sounds like the tale of the ugly duckling.' She returned to her notes. 'And it was last January, when your doctors confirmed you two could never have more children, that your marriage ended?'

I nodded. 'That's perhaps a harsh way to put it because it didn't happen overnight. It crept up on us. But yes, the decision was made on New Year's Eve. We'd been happy as a couple for so many years, but Kim couldn't face it any longer. Losing the babies hit too hard.'

Kim's words, *I'm leaving you*, had been painful at the time, but nothing like the pain of the two miscarriages and then the death of our son at just six months old. But as my emotional wounds bled and then festered, I came to understand who the real culprits were for spoiling my chance of happiness and a normal life. Sitting there in Dr March's room, I finally let myself go back ... back to the day when a group of bored teenagers let a new evil into their lives — and mine.

A crisp November day in 1974.

I'm feeling surprisingly buoyant. It's unusual for me to feel happy, so I use the good mood to fire up my daydreams of one day having my own business, being successful and wealthy, living in London. I even stretch it to include my mother living in a pretty little cottage somewhere, having survived her grief and her alcohol-induced oblivion.

I look down at the odd little dog scampering by my side — the source of my happy mood. Five days ago was my birthday and the little stray dog turned up whimpering and shivering outside our front gate. He isn't a puppy, just tiny and adorably cute — a miniature fox terrier or Jack Russell, I think, according to a book I found in the library. His name is Beano and he belongs to me now.

We're walking together around Hove Park. It's almost five o'clock and I should already be on my way home, but I'm lost in happy thoughts and don't notice how deserted the park is or how suddenly dark it's become.

'Bletch!'

I freeze. Familiar word, new voice.

I turn to confront my tormentors. The sight of them sends fresh alarm racing through me, turning my bones, muscles, tendons to disobedient jelly. I can't run, even though I'm desperate to.

The boys are wearing lurid red and green Guy Fawkes masks. And there's a stranger with them, a sorrowful clown's mask covering his face. It was his voice that called out. He's a man, not a boy.

'Who are you?' I ask.

'You can call me Pierrot,' he says and chuckles. 'He's a clown.'

I already know that. Beano is sniffing around the man's feet and gets a kick. He yelps and scampers back to me.

'Don't you touch him!' I order, suddenly inflamed with protective anger that overrides my fear.

I turn to Billy. 'Look, my mum's sick, alright? I'm just taking the dog out for a walk and I've got to get back. Please, I can't be late this evening. I don't want any bother.'

I watch in horror as Phil leaps forward and grabs Beano. My dog screeches in fear. 'Okay, stop now,' I say. Even to my ears it sounds frightened rather than commanding.

'He's a nice little doggie. Is he yours?' The man steps closer, his mask with its sad grin klaxoning all manner of warnings within me.

'Yes,' I whisper, catching a whiff of Brut aftershave. 'He's my birthday present.'

'Ah, how nice. So you wouldn't want anything to happen to him now, would you?'

I'm unable to speak as the meaning behind his creepy question sinks in. They're going to hurt Beano. I look pleadingly at Billy and Mike, still hiding behind their grinning masks, hoping to get through to them that this is moving onto dangerous ground. The boys' silence tells me they aren't too sure of that ground either. I seize on this and push again, directing my plea to their usual leader.

'Clive, please ... Just give me my dog and let me get home. We're all freezing out here.'

I can't tell whether or not Clive is registering my fear, but his red mask turns towards Billy's green one, suggesting he's uncertain of the situation.

'Anne.' It's Pierrot. I gasp with fear. How does he know my name? 'I assume you prefer Anne to Bletch? It's so much prettier. Or should I call you Annie?'

Annie's the name my father used to call me. Hearing it after so many years, and uttered by this hateful stranger, snaps me out of my terrified stupor.

'What do you want?' I demand, glad to hear my voice isn't shaking any more.

'You, Annie, it's you we want,' he says softly, almost affectionately.

My eyes narrow in confusion. 'Me?' Fat, ugly, short-sighted me? I want to laugh but I can tell the stranger isn't making a joke. I take a step backwards, my glance flicking to Beano who seems comfortable in Phil's arms. Phil is absently stroking him and I feel a small surge of gratitude.

'I don't get this,' I say, but a small voice in my mind is explaining it all very quickly and I realise what a precarious position I'm in.

'Come with us, Annie,' Pierrot coos.

I move my head slowly from side to side, unable to speak as the full realisation of what could be in store spreads through me.

Pierrot makes a soft tutting sound. 'That's a shame. I'll take him then,' he says, and reaches towards Phil for Beano.

'No!' I scream.

Billy is really the only one I know well enough to plead with. We've shared classes, teachers, track records. 'Billy, why are you doing this?' I ask.

Billy shrugs, not at all sure himself, but it's the man who speaks.

'See you later, Annie Bletch,' and, to my horror, he swings Beano above the ground by his lead. Beano gags, his legs cycling in thin air, his tiny body straining to breathe.

I scream and rush to rescue him, and find myself pinioned in Pierrot's arms, staring at that mask. 'Shut up!' he orders. 'I'll kill your dog if you don't do as we tell you.' I open my mouth to scream again and feel his hand clamp over it. 'Don't, Annie, there's a little life at stake here. Just do as you're told and both of you will be fine ... eventually,' and he laughs.

He pulls me towards the cement toilet block at the back of the park. I'm crying now, begging to see that Beano is alright. He ignores me.

'Are we safe, lads?' he calls over his shoulder.

A mumbled response confirms there are no witnesses and he shoves me into the cold, grey darkness of the row of toilet stalls with their permanent stink that no amount of disinfectant can remove. I feel the bile rising in my throat, but somehow force it back when I see Phil walk in clutching Beano. My little dog seems calm again, licking the hand of his new friend.

'Now, Annie,' Pierrot begins, fresh glee in his tone, 'I'm going to give these lads an education. We're a gang now. I've called us the Jesters Club — do you like our masks? Now, I want you to take these.' He holds out two small white tablets.

I recognise them immediately as Rohypnol. After my mother's suicide attempt, I'm the one who administers her drugs, and I'm very familiar with the little brown bottle that gives her the escape she craves. I shake my head and turn away.

'Take them!' His voice is less kind now and he forces a Coke bottle filled with water into my hand. 'Swallow them.'

'No!'

'Then your doggie dies. I'll throttle him right in front of you. Or should I stick this knife into his gut so you can see his blood oozing out onto the floor at your feet? It'll be a slower death for him, very painful.' He reaches into the back of his trousers and withdraws a vicious looking knife.

'Stop it,' I beg. 'Why are you doing this?'

Billy tries to say something but Pierrot snarls at him to keep quiet. 'I'm not fucking asking your permission,' he adds, then turns back to me. 'Drugs or dead doggie, Annie?'

I can feel the tension in this disgustingly smelly room and realise I'm not going to escape and Beano could die. I take the two tablets from Pierrot and swallow. I want to live, take Beano home, hug my mother, work harder at school.

'Uh-uh, Annie. Drink the water too. I want to see your throat moving as those tabs slip down.'

I do as I'm told.

'Good,' Pierrot says. 'Now, let's all be friends and have a nice chat. You, runt boy, keep a watch outside.'

Phil starts to protest.

'Do as I say and you'll get your go,' he orders, and turns back to me and takes my hand.

I want to pull away, I want to scream at Phil to run and get help, but I'm too scared. Instead, I watch as Beano's taken away from danger, relaxing comfortably in the crook of Phil's arm.

The drugs take about fifteen minutes to work. All the time, the four masked figures watch me intently. Pierrot is talking, explaining something about needing to borrow my body. It sounds as if he's speaking from the bottom of the sea. My peripheral vision fades and a strange warmth and buzzing wraps around my neck. It climbs into my head. I slump to the cold, damp floor.

I could see myself from above now, a large untidy heap on the toilet block floor. Thirty years had passed, but somewhere deep inside I was still that fat, unhappy teenage girl. I had tried to separate myself from her as a way of blocking out the pain but I could no longer hold her at a distance. I was Anne McEvoy. I no longer looked like that girl and I was no longer a frightened, helpless child, but from this moment I would blend the Anne of my memories with the Anne of today. I could no longer outrun my past.

'Anne, Anne!'

Someone was shaking her.

She stared at the person in front of her; it felt as if she was watching them from the end of a long tunnel.

'Let me get you some water.'

The tunnel began to fade and Anne realised she was still sitting in the comfortable bucket seat in Dr March's rooms. Her psychiatrist looked worried.

'What's happening to you, Anne? Articulate it for me.'

'I apologise, Dr March. I haven't been sleeping well lately. I'm fine. Truly, I am. I didn't eat breakfast and I've got a low blood sugar condition,' she lied. 'I didn't faint, did I?'

'You might as well have. You just disappeared, for want of a better word.'

'Well, as you can see, I'm fine.' She dug into her bag and pulled out a packet of fruit gums. 'Three or four of these usually fix me. It's because I didn't eat properly this morning.' She put two of the fruit gums into her mouth. 'Please, let's continue.'

The therapist frowned, glanced down at her notes, and continued reluctantly. 'Why didn't Kim want children earlier in your relationship?'

'I don't think he'd really thought about children to be honest, until I became pregnant. We'd been glued together for so long that I think he believed a child might change our relationship irrevocably.'

'And it did. You seem very calm, Anne, considering the man you've loved for so long is parting from you and the child you yearned for is no longer alive.'

Anne smirked inwardly. Very calm — killing calm, in fact. She pasted an expression of quiet resolve on her face.

'Parted,' she corrected. 'Kim and I are parted. In a way, I can understand why he needs to leave,' she added. 'The two miscarriages took their toll on both of us. It was so hard the first time. And then the second time, Kim was away, so he missed out on much of the trauma. I only told him about it when he got back and the baby had been gone a fortnight by then. I was trying to be strong for both of us, you see. Trying to protect him from the pain.

'Then I was pregnant again eight months later, and James made it. Both our grandfathers were called James and it felt such a solid name, as though he were here to stay, because they both lived into their eighties. So when we lost him when he was six months old ... well, it really broke Kim's heart. I think he blamed me for the pain, and for somehow not saving his son. He fell in love with James, you see, and he wasn't expecting that. He realised he really wanted a child bearing his name, his blood. And when the obstetrician told us I wouldn't be able to have any more children, it was the last straw for Kim. It wasn't about whether we loved one another. It was about grief. He's running away from the sadness. I understand that and I forgive him.'

Besides, it's not really Kim or the loss of my babies that ruined my happiness, she thought. *I was already ruined at fifteen.*

'And you, Anne. How are you coping with the loss of these precious little ones?'

Anne smiled grimly. 'I'm used to losing people, Dr March — my father and brother, my mother. I feel philosophical about our children. I wasn't meant to have them. And it began earlier than you think. I had a teenage pregnancy that ...' She paused for a moment before adding, 'Well, it failed. I've come to terms with not having children of my own during these past few sessions.'

She watched a flare of interest in the therapist's eyes at the mention of the teenage pregnancy but she had no intention of sharing any more with Dr March on that subject. She sighed. 'Which is why this will be our last session, Dr March.' And that threw the doctor off from her logical next question into what she did say.

'Last?'

'I'm here to say goodbye. I don't believe I need this therapy any longer.'

Dr March held her patient with a direct gaze. 'Are you sure, Anne? I know that living abroad makes the travelling difficult —'

'No, it's nothing to do with that, Dr March,' Anne cut in. 'I realise what I need to do is face my demons myself.'

'That's excellent, Anne. But perhaps you need a guide to do that.'

She shook her head firmly. 'No, this is something I intend to do alone. Thank you for all of your care and counsel the past two years.' She smiled brightly, loading it with confidence as she stood and offered her hand. 'I'm taking control of my life and fixing what should have been fixed a long time ago.'

15

Jack felt beat. It had been another long day and he found himself once again slumped in his sofa, his energy rapidly being sapped by the welcoming softness of the cushions that just begged him to close his eyes and sleep. But he knew he had to get up, heat the grill and cook the two fat field mushrooms he'd grabbed at Highgate Village's small greengrocer on the way home. The best he could do tonight was to press the meaty mushrooms between a ciabatta roll with some Dijon mustard and perhaps some rocket if any was still lurking in the crisper. That would be dinner ... if he could raise his fatigued body from the couch.

As he imagined the smell of grilling mushrooms his mobile rang and he closed his eyes with a sigh. Dinner would have to wait. He glanced at the screen as he pressed the button. 'Yes, Kate.'

'Sorry to disturb.'

'You're not,' he lied.

'But I figure you're at home, so —'

'I could be anywhere, with anyone, clubbing even ...' He heard the pause and smiled to himself.

'Right, yes, sorry.' Her tone was no longer so certain.

He made it easier for her. 'But as it happens, I am at home, just trying to find the energy to move from the couch where I landed a few minutes ago.'

'I know the feeling. I just wanted to let you know, sir, that I've spoken again with Eva Truro, Fletcher's old English teacher.'

'And?'

'It's all fixed. I'm seeing her tomorrow at noon.'

'Okay, that's good.'

'Seems like this female killer idea has legs.'

'Yes, your instincts are right on the mark. And if Sarah gets a lead on these cold cases, I want you to take her to Sussex with you. Drop her off in Brighton.'

'I'm going to Hurstpierpoint,' Kate replied. 'It's not as far as Brighton.'

He could tell how hard she was working to keep her tone as pleasant as she could, but still he heard its edge.

'I know, but take her all the same. She can catch the train from Brighton back to you at Hurstpierpoint station for the return journey to London, or work it out whichever way suits, but give her a lift.' His tone said there was no negotiation on this.

'Yes, of course.'

'Was there anything else?'

'No. Again, I'm sorry to have disturbed you.'

'I told you, you didn't. I'm just sitting here thinking that I should fix myself something to eat. And if you haven't already, then I suggest you do the same. I know you're as tired as I am.'

'I will. Er, night, Jack.'

There had been absolutely no need for that call, Jack realised. Kate had called him for the sake of it. He wondered why. Perhaps she was still smarting from the way he'd given Sarah the limelight. It was important that he didn't favour Kate over the others. It would be easy to, of course, because she was fast, smart and in his opinion the best detective on the team. But once petty jealousy began to breed amongst a small group, it was a very short hop to contempt and then he'd be dealing with squabbles all day when what he needed was a slick team working cohesively. No, it had been important to draw a circle around himself today so that Brodie and even Sarah understood he ran a tight but fair command, and to show that Kate stood on the outside of that circle, just as they all did.

He sighed and stood, stretched as he yawned, then reached for the bag of mushrooms that he'd dropped on the sofa beside him as he arrived home. The landline rang. He closed his eyes briefly in dread.

'Jack Hawksworth,' he said.

'Ah, formal then,' said a voice that he took a moment to recognise.

She helped him. 'It's Sophie.'

'Sophie, hi,' he said, genuinely pleased. 'I'm sorry to sound so abrupt — it's been a long day — and I'm equally sorry I haven't called.'

'That's alright. I thought I should confirm tomorrow's theatre tickets.'

'You got them. Well done.'

'Are we still on?'

'Absolutely,' he said, feeling a thrill of delight that there was something in this draining week to look forward to. 'I've booked a table at Wan Kei in Chinatown for six-thirty — is that okay?'

'Perfect. I'll see you there, shall I?'

'Will you be alright to —'

'Jack, don't start. I'll be fine. I'll see you outside the restaurant at six-thirty. Don't be late or I'll make you do more than pay for dinner.'

He smiled. 'I won't be late, I promise.'

★ ★ ★

Sarah arrived at the office before Jack had even unravelled his scarf or taken off his thick jacket.

'Wow, you're early,' he said, glancing at his watch as he put down the cappuccino he'd picked up on the way into the Yard. 'If I'd known, I'd have brought you one too.'

'That's okay, sir, I don't drink coffee.'

'Right,' he said, a flicker of a smile touching his mouth. 'What's got you in with the birds then?'

'Remember that former senior policeman I was trying to track down in Brighton?'

'Sergeant Moss, is it?' he said, taking a sip and feeling the rich caffeine hit the spot.

'That's the one. Well, he and I have been playing telephone tag but we finally spoke last night. I would have contacted you immediately, sir, but didn't want to disturb you. I think we might have something.'

'Sarah, always disturb me — I'll never mind, okay?' he said generously, thinking about Kate's call. 'So tell me what you've got for us.'

Sarah pushed her glasses further up her nose. 'It's an abduction case from the mid-seventies — Sergeant Moss said he'd be happy to talk to me about it and he's going to dig up the file. Says it's bothered him all these years, involved a teenage girl. The timing suits — it happened in the summer of '75. My gut tells me it might yield something.'

'Alright, good job, Sarah, it's all yours. Run with it and get yourself down to see him, but first we'll have a briefing here — I see Cam, Swamp and the others are dribbling in. Hang on.'

He motioned to Kate who had just arrived, bringing a gust of Rive Gauche perfume in with her. He liked the scent, always had. 'Morning, Kate'

'Sir?' she replied crisply, no doubt also remembering the previous evening's unnecessary call.

'Sarah's on to something. As we discussed I want you to take her to Brighton today. Use a pool car.'

Sarah looked at Kate and back at her boss. 'Sir, I don't mind catching the train. I could be —'

'Listen to me, both of you,' Jack said, and there was a new edge to his tone that neither had heard previously. 'We are working on a serial murder case, which, I'm sure you both agree, doesn't seem to be over yet. There are possibly more corpses coming our way — at least two, we're all guessing. The Super — rather predictably — wants the killer caught, but I'm getting the impression that neither of you is cooperating as fully with each other as I'd like to achieve the Super's goal. Take this time on the journey south to work it out, would you? Come back with good news from your respective tasks and a new attitude towards one another. Otherwise, one of you is gone. And don't be too sure about which it might be. I'm not blind or deaf. I see the sneers and I hear the undertone. It won't do. Not when I lead an operation. Is that understood?' He eyed them both but he hoped Kate felt the greatest burn from his scorching words, because he knew the animosity was mostly one way, from her. But he wanted to sound impartial at this stage.

'Yes, sir,' they both answered, glumly.

Jack softened his tone. 'Then get on with it, and bring back something that can help us break this case apart.'

Jack moved into the main operations area and got his team's attention. 'Alright, everyone, you know what we're doing. It's called legwork. I want to know everything we can about the schools and teenage lives of the two victims. I want to know exactly where Sheriff lived in this place called Hangleton and who he hung around with. We must find the stammerer — start hunting down a William Fletcher or Billy Fletcher. I need a deeper connection made between Sheriff and Farrow by close of today — what they got up to that might be prompting revenge killings now.

'Split up the plod work between yourselves and go at it. I'm going to see the Super and explain where we're at for his press conference tomorrow evening. By tomorrow lunchtime I want to be able to give him something to start working with, and I want this whiteboard filled with information.'

A chorus of mumbles greeted his urging and people started moving off to their respective work areas. Jack headed into his own office, hoping to get some thoughts on paper for his meeting with Martin Sharpe.

Joan followed him in and spoke quietly. 'Jack, are you ignoring the messages from that Deegan fellow in the Ghost Squad?'

He looked at her, irritated. 'What's that all about then?' he demanded, equally softly, for her hearing only.

She shrugged. 'He gave nothing away. Said you were to phone him.'

'He can whistle Tipperary backwards. I'm busy.'

'He was rather insistent,' she warned.

'Well, Deegan can kiss my ar—'

'Now, now, Jack. Don't make me report you for vulgarity.'

He found a smile for her. 'If he rings again, keep him off my back for now, could you? Lie if you have to.'

She tsk-tsked as she left.

'Please?' he called to her retreating back.

'I call in my favours from time to time, Jack,' she said over her shoulder and he knew she would do her best to protect him. 'Now go and see the Super, he's waiting for you.'

* * *

The screen she was in front of put itself to sleep and Anne stared back at her reflection, wishing once again that she'd never felt her maternal clock tick over, wished she'd never mentioned babies or being a family. If only Kim had stayed, or if only she'd been able to keep one of the little ones alive, she might have remained solid, grounded, in control. But their son had died and Kim had left. He said it was to go travelling for a year, to recover his equilibrium, but Anne knew it was a way of giving her sufficient time and space to graciously move out of his home in Brittany and settle herself back in England.

And now she had entered a very new and dark place. She felt as though she was staring into an abyss and whispering at her from its depths was the Jesters Club, still laughing at her, still calling her Bletch, still stealing her life from her.

Had Dr March been aware of Anne's teenage trauma, she might have begun pushing some alarm bells. But no one knew. No one except Anne and the Jesters Club. And so now Anne was taking charge and putting things right.

She'd had so many plans at fifteen — to leave Hove, go to London and make something of herself. But the Jesters had changed everything, and their evil smiles had stretched across the decades to torment her again, triggering all the rage and despair she had buried all those years ago. And now she wanted vengeance.

She bumped the keyboard accidentally and the screen came back to life, dragging her out of her dark thoughts and back to the present.

What had she been thinking about? Ah, that's right, sad old Clive, who had remained in a time warp; not leaving Hangleton for many years, getting nowhere fast as a tradesman, working for a glazing business on contract work that paid reasonably well, but so infrequently that he had never been able to lift himself beyond the council estate where he'd been born. When his father had died he'd moved with his mother to a small two-bedroomed flat in Harmsworth Crescent. The old girl was still there, almost blind, desperately needing professional care. It had been a simple case of looking up all the Farrows in the phone book who lived up Hangleton way. There had been only three, and Anne's brilliant recall from as far back as junior school told her that Clive's mother's name was Nancy and there was only one P & N Farrow living in Hangleton. Right enough, a phone call from a fake marketing company had told her there was now only Nancy in this dwelling. Two days later Anne had made her second call, this time as an old schoolfriend, with a made-up name, trying to put together a reunion of Goldstone Junior School. Nancy had been very helpful, not only giving her Clive's address in London but also where he worked.

'When did Clive move to London, Mrs Farrow?' she had asked innocently.

'When he met Lisa,' Nancy had said, as though Anne should know who Lisa was. 'A nice girl who suits our Clive — you probably know what I mean.' Which had sounded to Anne as though Lisa was a few pennies short. 'But her people are in London and she's got a steady job at a department store. Didn't want to move down south so he's gone there, you see?'

'Must be hard without him.'

'I do miss him. Clive's a good boy.'

Not quite as good as you think, Nancy, Anne thought but said instead: 'And this place where Clive works, er, Pony Express, is he enjoying it?' Not that she had cared.

'I wouldn't know, dear. I don't see him and he doesn't even ring much anymore. If you speak to him though, ask him to call me would you love, because there might be a place for me at that nursing home.' She didn't say which one. 'He's best outdoors and not working too closely with others — if you knew him at school I think you know what I mean. He's one of those people who delivers things for companies.'

'A courier?'

'That might be what it's called, dear. He doesn't earn very much. I think they're living in a council flat.'

And so, despite his slowness of mind, the once small flame of ambition that had once flickered in his youth had guttered and spat and finally died. Clive did indeed sound like he'd remained the loser he was in his youth and Anne had convinced herself that she had done them both favours by ending his ordinary life and its dark secret. He had died sobbing like a baby and she had felt nothing for him. Clive had been cruel to her and, in her opinion, deserved to know how it felt to be alone and frightened and fearing that your life was about to be stolen by someone else.

He had swallowed the water gladly, begging her not to hurt Lisa.

'I didn't rape you. None of us did. Only he did and only he attacked you that second time,' Clive had blubbered to her in the back of the van.

'I don't care that you didn't! You should have stopped him, Clive … both times. You helped him to abduct me! You should have helped me against him. You let my baby die, you bastard. Now you're going to pay for your cowardice.'

'Lisa and I were hoping to have a baby together next year,' he had slurred through his sobs. 'I'm sorry, Anne. I'm sorry about your baby.'

'Me too, Clive,' she recalled saying, 'Now hurry up and go to sleep.'

'He looked like him,' he said suddenly.

'Who did,' she had murmured, disinterested in his waffling.

'The baby. More like him than you.' The lids of his eyes lowered. 'You look amazing now though . . .' His voice trailed off.

Anne stared at him. 'You saw the baby?' She shook Clive. 'The baby, Clive, What do you know?'

'What baby?' he had slurred. He had reacted swiftly to the Rohypnol; time had been so short and she'd certainly given him a huge dose.

'*My* baby! I was pregnant. Is that too poetic, Clive? The child you forced on me when you raped me. The child you let him kill.' Her voice had broken on the final word.

But there was no more time. Perhaps she'd miscalculated for Clive had suddenly slumped; headed into the safe, dark escape of oblivion.

Anne had let go of his jacket, thrown open the back door of her van and retched. Hot, acid vomit gushed past her throat and splattered the bushes on the fringe of the park. She had planned to drag Clive's body into the wheelie bin she had in the van with them and then push his corpse to the toilet block where she had planned to dump it . . . just as they had left her thirty years ago.

She had sucked in the cold February night air, wiped her lips with a tissue and let the breeze dry her eyes momentarily. It was too late now. She couldn't wait for him to wake up and then re-start her interrogation. She decided that either she killed him and moved onto her third victim or she would give up on this trail of revenge altogether.

She had to keep going. She had to find Billy now and learn what he knew about Peter. What had they done with his body? Clive was no use to her any more. And Clive had never cared. It made no difference to her now that he was sorry. Anyone can apologise when their life is in the balance. Anne had coldly reached for the knife and, choosing the spot she knew from her research would ensure death, she had pressed it slowly, calmly into her prey's quivering flesh, burying it to the hilt.

Anne shook herself out of her trancelike state and back to the present. She had to find Billy and Phil and through them, her main tormentor, Pierrot. She'd savour his death last. She hoped with all her heart that he was alive, well, and watching the news with increasing fear.

Billy wasn't to be found on the 'Schooldays' website that had led her so easily to Mikey, and she'd already worked through the Fletchers in the Brighton and Hove phone book. None were connected with Billy. Where else to look? The school could be an option. She knew it had changed its name to Blatchington Mill at some point, but surely they'd still have records of past students stored somewhere. Or perhaps she could track down some of the teachers. She and Billy had both had Mrs Truro for English — one of the few classes Billy had actually worked in. Anne reached for the phone books again.

'Oh, what a coincidence,' Mrs Truro said when Anne had explained the reason for her call, and given the old lady a false name. 'You're the second person to ask me about that lad in as many days.'

'Really?' She felt her stomach clench.

'A reunion, how lovely. Have you found many of the others from the class of '76?'

'I'm getting there, Mrs Truro.'

'Funny that I don't remember you, Debra. I never forget a name and I don't recall you in my English class.'

'Well, I remember you, Mrs Truro,' Anne said. 'I used to sit at the back; I was very quiet, rather forgettable I'm sure.' She gave a soft laugh. 'Um, so is someone else organising a reunion then?'

'Oh, not at all,' came the reply. 'I'm helping the police with some inquiries.'

'Police?' The first tentacles of fear wrapped around her body. They were moving faster than she'd anticipated.

'You probably recall that Billy was friends with Clive Farrow?' Mrs Truro went on. 'And with Clive being murdered in that terrible way, the police are looking for people who might have some connection with him from the past.'

'Clive Farrow always frightened me a bit,' Anne said, her voice apologetic. She could hear in the pause that her old teacher believed her memory must be failing. Mrs Truro knew that Debra had known Clive just by that comment.

'Did those boys pick on you?'

'No, Mrs Truro. I escaped their notice for the same reason I did yours, but most of the people in our year were scared of them — not Billy so much, but Clive was unpredictable.'

'You're right, and that's what I told that DI Carter who rang last night. At least Billy Fletcher seemed to pull himself together. He actually did quite well in his English exams.'

'Of course. So you have no idea where I might hunt him down to send an invitation to the reunion?'

'No, Debra, I don't. Although after the police called last night it got me thinking about Billy again and I do seem to remember something about him applying to Canterbury. What about you, dear?'

'I did a business diploma at Brighton Tech and then ended up working in Manchester,' Anne lied. She didn't want to prolong the call any further than necessary. 'Well, I'm sorry for disturbing you but thank you for your time. It's been nice talking.'

'I'm sorry I can't help you.'

'Don't worry about it. And would you mind not mentioning my call to anyone?'

'Why ever not?'

'Well, I'd like to keep it as a bit of a surprise when I call — a blast from the past sort of thing.' Anne knew she was clutching at a very thin straw.

'Debra, until last night I've had nothing to do with anyone from Russell Secondary in almost twenty years. I'm hardly likely to suddenly be talking to your peers, am I?'

It was said frostily, but not unkindly. Anne remembered Mrs Truro's wintry gaze all too well and would have liked to tell her how much those English Literature lessons had meant to her. They were a life raft on an ocean of misery during her school years. But that would really set the old girl's mind working. Better that she believed she simply couldn't remember this girl called Debra.

Instead she simply said, 'No, you're right. Thanks again.'

'My pleasure.'

Anne put the phone down and bit her lip. No time to think — it was already ten-twenty. She probably only had hours to hunt Billy down before the police got to him. She reached for the phone again and, after checking with directory enquiries, connected to Canterbury University. More lies later she had established that a William Fletcher, ex-Russell Secondary, had studied English and psychology there. With a bit of arm-twisting, she had managed to ease from the man in records Fletcher's parents' address in the 1980s. He wouldn't give her the full details, but said it was a home on the Hangleton Council Estate.

Anne pulled out the Brighton phone book and rang the Brighton and Hove Council, using her earlier story of tracking down Billy Fletcher for a school reunion.

'Let me put you through to someone who might be able to help,' the receptionist said.

There was a click and a ringing tone, then a new voice answered. 'Jenny Newton.'

'Hello, Jenny, it's Catherine here, I'm hoping you might be able to help me with an unusual request.' Anne worked hard to load a big smile into her tone. 'I'm really sorry to lump this on to you but the receptionist said if anyone can help me with this, you can. Apologies — you drew the short straw.' She laughed.

'I'll do my best,' Jenny offered cautiously but Anne sensed the woman was flattered.

'Well, I'm originally from Brighton ... Hove actually. I lived in Hangleton but I've spent a large chunk of my recent life overseas.'

'Yes.'

'And I think my mid-life crisis is wanting to reunite the class I graduated with after A levels.'

'Oh, that's nice,' Jenny said, her tone warm. 'My mid-life crisis was far more selfish. I wanted to have a totally indulgent holiday in Paris at the George V Hotel.'

Anne leapt in enthusiastically. 'I lived in Paris,' she lied. 'And I dined once or twice at Le Cinq.' This part wasn't a lie. Kim had treated her to a few days in Paris and an exquisite dinner at the celebrated dining room to mark one of their wedding anniversaries.

'Oh, you lucky thing. I adore the place,' Jenny said wistfully. 'So, how can I actually help?'

'Thanks, Jenny, you see I've got one more person on the list to tick off but do you think I can find him? The thing is, Billy was the class clown who kept us all laughing. Everyone loved him. I really want him to be there. I've tried his old address — he used to live on the Hangleton Council Estate — but I just can't seem to track him down.'

'Right, well, he would have been a minor then. It's unlikely he's still in a council house in Hangleton himself. I'm not sure how I can assist you.'

'I just thought if I could find the family — hopefully his parents are still around — then they might be able to help me get in touch with Billy.'

'Oh, I see.' She paused and Anne could hear her reluctance. 'Um, well, that is a bit unusual. We don't give out personal details.'

Anne moved back to safer territory. 'How long did you have in Paris, by the way?'

'Oh, it was two magnificent weeks in the end. It rained for a few days of it but it didn't really matter.'

'I know, Paris is very beautiful in any season. I particularly liked it in winter when all the crowds had gone. So, are you able to just see if you've got any Fletchers?' Anne held her breath.

'Alright, give me a moment.'

Jenny returned after several long minutes. 'Sorry to have kept you.'

'That's fine. I really appreciate anything you can do.'

'There were some Fletchers on that estate, but they left some time ago. I don't know what happened to Mrs Fletcher, but it says that Mr Fletcher is now in a council nursing home.'

'Okay, so I'm still no closer,' Anne said, deliberately sounding crestfallen. 'Look, thanks, Jenny —'

'Wait,' Jenny said in a conspiratorial tone. 'I can give you the name of the nursing home if you think that might help? I can't see how it can do any harm, really. Just don't tell anyone where you got it, okay? Hopefully Mr Fletcher can direct you to his son.'

'Oh, that's brilliant, thanks. Billy was everyone's favourite and I would hate for him not to share in the fun after all this trouble I've gone to to set up a reunion.'

'I understand.' Jenny read out an address in Hove and a phone number. 'Well, good luck with hunting down your old school chum and I hope the party is a great success.'

'Thanks, Jenny, you've been so kind. I won't tell a soul, and I hope you get back to Paris soon. Why don't you take a romantic weekend every year?'

The woman laughed. 'I'll tell my husband that idea.'

'You do that. Take care.'

'Bye.'

Anne put the phone down and grinned. Should she go and see old Mr Fletcher? Yes. But first she needed to do some training. She needed to stay strong and fit. Lugging the near-dead weight of Mike and Clive had almost killed her — the irony of that thought amused her. She drained the cooling cup of brewed coffee. But the van made all the difference and she'd taken a lot of care in planning the two drops of the corpses. The wheelie bin and council worker clothes had been an inspired disguise and although getting Clive's body into and out of the bin had left her perspiring, the council bin did most of the work.

Michael Sheriff had been easier. She had simply rolled the body out of her van on that freezing Thursday morning in one of Lincoln's loneliest places, the covered laneway she had observed for a week. This twitten held special significance for her, but it was hardly noticed by the residents on the fringe of Lincoln's old quarter except for occasional use as a shortcut. A few stones had taken care of the streetlights the previous night and so Anne's ugly deed was over in moments and the van had gone.

As for the London drop, she knew the pattern of use for the public toilet facilities in Hackney, including the preferred days for the regulars who went trolling for action. The very early hours of a wintry Monday morning was always best and so Clive was laid out in his fetid morgue without interruption.

She'd need to do the same level of intense planning for Billy, once she knew where he lived and worked these days. Anne got up from her computer screen and stretched, heard her bones grumble and click. It was fortunate she was still so fit — that's what nearly thirty years of regular training did for a body. She could do fifty one-armed press-ups without blinking but all the same, she had worked even harder on maintaining a sleek look to those muscles or people could notice all that bristling upper strength.

It had taken a lot of pain and determination to create the body she had now and she had no intention of ever returning to the overweight, unhealthy girl she'd been in her teenage years. Whenever she felt like skipping a training session, Anne remembered her old school photograhs, saw herself fat, scowling and plain. Cosmetic surgery had helped — as did the strict eating regime she kept to — but the hardest yards were on the bike, treadmill, rowing machine, cross-trainer and other pieces of equipment that kept her strong, lean and sculpted.

She stood up and stretched, felt her shoulders click and promised herself a massage sometime soon. She put on her running clothes and trainers, pulled her hair back into a ponytail and went to the door.

16

Kate, still stinging from Hawksworth's rebuke, had grabbed the pool car keys and was already waiting in the unmarked Ford for Sarah, who arrived two minutes later, juggling anorak, files, and the sensible backpack that passed for a handbag.

'You don't mind me driving?' Kate said, as she turned the ignition. She had no intention of relinquishing the driver's seat anyway — it was simply something to say to prevent an awkward silence.

'No, I can look over my notes.'

Kate reversed. 'Hope you like U2?' She pushed a disc into the CD slot.

'Don't know them.'

'You're kidding, right?'

'No.' Sarah shrugged.

'So after a long day, what do you tune out to?'

'Mozart would be my first choice,' came the reply, the tone superior.

Kate didn't react. 'And if not Mozart? How about your choice in contemporary music? The Carpenters?'

Sarah frowned, suggesting to Kate she didn't know who The Carpenters were. Kate grimaced — even her sarcasm was lost on the DS.

'I like Simply Red,' Sarah offered.

'Okay,' Kate said, surprised. 'I like Mick too.'

'I like the old stuff best. These days he seems to just churn out covers of other old rockers.'

'Yeah, what a rip-off,' Kate said in spite of herself. 'Harold Melvin and The Bluenotes, then The Stylistics.'

'Not nearly as bad as stealing Bob Dylan's song.'

Kate nodded. 'Not that I'm a Dylan fan, mind you. Aren't you too young for such miserable music?'

'No, I love Dylan, and I'll admit Mick sang it well, but there are some songs that are sacred.'

Kate grinned. 'Like "Tie a Yellow Ribbon Round the Old Oak Tree"?'

Sarah winced as she laughed. 'Where did you drag that up from?'

Ah, so she did have a sense of humour. Taking advantage of the lighter mood, Kate attempted to clear the air. 'Look, I was embarrassed upstairs by what the chief said to us both. I hope you don't think I'd ever undermine anything you do.'

'No, I wouldn't think that, and he was suggesting I'm as much at fault, so I should be apologising too.'

'I know you're ambitious, and I know you're damn good at your job, so ...' Kate shrugged, not sure what she was trying to say. 'So if I can help, just ask, okay?'

Sarah nodded. 'I will. Thanks.'

Kate hummed to the soundtrack as she negotiated her way through the London traffic, searching for every opening that would get her a moment faster onto the A23 to Brighton.

'I don't listen to Mozart and I do know who U2 is, by the

way,' Sarah admitted. 'Sometimes it helps to play dumb. People expect less of you, pigeonhole you.'

Kate glanced at her, surprised. 'And that's good?'

'Yep, especially when you surprise them.'

'Very cunning.'

'We're still very much in a man's world, don't you think, Kate?'

'At the Yard, you mean?' Sarah nodded. 'I want to be the youngest female DCI at NSY.'

'After me, you mean?'

Sarah grinned. 'After me, you can go first.'

Kate replayed it in her mind, frowning, then nodded. 'Clever.'

'That was my Uncle Cecil's favourite saying.'

'I like Uncle Cec.'

The traffic thinned as they got closer to the feeders that would take them on to the road to Brighton.

'Truce?' Kate said into the silence.

'We were never at war, but yes, of course.'

Kate relaxed. She'd done what Jack expected of her.

'So what's the plan?' Sarah asked after a few minutes of far more comfortable silence between them.

'I'm seeing Clive Farrow's old schoolteacher at twelve. Fingers crossed, she's going to identify Billy Fletcher in our foursome photo. Perhaps even give us the name of the fourth boy.'

'Is Fletcher our next victim, do you think?'

'It's still too early to say, and certainly too soon to alarm him until we know more, but yes, I think it's likely that within the next forty-eight hours we'll be putting Fletcher under close security. What time's your appointment?'

'Sergeant Moss said I could come any time, that he'd be in all day.' She looked at her watch. 'We're cutting it a bit fine to drop me in Brighton and for you to get back to Hurstpierpoint, wherever that is.'

'It's in rural Sussex.'

'How long will it take to get there?'

'From Brighton about half an hour or so.'

'Just drop me near a station. Really. The Brighton line is direct and I can hop into a taxi at the other end.'

Kate thought about it. It was very tempting. She really didn't want to be late for the prickly Mrs Truro. 'I've got a better idea,' she said. 'Why don't you come with me to Hurstpierpoint? I'll only need five minutes with the old schoolmarm, I promise. Then I can drive you to Brighton for your appointment.'

'That sounds very workable . . . it's also kind.'

'I'm not all bad, you know.'

An awkward pause ensued and it was Sarah, surprisingly, who broke it. 'I think I'm jealous of you. There, I've said it.' She looked down, fiddled nervously with the coat in her lap.

Kate politely feigned surprise. 'Jealous?'

'Don't ask why, Kate, you already know.'

Kate did. She would be treating Sarah badly if she pretended not to. 'Sarah, I can't help the way I look. Well, that's a lie. I do help the way I look — I work on it — but I can't help what the cards dealt me, if you get my drift.'

'I know. My feelings are irrational and pointless.'

'Not pointless,' Kate said, turning her head hard right to see oncoming traffic. 'Bugger, hang on.' She held her nerve and swung out into it. 'Sorry, they're not pointless — why don't you do something about it?'

'Like what?'

Kate wanted to say, 'Like everything', but instead she said, 'Whatever you want to improve. You can change anything. Start with clothes. It's easy and painless, other than to your wallet.'

'I wouldn't know where to begin,' Sarah said, huffing theatrically.

Kate smiled. Sarah was showing a decidedly different side. 'You're funny when you want to be.'

'It's a defence mechanism.'

'It's good. Use it more. Let the guys around the office hear it — they'll appreciate it. It's a really handy weapon. And it shows you have personality, whether or not you want them to explore that. Blokes hate wishy-washy women. And wit can cut as well as amuse. It'll stop them using you as a doormat.'

'DCI Hawksworth never makes me feel like a doormat.'

'No, but he's something of an exception. So, no man in your life?' Kate asked brightly.

'No. Don't need one.'

Her comment was met by a look of incredulity. 'You don't have to need one to want one,' Kate said.

'And I don't have to want one because you think I need one.'

'What does that mean?'

'I mean that having a man simply to make me feel like I'm normal is unnecessary. I don't need someone to take out the rubbish, fight off spiders or keep me warm at night.'

Kate shook her head in wonder. 'And what about love, Sarah?'

'Well, that's different. I've never experienced it. Have you?'

Now Kate flicked her a sharp glance. 'I'm engaged, or hadn't you noticed?'

'Do you love him though? Really love him?'

Kate hesitated as the other night's cutting words from Dan returned. 'I . . . I don't know what you mean.'

'Well, I believe in heart-stopping love at first sight. If I can't find the man that does that to me, I'm not prepared to settle for second best. Listening to your hesitation, apparently you can.'

'Fuck you!' Kate said, shocked at her colleague's bluntness. 'What would you know about it?'

Sarah shrugged again. 'Nothing. I know nothing about love, as I said. Until it happens I won't know the joy or pain of it. I'm really sorry, I shouldn't have said what I did. I'm not very good in conversation as you can see. I'm far too honest. That's why I work hard to keep my mouth shut at work, only speak when I'm spoken to.'

'No! Sorry won't do. That was really vicious.'

'Well, you never talk about your fiance, Kate. It strikes me that someone who's in love and about to be married usually talks about little else.'

'So what if I don't want to be boring?' Kate realised her voice was raised and brought it under control. 'What if I want to be professional and separate my private life from work?'

'It's just that you *never* mention him. And when I asked you if you loved him, you struggled to answer.'

'I didn't struggle.' Kate hated to hear herself sound so defensive.

'You didn't answer.'

'What is this — the third sodding degree?'

Sarah didn't reply, but undid the window to let in some freezing air.

'Blimey!' Kate said 'You try and help someone, try and do the right thing, and you —'

Sarah swung back. 'This has got nothing to do with helping me, Kate. This has everything to do with being seen to be doing the right thing. DCI Hawksworth said jump and that's what you're doing.'

'He is our boss, or hadn't you noticed?'

Sarah wound the window back up. 'I just don't want you kidding yourself that you're extending the hand of friendship. You're simply following orders.'

Her words stung. 'It's what I do, Sarah. I follow orders. He wants us to get on and I want to be able to look him in the eye and say I did my best. Pity about DS Jones and the chip on her shoulder, though.'

'What chip?' It was Sarah's turn to be defensive.

'I don't want to talk about this any more. I'll drop you off at Hassocks station and you can find your own way to Brighton.'

'The DCI said to drop me in Brighton.'

'I don't care what he said.'

'So you don't follow orders then? You're selective about what you do and don't do, depending on how it makes you look. I've heard that termed as shallow.'

Kate wasn't going to take this any more. She checked her mirrors, screeched into the left lane and pulled in at the next lay-by. 'Look, what is your problem, Detective Sergeant?' she demanded, glaring at her passenger.

The wind seemed to go out of Sarah's sails.

'I don't know,' she said. 'I'm very much out of my comfort zone. I'm probably best left behind the computer, digging through data. DCI Hawksworth's got me all wound up, making me believe I'm capable of anything, but I'm really a behind-the-scenes person.'

'How does that justify attacking me?'

'You attack me every day.'

'What?'

'I'm plain and I accept it, but I'm not stupid. I see your sneers and glances. I miss very little because, you see, what I don't have in looks, I make up for in brains.'

'Modest too,' Kate snapped.

Sarah pulled an expression suggesting she didn't care. 'I'm clever and I'm also honest. I've never much worried about being popular.'

'That's obvious.'

'You, on the other hand, desperately want to be noticed ... especially by DCI Hawksworth.'

Kate sneered, horrified that she was so transparent. 'I think your radar is off beam and I resent what you're implying.'

'I'm not implying anything. I'm saying it. I told you, I'm always honest.'

Kate wanted to pull rank but was too unnerved by the DS's accuracy regarding her own attitude to Jack. Instead, she looked at Sarah with a wounded expression. 'What do you hope to gain by this? You reckon it looks good to be arguing with a senior officer?'

'I didn't start an argument. I simply asked you a question and then answered a few. It's not my fault if I've hit an artery and you're haemorrhaging.'

'Alright!' Kate shouted, derailed by her colleague's far cooler demeanour. 'I don't know how I feel about Dan. Okay? We're getting married in a few months and suddenly I don't know if I want to go ahead but I feel like I'm in too deep. I have to marry him because I don't know what to say that could stop it without causing too much pain. Dan and I have been together for years. My family loves him and his family loves me. Dan's sweet, he's kind, he's ...' She shook her head miserably, searching for what to say next.

'Not Jack Hawksworth?' Sarah offered carefully.

Kate's voice sounded like ice when it came. 'What is that supposed to mean?'

Sarah didn't flinch. 'Your problem with Dan is DCI Hawksworth.'

Kate prided herself on being strong emotionally, but tears came now. No sobbing or heaving, just heavy tears rolling down her cheeks as she desperately tried to find something biting to say to Sarah. But nothing came because nothing ever hurt more than the truth. And Sarah's barb had gone straight to the heart of the matter.

Sarah looked mortified. 'Oh, DI Carter ... Kate, I'm sorry, I'm so sorry.'

'No, you're not, and don't be,' Kate said grabbing hopefully for tissues from her pocket. She found none and reached for her bag instead. 'This whole wedding thing is making me emotional.'

Sarah gave a soft sigh. 'I didn't mean it.'

'Yeah, you did.' Kate gave a mirthless laugh. 'And the worst part is, you're right. Well, not completely, but you're on the right track. I don't feel that Dan and I are good together any longer. DCI Hawksworth, if you must know, is more the type I think would suit me.'

'What type is that?'

'Oh, you know ...'

'Tall, dark and handsome?'

'Shut up.' Sarah apologised with a shrug. 'Hawksworth's character,' Kate went on, 'his whole persona highlights for me what I'm looking for in a man.'

'So the chief's inadvertently done you a favour — preventing you from a marriage that's bound to fail because you're not going into it wholeheartedly. There's nothing wrong in that. It's honest.'

Kate stared out at the road, unable to respond for a few moments.

'Until this moment, I hadn't been able to crystallise my thoughts,' she said eventually, 'but thank you, Sarah, for being a total bitch and helping me to see my way more clearly.'

'Don't mention it. I told you: blogsy but bright.'

Kate sniffed. 'Well, it's up to you. You can change the blogsy bit. Go out and buy yourself something that smacks vaguely of slutty — something low cut, red perhaps.'

'I could never wear anything that vulgar.'

'Well, you wear that anorak.'

And both of them burst into laughter.

'Friends?' Sarah offered, clearly keen to build some bridges. She held out her hand now.

Kate nodded. 'Let's start again.' They shook on it. 'I hope I can trust you, DS Jones.'

'You can. Blogsy, smart, vulgar anorak and takes secrets to the grave, I promise.'

'Good, because I need to work out the Dan thing without it being complicated by work gossip.'

'I don't do gossip — you should know that by now. I hope you sort it out soon. It wouldn't be fair to break his heart at the altar.'

Kate sighed and glanced quickly at her face in the mirror before readjusting it to see the traffic. She indicated and merged into the lane. 'Come on, Jones, enough melodrama. We've got a killer to catch.'

17

'Mrs Truro? I'm DI Kate Carter, and this is DS Jones.'

'Do come in,' Eva Truro offered, stepping back from the door of her neat home with its tidy front garden of pruned rose bushes. 'Can I get you ladies something?'

'No, thanks,' they said in chorus as they entered her sitting room. It smelled of potpourri and furniture polish.

Kate smiled. 'We've got another appointment in Brighton and I think you've got a lunch to get to, haven't you? We mustn't hold you up.'

The former teacher nodded. 'Please, sit down.'

The two detectives perched themselves side by side on a two-seater sofa with a busy pattern of cabbage roses. Eva Truro did not sit but stared down at them from on high through her bifocals. Kate opened the folder she'd brought and took out a photocopy of the photograph of the four smiling teenagers. She handed it to Mrs Truro, who suddenly looked every bit the formidable teacher she had once been.

'I need to know who you recognise in this phograph, Mrs Truro.'

'Ah, yes, let me see.'

Kate and Sarah held their breath while the older woman frowned thoughtfully at the piece of paper and held it up to the light.

'I recognise only two,' she began, 'although this one looks a bit familiar for some reason, but then it was three decades ago ...' She trailed off.

Kate sat forward. 'Which two can you identify?'

Eva Truro moved to stand alongside the sofa. 'This one,' she said, pointing. 'That's Clive Farrow. And this,' her finger slid over to the third boy in the picture, 'is Billy Fletcher. Good-looking, isn't he?'

Kate stole a glance at Sarah. They'd got what they came for.

'And you're absolutely sure?' she said to the teacher. 'I'm sorry, I have to ask you that.'

'Of course I'm sure, DI Carter. I don't forget faces, which is why this smaller, more baby-faced fellow troubles me. I could swear I've seen him — and if I'm honest, even this boy here,' she pointed to Sheriff, 'is vaguely familiar, but I'm sure he didn't go to our school.'

'We're very pleased to have Billy identified, Mrs Truro, and grateful to you for your help and time,' Kate reassured. 'I'll give you my card.'

She dug into her wallet and found one, annoyed that it looked a fraction dog-eared. She noticed how their prim host greeted it with a soft look of disapproval.

'Call me any time,' Kate continued, 'and especially if you can remember anything about this third boy, the smallish one.'

'Is he important?' Mrs Truro smoothed out the edges of Kate's card as she spoke.

Kate couldn't lie. 'Well, of these four, two are already dead. This is Michael Sheriff,' she said, pointing to the boy next to

Clive. 'It's very possible that Billy and this fourth person you think you recognise could be under some threat.'

'I see.' The older woman frowned. 'In that case, why don't you try and find out more about the reunion that the school is planning?'

'Reunion?'

'Yes, there's a girl called Debra ... oh, what was her surname now? Um, Debra Free, I think she called herself, although I don't remember anyone of that name in the school.' She shrugged. 'But I'm not perfect. If I saw her face-to-face, I could soon tell you if she was a former pupil.'

Kate stared at her. 'What about Debra, Mrs Truro?'

'Oh, well, as far as I know she's organising a reunion. Asked me for help in tracking down Billy Fletcher and —' She stopped, startled, as both detectives' faces lit up with keen interest.

Kate was on her feet. 'Asked for your help? When was this?'

'Why only today. She rang wanting to find out whether I knew where Billy Fletcher had gone after his schooldays. She's pulling together a class —'

Kate couldn't wait for the older woman to finish. This was too important. 'I'm sorry, Mrs Truro, but did you get a return number or any other information about this Debra Free?'

Now the woman looked defensive. 'No, why would I? I had very little information to give her anyway.'

Sarah noted Kate's rapidly increasing impatience with the older woman and spoke up. 'It's just that this Debra could possibly help us with finding Billy,' she explained, skirting the truth. 'She may even have already found him,' she added grimly.

'I see. Well, I know nothing about her as I've just told you.'

'But what did you tell her?' Kate asked, her tone hardening with barely controlled exasperation.

The older woman's eyes narrowed. It was obvious that she didn't appreciate DI Carter's persistence or her manner.

Sarah leapt in again. 'Mrs Truro, this information could save someone's life.'

'Do you mean to tell me the stranger who called this morning could be the killer you're hunting?' she demanded, aghast.

'No!' Kate cut in. 'No, we're not, but this woman is the first real lead we've had. She might be well advanced in her search for Billy Fletcher and if she can help us to find him, then yes, DS Jones is right, it could possibly save another life.'

'So Billy is next?'

'We don't know, but we have to make sure that he's protected,' Sarah soothed. 'As we said, two of the boys in the photo are already dead. It's logical for us to believe the other pair could be in danger and we're just pleased you may have something that could help.'

'Yes, of course,' Mrs Truro replied, appeased. She adjusted the collar of her neat, freshly starched blouse and primped her soft silver curls. 'I'd like to help the police but all I can tell you is what I told the Free woman earlier today and that's that I believe Billy applied for Canterbury University. Whether he succeeded, I cannot say. Billy was a determined young man — you have to be to overcome the setbacks that a stammer can create — and I'd suggest he probably did succeed in his desire to go to university and make a go of life.'

'Thank you, Mrs Truro,' Sarah said. 'You've been most helpful.'

Kate nodded. 'Thank you for the identification. Please call at any hour if you think of anything connected with these boys, no matter how unimportant it may seem. Sometimes the clues are in the trivialities.' She forced a smile, shook the woman's bony hand and headed towards the door.

Sarah followed suit, smiling warmly. 'We are most grateful for your time today. And DI Carter's right: anything small that you can remember about Clive and Billy is helpful, particularly where any bullying might have occurred.'

At this Mrs Truro scoffed. 'Oh, they were often accused of it, I'm afraid, but I'll think on what you say.'

'Thank you. We can see ourselves out, Mrs Truro.'

Inside the car, Kate was seething. 'Can you imagine what a witch she must have been as a teacher.'

'I think you're too touchy. She's just meticulous, that's all, and that can be annoying for someone who's always in a hurry.'

Her words were carefully chosen but Kate could hear what was really being said.

'Okay, so I'm impatient, I admit it.' She paused, before adding, 'Thanks. You were good back there.'

'Well, someone needed to go gently.' Sarah saw Kate frown, no doubt recalling DCI Hawksworth's 'tread softly' advice, and added, 'But there are times when firmness is required and I don't think we'd have got this info about Debra Free if you hadn't pushed.'

Kate smirked. 'I think you're being generous, but I'll take the compliment. You should apply to work for the commissioner's PR team — you're very good at diplomacy.'

'No, thanks. I like working with HOLMES and its lovely, hard facts.'

Kate turned on to the A23, slipping the car into fourth. 'So, tell me about this cold case you're so excited about. We've got half an hour's drive to Brighton. But first, let's ring the DCI and tell him we've got a firm ID on our stammerer.'

18

Anne had caught an express train to Brighton and was now queueing for one of the big black taxis that swung around the concourse at the station.

While she was waiting, she made a call on her mobile.

'Hello, it's me, Mrs Shannon, Sally. How are you?' She listened patiently to the old lady's response. 'I'm fine, thank you. I just wanted to let you know that I'll be using the van in the next couple of days, alright?... Yes, catering again. ...No, I'm not sure when at this stage, but I've got my key to the garage so I have no reason to disturb you. I just don't want you wondering what the noise is or who might be moving around in there. Did you get the forty pounds I sent last month?'

Mrs Shannon took her time explaining about the money. 'I'm glad it's arrived and I'll post another forty today if that suits?... No, I won't be telling anyone, Mrs Shannon, your pension is safe, I promise you. This is our little secret okay?... Alright then. Thank you, and look out for the money. Don't spend it all at once.' The old girl was chuckling as Anne ended the call.

Her turn came and she climbed into the back of a cab, called out the address to the driver.

'That's a nursing home, right, luv?'

'Yes,' she replied, putting on a pair of sunglasses. She was glad she was wearing the sleek Cleopatra-style wig today, as the driver's eyes kept flicking to his rear-vision mirror. She knew taxi drivers were notoriously observant.

'Got a relative there, have you?' he asked.

'Er, yes, an old uncle.'

'Down from London?'

It wouldn't pay to lie; he probably knew the train timetable off by heart. 'Yep, a quick hurtle down to check on him.'

'Want me to wait?'

'No, that's alright, but thank you,' she said, settling back and hoping he'd take the fact that she was staring out of the window as a sign that she didn't care to chat. Sadly, she'd scored a busybody.

'What do you do then?' he asked.

'What do you mean?'

'For a crust?'

'I'm an interior designer,' she answered crisply.

'One of those paint and furniture type people?'

'Yes,' she replied wearily, 'you could describe it that way.'

'I like to change the colour of our lounge each year, actually. This year I've gone red.'

Must play havoc with your hideous brown velveteen sofas, Anne thought unkindly but said, 'That's very brave.'

'Oh, it's a big joke in our house. Everyone holds their breath to see what colour I'll choose.'

A riot. 'How far is the nursing home?'

'About four or five minutes away.'

'Good. You don't mind if I make a call?' she said, waving her mobile.

'No, luv, go ahead.'

Anne thanked whomever was listening for small mercies as she dialled her home answering machine and had a conversation with herself that got her to the gates of the nursing home.

Inside, she asked to see Mr Fletcher.

'Roy Fletcher?' asked the wide-hipped woman behind the reception desk.

Anne glanced at the woman's badge. 'Yes, Ruth, that's right.'

'Well, old Roy's busy today. Hope you don't mind queuing,' she said brightly. 'You'll find him —'

'Sorry, what do you mean?'

The woman grinned. 'Nothing, luv, only that he's already got someone with him.'

Anne froze. 'Er, do you know who?' she asked.

'No idea, sorry.'

'It's just that he may not want to be disturbed. I could come back.'

'Hang on, Eileen may know. Eileen?' she called out to another woman squeaking across the lino floor in her flat white nurse's shoes. 'You've just finished the afternoon tea out there, haven't you? Who's with Roy Fletcher?'

'His son, William,' came the reply.

Anne felt her stomach do a flip. 'Billy?' she choked out.

Eileen looked at her, frowning. 'I only know him as William.'

'We went to school together,' Anne said, dragging her spiralling thoughts under control. 'He was Billy back then.'

'Small world,' Eileen said, grabbing her coat. 'I'm off, Ruth. Can you point this lady to where Roy is?'

'I was just about to,' Ruth said, then turned back to Anne. 'Alright, sorry about that. What's your name?'

'Look, I've just realised I've left something important in the taxi I came in,' Anne said. 'I'll be right back, just got to make a call.' She waved her mobile and moved quickly towards the main door.

Outside, she took a deep breath. She needed to find a secure place to think. Fortunately, there was a small green area opposite the nursing home and there, on a bench, her eyes riveted on the doorway she had just escaped through, Anne planned her next move.

Stay calm. This shouldn't frighten you. This is lucky, she told herself, *you don't even have to find him. He's given himself to you. It's meant to happen.*

Anne couldn't fail to see the irony of her present situation. Here she was, all but trembling from fear that she'd nearly walked straight into Billy Fletcher, when her intention was to hunt him down anyway. Her mouth pulled itself into a tight, mirthless smile. At what point, she asked herself, had she separated from the person who wanted a quiet, anonymous life to the Anne capable of such rage that she could take a man's life? And not just one. But these people had raped her, taken away her innocence forever, and then followed it almost nine months later with the ultimate cruelty. Despite the years she'd spent ignoring the past, that terrible night was never far from her; always waiting to engulf her and take her back to West Pier.

It was a hot July day and scorching in the bakery. Anne was working until four-thirty and thanked her lucky stars the bus home stopped right outside the shop. She touched her belly, as she did a thousand times a day it seemed. She'd been on her feet since eight and the baby was restless, kicking furiously and making her feel queasy. But as another satisfied customer left, mentioning to the manager that the young pregnant woman behind the counter was 'very friendly and served customers well', Anne had never felt happier. Perhaps the Jesters had done her a favour in a strange, painful way. Their night of torment had changed her life, and although she regretted that she would likely now never have the chance to use the sharp intelligence she possessed, work in London, have her own lovely place, she had at least found a new sense of direction.

She'd put that night behind her, buried it in the deepest part of her, promising herself she would never think on it again. But it was all so vivid now. After years of shutting it away, she could remember it in bright, horrific detail.

She had woken up slumped in the toilet block, feeling groggy and sore. Beano was beside her, dead. He'd been stabbed. Dear little Beano. She knew who would have done the stabbing, but as far as she was concerned, all of them were to blame for his death. She had scooped up his stiff body and sobbed into his fur.

Somehow she'd got herself home and stood in the shower, waiting numbly beneath the icy needles of the water while the immersion heater rebooted itself and the hot water returned. She stood through three separate clicks of that cycle, trying to come to terms with what she now understood had occurred. She flinched at the spike of pain between her legs. It felt as though she'd been ripped open. Her tears had joined the water of the shower, along with the helpless stream of urine that burned as it passed out of her and down her legs to stain the water at her feet.

She couldn't see those boys again. She couldn't go back to school. She was old enough at fifteen to leave and work. She would get a job in Brighton, far away from Russell Secondary Modern. And she would work shifts that avoided school arrival and departure hours. She would make herself invisible and her tormentors would forget about fat Anne who they'd raped. A scrawled note had been left in her pocket. *Thanks for a good time. Happy Birthday! Sorry about the dog.* it said and it had been signed with the name of clowns — *Pierrot, Coco, Bozo, Cooky* and *Blinko* — and underlined beneath — *The Jester's Club*. Had they all had their fun whilst she was unconscious? Which one hadn't worn a condom? Perhaps it was for the best that she had been so out of it; she couldn't imagine how she would have survived if she'd been a witness to her own attack.

And she'd done just that. She'd left school and got a job at Forfars the Bakers in Western Road. She didn't notice that her period didn't arrive in November or December because menstruation was still new for her. But by January she'd realised the same bag of pads were still in the bathroom cupboard and so she'd found the courage to talk to her mother, who had taken her to the doctor for a blood test. Anne was pregnant.

The revelation had sparked an intense love within Anne. She knew her son or her daughter was now her purpose in life. She was going to be a great mum, and she was going to give her child everything she possibly could, but mostly she was going to lavish it with affection. She had daydreamed of pushing a pram in the park, playing with her infant in the sandpit, taking him or her onto Palace Pier — pity West Pier was closed, she thought sadly. They would go on regular daytrips into London and see the sights, and perhaps she could learn to drive and save enough to buy a little car and they could go off on picnics.

The baby stretched and a new pain, like a cramp, accompanied it. She sucked in her breath and waited for it to pass.

Her manager, Angela, glanced over. 'Alright, Anne?'

'Ooh, I think it's a boy.' Anne grimaced, straightening from bending slightly at the discomfort. 'He's going to play for Brighton and Hove Albion, I'd say.'

'Sea-gulls!' the manager chanted and they both grinned. 'Anne, you look ready to burst,' Angela went on. 'Go home, take an early mark.'

Anne stared at her. 'Are you sure?'

'Yes. I can manage with Lesley and Sharon for the next couple of hours. Go on, you've worked hard today.'

The pain grumbled again. She was feeling a bit nauseated suddenly and the thought of getting home earlier was a gift from the heavens. 'Okay, if you're sure then.'

'Hurry up and leave before I change my mind,' the older woman called over her shoulder.

As if she was further blessed, a bus came along almost straightaway and Anne clambered on board. The bus lurched away before she'd sat down and she was thrown into a seat, apologising to the man next to her for all but falling onto him.

She bought her ticket from the conductor, then sat back and allowed her mind to wander. If it was a boy she was going to call him Peter, after her dad. She had no idea for a girl yet — perhaps Lucy. She smiled. Her choices were from the Narnia books, which she'd loved since she was ten. *And look at me now*, she thought, *still a kid myself but about to have my own child*. She hugged her belly with pleasure and it seemed to answer her with a fresh wave of the odd sensation that wasn't really pain but wasn't altogether comfortable either.

When she got home, her mother was slumped on the sofa in her usual stupor. Anne realised it'd be up to her to organise their evening meal. She should be used to it by now, but her mother had rallied a little at the news of an impending grandchild and so it hurt more than ever to see her ongoing dependence on the gin bottle. Anne had been feeling like fish and chips all day — the walk would do her good.

On the way back from the shop, she called into Hove Park, where plenty of people were walking their dogs and enjoying the balmy evening. Anne found a bench and savoured her dinner, feeling a tad guilty that her mother's meal would be soggy by the time she returned with it. Then again, there was every likelihood her mother wouldn't bother to eat anyway.

She noticed a pale green car cruise by slowly, then her glance slid away to where a couple were teaching their puppy some obedience commands. She smiled, remembering Beano. It was only the news of the baby that had blunted the pain she'd felt at losing him. *Everyone I love dies on me*, she thought. *Mum's next.* And then she thought of her child. *If I love him too much, will he die on me as well?* The fish felt like a wad of cardboard as she swallowed it. *No*, she reassured herself. *No harm will come to Peter.*

The park was emptying and Anne roused herself to make tracks for home. She sighed, stretched and glanced again at the main road. The traffic had thinned dramatically since she had last looked and she noticed the pale green car again, driving close to the kerb. It had to be the same car, surely. It was old, a bit battered in places, and she thought she could see several people inside. She knew she was probably being jumpy, but she was relieved to see it cruise past the park and out of sight.

A lone seagull shrieked overhead. *Hoping I might toss a chip your way, eh?* Anne thought, and as she did so, a fresh contraction announced itself. This time it hurt, intensifying to the point where she was holding her breath and had to lean against a nearby fence. Eventually, she recovered herself, holding her mum's warm fish and chips and her purse close, wondering how long before the next one or whether it was a one-off. She couldn't be going into labour. Peter wasn't due for weeks.

Now she felt frightened. She needed to get home quickly. She decided to cut through one of the side streets that led off the park. There was a twitten at the top that would take her through to the main road where she could get a bus or, better still, a taxi. This was definitely an emergency and she'd kept a couple of pounds in the back of her purse just in case.

She tried to hurry her heavy body along the short road that led to the twitten. She could see its opening now, could hear the cars speeding by on the main road at its end. Yes, she'd be fine. There was a phone box there too, so she could call a taxi if the pain got too bad.

She crossed the road to enter the small flint-roofed lane, then heard the sound of a car rolling to a stop behind her. She turned to see the pale green car she'd noticed before, a Cortina. Spilling from it were Billy Fletcher and Clive Farrow. It was a nightmare, but one Anne knew there would be no waking from. Letting out a cry, she hurtled as fast as her swollen body would allow down the tiny laneway, the slap of her shoes echoing noisily off the tall flint walls.

To Anne it seemed as though she was moving at high speed, but the end of the walkway never seemed to get closer. The boys caught up with her all too easily.

'Billy, don't!' she begged, seeing the grotesque clown's mask he'd pulled over his face, its wide smiling mouth intimidating and sinister. A ridiculous thought flashed into her mind amidst her fear: *I suppose you can't get Guy Fawkes masks at this time of the year.*

Billy slurred something about having a party and Clive giggled. Anne knew the sound of alcohol talking, had heard it often enough at home. 'You're drunk. Billy, please ...'

'Shed-urp!' It was Clive; he was far drunker than Billy, it seemed.

And then new footsteps. Measured, in no hurry. She knew who it was going to be without even turning.

'Hello, Annie,' Pierrot said gently. 'We thought that was you in the park. I saw you quite by chance earlier today, coming out of a bakery in Brighton. Imagine my shock at seeing you with that huge belly — too much of a coincidence for your baby not to belong to the Jesters Club. So I found the lads after school and we've been celebrating ever since. And we just had to say hello to an old friend.'

'Leave me alone!'

'Hush, Annie. We're allowed visiting rights to our own child, aren't we?'

This made all the boys laugh. Phil staggered towards her, his clown mask askew. 'Where's Beano?' he asked, his words running into each other.

They'd all grown, even Phil. Billy was much taller than Pierrot now, and Clive was as huge as Frankenstein, but thinner. It occurred to her to ask Mike whether he'd taken to smearing Nivea on his lips these days now that he could smile so brightly, but she doubted he'd get the jibe. He wasn't so quick he'd know she was referring to his hideous clown mask.

As if he could read her thoughts, Mike threw an insult of his own. 'You've got even fatter,' he slurred. 'I didn't think that was poshible.'

'She's pregnant, idiot,' Billy corrected.

'Yes, but to whom, I wonder?' Pierrot mused. There was no waver in his voice; presumably he'd not been drinking himself.

'You've got them drunk,' Anne accused. The boys giggled.

'We're a gang,' Pierrot said, sounding injured. 'I'm their teacher. I'm introducing them to lots of experiences. Tonight it's a celebration with you, Annie. The boys want to set things straight.'

'Not bright enough to play with people your own age?' Anne sneered, sounding far braver than she felt. She looked into the leering faces of her tormentors and the simple, steady, happy world she had built this year crumbled about her. *Not again. Please, dear god, not again.*

'Come on, Annie, come with us,' Pierrot urged.

'No!'

She tried to move away but hard fingers dug into her. They were too big, too strong. She vomited instead, over Clive's shoes. Horrified, he hit her. Not a slap but a full punch that caught her in the chest. She felt something crack, a rib perhaps.

Anne began to cry. Pain was moving in on her in a long, rolling wave and she could feel her baby squirming. A fractured rib meant nothing to this. She lowered herself to the floor of the alley and wept.

Pierrot heaved her back to her feet, making tutting sounds at Clive. 'Don't hurt her. She's our little mum.'

This time Anne couldn't scream, for the contraction was so intense it was all she could do to hold her breath and deal with the pain. She was aware of the boys pulling off their masks. Why they even bothered with them she didn't know. It was only Pierrot's identity that was a mystery. They held her upright, moving her along the twitten towards the car.

'Everything alright?' A new voice.

Anne wrenched her head around to see a man walking a dog. She tried to speak but couldn't; the pain had her fully in its grip now. All she could do was groan, and that just helped Pierrot's explanation.

'My wife — we're having a baby and we think it's coming right now. I'm rushing her to the hospital,' he said.

Anne shifted, desperate to get a look at her captor's face, which she realised was now unmasked. He was turned away from her, waving to the man with thanks, but she caught a glimpse before he pulled on the mask again: he had very dark hair and pale skin from what she could tell. And she was sure his voice held an Irish lilt.

They bundled her into the back seat of the Cortina, Clive and Billy flanking her, Billy pulling a hood over her head. Mike and Phil shared the front seat, she could tell from their voices. Clive, on her left, tied her wrists together with something.

'Why are you doing this?' she screamed through tears. The hood smelt of food — a bit like the bag the Christmas ham came in, she thought. Perhaps she looked liked a pig herself, all trussed up ready for the kill. She was sure she was going to vomit again.

'I told you, it's a surprise party and the boys don't want you to see anything until we're there. Here, tape her mouth,' Pierrot said. 'Can't have her drawing attention to us now, can we, boys? And push her down on the floor between you.'

The boys were too drunk, she realised, to comprehend how dangerous this was becoming. She helped them by moving herself down onto the floor. She wasn't going to invite Clive's fist again. The pain at her ribs exploded.

'I think I'm going to throw up,' she warned before the tape was applied.

'No, Annie, no, you won't,' Pierrot soothed, his tone sickeningly gentle as his hand reached back to pat her head. His next words sent shards of ice through her trembling body, freezing her into silence. 'We'll take care of you . . . and the baby.'

Anne had no idea where they were going. She tried to follow the twists and turns of the car but was too rattled to concentrate hard enough. She gave up and focused instead on the pains that were coming more regularly now. She groaned, her lips pulling against the masking tape over her mouth.

The car began to slow, and finally Pierrot parked. She heard him turn to her. 'Now, Annie, we're going to take off that hood.'

It was done. She looked up at them fearfully. From her spot on the floor, she could see it was inky dark now. She could hear the sound of waves and smell salt air. They were at the seafront in Brighton. She turned her head and saw the bright lights that her father used to bring her to admire when she was very little. Their happy fairytale glow mocked her misery.

As the boys piled out of the car, ideas for escape came and went in her mind like flashes from a sparkler. One moment bright and burning with potential, the next, extinguished. She ran through several scenarios, all ludicrous, from kicking whomever grabbed her first, then blindly running down the promenade and hoping to crash into someone, to somehow twisting away the moment they got her out of the car and racing towards the sea. They might lose her in the dark or she could drown herself. Better than whatever they had in store for her. It finally occurred to Anne to simply cooperate. No struggle, just make it easy on them, and perhaps they'd let her go. She survived last time. This time she had a baby to protect, and his life, no matter at what cost to her, was all that mattered.

She heard locks and chains rattling and then a gate swing open.

Pierrot was back, peering into the car, his freakish mask hiding his face. 'Anne, do you see this knife I have in my hand?'

It was concealed up the sleeve of his shirt, just the tip showing. She remembered that blade. It was the one that killed Beano. She nodded.

'There's no one around because there's a storm brewing,' he went on. 'The promenade's empty — all these lights on for no one. But you never know your luck in a big city, do you?' Again she nodded, hoping that was the right answer. 'So, if you do anything you're not supposed to do, I'm going to stick this knife into your belly. Do you understand?'

Her head bobbed frantically.

'Good girl. Now, when you get out, you just act natural, okay? I'll put my arm around you and we're going to act like a normal couple out for a stroll on Brighton Beach. Can you do that?'

212

She nodded again, imagining just how abnormal a couple they really looked — his mask a most romantic touch. He ripped the masking tape off her mouth and the sting made her lips feel as though they'd grown to ten times their normal size.

'I want you to tell me that you understand,' he urged.

'I do,' she said, trying to please yet desperate now with pain, 'but you need to know that I've gone into labour. The baby's coming.'

He paused, considered what she'd said. 'Are you sure, Annie?'

'He's early. But he's coming, I tell you. I began having the pains in the park and they've been getting worse and closer together. That means I'm in labour. I've been to classes, I know what's happening. I've got to get to a hospital.'

He hesitated again, calculating, then said, 'I can't let you do that.'

'My baby is being born!' she cried, the wind whipping her words away. 'He's early, he'll need special care from a hospital or he could die.' She was past caring about herself now. If he was planning to rape her again then she wished he'd just get on with it, but she wanted him to do it near a hospital so she at least had a fighting chance of delivering Peter safely.

'What do you want from me?' she asked in frustration.

'Something I gave you, Annie. I want it back.'

'I took nothing from you. You took my life from me,' she whispered, tears coming freely again now.

'Hush, now. Remember your promise.'

Anne was tempted to let rip with the biggest scream she could muster, especially now the latest contraction had passed. She was sure she hadn't long before the next one arrived. She felt Peter move inside and it reminded her once again of the chance at happiness she had, of how much she loved this child and how much she wanted him to live. *Cooperate*, she told herself. It might work out.

Reluctantly she took Pierrot's hand, forced herself not to recoil from his touch when he put his arm around her enveloping her in a haze of Brut and perspiration and another smell, an unpleasant one. It was tobacco, she realised. Pierrot must be a smoker.

She walked carefully alongside him and only then realised where he'd brought her. *West Pier!* Its colourfully lit facade now appeared suddenly sinister. The place she'd always loved had become a place of dread.

'West Pier's closed,' she said, confused.

'Not to us, Annie,' and he led her through the wooden gate and locked it behind him with a key.

The pier had been closed this year sometime. She recalled all the drama surrounding its closure. Everyone in the bakery and all the customers talked about it non-stop for a while. And she'd learned from reading *The Evening Argus*, which she did regularly, that West Pier was built as far back as 1866. She'd ridden on its red and white striped helter-skelter when she was four and loved looking at the sculpted goddess faces around its windowpanes and, more fascinating, its timber serpents coiled thick and colourful around all the lampposts. Although bombings during the war had done their best to destroy it, the West Pier had withstood the onslaught, but it was the ravages of time and weather that had finally closed one of the most popular spots in the whole of southern England.

'Don't you love the pier?' he said conversationally as he pulled her closer still. 'Too dangerous to keep open, they say. Such a pity. I spent the best times of my childhood here.' She heard a wistful note in his voice, but it was banished quickly. 'Come on then, Annie. Let's get you inside, shall we?'

She saw that the knife was now so close to her tummy that it was probably resting against Peter's head. It wouldn't take much to kill them both, she thought, and the grief hit her again. She started crying, and this time he didn't soothe her as before but simply bundled her into what had once been the magnificent concert hall. Now it was just an empty shell.

Mike swayed towards them on unsteady legs. 'Hey, Fl—'

'No!' Pierrot roared into his face. 'No names!'

He shoved Mike away, flicked a lighter and lit a candle he'd pulled from his pocket. He wedged the candle between two broken pieces of decking.

Anne wasn't watching him though, her attention on Mike Sheriff, wounded by Pierrot's tone. *Go on, Mikey, get the others going as well*, she silently urged. Hope flared.

Billy, who seemed to have sobered up slightly, walked to where Pierrot was lighting another candle. 'Can I have a word?'

'Yep.' Pierrot didn't turn.

'We don't want to do this any more.'

'What don't you want to do?' Pierrot stood.

'This!' Billy said, pulling off his mask. He pointed at Anne. 'This party thing. It's stupid. Sorry, Anne. I'm sorry for all of it.'

The others moved towards her, all unmasked now. Phil spoke, his voice croaky, newly broken. 'I didn't agree with the dog being hurt, and I'm not interested in all of this. I never was. I'm going home.'

'Yeah, me too,' Mike echoed, sneering at the man who'd been their leader just moments ago. 'We're still young enough that girls will give it willingly,' he taunted.

Pierrot didn't rise to the bait. Instead, he removed his mask and pointed to a sack on the timber floor. 'Here, lads,' he said. 'Over there.'

Anne stared at her abductor's face in the shimmering glow of the candles. He looked so ordinary — scruffy dark hair, pale skin, blue eyes. How could she describe him, she wondered, if the police asked her. And then the realisation hit her with as much force as Clive's earlier punch. If Pierrot had removed his mask, he was no longer frightened of her seeing him. And if he didn't fear her identifying him, it probably meant he intended to kill her. She began to sob again but everyone ignored her.

'What is it?' Clive said sulkily, staring at the bag.

'Take a look, it's all I promised.'

Phil moved the fastest, digging into the sack. 'More booze, smokes, chocolates, crisps, beer!' He began to laugh.

'Chocolate,' Clive mumbled and ripped into a block of Cadbury's.

Anne closed her eyes with a fresh wave of despair. The storm was whipping up outside. No one would hear her. There was no hope any more. A new contraction hit her and she sank to the floor of the concert hall, looked up to its once glorious, now damaged roof and prayed it would collapse right now on top of her. Kill her, kill them all, before Pierrot had a chance to hurt her again. Or, worse, hurt Peter.

He turned to her now, his eyes glittering. 'That baby is mine, Annie,' he said. He gave a small, harsh laugh. 'I can't believe it, but it's true.'

'He's mine,' she defied him.

'You can't keep him, Bletch,' he whispered, stealing a glance at the boys.

Anne began to pray.

Anne came to full consciousness, her eyes fluttering open at the sensation of raindrops falling on her face. Pain hit her so hard she cried out. And then she remembered in slow-motion and in horrific detail what had happened. She turned her head and retched. There was nothing left inside her; she had lost it all during the night, when Pierrot had first jumped on her belly.

She remembered him screaming at her — long after the four boys had fled — that he and his wife had wanted a child for so long and now she'd stolen that from them. He had called her a slut, a whore, a slag. Anne touched her belly now and felt the flaccid flesh that moved like the bread dough at the bakery. Her body was a deflated balloon, its womb empty of its precious life. She had hoped the whole thing was a nightmare, but as she lay there in agony, the world spinning around her, she remembered it all in stark clarity. The tiny body dangling from Pierrot's bloodied hand, her tormentor's laughter as he told her her baby was dead.

She began to scream relentlessly, the bloodcurdling keening finally rousing an early morning passerby and, ultimately, the police.

She remembered lovely Sergeant Moss clearly. He so badly wanted her to give him the information he needed. He knew she'd been been coerced, abducted — said as much — but she wouldn't give him a thing. It was her own fault that the police couldn't help her. But then that was such a terrifying time. She recalled now how she couldn't think straight that day.

Anne shook her head free of the memory. Her pulse was racing, and she was gasping for breath. She put a trembling hand to her forehead. It was clammy. Memories could still reduce her to a shaking wreck.

She looked around, concerned that someone might have noticed her distress. She couldn't afford to stand out now, not when she was so close to her target. She took a deep breath and got to her feet. She would make them all pay. And Billy Fletcher was next.

19

As they reached Brighton, Kate stuck her earpiece in and dialled the operations room. 'Find out where we're going on the street map, would you?' she said to Sarah while she waited for the call to connect. Sarah obediently found the directory in the glove compartment and looked up the address she had written down for Moss.

'Hi Joan, it's Kate.' She paused while Joan passed on her own message. 'Good, I'll let Sarah know. Is the DCI there? . . . Thanks.'

She looked over at Sarah who was waiting expectantly, then put a finger in the air to stall her.

'It's Kate, sir. Yes, sir, just heading into Brighton now. . . . Er no, we decided to do both calls together. Just wanted to let you know that we have a firm ID on Fletcher, which puts him in a precarious position. We need to find him.' She quickly relayed everything they'd discovered. 'I agree, we should start there, even if it does mean ringing every W Fletcher in the book. Okay, sir . . . Yes, she did, thank you. Bye.'

She hung up and turned to Sarah. 'He's going to start the hunt for Fletcher, and Joan said to tell you that your clown theory is right. Apparently the DCI rang one of the oldest touring circuses in Europe and got on to some ancient clown academy in Italy. Clowns are highly suspicious of blue and don't even carry that colour in their make-up boxes. Blue on the face is considered the worst kind of luck. In their words, death on stage — meaning they're going to dip out and not make a single person laugh.'

Sarah punched the air. 'Yes!' Then she frowned. 'I don't know how that brings us any closer to the killer though.'

'Maybe he or she trained as a clown or always wanted to be one?' Kate suggested.

Sarah wrinkled her nose at the idea. 'Then why smear blue paint on someone else's face? No,' she shook her head, 'if we follow the theory, then the killer is calling the victim the clown, giving him the bad luck. Death to them, in other words.'

'Or telling them their luck's run out,' Kate said, and then looked at Sarah, knowing they'd stumbled on something. She braked before she ran straight into the back of another car. 'Oops, sorry.'

'That sounds closer, doesn't it?' Sarah said, thinking it through some more. She bit her lip. 'But why? Why clowns in the first place?'

'That's the sixty-four-million-dollar question. Tell me where we're going.'

Sarah gave directions and they finally drew up outside a small house near St Ann's Well Gardens. 'This should be it,' Sarah said, 'number eighteen.'

'Come on then, maybe your ex-sergeant will fix us a cup of tea.' Kate looked at her watch. They'd missed lunch and it was way too early for dinner. What she wouldn't give for a custard cream right now.

Former Sergeant Moss met them at the front door before they'd even let themselves inside his gate.

'DS Sarah Jones and DI Kate Carter,' Sarah said. 'Are you Sergeant Moss?'

'Just Mr Moss these days, DS Jones. In fact, call me Colin, I answer to that more happily.'

He shook their hands and showed them into the house, where the chocolatey aroma of tobacco permeated the hallway. He guided them into a sitting room, cluttered with family memorabilia and silent save for the ticking of a very old clock.

'My wife's going to put the kettle on. Can we offer you girls a cup of tea?'

'Thanks,' Sarah said, taking the lead. 'White and no sugar is fine for both of us, right?' She looked at Kate who smiled her thanks.

A woman who looked like every childhood story's grandmother bustled into the room. 'Tea?' she asked.

'This is my wife, Alice,' Colin Moss said. 'Meet DS Sarah Jones and DI Kate Carter.' The women nodded at each other. 'All of us want tea, my love. And a very simple order: three with milk and no sugar.'

'And perhaps some home-made shortbread?' Alice Moss said, a glint in her eye.

Kate liked them both immediately. 'Your pipe's unlit, Colin,' she said to break the ice. 'Don't miss out on our account.'

He gave a soft chortle. 'I miss out entirely, DI Carter, my lungs can't handle it any more. But I simply can't shake the habit of the old favourite hanging from my mouth.'

He turned to Sarah. 'So, DS Jones, your call has opened up a very old wound.'

'I hope not too painful?'

'Agony actually, but necessary. It's been festering, as I mentioned on the phone, for far too long and it bothers me to this day that we didn't do more for the girl in question. It was that pile-up on the road up to Chanctonbury Ring that distracted us. An idiot was watching the burning torches of some pagan ritual or other and lost control of his car, ploughed into other cars and it quickly became a war zone. All spare units were called in to help because it was remote and the dead of night. Just directing traffic to get ambulances up there was a nightmare. It took up all our time and resources for days.'

Sarah nodded. 'You said you have a file, Colin?'

'Here it is,' he said, gesturing to the table in front of him. 'It's the only item I ever took from the station, although everything in there is a copy. If you need the originals, they're with Lewes.'

'Thank you,' Sarah said. 'But would you mind telling us everything you can? The file will be very helpful, I'm sure, but you met this girl, you were there.'

He nodded and stood to open the door for his wife who was arriving with a tray laden with their afternoon tea.

'This is very kind of you, Mrs Moss,' Kate said. She'd been deliberately quiet, determined not to steal Sarah's thunder, even though she was desperate to hit Colin Moss with a barrage of questions.

'Oh, don't mention it, dear. We get so few visitors these days that it's nice to lay a tray properly again. And anyway,' she said, a smile in her voice, 'if you skinny girls would just eat all these biscuits, you'll save my Colin another inch on his waistline.'

'Oh, go on with you,' Moss said. 'I love your shortbread as much as I love you, and you wouldn't have it any other way.'

Alice Moss left them to their tea and conversation but not before throwing her husband a private smile. Kate saw it, and knew she wanted exactly that for her and Dan . . . yet deep down recognised they would never have that kind of connection.

'How long have you been married?' she asked.

'We've just celebrated our golden wedding anniversary,' Colin said proudly. 'Fifty years last Sunday. I'm going to take her on a European cruise called Classic Capitals. First it was our children, then my work — we never got around to fulfilling my wife's dream of seeing all the major cities on the continent.'

Kate smiled. 'That's lovely. Make sure you do — no excuses.'

He saluted. 'I never argue with a woman. Help yourselves, ladies, please. I'll pour as I tell you what I know.'

He stirred the contents of the teapot before filling their teacups.

'The girl's name was Anne McEvoy. She was fifteen when the attack occurred. It took place at West Pier and an angler raised the alarm — the Brighton fishermen took on a sort of loose security role for the pier when it was formally closed, you see? They had keys, kept an eye on things.' The detectives nodded. 'From what we can gather, Anne had been heavily pregnant, and although she wouldn't speak much to us, the angler who found her told us that she said she'd been attacked and her baby had died. She said nothing else, refused to talk to the police or any of the medical staff.'

Kate frowned. 'Why?' she asked. 'What happened?' Even as she spoke, she knew he had no answer for her or Anne McEvoy would not be a cold case.

'I can't tell you. That's what makes it so frustrating. She worked at a bakery and was, according to her co-workers, very much looking forward to motherhood. Her manager told us that Anne had once confessed that her life had been pretty miserable until she became pregnant but that she was sure the baby would change everything, give her every reason to love life.'

'How sad,' Sarah said.

He nodded. 'She was a sad girl. She was a chubby sort, you know, and no oil painting, but I could sense spine in her. Not toughness, just that she had courage.'

Sarah sat forward. 'So do you think it was fear that prevented her from saying anything?'

'Fear alone? No. But she was certainly fearful. I think her body and mind were in shock. The baby hadn't been quite full term, according to the hospital notes. When I saw Anne, she was on a drip, very bruised. The doctor said she'd been bashed around, that something heavy had landed on her abdomen.'

'The baby?' Kate asked.

He shrugged. 'Never found.'

Both women looked at him, incredulous.

'We did everything from putting up posters to doorknocking but no one came forward with news of a newborn child. I'd hoped it might turn up on someone's doorstep, but the trail was cold from the moment Anne was found.

'The doctor thought she might have thrown the child and the afterbirth into the sea, but we discounted that idea as it didn't explain the battering she'd suffered.'

'And Anne wouldn't tell you anything herself?' Sarah asked.

'She wouldn't give us any details other than her name. It meant we were able to track her mother down — her father and baby brother died when she was a child — and that's where the story gets even more tragic.'

Colin Moss looked sadly at the two police officers. 'Anne's mother was found dead in her house later that day — an empty bottle of pills at her bedside. She'd washed them down with a bottle of Scotch.'

'Nothing suspicious?' Kate wondered aloud.

He shook his head. 'It was largely agreed that the news of Anne's attack and subsequent loss of the baby prompted her suicide. After telling her that her daughter had been found on West Pier, taken to hospital, believed attacked, our people offered to send a car but she asked them not to, said she preferred to make her own way to the hospital. She never arrived.'

'Did any of your people say anything about the baby?'

Moss grimaced. 'Didn't have to, I suppose. She likely guessed by what they weren't saying. I gather she was an unstable woman so who knows what thoughts went on in her mind. She'd already lost a husband and child in traumatic circumstances and no doubt she felt she might lose her daughter and grandchild.' He put down the teacup he'd been cradling to his chest. 'The East Sussex police didn't see Anne again,' he continued softly. 'By the time we returned to the hospital, it was evening and Anne had disappeared. All our attempts to locate her came up wanting. The manager at the bakery where Anne worked told us that on the day in question she'd given Anne an early mark and the youngster had left on a very happy note, telling her she might treat herself and her mum to some fish and chips with the day's wages.'

'And Anne's school?' Sarah prompted.

'She'd left school the previous autumn, around the time of her pregnancy. Apparently she was a top student and the school principal had tried to persuade her to stay on for her O and A levels. They had no idea who had fathered her baby — in fact, none of the teachers or staff had known she was pregnant — and none of the children could help either. They didn't know she had a boyfriend — they described her as plain, bespectacled and very overweight. According to all, she was a clever girl who should have been at a grammar school, and a loner. One teacher said she suspected that Anne was "receiving some attention", as she put it, but thought it was just foolish boys larking around. Anne would likely have said something otherwise.'

The two detectives glanced at each other. Moss gave them an enquiring look, but Kate nodded to him to go on with his story for the moment.

'The case became a sort of personal mission,' Moss said. 'I spoke to the fisherman who looked after West Pier's security, "Whitey" Rowe, and he told me there were only three keys for the gate. He kept one permanently, another was kept at the kiosk for emergencies, and the final spare was circulated among the fishing community — a sort of you-scratch-my-back-I'll-scratch-yours arrangement. According to my notes, Whitey had his key with him all night, and when he did his rounds at the Pier around nine-thirty all was quiet. He'd enjoyed a spot of fishing and gone home at ten-fifteen. No sign of Anne or her baby. It was as if she had never been there.'

'So what happened next?' Sarah asked.

'The case was kept open, but as time wore on it was filed away in the "Unsolved" cabinet at Brighton police headquarters.'

'What do *you* think happened?' Sarah said. 'Pretty hard for a baby to disappear without someone noticing. A baby cries a lot, after all.'

'The doctor who admitted Anne firmly believed the infant was thrown into the sea from the pier.'

Kate flinched. 'So possibly the father, not wanting the child, took it upon himself to get rid of it?'

Moss nodded. 'Which means he was perhaps too young to cope with a baby, or was trying to protect his reputation. Or the attack was an accident and they needed to get rid of the evidence.'

'An accident!' Kate exclaimed. 'How could you not notice that the girl you're attacking is heavily pregnant?'

Sarah picked up the thread. 'Colin, you said "they" — what do you mean?'

He hesitated. 'I could be wrong but I never believed this was an attack by one person.'

'Why?'

'We scoured the pier's concert hall where Anne was found. It was pretty much a ruin in 1975 and closed off to the public. Yet we found sweet and chocolate wrappers there and empty bottles of alcohol.'

'Pretty normal sort of rubbish,' Kate commented.

'Yes, DI Carter, but the wrappers were all current designs and fresh, and all found in one spot. The discarded chewing gum was still sticky and the bottles of alcohol were still wet inside. In my opinion, there was too much debris for it to have been consumed by one person. I mean, he could have, but it struck me as odd and the feeling that there was more than one perpetrator has never left me. Frankly, there was enough debris to suggest a small gang.'

The women exchanged glances again, which told him far more than any words could.

'So why don't you tell me what you've got and how this might relate to my Anne,' he finished.

Sarah looked to Kate who nodded, deferring to her to do the briefing. Sarah spared Moss none of the details of the recent murders. Jack had authorised her to tell him everything. When she'd finished, a silence hung over the three of them — as cold as the half-drunk pot of tea on the table.

'Four of them,' Moss finally murmured. 'That poor girl.'

'Of course, we can't be sure exactly,' Sarah added. 'These two cases certainly fit together nicely, and the timing is right, but it still remains hypothetical. We have nothing concrete to tie them together.'

He ignored her prevarication. 'So Anne is hunting them down, eh? I told you there was something more to her, although it's a long time to wait for vengeance.'

'Colin, I think our DCI would appreciate being able to speak with you face to face,' Kate said. 'Fancy a trip to London?'

At his wry smile, she added, 'What about your wife?'

'Oh, she'll be fine. Her sister and brother-in-law are staying with us at the moment — hence all the shortbread — so she won't be alone. Er, do you mean now?'

'Sooner the better,' Kate admitted. 'This does all sound a bit too neat to ignore as mere coincidence, and there's the concern of a third corpse turning up. We've got a car here, so we could drive you into London now and have you brought back this evening by, say, eight o'clock. Is that going to suit?'

'Let me go and change,' Moss said. 'I've always wanted to go to the Yard — can't arrive at headquarters in my scruffies, can I?' He grinned. 'Eat those wretched biscuits, ladies, please, or I'll have some explaining to do.'

20

Anne, having recovered her composure, watched, fascinated, as a much older Billy Fletcher emerged from the nursing home. He stretched on the stairs beneath the watery sunlight of this suddenly mild March day. Not that it would last, but it was uplifting to feel that soft warmth, she thought, as she saw Billy reach into his coat pocket and take out a box of cigarettes. He lit one, then dug into another pocket for his phone. He punched in a number, inhaled deeply on his cigarette, put the phone to his ear and waited for the connection. Billy looked even more handsome than Anne remembered; the lines of the decades had only added to his attractiveness. He wore his dark hair short and had a close-shaved beard. His clothes were expensive and stylish. All in all, he had the air of a confident, wealthy man.

Anne surreptitiously removed her wig, hid it in her bag and fingered her own hair into some order. She took off her coat and turned it inside out to change it from a cream trench coat to a chic black one. She added a silk scarf from her bag and took a moment to apply some lipstick and check the rest of her make-up. She needed to look good.

She could hear Billy wrapping up his conversation, so she walked across the grass and then the road as though she was going into the nursing home.

'Billy Fletcher?' she exclaimed, feigning amazement and stopping at the foot of the stairs that led up into the home.

He turned to her, phone still to his ear, his expression one of surprise. 'Er, yeah,' he stammered, then into the phone, 'I've gotta go. I'll call you later.'

He frowned at Anne, a question in his eyes. 'Sorry, do I know you?'

She laughed delightedly. 'Oh, look closer, Billy? You should remember me from schooldays.'

He stared but his expression remained blank.

'Okay, let me give you a clue. Does the nickname Bletch help?'

The recognition that finally came stretched across his face with a look of wonder. 'Anne McEvoy? It can't be.'

'One and the same.'

'Bloody hell! You look amazing.' He clicked a button on his phone and slipped it back into his coat pocket.

'Thank you,' Anne said, all smiles.

'What have you done to yourself?' he asked, clearly impressed, his glance taking in the knee-length charcoal grey pencil skirt that showed off her slim, toned legs. She noticed how his eyes flicked to the tiny glimpse of cleavage she was deliberately showing, having undone the button on her silk lilac shirt as she crossed the road.

'I grew up,' she said.

He whistled. 'But you were so fa—' He stopped, embarrassed.

'I know, you told me often enough.' She stepped closer. 'I've looked like this for years, although it's harder to maintain these days. It's quite a health routine, let me assure you.' She laughed delightedly at his shocked expression. 'When did we all get to be in our forties, eh?'

'You look amazing,' he repeated, unable to help himself. And then she saw his expression cloud as memories ghosted into his mind, reminding him of his former relationship with Anne McEvoy. 'What are you doing here?' he said carefully and she saw him swallow hard. No, Billy had not forgotten any of it.

'I visit an old friend of the family infrequently. What about you?'

'My dad's in here.'

She smiled, ensuring he felt the full force of its warmth. 'It must be fate — we were destined to meet.' She glanced up the stairs, praying none of the nurses would see her. 'Listen, are you free?'

'What do you mean?'

'I mean, are you rushing somewhere? Perhaps we could have a cup of coffee or something?'

'Um ...' His gaze flicked nervously up and down the street. He looked embarrassed again.

'Oh, come on, for old times' sake. How often do you get to meet someone from your teenage years?'

'Anne, it's been a long time but I can't help feeling odd about seeing you. I don't really know what to say to you about ...' His voice trailed off, then, to his credit, he rallied. 'About what happened all those years ago.'

'You mean the rape?'

Billy blanched. 'I ... yes ...'

'Billy —'

'It's actually Edward these days.' His voice was suddenly strained. More memories, no doubt. 'I, er, I changed to my middle name. No one knows me as Billy these days — other than my dear old parents and they agreed to call me William.' Again his gaze roved. He was feeling very awkward.

Good, Anne thought. 'Alright ... Edward ... Look, let's just ignore the past. Something awful happened. It was thirty years ago and I've moved on.'

'I find it impossible that you can stand to talk to me.'

'Let's talk somewhere else. We're blocking the doorway, I think.' Billy allowed himself to be walked a few metres away from the nursing home. 'Look, it's such a surprise to see someone from the past. I'm happy to have a chat over a cuppa — why can't you be?'

'Anne, I can't pretend it didn't happen and act perfectly normal with you.'

'Why not?' she asked brightly. She couldn't lose him now. 'I can, and I was the victim. This is good for me. I've never seen anyone from my schooldays — I'd really love to hear about your life.'

He stared at her, baffled. 'No grudge?'

She crossed her heart. 'I promise. Don't get me wrong, I've had a lot of therapy, but it was a lifetime ago, and really, I remember very little of it.'

He shook his head, understandably unnerved. 'This is very awkward. You know I didn't —'

She pulled an expression of mock exasperation. 'Come on, we can do this over a cup of coffee — or better still, ignore it and talk about what we're both up to today. Yes or no?'

Could he resist her? She was sure she'd marked him right, had employed just the right amount of sex and confidence to lure him into her web. Billy was a handsome, virile-looking guy and he didn't have a ring on his finger. She was certain he wouldn't pass up the opportunity to be seen with a gorgeous woman.

'Okay,' he said reluctantly and Anne knew she'd cornered him. 'What about your friend?' He pointed with his thumb over his shoulder to the nursing home.

'Oh, I can come back any time. I'd kill for a hit of caffeine right now.'

He shrugged. 'Do you have a car?'

'No, I came by taxi. What about you?'

'Hop in,' he said, squeezing the button on his car keys. A sleek black car close by lit up.

Anne raised an eyebrow. 'I see you've done okay,' she said, sensing it was what he'd like to hear.

'Yeah, cheers, I have.'

He opened the door for her and Anne made sure he got a lingering look at her legs, bending deeply into the seat so he could also have a peek at her lacy bra beneath her shirt.

He joined her in the car. 'Looks as though you've done okay too.'

'Oh? What makes you say that?'

He smiled. Billy had lost none of his boyish charm. Seeing him grinning at her shot Anne straight back into the days of fear. She had to force back the anxiety and dig deep to paste a similar look of pleasure onto her own face.

'Well, expensive clothes, no doubt very pricey perfume and loads of confidence,' he said. 'Money breeds confidence. I know from my own experience.' He winked. 'There's a pretty good cafe near Hove Park —' He looked at her, suddenly mortified.

'No, not Hove Park,' she murmured, carefully not showing any overreaction. 'Somewhere on Church Road perhaps?'

'Yeah, okay, I know somewhere.' But the chasm had opened between them. She felt his awkward silence descend upon her. He shook his head again. 'I must be mad ...'

Anne waited, wondering at the best approach. She had almost lost him again.

'I don't know what to say,' he finally added, and swerved the car over to the kerb. 'Let's not do this.'

'Billy — sorry, Edward ...' Anne loaded her voice with a gentle, soothing tone. 'Please, I've dealt with it,' she said softly. 'I've had help over the years and one of the main things my therapist told me was if I could ever meet one or two of the boys involved, it would help enormously towards my healing. I've never had the chance until now.' She reached out tentatively and placed her hand on his wrist. Took it away again almost immediately.

'You're serious?' He looked to where her hand had rested. 'How can you possibly forgive us?'

She took a deep, shaking breath. 'It was either that or kill myself. I chose to live, chose to move on. And today, seeing you again, reinforces that I have moved on and built a good life. I've never been more satisfied or focused.'

Anne smiled. Billy could never understand how much she meant those final words, although he'd soon find out.

'You're amazing, Anne.'

'That's the third time you've said that.' She smiled warmly at him. 'But thanks, it means a lot. So, come on, tell me about yourself. Are you married?'

She felt intense relief as Billy indicated right and pulled smoothly into the traffic of Sackville Road.

'Divorced. I'm enjoying bachelorhood again. You?'

'Divorced,' she grinned, as if to say snap. 'But happy,' she went on, keeping it simple. 'Do you live in Brighton still?'

'Hastings at the moment — for about three months probably.'

'Oh, not too far from your dad. That's good.'

'I'm in hospitality. I've set up a chain of B&B self-contained accommodation throughout East Sussex and I'm now moving into franchising the name so guesthouses can use it. I'm doing up some apartments in the Hastings area just now — "the new Brighton" they're calling it.'

'That's fantastic, congratulations.'

'What about you?'

'Interior design. I have my own business and work for well-heeled London clients who want to know whether a colour called broken white, for instance, works better for them than eggshell white.'

He laughed and Anne heard the relief in his voice. She knew her attitude confused him but she had to get this right.

'What about this place?' he asked.

Anne saw that it was a nondescript cafe. Perfect. 'That's fine.'

Billy parked close by and within minutes they were seated opposite each other at a wooden table that wobbled. A small silk pot plant sat next to a bowl stuffed with packets of sugar.

Anne reached for a sachet of sweetener as their coffees arrived. Over a couple of very ordinary cappuccinos, she fabricated the past three decades of her life for Billy, carefully steering well clear of their schooldays, keeping her voice light, her humour sparkling. She could tell he was unsettled, but also helplessly captivated by the lovely-looking woman opposite him.

'I've travelled a bit too,' Billy said, after she'd finished telling him about living in France.

'Oh?'

'Yeah, I've just come back from six months on the other side of the world.'

No wonder he hadn't heard about the other murders. She had been waiting for him to mention them. Seemed her luck was running. 'Holiday?' she asked.

'Bit of both. I'm a ski freak. Discovered it about ten years ago and decided I wanted to do some skiing in New Zealand. I ended up staying longer, touring Australia, and stopped off in Asia to look at the health spas. No one does it better.'

'And did you pick up much for your own business?'

He nodded. 'The spas in Thailand were magnificent. Once this franchising thing is up and running, I want to take a look at setting up some luxury health resorts. The holiday itself was brilliant, especially Queenstown. They filmed *The Lord of the Rings* there and all over New Zealand. Did you ever see it?'

He was gabbling, still a bit nervous.

'No, but I've always wanted to get to that part of the world,' Anne said, draining the last of her coffee. 'I should get some info from you. Are you in town for a couple of days?'

'No, I'm driving back to Hastings. Why?'

She shrugged, making sure her breasts pressed against the silk shirt. 'Oh, I just thought I could hear more about your trip over dinner.' She saw him open his mouth to say something and waved a hand in apology, 'Of course, you've probably got a lot to do —'

'No,' he interrupted. 'If ... if you don't feel funny about us having dinner, I'd love to.'

'Tomorrow evening?'

'So you're up for a day or so?'

'Several,' she lied and smiled, knowing it was the perfectly timed tease.

'Shall I meet you in Brighton somewhere?'

'Sure. Is seven okay?'

'I'll book a restaurant,' he said.

'No, let me. My treat,' Anne insisted. 'Give me your mobile number and I'll text you the details.'

Billy looked bemused — probably unused to a woman taking charge, Anne thought. He gave her his phone number, which she put straight into her mobile.

She glanced up from the keypad. 'I hope you don't mind, I've put you under Billy — I can't think of you as Edward.'

He looked mildly embarrassed. 'It's okay. Just don't call me that in public,' and they both smiled. 'Right, let me get you back to the nursing home.'

'No, look, I'll go up there tomorrow. Now that I'm already this close to town, I'll do some shopping. I love the Lanes and never get enough opportunity to enjoy them.'

'Pick up some nice pieces for your clients, I suppose, and sell them for twice the price?'

'Yes, that sort of thing,' Anne replied sheepishly. She held out her hand. 'Well, until tomorrow then. Look out for my text.'

'I already am,' he said, a little more confident now, a hint of brazenness filtering into his voice. She remembered that tone well.

'I hope you don't mind me mentioning that I'm really impressed you've lost your stammer,' she said as they moved out of the cafe onto the pavement.

Billy's expression lost its assuredness. 'You never lose it, Anne. It tends to come back when I'm under a lot of stress or anxiety.'

'The divorce?'

He nodded.

'Well, you're obviously very happy and stress-free now,' she said, imagining how she was going to bring that stammer back in force. 'If I didn't know you, I'd have no clue. See you tomorrow.'

She gave him a last coquettish smile, a small wave, and then she turned and walked away from the man she was going to kill tomorrow night.

21

It was just before six by the time the Operation Danube team congregated in the operations room. Kate was starving and more than grateful to see the tower of bulging sandwiches DCI Hawksworth had ordered up from the nearby delicatessen.

'Thank you for coming, Colin,' Hawksworth said for everyone's benefit. He'd held the full team back late so they could hear Moss's tale. 'But we can't have you talking on an empty stomach.' He gestured to the food. 'Please, let's have a working supper.'

Colin Moss had enjoyed his tour of New Scotland Yard but now wore a serious look that indicated he was ready to get down to business.

'Before we hear Colin's info,' Jack went on, 'you need to know that Kate and Sarah's trip to Hurstpierpoint has delivered us a firm ID on William Fletcher — known as Billy. He's this fellow in our photo, the good-looking guy, the stammerer that Clive Farrow referred to. According to Mrs Truro, Billy's old schoolteacher, she seems to think this fourth boy is familiar but couldn't give us a name. I don't have to impress upon you how important it is that we find not only Fletcher, but this fourth guy too. We have to assume both are now at risk.

'Alright now, everyone, sitting next to Sarah we are very fortunate to have former police sergeant Colin Moss. He was with the Brighton Police before he retired and he's joined us this afternoon to tell us about a cold case that Sarah's instincts have led her to. If she looks a bit fidgety, it's because she thinks we're on to something that could break open our serial killer case.'

Everyone stared at Sarah and Jack winked at her. He was pleased her instinctive work had paid off, and was especially glad to see the two women seemed to have sorted themselves out.

Once again Moss told his story of Anne McEvoy. He was greeted by a heavy silence when he finished. DCI Hawksworth broke it.

'A tragic tale and one, unfortunately, that fits all too neatly into the scenario we are working with. I agree with Kate that it is too much of a coincidence for us to ignore that Anne McEvoy may be taking her revenge. Kate, I think you should call Eva Truro again — all of the teachers for that senior school if you have to — and establish whether she recalls Anne McEvoy.'

Colin Moss interrupted. 'Is this Russell Secondary? I can probably save you a call and some time.'

'Yes, Farrow and Fletcher attended that school,' Kate answered.

'Well, it's now known as Blatchington Mill, but Anne McEvoy definitely attended Russell Secondary. She left in October 1974 when she was nearly fifteen.'

Jack felt a tingle of excitement zip through him like an electrical current. His gut was sending a bright message that this was it. They were definitely on the right trail.

'Right, all the more reason to find Fletcher and the fourth person in our photo,' he said. 'Everyone is to turn their attention to this. We need to contact the doctor who examined Anne that night — do we have a name?'

Moss nodded, he didn't have to consult the file. 'His name is Dr David Whitworth. He was in his late twenties back then so he should still be knocking around. I am, after all.' His quip won a flutter of polite laughs.

Both Cam and Bill had questions about the debris that had been found, which the former policeman was able to answer in detail because he'd personally visited the scene of the crime.

'Definitely teenage debris. Chocolate bars — you know, Mars, Bounty, Galaxy, as well as Opal Fruits, pear drops, milk bottles, chewing gum — that sort of thing. As for the alcohol, it was vodka and beer, plus there were lots of 10-pack cartons of cigarettes. They did them in those days.' He shrugged. 'All the sort of stuff teenage lads would enjoy.'

Sarah was studying the file. 'Colin, it said in the notes that there was also a tin of tobacco found.'

Moss sat forward to pick up another sandwich. 'Yes, a bit baffling that. There were no cigarette papers found, just the tobacco. It could have been anyone's, of course, but it was relatively full and fresh, suggesting it hadn't been lying around for a while.'

'Not the sort of thing teenagers would go for,' Bill said.

Brodie shrugged. 'Teenagers will try anything.'

'Yes, but there wasn't any associated litter there,' Colin added, agreeing with the older detective. 'If those boys were throwing around their sweet wrappers and beer bottles, then you can be sure we'd have found stubs of roll-your-own cigarettes, used papers and so on, but there was none of that. Just the tin. It always bothered me — still does.'

Jack finally aired what he'd been thinking the whole time Colin Moss had recounted the sorry story of Anne McEvoy. 'If you work with the hypothesis that these boys and Anne were on the pier together, are you suggesting there could have been someone else, someone older, involved as well?'

A fresh silence descended. Moss and Hawksworth stared at one another. The older man confirmed Jack's fears.

'I'm guessing, of course, but yes, that's been at the back of my mind for nearly three decades. I just needed someone else to think it, say it. No one at the time agreed with me.'

Hawksworth blew out his cheeks. 'An adult. So what we're saying now is that an older man may have been there, possibly orchestrating the attack.'

'Perhaps even the original rape and, arguably, the early birth of a baby,' Kate said, her tone vicious. 'How cruel.'

Hawksworth lightly touched her sleeve. 'Just a theory, Kate. It's all we have at the moment.' He noticed how she removed her arm as if burned, wondered at it briefly, but took up the thread again. 'Colin, did you find out anything much beyond Anne's schooldays . . . even after you'd lost track of her?'

'No, I'm very sorry to say, but not for lack of effort. Anne disappeared as though she'd never existed, her mother was dead, and there were no other relatives that we could find. She never contacted anyone from the bakery. I kept her file open for two years, hoping I'd get a lead from somewhere, but she'd covered her tracks well. I retired in '77.'

'You did everything you could by the sounds of things,' Jack said. 'If these murders are Anne's work then at least you get to close that file now, Colin.'

The older man nodded. 'What a sad life she's had.'

Jack looked at Sarah. 'You go through that file and pick out anything that we can work with. Colin, are you comfortable about DS Jones staying in touch with you?'

'Anything to save me from touring with my in-laws,' he offered, smiling at Sarah.

'Good,' Jack said. 'I also want you working on that blue paint, Sarah. Use the database — see if there have been any incidents with blue paint previously.' Her expression said it was unlikely but he persisted. 'There's a clue in there somewhere, even if she didn't mean for it to be important to us.'

'Yes, sir. Can I just check something on that?' Sarah pushed her glasses back up her nose. 'Colin, I don't suppose there was any blue paint found at the scene that isn't mentioned here on the list?'

Moss frowned and shook his head.

'I mean, I realise it was 1975, and I'm not having a go at the policework,' Sarah went on, 'I'm just wondering if you're able to recall any cans of paint.'

'Well, the pier was a sort of greeny blue, but I'd think it highly unlikely there were any cans of paint lying around.'

'This is a very bright blue,' Hawksworth said, pointing to the ghoulish photos behind them.

'Oh, yes, of course,' Moss said. 'Then, no, definitely not. I walked the whole concert hall, looking for something that would give me answers to Anne's abduction and her disappearance. Definitely no cans of paint, and no splotches or signs of that colour anywhere. What does it mean?'

Jack looked to Sarah — it was her theory after all.

She shrugged. 'Well, the closest we can get to something of a macabre nature is that clowns are deeply suspicious of the colour — afraid of it, in fact. It signifies bad luck, death on stage — meaning their act bombs — but I reckon it could be even more sinister than that, as in death itself. That's why we're hoping to make a link between that and the blue paint on our victims. The fact that it's smeared on their faces is significant, especially that it was applied by their own fingers.'

'Like clown make-up,' Colin finished.

'Exactly,' Sarah said. 'Although it's still only a theory.'

'I'll think on it, something might surface.' He looked around at the other members of the team. 'So, let me get this clear: you are now working on the supposition that Anne McEvoy has re-emerged to stalk and kill two of the boys, now men, who raped her?'

Everyone bar Jack sat back and shared sheepish, awkward glances. There was a pause before the answer finally came. 'Yes,' Jack said.

'And that she's now likely hunting down the other two from this photo?' Moss added, gesturing at the picture of the four grinning boys that was pinned to the board nearby.

'Yes.'

'And that it's plausible she would hold this grudge thirty years on?'

Jack leaned forward, his fingers entwined on the table in front of him. 'I'm going to leave that to the clinical psychologist we're working with, but he thinks it's plausible. And listening to your tale of what Anne McEvoy suffered, I'm of the belief that no woman forgives the slaughter of her child — if that's what occurred. She'll take that hate to the grave. And if these are the men that raped her and then attacked her again with the intention killing the child they inflicted upon her, I don't feel much pity for them.'

Jack felt the atmosphere thicken around him. He knew he shouldn't have revealed his feelings quite so openly.

Moss stared at Hawksworth, betraying nothing of his own thoughts. 'I heard you were one to move whole cases forward on gut instinct, DCI Hawksworth, but I'd caution that you may need some facts to back this one. Anne, if she's alive, is forty-four.'

'Have you checked into me?' Jack said, his tone smooth.

'Yes, I did. I don't care to work with people I don't know much about. You come with glowing praise.'

There was a pause before Jack gave a twitch of a smile. He didn't care much for being investigated but he also knew he needed to show respect to this still-sharp former policeman. 'Is there anything else you can tell us about Anne?' he said.

Moss finished his coffee. 'It was a long time ago and I probably spent little more than five minutes in her company. She'd been beaten up, she was frightened and angry, and silent. There's very little else I can give you on her, other than she had long dark hair and her eyes were an intense blue.'

'She sounds striking,' Jack said.

'No, not at all,' Moss countered. 'Apart from her eyes, Anne had the plainest of features and, although the word probably isn't politically correct enough for New Scotland Yard these days, the girl was fat. She wore heavy glasses with thick lenses as I recall — they found them broken in one of her pockets, along with a little change and a door key when she was first picked up. We've presumed she stole the money for a taxi from the hospital to her house, discovered her dead mother — a drug overdose — and then she was gone. Vanished.'

'What happened to everything?' Cam asked.

'The house, you mean?'

Cam nodded.

'You know, I don't have the answer to that. The father — a local GP — and her younger brother were killed in an accident when Anne was very young. After her mother's death, it all probably went to Anne.'

'What a miserable life,' Kate said.

Moss nodded. 'It's why I always felt so badly about this case. We didn't do enough for Anne. She'd already had a sad life, and our ineptitude in looking after her made it worse — apparently turned her into a killer.'

Moss's final words bit deep and Jack was reminded of his Super's caution. He wondered if he should heed that warning now, stop himself taking too great a leap of faith.

He cleared his throat. 'Cam, why don't you look into the house and family belongings? See if you can find out more.'

'Right, Hawk.'

'Well,' Jack said, leaning back, 'this has been valuable. Thank you, Colin, for all the information and especially for your time and being kind enough to come down to London. I'll organise for you to be driven back now, if that's okay? Bill's offered to take you as he's got an early morning meeting with Sussex Police over at Lewes.'

Moss nodded. 'Say hello to Lou Stanton from me,' he said to Bill before returning his gaze to Jack. 'It was my pleasure to help, DCI Hawksworth. If you find her, will you let me know?'

'Of course,' Jack said. 'Although I have a feeling she'll find us.'

'If it is her,' Moss cautioned again quietly.

He and Bill departed after a round of handshakes and further thanks to Kate and Sarah, leaving the others to stare at the debris of their supper.

'I think it's her, sir,' Kate reassured.

'We've only got two bodies, a theory and a cold case to go on,' he replied.

Kate tried harder. 'We have stains at the West Pier scene that the police file says were birthing fluids. We know Anne has very good reason for hating these men.'

Jack sighed.

'Sir, there are too many coincidences,' Sarah persisted. 'Moss is being cautious because that's probably how he is in life.'

'And I'm not?' Jack asked, no accusation in his tone.

'I didn't mean it like that, sir. I simply meant that you're prepared to go out on a limb, which may save someone's life because you don't wait for all the answers. You make the bigger leaps.'

Jack wondered which of his critics, or indeed his supporters, Sarah had been listening to. 'And if we're way off track, I could be as good as killing someone right now.' He rubbed his face to rid himself of doubts and then sat up straight, arching his back. 'What time is it anyway?'

His watch told him it was nearing six-forty-five, and his instincts told him he should be worried about that for some reason.

'Right, you've all put in a big day, so thanks, everyone. It will all still be waiting for you in the morning,' he said.

'Tomorrow's Saturday, sir,' Kate reminded.

A phone began ringing.

'Saturday? Blimey, I'm losing it,' Jack admitted and stood, stretching again as Kate reached for the phone. 'Cam, you're working tonight, right?'

Brodie nodded. 'I'll be here.'

'Who's on tomorrow?'

'Me again, and Swamp's in Brighton. Sarah's in, I believe.' Sarah nodded.

'It's your extension lighting up, sir,' Kate called to Jack before answering. She paused, then said, 'Yes, he's here.' She turned to Jack as the rest of the team began packing up for the night. 'It's for you.'

'Who?' he mouthed as he took the phone.

'Someone called Sophie,' she said sweetly. 'She's wondering if you're planning on standing her up tonight.'

'Oh bugger! It's Friday!' Jack said, wincing as he covered the phone. Everyone but Kate laughed.

'Hot date?' Cam asked.

'Shit!' Jack exclaimed again and realised he couldn't move away from Kate's desk. She packed up around him. 'Hello,' he said into the phone, awaiting a barrage of abuse.

'Hi there. It's quite cold out, you know, and if you don't hurry I'm going to take this guy up on his offer to go clubbing.

His name's Andy and he smells and doesn't seem to mind my wheelchair.'

'Sophie, I'm so sorry,' he groaned. 'Where are you?'

'Where we arranged to meet fifteen minutes ago.'

'And where was that again?'

He put a plea in his voice and noted Kate's look of disdain as she reached beneath his arm for her bag. 'Good night, sir,' she said crisply, but all he could do was nod because Sophie was speaking again. *Why did Kate look so angry?*

'I'm outside the Chinese restaurant you booked,' Sophie said. 'I don't mind going to the theatre alone, Jack, but I refuse to sit at a table alone, especially if I don't have a guarantee you're on the way.' Again her voice held only amusement.

He couldn't believe she was being so decent about this. 'I'm coming, I'm coming,' he assured. 'Give me twenty minutes. Please, go inside, order a drink — order one for me too — and some food. I'll be there before the ice melts in your glass, I promise.'

He heard her deep chuckle and liked her all the more for that laidback attitude. Any other woman, in his experience, would have been screeching at him by now.

'You're being fantastic about this, Sophie. I can explain, but thank you.'

'I'm a doctor's daughter; it's in my blood to understand other people coming first,' she said, and he could hear the smile in her voice. 'Hurry up!'

22

The vintage '63 MG pulled up outside an old terraced house in Rottingdean, just three miles from the Brighton city centre. Its driver nimbly jumped out, ran up the front steps and eased his door key into the lock. He smiled as a familiar aroma greeted him.

'Helloooo. It's me!' he called.

Clare Flynn emerged from the kitchen. 'Why didn't you tell us you were coming? I could have cooked for you.'

He grinned again. His mother had lived in England since she was nine, but still had that hint of an Irish lilt to her voice. 'I didn't know I was coming, Mum, until I got off work early. And anyway, you always cook enough for an extra person.' He kissed her, gave her a hug and the flowers he'd brought.

'Oh, thank you, darling. Why do you spend your money on me and not that young woman of yours? I —'

She couldn't miss his wry expression as he cut across her words.

'Where's Dad?'

'In his shed. Where else would he be when I'm serving up dinner?'

He sniffed. 'What's cooking?'

'A lamb stew. We're cleaning up from the weekend when your aunts and uncles were here. You should have been here too, Peter.' She wagged a finger at him. 'You were missed.'

'I know. I told you, I had to do an installation at Burgess Hill. It was important, Mum, they'll have understood. I'll see them all next weekend at Michael's christening anyway.'

She touched his face affectionately. 'When are you going to give me grandchildren, Peter?' He grimaced and she knew when to stop. 'Go wash your hands.'

'Are you doing champ?'

'Of course,' she said over her shoulder.

'Let me just say hello to Dad.'

He walked through the familiar rooms of his childhood home and paused briefly to lift the lid of the pot on the stove and inhale the smell of onions mixed into the buttery mash. His mouth was already watering. He let himself out the back door.

'Dad?'

'Yeah?' came the muffled call. His father stepped out of the shed. 'Peter! Are you staying for dinner, lad?'

'Of course. What are you doing?'

His father bent down to pick up some fishing tackle and Peter noticed how he winced as he straightened. He hated to think of either of his parents as getting old.

'Are you alright?'

His father sighed. 'Oh, I'm just getting some stuff together. I thought I'd go fishing next weekend with Uncle Dougie, want to come?'

'Sure, if I'm not working. You haven't been fishing for years.'

'No, but I've promised myself to start up again. I used to bring fish home for the table twice a week before you came along.'

'You never told me that.'

'Didn't I? Well, I've only just realised how much I miss it. And life's too short not to do the things that please us, son. Your mother can make fish pie for us.'

Father and son grinned and both made lip-smacking noises.

'Is she screaming at me for dinner yet?'

Peter shook his head, feeling a fresh rush of affection for his parents. They talked about each other as though they were combatants sometimes, and yet couldn't bear to be apart. 'She told me to wash my hands. That's usually the prelude to the scream.'

'Pah! She knows I like to watch the news.'

'Well, I'm here now, so you won't get told off if you eat your dinner on your lap like a peasant.'

It was an old family saying and his father laughed as they walked towards the house.

'How's business?' he asked.

'That's why I'm here. I have some good news.'

Garvan paused, stared at his boy. 'The contract?'

'Let me tell you both together.'

'No, tell me now. I want to savour it myself.'

Peter grinned. His father could be quirky at times. Another reason to love him. 'I got the government account.'

He thought for an instant that his father was going to weep but saw him rein back the tears.

'Peter, that makes me very proud, son,' he said, his voice trembling.

He reached for his boy and pulled him close, hugging him hard. Peter's dark brown hair wasn't black like his father's and his skin wasn't as pale, but they had matching bright blue eyes. They were unmistakeably father and son.

'Let's have a drink,' Garvan said. 'We should have a toast.'

Inside, Clare was ladling the stew into a big dish, the champ steaming on a plate, a well of melted butter in its centre. 'Come on,' she said, waving a hand in exasperation. 'This'll go cold. Now don't say you want to watch the news.'

'Just the opening minutes, love, please.'

Clare sighed. 'Okay, okay, I'll bring it into the lounge. Just go and sit down.'

'I'll help,' Peter said, winking at his dad and wiping his newly rinsed hands on the kitchen towel. 'You go, Dad, or you'll miss the headlines.'

His father smiled conspiratorially and disappeared into another room.

'Your father gets a bee in his bonnet at times, I tell you.' Clare began setting up trays so they could eat off their laps. 'He's obsessed with those murders.'

'Which murders?' Peter asked, fetching cutlery and napkins.

She gave him a look of surprise. 'You can't be so busy you don't know about the two murders?' He frowned and she attempted to jog his memory. 'The one in London. Then they discovered it was identical to the killing up north of some poor fellow.'

'Oh, that — the murder in Lincoln, you mean?' Clare nodded as she put their plates onto the trays. 'Why is it so important to Dad, though?'

'Search me. They're saying it's a serial killer.'

'Two murders in two different counties gives us a serial killer?' Peter scoffed, placing glasses on each tray. 'Dad wants wine.'

'Wine? You know what the doctor said.'

'Mum, a glass of wine never hurt anyone and I've brought something special to go with your dinner.'

'You and your fancy stuff. I don't know where you get it from, son. We never had all this when you were growing up.'

'No.' He kissed her cheek. 'But if you didn't want me to enjoy the finer things in life, you shouldn't have given me such a good education or pushed me so hard.'

'Oh, go on with you. You were just clever. Take this to your father. Tell him to go ahead and eat like a peasant,' she said, handing Peter a tray.

He took it, noticing how she'd neatly folded the ordinary paper napkin on his father's tray but not on his, or her own. For all their gentle bickering, he knew how much they loved each other and it made him feel safe.

Peter arrived in the lounge to see his dad glued to the TV. It looked like a police press conference onscreen. 'Here,' he said, putting the tray on his father's lap. 'Don't let it go cold.'

'Shh,' came his father's reply.

Peter sat down to watch as well, giving his mother a smile when she came in with his tray.

'If anyone has any information that can help us with our inquiries, please call our incident room on the number now showing onscreen, or you can call freephone to Crimestoppers where your details will be treated anonymously,' a silver-haired policeman said. 'These are particularly brutal killings and anything at all, no matter how irrelevant it may seem, could further our investigation.'

The report cut to a reconstruction scene and a presenter's voice narrated: 'Clive Farrow was last seen at a fish and chip shop in Hackney in London's north. A witness saw him get into a red BMW Z3 Cabriolet.' A large man with dark floppy hair was shown balancing two packets of fish and chips and lowering himself carefully into the passenger seat of the car. 'The female driver had dark hair, and police believe Farrow left the area with her at around 7.10 p.m., supposedly on the way home to his fiancee with their takeaway dinner. He was not seen alive again.

He was reported missing at 8.32 p.m. that same evening. Police would like to question the driver of the BMW. Anyone who has any information pertaining to the scene, the driver or the car should please come forward.'

'Dad, I've got some bubbly,' Peter said. 'Do you want me to get it?'

'Just a minute,' Garvan said, his tone vexed.

'Dad!' Peter couldn't hide his exasperation. 'What's wrong with you? What's all this interest in murder?'

His father looked suddenly ashamed. 'I think I might have known that man.'

'What, that one? The bloke who got into the car?'

His father nodded and reached for the remote control to flick off the TV.

'Then you've got to ring the police,' Peter said, shocked.

His mother walked in with her tray. 'Police? What are you both talking about?'

'Dad knows the dead guy — the one killed in London.'

His father wore a pained expression. 'I don't know him for sure. I said I think I might have known him. I'm talking thirty years ago. I haven't seen him since. I'm no help, and only the name is familiar, nothing else.'

'Oh,' Peter said, 'then don't worry about it. That sort of information is no help to the police. Look, let me get that bottle — I need a drink. Tell Mum my news,' he said to his father.

'What news?' he heard his mother say as he stepped out into the corridor and reached for his mobile. He quickly tapped out a text message, added an X at the end and smiled. She should receive it moments before the rehearsal began. Peter couldn't imagine a happier moment than now. His good news about the contract meant steady, profitable income for the next five years at least. And Ally's acceptance into the Bournemouth Symphony

Orchestra meant she too was on cloud nine. Everything was coming together. They could buy a house in Southampton, get married, start a family. He just had to tell his parents.

He returned to the lounge brandishing a bottle. 'I lied,' he said, grinning, 'it's proper champagne!'

'Peter,' his mother exclaimed, putting her dinner aside so she could clutch her boy in a firm embrace. He assumed she'd heard the news. 'We're so proud of you, son. You must be excited.'

'I am.' Peter took a silent deep breath. It was now or never. 'There's more news.' They both looked at him expectantly. 'I'm getting married.'

Various eating implements went flying as Peter found himself hugged by two of the three people he loved most in the world. His mother began to babble. 'Patricia is going to —'

'Wait, Mum, please. It's not Pat.'

He had anticipated the expression of shock on his mother's face, but not the cutting silence that followed.

'Her name is Ally . . . er, Allison,' he went on.

His mother looked as if he'd made a joke she hadn't quite understood the punchline to. 'Allison?'

He ran a hand through his hair. 'Sit down, both of you.'

They did so, as robots might on command.

'This isn't easy for me. I hope you know I've never lied to you about anything.' They nodded, still robotic, although he could imagine the tendrils of panic fluttering through his mother's mind. 'Except this,' he added, rushing on with his tale before his mother could react. 'I broke up with Pat eleven weeks ago but didn't know how to tell you. She and I weren't meant to be, Mum,' he implored, watching his mother shake her head in disbelief. 'The night we finished, I went out alone, to a pub. I needed a drink. I knew we were over for good, but we both decided to keep it secret for a while. We needed some distance from each other before we could tell all of you. Anyway, I met a girl.'

'Peter,' his father began softly, but Peter spoke over him. He needed to get it all out.

'Her name is Allison Renn. She's a professional musician. She plays violin and has just been appointed to the Bournemouth Symphony Orchestra. I know that won't mean much to you, but those sorts of jobs come along once in a lifetime. Well, they chased Ally — she's that good, you see.' They didn't see, he could tell by the quiet shock still haunting the room. 'I came out of the pub and her car had broken down. She desperately needed a push but we couldn't get it going and she was running late for rehearsal, so I did something barmy. I drove her to Southampton. And I waited for her and brought her home. I fell in love that night,' he said, hoping that might melt them.

'And Pat?' His mother's voice was edged with bitterness.

'She's glad to be rid of me. I've told her about Ally and although that started another blazing row, she understands.'

'Understands?' his mother echoed incredulously. 'Sheila and I have already begun planning the wedding! What about our grandchildren?'

'Mum, that's all part of the problem. You and Sheila love the idea that your English-born son and her Irish-born daughter are going to marry and give you English-Irish grandchildren and we'll all be an even bigger, happier family eating champ and stew forever.'

'Our families have known each other all of our lives, Peter, since your grandparents came here from Ireland,' his father joined in. 'Do Sheila and Harry know?'

Peter nodded sadly. 'They will by now, I think. Pat was going to ring them just before they left from Dublin to come home this evening.' He shrugged. 'She didn't want to spoil their holiday.'

Clare stood, rolling a napkin around her fingers. 'You don't even know this girl. It's only weeks! Are you mad?'

'Madly in love, yes.'

'Pah!' his mother said, swiping the napkin at him and dissolving into tears. 'We loved Pat.'

Peter felt the burden of guilt settle itself around him like a smothering blanket. He had anticipated how hard it was going to be to tell his mother especially, but he resented the shame she managed to prompt in him, just with her injured expression alone.

'Yes, but I don't, Mum. It doesn't mean you and Dad have to stop loving her. You've known her since she was a little girl; the problem is, so have I. We're friends at best — and distant cousins — but we're not in love. Never have been, if the truth be told. The way I feel about Ally, I've never felt that way towards Pat.'

Clare began to sob and Peter looked to his dad for help, who couldn't help but move to his son's aid.

He put his arm around his wife. 'Come on, my love, now don't upset yourself too hard. We want our boy to be happy, don't we? No good him marrying someone for us — that won't do. Tell us about this girl, Peter,' he said, nodding at his son to say something and make it good.

'She's wonderful. You'll fall in love with her as I did. Look, I have a photo,' Peter said, reaching into his back pocket for his wallet and pulling out a picture of a slim, blonde-haired girl with a shy smile and clutching a violin case. 'I took this in Bournemouth the third time I drove her there.'

His mother sniffed. 'Very pretty, very English.' The words weren't unkind but her tone was.

Peter kept his own rising bitterness in check. 'Mum, if I'd married Pat, it would have been a sham — an arranged marriage — and it would have ended in tears, divorce probably. Is that what you and Dad would want for me? This is real between Ally and me. She's keen to meet you, but not until you feel comfortable. She knows all about Pat too.'

'And what do her parents think about you?'

'I haven't met them.'

'Well, what are they going to think of a girl who says yes to a man who asks for her hand after just weeks of knowing her?' his mother demanded. It sounded like an accusation.

'I don't know, Mum.'

'Why not?'

'Because I haven't asked her yet. I wanted to ask you both first. I wanted your approval before I ask her.'

His father looked suddenly ashamed. 'Do you hear that, Clare?' She nodded, also abashed. 'He's asking our approval. Son, this is your life. We trust your choices in all you do.'

Peter could see how much this was costing them emotionally. Perhaps the discussion about moving nearer to Bournemouth would have to wait.

'I promise you, you'll love her almost as much as I do,' he said.

His mother finally looked at him properly. 'Bring her around soon, Peter. We'll make her feel welcome.'

Relief flooded his veins. He wished he could interrupt Ally's rehearsal right now and propose on the phone. But he would wait — he wanted to see her cool grey eyes light up when he popped the question and offered her the sapphire and diamond ring he'd taken out a loan to buy.

He looked at his dad, conveying silent thanks, and again was struck by his father's surge of emotion. He hugged him, confused by how oddly his dad was behaving. Then he bent to kiss his mother, who silently stroked his back in lieu of the words she obviously couldn't find at this moment. They would have been hollow, for he could feel the disappointment radiating from her. Best they waited to say more.

He changed the subject. 'Dad, before I forget, remind me that I need my birth certificate. I need it to get the security clearance to work on the government account.'

He couldn't miss his father's glance at his mother or the flicker of alarm that passed across both their faces.

'Peter,' his mother said, 'we'll talk about that later. Come and eat your dinner before it gets cold. Champagne after, okay?' She sounded strained.

It wasn't worth arguing. Peter put the expensive bottle of French champagne into the fridge, returned to his seat and the tray of cooling food. His appetite had deserted him.

'So this security clearance can only be done with your birth certificate, is that right?' his father asked.

Peter nodded. 'I'm not allowed to work on the job without it. I need to show them the adoption papers too, before they can sign off on the contract.'

'Then we have a problem,' Garvan Flynn replied.

'Why?'

'Because we have no paperwork for you, son.'

2 3

Jack ran to his office, hoping the dry cleaning that Joan had very kindly picked up the day before, which he'd forgotten to take home, included his dark suit. He was in luck. No option but to wear the same shirt, but he'd take five minutes to shave again, perhaps change the tie — he always kept a more formal one strung around whatever handy hanging spot he could find.

Jack prayed none of the female staff would appear as he changed — to his knowledge it was only Cam holding the fort for the evening, but he still looked around constantly while putting on his clean suit. He ran to the bathroom with a toilet bag he kept on hand for those suddenly called press conferences the Super seemed to enjoy. 'I especially like to interrupt the media's lunchtime drinking,' he'd said to Jack often enough. Finally he was ready, dabbing on some cologne and wincing at the sting.

'Cam, I've got to fly,' he said, re-emerging into the main operations room.

'I hope she's worth it, chief,' Cam answered, not looking around from his screen. 'I'm going to see what I can find out about the McEvoys' family home.'

'Good job, Cam. Call me — er no, text me. I'll be at a show but the phone'll be on silent and I'll call straight back if it's urgent, okay?'

Brodie put a hand in the air to wave his superior off.

'Have one for me.'

Jack rang Sophie again from outside the Yard just as he was climbing into a taxi. He gave the driver the address. 'I'm in a hurry,' he added.

'I think I might have heard that somewhere before,' the cabbie replied good-naturedly, and then proceeded to take roads that Jack hardly knew existed as a good route to Chinatown.

'How's that ice going?' Jack asked as Sophie answered.

'I'm sucking it,' she said and giggled. 'To make sure it's gone before you get here and then you'll owe me big time.'

'I'm paying for dinner. It's a done deal.'

'You have no idea what my terms might be, DCI Hawksworth.'

He grinned. 'Whatever you want, but I have to tell you, this driver is a clever one — I'm almost at your doorstep.'

She made a sound down the phone as though she were sucking a sweet. 'Too late, the ice has gone!' she clicked off.

Jack gave the driver a ten-pound note and got out into the soft drizzle, not waiting for change. 'Thanks,' he called, and scanned the area for a flower shop. He couldn't bear to walk up to Sophie empty-handed, especially after treating her so poorly on a first night out together.

He entered Gerrard Street via the large, gaudily lit, red iron gates that guarded either end of the Chinatown strip and spotted a small florist, still open. *Just for emergencies like this*, he thought. Inside, he was greeted by a young girl still in school uniform.

'I need something really beautiful, really sexy, that says sorry and I think you're fabulous all at once,' he said, and smiled broadly when she burst into giggles. 'Can you help?'

'Yes,' she said, her warm, dark eyes twinkling, 'but I'll get my sister.'

An older, more stunning version of the youngster glided out from a back room. 'Hello,' she said brightly, 'I'm Lily. I've heard you're in trouble.' She smiled. She had the Asian woman's slim, elegant build that Jack found so provocative.

'Deep trouble,' he replied and the younger sister laughed again.

'Then there's nothing for it,' Lily said, 'it has to be the earliest pale pink tulips from Holland. Very, very expensive.' She teased him with another smile.

He pulled an expression of horror. 'Just how expensive?'

'Well, you are saying sorry, after all, and you want the instant forgiveness that only my tulips can provide.' She deliberately said the word as 'two lips'.

Wow! Lily was sexy; Jack could barely tear his gaze from her sparkling dark eyes to look where she pointed in the fridges.

'Alright, alright,' he said, beaten. 'Just make them look impressive.'

'They'll do it all by themselves, I promise,' Lily said, picking out a dozen magnificent stems. 'Get some pale pink and silver ribbon cut up, Alys,' she instructed her young helper as she moved back around the counter to arrange the flowers.

'They are lovely,' Jack admitted, knowing that was an understatement. 'I'll have to hurry you though, I've kept her waiting long enough,' he said, looking at his watch and groaning inwardly.

Lily had the tulips displayed in silver paper and cellophane in a blink and was soon swiping his credit card for forty-five pounds. Jack signed the docket after a look of horror and a groan for Alys's entertainment.

'Thanks, Lily, they're magnificent. Do you have a refund

policy? Can I return them if she's already gone or refuses to forgive me?'

Alys exploded into girlish laughter and her big sister gave him a wry look. 'By all means, I'd love them for my room,' Lily said. 'But we don't do refunds.'

He liked her, would have asked her out for a coffee if Sophie wasn't in his life. 'Wish me luck,' he said and the sisters obliged in a chorus.

Jack hurtled through the restaurant door and ran up the stairs two at a time, the evening's drizzle clinging to his suit like sparkly dandruff. He wiped it off his shoulders as he arrived on the fourth floor.

'I've got a booking for Hawksworth,' he said to the maitre d'. 'My guest is already seated, I understand.'

He was shown to their table. It was four minutes after seven.

'I ordered for both of us,' Sophie said as he arrived with his flowers. 'For me?' She looked genuinely delighted.

'I don't know how else to say sorry.'

'Eat. The curtain goes up in less than half an hour. I hope you like these dishes, tuck in. These tulips are stunning, Jack, thank you.'

He gave a shrug of dejection. 'And what you're going to do with tulips at the theatre, I have no idea. What an idiot I am.'

'I'll check them into the cloakroom,' she said breezily. 'I love them.'

'I'm glad,' he said, swallowing a gulp of the vodka and tonic she'd ordered him. 'Ah, no ice.'

'Told you,' she said and smiled. 'I hope that's your poison and I'm sorry we don't have time to linger over dinner.'

'Gives us an excuse to do it again.'

'Big day?'

'Full on,' he said, unwrapping his chopsticks.

'Do you focus on one case or several at a time — how does it work?' she asked, expertly lifting some vegetables into her bowl. 'This chicken is delicious, and have some of this,' she urged in between mouthfuls, pointing to the various dishes.

He grinned, enjoyed watching her eat. She looked dazzling tonight in a simple black dress with a sheer silver wrap. He had to wonder how she did it all herself. 'Your hair looks terrific like that,' he said.

'Thanks. I only wear it this severe when I'm trying to show off my hideously expensive earrings,' she said. 'Anyway, tell me about your day.'

He sighed and finished the vodka. Shame he didn't have time to order them a lovely crisp Gewürztraminer to go with their spicy Szechuan chicken. 'Sorry, I didn't answer, did I. Um, yes, many of us juggle several cases at once — that's normal. Sometimes, though, a case is big enough to require single-mindedness.'

'And which kind of case was it that kept me waiting?' she said, ladling rice into her mouth.

'I love the way you eat,' he admitted.

'Well, your tummy is going to rumble through *Les Mis*, I can see that,' she said defensively, but without heat.

'I'll manage. Perhaps we can sneak a Mars Bar in for interval?' He appeased her by beginning to eat, knowing he had barely minutes now to finish the food.

Sophie dabbed her mouth with a napkin. 'So go on, which type is yours?'

'Er, the second one,' Jack answered, trying not to spit food at her because his mouth was full and the meat was still hot from the sizzling plate it had been cooking on.

'Okay, so the bad one.' He nodded. 'Do you work in a team?' He nodded again. 'You strike me as a loner, Jack. Do you work well in a team?'

He swallowed, licked the juices from his lips. 'Yes, I believe so. I'm running this one, so I'd better be a team player.'

'Are there women on your team?'

'Three — no, four.'

'All support, I suppose,' she said wryly, draining her sparkling water.

'Not all. There's Detective Inspector Carter and Detective Sergeant Jones — I'm sure neither of them would consider themselves as support.'

'We'd better go,' Sophie said, looking at her watch.

'I'll get the bill.'

'Right, I'll just fix my lipstick — give me one minute,' she said, adroitly turning her wheelchair from the table.

'You look very beautiful,' Jack said.

She stopped and their gazes met and lingered. 'Thanks, Jack. I'm always a little embarrassed by my arms.'

He stared at her with incredulity. 'Why? They look perfectly lovely to me.'

'That's because you can't see them. I expertly hide them with three-quarter sleeves and dark colours, and in winter I get to drape beautiful shawls about myself or wear thick coats — I love winter.'

He heard the amusement in her voice. 'Sophie, you're perfect.'

'Not perfect,' she said, and a hint of sadness crept in as she looked briefly towards her legs, 'but I'll take that compliment and cherish it.'

It was the sudden stillness between them and not wishing to lose it that prompted him to continue in his direct way. 'How did it happen?'

She sighed. 'We'll be late.'

'Tell me . . . please.'

'Multiple sclerosis, diagnosed when I was twenty-two. Most people don't really understand it, so let's keep it simple and say that it can make my body very dysfunctional at times. I'm lucky, though,' she added brightly. 'I can get around relatively easily on walking sticks when I need to, but it wears me out faster — hence the muscled arms to stay stronger for longer. If I've got a big day ahead, I use the chair. And I always use the chair going out because I don't know what I might have to face.'

Jack regretted asking the question now on their first night out together. 'So you can move around freely?' he said.

'Not freely, no.' She grimaced. 'And not very well at the present time because I'm in what's known as relapse. Typically one of my relapses lasts a month or more. This one is taking its time, but for most of today I was on my feet — with my sticks. Just don't ask me to run or exert myself. I'm useless.'

The waiter arrived with Sophie's coat.

'I love the lining,' Jack said, pointing at the violet silk beneath the coat's blood-red exterior, more for something to say, having realised he was stepping into an area neither was ready for.

'Thank you,' she said. 'If you can't match it, clash it, I say.'

'Sophie, I'm sorry, I shouldn't —'

'No, don't be. It had to come up.' She gave him a soft look of sympathy. 'And now it's done with,' she grinned, trying to lighten his sudden glum mood. 'Besides, you should know the dodgy bits up front if we're going to enjoy sex at some stage.'

He looked up from the table, startled.

'I have a very obedient bladder so rarely an accident other than in relapse,' she went on. 'And my bowel is superbly trained and delivers on time, every day, so I don't go anywhere until Mr Bowel has had his say, then I'm safe.'

'Sophie, don't —'

'No, we've arrived at the inevitable point — a bit earlier than

264

I'd imagined — but let's do it. Is there anything else you want to know?'

Jack stared, deeply embarrassed, into her cool, almost unnaturally dark eyes, and strained for a response that could return their sparkly mood of just moments ago. 'Could you just clarify the bit about the sex?'

Sophie laughed, husky and joyous. 'That was the right question, Jack Hawksworth. Come on, pay the bill, take me to the theatre and I'll explain it in detail a bit later.'

Jack pushed Sophie in her chair into her apartment. 'Right,' he said, feeling more self-conscious than he could credit. 'We must do this again soon.'

She swung the chair around to face him and eyed him, slightly bemused, remaining silent.

'What's wrong?' he asked.

'You.'

He shook his head, gave a confused smile.

'Was *Les Mis* that disappointing on the second viewing, or is it that the multiple sclerosis thing was a major turn-off?'

He looked up from her carpet, shocked. 'Whatever makes you say that?'

The amusement never seemed to disappear from Sophie's tone. He envied her such composure. 'I'm surprised you didn't just give my wheelchair a big shove from the lift just now and wave me goodbye as the doors closed.'

Before he could register it Jack was suddenly crouched before her, his hands reaching for hers. 'Oh god, Sophie, I hardly notice the chair and I don't care why you're in it. I know a little about MS and that it affects sufferers in myriad ways.'

'Then you'll know the relapse still has a way to go. Soon the spasms will return and the chair will become a necessity rather than an aid — that's when I don't go out much and I get moody. I'm not much of a catch, to be honest, so flee, Jack, while you still can.' She smiled crookedly.

Jack squeezed her hands now as he leant forward and kissed her. It was a gentle kiss and it was welcomed.

'Sophie, I think you're beautiful,' he murmured thickly when they parted, and felt his desire inflame further when he saw a similar rush of longing reflected in her eyes. 'I've never met anyone like you, and even though every inch of me says you're dangerous, I feel compelled to know more about you.'

'Dangerous?' She frowned. 'Yes, a real thug in this thing.' She looked at him quizzically. 'Dangerous to who?'

'To me,' he said softly, mesmerised by the uncanny darkness of her eyes. 'To my heart.'

He hadn't meant to sound so dramatic but the stillness that suddenly hung between them was intense.

She held the silence a few moments longer, her gaze searching his — for guile, he thought. *And why not? Why should she believe me?*

'Tell me, Jack,' she said finally, 'how is it that someone who looks like you and acts like you isn't already married and mortgaged to the hilt, with a horde of beautiful children clinging to your long legs?'

It was the same question his sister asked regularly, and one he asked himself when he permitted self-indulgence. There would be no diverting Sophie with meaningless platitudes.

'The job,' he said grimly. 'I love it but it scares me. Right now I'm heading up a major investigation to hunt down a serial killer.' He hadn't meant to tell her this, but her question demanded honesty. 'I can't imagine how I could separate that role from life in the suburbs, going to children's school plays and picnicking at the weekend.'

She flinched. 'I had no idea. A serial killer?'

He nodded. 'I'm not permitted to discuss it, although if you've been paying attention to the news then you'll know the case. I know you understand that I can't say more, but we're on this person's trail, I think, we're close enough to smell them. I just have to make sure we protect the next victim.'

'But if you know who the next victim is, then surely —'

'We think we know,' he cautioned, then his voice softened. 'So how, with all that on my mind, do I find the time to love a family?'

She came back with the predictable reply. 'You can't be the first police officer to ask that question.'

'I wouldn't say many of us juggle the stress of our jobs with home life terribly successfully — especially in major crime. They do try but you'd probably be saddened by the number of senior police officers who are divorced or having problems in their relationships as a direct result of their work. I don't want to be one of those.'

'That's up to you then, surely?'

He frowned. 'No. It's not that controllable. The job spills into your life — you can't deal with what I do and not have it get under your skin. I control it to a point, but in instances such as this case, it becomes all-consuming. Look what I did to you tonight.' He shrugged. 'And then there's the danger of those I love being in the firing line, too.'

'Are you saying you're worried that the criminals you put away might take their revenge on your family?'

'I'm actually more worried about those I don't put away. Imagine us a married couple — I'd be constantly fretting that you were going to become a target as a means of getting to me.'

He saw the incredulity flit across her lovely face. 'Jack, you can't live like that. You can't miss out on life. Forget me — as I say, I'm no catch — but you've got to promise me that you won't let this prevent you from enjoying what life and love is all about.'

'You sound like you speak from experience.'

'I do — not that it's any of your business — but yes, I've had someone special in my life. He let me down, but that's by the by. Until then he'd been nothing short of perfect. I've moved on. I've let him go.'

'Now I'm jealous.'

'Don't be. I'm over him — that's why I can sound so grown up about it . . . and why I can kiss you like this.'

She pulled his head close and he loved the feel of her cool fingers running through his hair as he lost himself again in the touch of her lips.

'I'm not ready to ... you know,' Sophie whispered, embarrassed. It was the first time he'd heard her sound in any way tentative.

'This is enough for now,' he replied, and when he kissed her again, neither pulled apart. This time their kiss was deep and lingered long enough for Sophie to wrap her arms around Jack's neck and for him to lift her to the sofa. Jack vaguely registered how much heavier Sophie was than he'd expected; he smiled inside that she wasn't the frail woman he'd imagined in his dreams. He began fussing at her zip, suddenly desperate to see her naked. He'd never intended to do anything more, on this first date, than lose himself in her company, hear that seductive laugh and, just for a few hours, remove himself entirely from fear and death. He had dreamed of kissing her but now it was real. Her soft, urgent mouth made him lose track of time and his hands became reckless explorers. Every inch of her was soft and smooth. She smelled delicious, her skin was cool, her hair silky against his face.

He couldn't remember, but they'd ended on the floor during Jack's grateful release when Sophie had moved her attention from his lips and focused it elsewhere. She had silenced him when he'd made the initial move to give her the same tender treatment, turning coy and pulling a blanket down to cover herself, claiming she was chilled. Jack did not press her. Sophie would choose her time and place in the same way she had decided it was the right moment to offer him such generous affection. He'd be lying if he didn't admit to feeling slightly cheated but the guilt was momentary and he surrendered to the deliciously cosy fug of semiconscious slumber that seemed to arrive once Sophie had quietened his protest and pulled his arms around her.

It was his phone that finally roused them, alerting him to a message. It was Kate. Even her texts sounded twitchy. He kissed Sophie's ear and she smiled contentedly. 'I should go,' he murmured.

'You've crushed my disgustingly expensive designer gown. I'll have to exact payment.'

'Name your price,' he said, nibbling her earlobe.

'Dinner again, more leisurely. Your place, perhaps.'

'No way. I can't compete with this lovely space, this soft carpet, so gentle on our skin with no rash for me to explain at work.'

She laughed again. 'Alright, my place and —'

'I'll bring everything, including the wine, and cook for you.'

'Done,' she said. 'Now go.'

'Tonight?'

'Er, no, not tonight. How about Sunday or Monday?'

'You're going to keep me waiting that long?' He feigned despair.

'I'm really sorry but I have to go out of town for a day and a night at least.'

'Work?'

She shook her head. 'My mother. I haven't seen her in a couple of months and I've promised this weekend. I reckon I can be back by Sunday night though, at a push.' She paused, then added, 'If you make it worth my while.'

'Pan-fried Atlantic salmon, sweet potato wedges and a spinach salad with pine nuts, followed by my exceptionally good chocolate brownies. Or, if you want a proper winter meal, I can do you a hearty lamb stew in minted cider and then the world's best apple crumble.'

'Good grief, I want it all!'

He laughed and pulled on his trousers. 'Let me help you,' he said, feeling even more shamefaced at her disarray, the empty wheelchair not so far away.

'No, don't worry. It'll take a while to get some feeling back in my legs.'

'What?' he exclaimed.

'It's alright, all normal. A tumble with you on the floor is fun but not necessarily good for me. I'll be fine. I'll get myself together over the next few hours. And I'll look forward to seeing you tomorrow evening. Are you sure you can see me so often — I mean workwise?'

He nodded. 'Sophie ... listen, about last night ... I'm sorry if I seemed distant.'

She grinned, groaning slightly as she sat up and leaned against the sofa, careful to pull the soft blanket around her bare shoulders. She shivered theatrically. 'Sorry, I can't afford to get too cold or stiff. Don't apologise, last night was lovely and it was all my choice in case you hadn't registered that. I just wasn't sure, you know ... didn't want to push you somewhere you didn't want to go.'

'No, you misunderstand. That's why I need to apologise. My mind *was* elsewhere in the taxi home. I was thinking about the case and something clicked into place … well, might have anyway. I know you were feeling uncomfortable when I brought you home and seemed so reluctant. It was the case dragging at my thoughts.'

'The thing that clicked into place,' she said, 'will it help you go forward?'

'I'm not sure. It's such a vague element. You don't have any insight into the significance of the colour blue, do you?'

She frowned. 'Blue? Well, as a property developer I do know that a lot of people love the colour, but we deliberately never paint any rooms blue because many people are superstitious about it.'

'Really? I mean, I know people used to be superstitious, but still?'

'Absolutely. I've always had a love for history and so I know where it stems from, but for most people it's probably something from childhood that their granny mentioned and it's stuck. Blue is a colour that's associated with magic and it's considered unlucky by anyone on stage, for instance.'

'Yes, that's right,' he said eagerly. 'We've been discovering this. Clowns too, apparently.'

'Clowns especially,' Sophie said, dipping her chin in a nod of congratulation. 'I'm impressed that your team is so knowledgeable about history. I'm sure I'm right in saying that the traditional clown would never use blue in his make-up.'

'You're right. And that's what triggered my "moment" in the cab.'

'You'll have to fill in the blanks, Jack,' Sophie said, arching her eyebrows to show him she was lost in this conversation.

'What? Oh, sorry, well, it just got me thinking that the whole frontage of the florist where I bought your bouquet was painted blue. They're a Chinese family — I was wondering whether they might be able to throw any insight into the use of that colour. Perhaps it has special meaning for Asians.' She pulled a face to suggest he was reaching. 'I know, but blue paint is significant or why else would something so odd be involved in a murder scene?'

'Murder scene? Where was the paint?'

'Pardon?'

'Well, if it's in its tin, it loses relevance in a way. Where exactly was this blue paint?' she said, her words disappearing into a wide yawn.

'Don't give it another moment's thought.' Jack smiled, mindful of protecting facts that the public was not yet privy to. 'I'll get going. Is seven okay for Sunday?'

'Already looking forward to it.'

24

As Jack rushed out of his apartment on Saturday morning and took the hill down to the tube station at a steady jog, he had no idea that he was passing Kate in a coffee shop in Highgate Village.

Anne, meanwhile, was checking her reflection in her bedroom mirror. A small overnight suitcase was open on the bed and two rolls of tissue paper that contained wigs were at its side, yet to be packed. She had banished all other thoughts from her mind; today and this evening were all about Billy. She knew the police were closing in on him — they had to be — and Phil would be next. However, with Billy changing his name to Edward, the confusion generated might just buy her the few hours she needed.

She'd already booked ahead at St Catherine's Lodge in Hove under an alias, but had made no restaurant reservation. Billy would never make it to dinner, she thought, a fresh coldness washing over her as she began to mentally prepare for the next killing.

The jeans and hooded sweatshirt looked perfect; her hair pulled back in a clasp with wisps breaking free to fall carelessly around her face. No make-up and that good skin of hers ensured her freshly scrubbed appearance belied her age. This morning she was a caterer and needed to pick up her van from Mrs Shannon's garage. Anne didn't have to send her as much money as she did but the regular cash kept the old girl's lips tightly zipped. She was probably happily counting her latest windfall right now.

Jack's phone vibrated next to his chest as he ordered a cream cheese and smoked salmon panini at Giorgio's, to go with the long black to wake him up.

'Thanks, Lucia,' he said to the Italian waitress.

She winked as she began preparing his takeaway breakfast. Lucia liked men in uniform, and had once quipped to a co-worker that even though Jack was a plainclothes officer she'd take him in a frilly tutu, if that was what he chose to wear.

He flashed her a smile as he answered the phone. 'Hawksworth.'

'Did you have breakfast?'

He felt a spike of warmth move through him. 'You didn't offer.'

'You were in a hurry.'

'I'll always make time for a quickie.'

'Are we talking about food, Jack?' Sophie purred.

'I'm very hungry,' he added and heard her laugh softly down the phone. 'Thank you again.'

'It was a pleasure. So where are you? It sounds too noisy for work.'

'Ordering breakfast.'

'I hope she offers only food.'

'I'll tell the gorgeous Lucia you said that,' he threatened and watched the waitress blow him a kiss across the counter.

He dug into his pocket and handed over a ten-pound note. 'They do the best paninis in London here and with any filling you want,' he said loud enough for Lucia to hear as she wrapped up his sandwich and placed a lid on the coffee.

'Goodie, try them on baked beans and Mars Bar.'

'Very amusing. So what time are you leaving?'

Sophie paused. 'Pardon?'

'Your mother. What time are you headed off?'

'Oh! Sorry, my head's all over the place today, I forgot I'd told you. See what a bit of long overdue sex does to a girl?' Jack chuckled deeply. 'There's a Virgin train from Paddington at five past ten, I've got a reservation on that one. First class — I need the sleep. How about you? Will you keep awake on the case?'

'Not sure I want to even go to work,' he sighed.

'Things aren't stalling though, are they?'

'No, not really. In fact, we hooked up with an old policeman who's helping us with a crime that goes back several decades, can you believe. We think it has a bearing on these murders.' He heard only silence. 'Sophie?'

'I'm here, sorry, trying to do two things at once. So a cold case — is that what you call it?'

'Yes. One of our diligent diggers at the Yard dug far enough back to turn up something.'

'Well done. Sounds like you're on his trail then.'

'Or hers.'

'No! A woman?'

'Who knows? Anyway, look, I'm not supposed to discuss anything.'

'Who am I going to tell, Jack?'

'I know, I know, but protocol and all that. To answer your question, I don't want to go to work because I'd rather spend the day with you.'

She gurgled a laugh. 'I know. I promise I won't stay away too long. But I can't let Mum down.'

'Give me the landline number.'

'Oh, just use my mobile. It might as well be an appendage anyway.'

'Well, give me an address. I might suddenly want to send you flowers.'

'You gave me flowers yesterday. Don't waste your money, Jack. I'll only be away from London for a day, really.'

'Sophie, don't ruin my fun, please.'

'It's your money. It's called The Haven — I know, I know, and it even looks like a chocolate box. School Lane, South Molton and then just Devon will do. But, Jack, I'd rather we went to a show again than more flowers, truly.'

'You get there safely and be nice to your mum. Can I call you?'

'Sure. But I'll call you straight back if you hit my voicemail. Mum can be a bit all consuming.'

'Alright, looking forward to Sunday night, if you make it back. Speak later.'

He waited to hear the line go dead, then picked up his panini and coffee, waved farewell to Lucia and turned straight into the barrel chest of a police officer he recognised.

'Don't spill your coffee, Jack.'

'DI Deegan,' he replied, his good mood instantly souring.

'DCI Deegan, you mean.'

'Congratulations.' Jack made to leave. 'Excuse me.'

'Er, before you go, Jack.'

'DCI Hawksworth, you mean.'

Deegan gave him a smirk. 'I'd like a word.'

'Make an appointment.'

'I thought I'd keep it low key.'

'Why, Roy? Is this work or personal?'

'Bit of both, Jack.' He shrugged embarrassment, which they both knew was feigned.

'I'm not sure if you know but I'm heading up Operation Danube. We're pretty flat chat at the moment — breakfasts on the run, that sort of thing.' Jack held up his coffee and made the effort to keep any trace of sarcasm out of his voice.

Deegan nodded. 'Oh yes, I know exactly what you're working on. In fact, I know everything you do, Jack.'

Hawksworth frowned. 'What do you want?'

'I want you squirming, constantly wary, and my gut instinct tells me that's the feeling you're going to get used to in coming weeks.'

'What are you talking about?'

'We're talking about your conduct, but look, don't worry. You're too busy, as you say. I tried to keep this a quiet chat but if you want me to come up and visit you on the twelfth floor and speak to you in front of your colleagues, by all means. I'd like to see that view.'

Jack lost all patience. 'Deegan, what are you up to?'

'My job, Jack.'

'Which is?' He knew but he was buying time.

'Oh, haven't you caught up, yet? I've been with the Ghost Squad for a couple of years.'

'Ghost Squad,' Jack said sardonically.

'Mmmm, that's right. And you know what we guys and gals like to do over at DPS.'

'Yes, I know, but I don't see what the Directorate of Professional Standards has to do with me.'

'Oh, it has everything to do with you, DCI Hawksworth, because I'm going to recommend that you be put under investigation.'

Jack moved from disdain to outrage. 'What?' he roared.

People began to look around.

'I thought it only fair you should know.'

'I wish I knew what the hell you're banging on about, Deegan. Now either make sense or fuck off out of my face. I've got work to do.'

Deegan grinned. It was sly and didn't reflect in his hard, calculating eyes. 'So have I, Jack. I'm sure we'll be talking again shortly but let me leave you with this thought. Liz Drummond might have left the Force ten years ago but she didn't leave it empty-handed.'

Jack stared at him open-mouthed.

'Later, Hawk,' Deegan said, loading the nickname with derision, then he was gone.

Kate fidgeted with the froth on her morning cappuccino. She wondered yet again what she was doing here in Highgate Village. She should be at the Yard, taking her theory up with her boss in the appropriate manner, not stalking him in his own suburb. *But then this has nothing to do with work, does it, Kate?* she thought, defiantly ripping the top off a sugar packet and tipping the contents into the cup. She stirred angrily.

She'd slept little, wrestling all night with her thoughts. Dan had come home briefly, planning to head out again after a quick change of clothes to meet up with some friends. She'd given him stick about the mess that morning and the fact that he hadn't taken her out to dinner or a show, to a movie or even a local cafe in so long she couldn't remember the last time. She'd asked for trouble taking that tack. It didn't help her irate mood, of course, that Dan could remember all their recent movie outings. His terrific memory had made her even angrier and she'd asked him if he could see a pattern emerging. When he'd stared at her silently, puzzled, she'd hurled back: 'Fantasies, Dan! No sense of reality . . . just like your life and this sham of a relationship.'

That was it, he'd stormed out. Her fury at him turning his back on her when she felt she most needed him to love her had prompted Kate to walk out of their home herself, and stay away. Her acid thoughts in the lonely hotel room had inevitably turned to Jack and the Marvin Gaye fan, and the only saving grace for the ugly evening was a fresh theory about the case that had come to her while softly weeping about her love life being such a mess and her chance at having a family seemingly non-existent.

Hours later, showered and hoping the make-up covered her puffy eyes, she armed herself with this new notion about the killer's motives and convinced herself she wanted to run it by DCI Hawksworth but didn't feel like airing it for everyone's scorn. Hence the trip over to Highgate. Even she could hear the lie echoing through her thoughts.

'Penny for them,' a voice said. Kate looked up. It was the older waitress, who'd served her. 'Something wrong with my coffee?'

'Lost in my thoughts, sorry.'

'You look miserable and it's only just past seven in the morning. You must have got up before the birds, my girl. Want a triple chocolate dream biscuit? We made them last night — guaranteed to perk you up and unbelievably good.'

'Not good for my hips though,' Kate replied sternly, for her own benefit more than the woman's. She sipped her coffee, relished the hit of sugar. 'This is good, thank you.'

'Got stuff on your mind, eh? Well, cheer up, girl. Being miserable won't solve it.'

Kate gave a half-hearted grin. The woman — probably the owner, she realised — obviously wasn't going to let her stew quietly. 'My boss lives here somewhere — I think his place is just around the corner. I should see him at work but I'd hoped to have a private chat, and yet it feels a bit un-PC, you know, to come to his home. What would you do?'

She swallowed the rest of the coffee — it wasn't hot any more but it was decent enough not to waste, and at four pounds she couldn't afford to. *Bloody Highgate prices!*

'Depends how honest you are.'

Kate looked up, puzzled. 'What do you mean?'

'Well, *are* you stalking him? If you can't honestly say you're not, then it's not right you visit where he lives. If you genuinely need to talk to him quietly and your conscience is clear, where's the problem?'

Bull's-eye. Definitely not the dumb waitress.

'Yeah, you're right,' Kate said, standing up, deciding to head straight into the office. Her conscience certainly was not clear. Not with the way she was feeling at the moment about Dan, about Jack's new romance, about her own life.

'What do you do?' the woman said, gathering up the detritus of coffee things on Kate's table.

'I'm with the police.'

'Oh, right,' she said, clearly surprised. 'You look like you're in fashion or something. Hang on, your boss isn't that lanky, drop-dead gorgeous guy, is it?'

Shit! 'Um, no, doesn't sound like him. He's bald … and paunchy.'

'Oh, okay, 'cos there's this dark, good-looking sort who comes in here some weekends. I saw him once being dropped off in a police wagon, and not so long ago he dropped his wallet in here and I saw the ID. I'm sure it said Detective something or other.'

Double shit! 'I don't think it's my boss — wish it was,' Kate said with a contrived air of wistfulness. 'Thanks.'

She left hurriedly, her cheeks burning. In her disquiet, she turned in the wrong direction for where her car was parked.

Rather than look like the goose she was certainly being, Kate kept walking, following the road around, hoping she could keep turning left and find her way back to her car. Except there were no left turnings and she had to keep walking, finally finding herself at an entrance to Waterlow Park. It was beautiful in the watery winter sunlight and she envied Jack his sumptuous surrounds. Some good came of your parents' death then, she thought uncharitably. No matter how well paid he was, no DCI could live here solely on his earnings. She'd heard rumours that Jack was very well heeled as a result of the accident. The roadster he sometimes reluctantly brought into work was testimony to that, together with his address.

She sat down on a bench to gather her thoughts but jumped when her phone rang. She wildly hoped it was Jack but could see who it was on the screen of the mobile. She pressed the button but didn't say anything.

'Kate?'

'Yes?' she said finally.

'Where are you?'

'That's my business.'

'It's not right that you don't come home.'

'It's not right that you treat me as you do.'

'How, Kate? How am I treating you?'

She sighed. Sick of herself and her gripes and her sudden overwhelming sense of bitterness. 'Dan, I don't want to do this. Last night was enough, okay?'

'Look, we've been building to this for ages. We've both felt it, so don't tell yourself otherwise. Let's get it out, whatever's bothering us.'

She didn't want to. Didn't want to remember how close to the truth Dan had been. 'You do recall your accusation from last night?' she said, the memory of his words hurting her again.

'Am I wrong, Kate? Aren't you infatuated with your boss?'

'That's so ridiculous!'

'You talk about him so much.'

'And you talk about Darth Malek from your stupid "Star Wars" game — at least Jack's real. And anyway, you never stop talking about that woman, Gail, at your office. I don't accuse you of being in love with her.'

'Gail's forty-seven, Kate,' he said and she heard the sarcasm. 'And besides, I didn't say in love, I said infatuated — there's a difference.'

'Oh yeah?' Kate sneered.

'If it's just an infatuation, then I can win you back, Kate. If it's more, I can't compete with poster boy.'

'Don't call him that.'

'Why? Does it upset you?'

'Because he doesn't deserve it, Dan. He's innocent and he's a good boss. Jack's seeing someone and this is just a fabrication in your mind. You need to blame anyone but yourself for the fact that our relationship is breaking down.'

There, she'd said it. She realised she was breathing hard, the pain in her chest from tears held back was threatening to explode and then the dam would burst and release a torrent. She had to regain control.

His voice came out broken. 'So our relationship is breaking down — it's over — is that what you're saying?'

She sniffed. 'It doesn't need me to say it, Dan. It's what we both know. People in love don't behave like we do.'

'Oh, and how do they behave?' He was getting angry now.

'They don't just share the same bed, Dan. They talk, they go out, they make love, they want to be with each other every minute of the day. They think about no one else.'

Silence greeted her outpouring and she felt the tears sting in her eyes at the treachery in her own words. Admit it or not, Jack

Hawksworth was the catalyst for this. She and Dan were breaking up, she could feel it happening in this phone call, and the worst part was, she just wanted to get it over with.

'The thing is, Dan, I'm not blaming you — we're both in this together. Maybe it's our work, but things don't feel right.'

'Kate, don't do this. We're supposed to be getting married, for god's sake,' he beseeched, all anger gone. 'Our parents ...' He stopped, his voice already ragged.

'I'm sorry, Dan. We can't commit to marriage just because our families love us together.'

'So we change. We'll move as we planned. I'm earning enough now — you can have your more swanky London address. You'll need to change your job though, Kate. I don't mean leaving the Force but you can't work with that Hawksworth guy. I don't trust him.'

'Well, just for the record, I do. And, you see, I don't believe we are good together any more and I don't want the life that you're shaping for me.'

'And he can give you the life you want, I suppose.'

'Dan! Shut up about my boss. He's got nothing to do with this. This is about us and how wrong we are.'

'I don't believe you. Where are you?'

'Why?'

'I can hear birds.'

'I'm in a park ... somewhere to think.'

'Which park?'

'I don't know.'

As if by divine intervention, a voice suddenly asked, 'Excuse me, is this Waterlow Park?' Two older people looked down at her, their worried faces telling her they had probably been lost for a while.

She felt sick. 'Yes, it is.'

'Do you know where Cumberland Street is?'

'I'm sorry but I don't. I don't live here.' They looked so anxious, Kate felt obliged to help. 'Just give me a moment, please.' She spoke into her phone again. 'Dan? I've got to go.'

'Waterlow Park. That's Highgate. Where he lives, right?'

'You're getting this so wrong.'

'We'll see.'

'What's that supposed to mean?'

'Are you coming home tonight?'

'I've got to go.' She smiled, embarrassed, at the waiting couple.

'Yes or no?'

'Yes. See you later.' Kate snapped the phone shut. 'Now, let's see if we can't find Cumberland Street for you,' she said to her audience, adding a brightness to her voice she simply didn't feel.

Dan's world was collapsing in Stoke Newington. Kate had been acting oddly of late. Nothing he could put his finger on — she had just seemed preoccupied in recent days. Very moody, very distant. She didn't want affection from him, and all she had for him in return was grumbles. Suddenly nothing he did was right. And yet he was doing nothing differently. The difference was Kate and her involvement in this case — this Operation Danube that she was working on with Mr Fabulous. He'd started calling Hawksworth that after seeing him on one of the news bulletins. He dressed sharply for a cop — that ridiculous pale-striped shirt. Dan would get laughed at if he turned up in that garb. But he could tell Kate loved it. She'd told him to be quiet in no uncertain terms that night. That was when it had sounded like she cared about her boss. Now he was sure she cared in a completely different way. He'd inadvertently hit an artery with his barbed comments that were simply meant to poke a bit of fun. Now their relationship was haemorrhaging. She was secretive, remote, suddenly dressing very sexily for work, wearing perfume — even though she knew it made him sneeze. He rang Gail.

'You could be imagining this all, Dan,' she said when he'd finished pouring out his sorrows. 'You've got no proof, have you?'

'No, but I live with her, Gail. My gut tells me she's nuts about this guy.'

'Well, what do you want to do?'

'I don't want to lose Kate. We're supposed to be marrying any minute — instead, tonight I imagine she's going to talk about who keeps the CD collection! I don't know what to do.'

'She knows you love her?'

'Of course.'

'How? We girls like to be told.'

'She's a detective, she's not soppy like that.'

Gail laughed down the phone. 'Makes no difference, Danny boy. Tough or not, every woman wants to know her man's crazy for her.'

'What am I going to do?' he moaned.

'Go see him,' she said.

'What?'

'Go have a chat with him and suss him out. Man to man. You'll know the moment you clap eyes on him. If he's brave enough to see you, that is. If not, there's a good chance there's something going on.'

'I might take a couple of days off to sort this mess out.'

'Come in next Wednesday — that's two official days off. You've got so much leave due you anyway.'

'Thanks, Gail. Have a good weekend.'

'Any time, honey.'

Dan went looking for anything on Kate's desk at home that would give him information. He found her diary. She didn't keep a daily record of anything as far as he could tell, other than the usual dental appointments and so on. He knew she had two diaries — this one and the slimline one she tossed in her choice of bag for the day. The bags changed frequently, depending on the day's outfit. Her current obsession was some tiny silver designer thing that had cost a small fortune. The bloke in the boutique had carried it to the till as though he was holding something so fragile and priceless it may soil if a customer looked too long at it. Kate had said she wanted it more than anything and at that price he had chosen to make it a wedding gift. Not that it sounded as though there was going to be a wedding any longer.

His mind was wandering. The slimline diary was definitely with her and that was the one more likely to hold personal appointments. He banged his fist on her desk in frustration, dislodging some paperwork that in turn revealed her address book. Kate was methodical, entering every important address into this 'bible' as she called it. He snatched at it, ran his finger down the letters and found the H section. There, in big letters, was an entry for Jack Hawksworth — his home address and phone number, circled several times. Dan scribbled it down on a post-it note, grabbed his wallet, car keys and coat, and was out of the door in less than a minute.

25

Jack was so rattled by Deegan's couched accusation and the announcement that he was being investigated by the Ghost Squad that he decided not to go up to the ops room after all. It wasn't as though they couldn't reach him easily enough. Instead, he called Brodie and learned that Billy Fletcher was still to be found. He told his DI to contact him immediately anything broke and said he was nearby; used the excuse that he was running some urgent domestic errands.

He wasn't sure what to do as he sat outside Giorgio's and chewed on the panini that suddenly tasted as appealing as cardboard. The coffee helped. Jack thought about just going home but that didn't feel right. He absently made a decision to head for Westminster Cathedral, barely a couple of minutes' walk away, where he could reflect in peace on what Deegan could possibly have meant about Liz Drummond, and work out what to say to Superintendent Sharpe about this sinister development.

He walked towards the cathedral but ultimately found himself staring at the bookshelves in Waterstone's. Feeling very much on automatic pilot, he was pulled towards the fantasy fiction shelves — perhaps he could just sit in the park with a book. He picked out

Assassin's Apprentice, weighted it in his hand as a new idea clicked into place. He gathered his wits again and checked his watch. It was the diversion he needed. He could think just as easily on the underground.

Jack paid for the book and then was moving, dodging the shoppers on his long legs that carried him swiftly to Victoria Station and down into its belly towards the District or Circle Line, whichever would get him fastest to Paddington. His luck was running: a Circle train had just disgorged its bounty and was swallowing up its latest horde. He stood by the doors watching as the seven stops rolled by. Notting Hill and Bayswater arrived and passed and then he was off and running, entering Paddington Station at full trot. Jack scanned the flicking boards for trains to Devon and felt his heart surge when he found Sophie's train was running late, hadn't even pulled into the platform yet. He was going to make it, be able to see her again, give her a kiss and a favourite book for her to enjoy on her train ride southwest. And for just a short while he would rediscover his bright mood and forget Deegan's threats.

He began scanning all the impatient faces lining the platform. There was no sign of a wheelchair. Jack flashed his badge at the platform entrance — not that the dull-eyed attendant could give a damn — and, as the train finally pulled in, strode up the platform looking for Sophie, who would hopefully throw her arms around him and make him feel warm and loved again.

She was nowhere.

He returned to the gate, now swarming with Saturday shoppers. He waited until all the passengers had boarded, until the whistle blew and the train reluctantly heaved itself away from the terminus and back out into daylight. Definitely no Sophie. He dug in his pocket for his mobile and let her number ring, pleased to hear her voice again — even though it had been barely hours.

'Jack! I was just thinking about you,' she said and his smile widened.

'Seems I can't leave you alone.'

'I'm glad to hear it. Everything okay?'

'Yes. I just wanted to give you something small to take away but I missed you.'

He could imagine her frowning. 'Missed me? Where?'

'At the station.'

'What station?' There was a hint of alarm in her voice, he thought.

'Paddington. I wanted to catch you on the platform, surprise you.'

'You came to Paddington to see me?' she asked, incredulity replacing alarm.

'It's official — I'm a stalker.'

'Well,' she said, pausing, 'I don't know what to say. I'm, um, flattered. What did you want to give me?'

'A book for your journey. It's a favourite of mine.'

'Oh, how thoughtful. And your favourite ... damn!'

'Yes, I'll just have to give it to my other lover now.'

She laughed, all the breeziness back in her tone as she said, 'Don't you dare! I think favourite books reveal plenty about the reader. I want to read it and shall claim it as rightfully mine on Sunday.'

'If you make it back in time,' he cautioned.

'I promise to.'

'So did you catch the train in the end? It was running late, I don't know how I missed you.'

'Well, I feel horribly guilty now, Jack, but I took an earlier train. I'm halfway to Exeter already.'

Jack made a sound of indignation. 'And to think I ran all the way to the Victoria tube.'

'Sorry,' she said, amusement in her voice. 'I'll make it up to you.'

'Promise?'

'With knobs on.'

'Okay, better let you go. Enjoy the trip.'

'I'll call you, and thanks for the nice thought. What's the book called, by the way?'

He told her.

'I'll look forward to it.'

He heard the dial tone and was about to turn away when the station attendant gestured at his warrant badge and said, 'Handy, those. Free travel, entry anywhere, man.' He clicked his tongue, impressed.

Jack winked an acknowledgement. 'What time did the earlier train to Exeter leave?' he asked, more for something to say than really needing to know.

'Isn't one.'

He frowned. 'Oh? A friend I'd hoped to catch before she left just told me she took the earlier Virgin train. Perhaps half an hour earlier?'

'There's only a Great Western train before the one you've just seen pull out and that's at seven-thirty, man.'

'No, that's too early and she definitely said Virgin.'

The man shook his head, began rattling a rhythm with his fingers on the knuckles of his other hand, his gaze drifting. 'First Virgin train of the day just left, man, next one after twelve. Nothin' in between.'

Jack nodded. 'Okay, thanks.' He walked away, puzzled. His phone distracted him with its low tone and he recognised the number. 'Hello, chief.'

'Jack. How's things?'

'Alright, thank you, sir. There's no news as yet — beyond

what you already know about the cold case — but I'm hoping to hear more over the day. I'll call the moment I have something.'

'Excellent. Well, I'm at home — promised Cathie I'd do some gardening with her.' Sharpe gave a snort of disgust. 'Call me any time you know more. In fact, why don't you come over, share a glass with us?'

'Sounds nice, thank you.'

'Cathie's yelling that you should come over for a meal.'

'That's okay, sir, the drink sounds good. Can I call you?'

'Sure. What's up?'

Jack hadn't realised he sounded as though anything might be up but perhaps the old man knew him better than he thought. And Sharpe was his best ally. He came clean. 'Had you heard that Deegan had moved over to the Ghost Squad?'

Sharpe sighed. 'Yes, he's not the right fit for the Ghost Squad. I wish someone had thought to ask me.'

'He's made DCI.'

'He's ten years older than you, Jack, you can't mind.'

'I mind only that he staked me out at Giorgio's. Ruined my breakfast.'

'The Ghost Squad staked you out? What's going on?'

'He's gunning for me, sir — well, according to Deegan, he's hoping to put me under formal investigation.'

Silence greeted this.

'Sir?'

'What for?'

'He didn't say. Actually, that's not true — he said something appropriately cryptic that was meaningless to me. But he was clear that he's planning to make my life difficult.'

'Your nose is clean isn't it, Jack?'

'Squeaky.'

'Then Deegan can go to hell. Leave it with me.'

'Er, sir, let's just leave it alone for a while. See where it goes.'

'I'm happy to call —'

'I know. But I think we should let Deegan make the move. If he thinks he's got me spooked and running to you, it doesn't look good.' He hoped his Super wouldn't press it. 'Everyone knows Dad and you go back a long way. You've looked out for me long enough, sir. Let's see what happens.'

'I understand. Let me know when we can see you over the weekend. We'll talk then. In the meantime, watch your back.'

'I will, sir.'

Jack clicked off the phone, found himself close to the ticketing office. There was only one person in the queue. While he dithered, wondering just how paranoid he was being, the person was served and vacated the window.

'Yes, please?' the attendant said, eyeing Jack balefully.

He couldn't back off now. 'Um, can you tell me which trains run from Paddington to Devonport, please?'

'Which days?'

'Today. Saturday.'

Jack watched the man's fingers rattle on the keyboard.

'Saturday ... Saturday. Ah, here we are.' He gave Jack the identical times the platform attendant had.

'So, nothing between seven-thirty and ten-oh-five on any line?'

'No, not even from Waterloo.'

Jack shook his head. Sophie had no reason to lie to him, especially after their evening together. 'Tell me, are you hooked up there to reservations?'

'This *is* the ticket office, sir,' the man said, his tone droll.

'I mean, can you check on a reservation?'

'Only if it's yours, sir,' he replied.

Jack took out his warrant card, spun it beneath the glass divider.

The ticketing officer gave him an ironic smile. 'I'll get my manager.' He put up a use–other-window sign at his counter and indicated the side entrance with his chin. 'Come inside.'

Jack waited while his credentials were shown to a large woman with what looked like a million tiny beaded plaits flowing off her scalp.

'Scotland Yard?' she said, coming towards him and beaming with lips glossed blood-red. 'This *is* exciting. How can we help?'

'Can you look up a reservation for me, please?'

'Someone been naughty?' she said, her eyes twinkling. 'I'll handle this, Les, thanks.' She sat down at the man's terminal, her long immaculately-painted nails poised over the grubby keyboard. 'What name?'

'Fenton.' He spelled it out. 'First name Sophie, with a "ph". She was travelling from here to Devon today.'

She keyed in the name, shook her head. 'No Sophie Fenton booked on any services today out of anywhere, but she could have purchased a ticket for a non-reserved seat, paid cash and we'd be none the wiser.'

'Yes, of course. I'm just taking precautions.'

'Hey, you look familiar.'

Jack squirmed, forced a grin. 'I don't think so.'

'Wishful thinking maybe,' she replied and gave him a lascivious look.

'Right,' Jack said, suddenly uncomfortable. 'Thanks ... er, Mabel,' he glanced at the badge on her breast and looked away hurriedly. 'I appreciate your help.'

'Ask for it any time, but make sure you ask for me only,' and she gave a snort of laughter to his retreating back.

Standing across the road from Coleridge House at Highgate, Dan glared at the facade of the mansion apartments. He contemplated ringing Kate again, gripped by a bitter sense of triumph now he was here. His imagination spun out of control as he contemplated that a call may find her rolling around on her boss's sheets up there. He flicked his phone shut, crossed the street and entered the apartment building. It smelled of potpourri and money. He grimaced, realising only now that using the lift would require a security card.

He stood there, staring at the floor numbers with impotent fury, when the lift chugged to life on the fourth floor. A few moments later the doors opened and a woman stepped out. She glanced at him only briefly and walked past.

'Er, excuse me,' Dan said. 'Sorry to disturb you but I need to reach Jack Hawksworth, except I can't get up in the lift.'

'You need one of these,' the woman said, holding up a keycard, a strong foreign accent colouring her speech.

'Yes, I realise that now. It's an emergency actually. I have to deliver something — er, he asked me to push it under the door.'

'You work with Mr Hawksworth?' She pronounced her 'W's with a hard 'V' sound. German, no doubt.

'DCI Hawksworth, yes, er, at Scotland Yard,' Dan said.

'Why not go there?'

'I'm supposed to leave what he needs somewhere private.' Dan had no idea what to say if she suddenly demanded to see this thing he kept referring to. 'We're working on a secret case.' If this was any other situation, Dan would have laughed at the ridiculously childish lie. But the German woman's expression didn't flinch.

'Ja, I understand. I heard he works on this important case.'

'May I borrow your card to —'

She held up a hand, began moving towards the door. 'No, no. My card, it is not lent to anyone. Anyway, I don't think he's at home. You should make another arrangement. Ring him on his mobile phone.'

'How do you know he's not at home?'

'Because I assume you've already tried ringing upstairs,' she said flatly. 'Excuse me, I must go.'

Dismayed at how easily his plan had been thwarted, Dan watched the German woman hurry out. She used the fire exit, which was odd, he thought, but then so was she. His phone rang. 'Dan Rogers,' he answered distractedly.

'Dan, hi, it's Jack Hawksworth here. I'm Kate's DCI at the Yard.'

He was stunned. 'Yeah, I know you are.'

'Oh, right. Look, she tried to reach me but I was a bit tied up and now I'm having no luck getting back to her.'

Dan snorted. They really did take him for an idiot. 'Yeah, I'll bet you're tied up. Just roll over and talk to her, mate!'

'Pardon?'

'You heard.'

'Dan?'

'Don't call me Dan as though you know me, as if we're friends.'

'Er, look, I'm not sure what's going on here, or what you think is going on, but I'm Kate's boss and I'm simply trying to return her call.'

'Pull the other one. I'm going to have you reported, Hawksworth.'

'Now, just a minute!'

'No, this is bullshit! Why was Kate in Highgate this morning if she wasn't with you, you sod?'

'Highgate? I don't know what you're talking about. I have no idea where she is, which might explain why I'm calling you.'

Dan ignored him. 'She didn't come home last night. She rang me this morning from Highgate. I'm standing outside your place right now. If I could, I'd get up into your rich boy apartment and beat the shit out of you before I trash the place.'

He instantly regretted that comment. He was incapable of beating up anyone, and he certainly wouldn't be testing his unknown fighting quantity on a senior policeman. He waited through the terrible pause, berating himself for how stupid he sounded and how ridiculously this situation was spinning out of control. Why did Hawksworth have to ring him at this time of all times?

He wasn't prepared for compassion.

'Dan, I'm really sorry, but whatever's happening between you and Kate is nothing to do with me. Listen, come over to the Yard — can you do that?'

'Why? Going to set your people on me?' Dan said sulkily, wishing he'd held his tongue.

'No. I think you've watched too many cop movies. Let's have a drink. I'm not normally one for a Ruddles quite this early, but it's nearly eleven and I can pretend it's high noon if you can.'

Dan hadn't expected this tack. 'I don't drink alcohol.'

'A soda water, then. Orange juice, coffee, whatever. Let's talk about what's worrying you and perhaps we can find Kate in the meantime. I'll help you.'

This didn't sound like a man who was cuckolding him, but then he wasn't eyeballing him and everyone was a better liar via phone. That said, Hawksworth's offer was probably more than he deserved, given the accusation. 'Where?' he said.

'Our local at the Yard. The Old Star, near the station. Don't drive, it will take forever. If you're at Highgate, then hop on the tube at the bottom of the hill. I'll meet you in there in half an hour, okay?'

'Right.'

Dan snapped his phone shut, a mixture of humiliation and remorse flowing through him now. He left Coleridge House, turned right towards the Village and the trek down the hill.

He tried Kate one more time and was surprised when she answered.

'So where are you now?' she demanded. 'I'm home, but you haven't even bothered to stay around to save our relationship.'

'I'm in Highgate.'

'Highgate?' she shrieked. 'What the hell are you doing there?'

'Trying to find you. So is your boss.'

'What? I've only just this second turned my phone back on. Dan, you haven't been speaking to Jack, have you?'

'Jack, is it? Yeah, I've been speaking with him — we're old pals. In fact, right now I'm on my way into the city to have a drink with him at the Old Star.'

'You're not serious?'

'Deadly.'

'This is madness. I'm at home, waiting for you.'

'And we'll be in the Old Star, waiting for you. Apparently you've been trying to reach him.'

'Yes, that's right.'

'I feel like I'm being set up, Kate. You two could surely come up with a better plot than this.'

'You're acting so paranoid I could throttle you. If you embarrass me in front of my work colleagues, Dan, I won't forgive you.'

'Too late.'

He heard the line go dead and wasn't surprised. Kate wasn't one for idle threats. He had a few stops on the tube to decide just how repentant he was prepared to be.

26

Jack stared into his lime soda and contemplated how a morning that had started out so spectacularly, with his arms wrapped around a beautiful woman, could wind up so catastrophically before noon had even struck. His thoughts moved to Deegan's threat and he briefly considered calling Liz. Not that he knew where to find her — but he was a senior policeman, and there were ways. It had been years since they'd spoken and even longer since they'd seen one another. It was as though Liz was from a previous lifetime and he decided to let her remain there. Let Deegan do the muckraking; Jack wouldn't dignify the man's menacing attitude by reacting in precisely the way Deegan hoped he would. If the mud was coming at him, it would arrive soon enough, but he was pretty sure there was nowhere for it to stick. Did Deegan bear him some sort of grudge? Probably, and the man was obviously using his new position to push it.

He saw a dark-haired man wearing rimless glasses enter the pub and glance around. Jack had no idea what Dan looked like, so he waited, but gave the guy eye contact, and right enough he walked over, slumping into the chair opposite.

'Thanks for coming,' Jack said, holding out his hand.

Dan didn't take it. 'I've spoken to Kate.'

'Good. What can I get you?'

'Flat white.'

Jack caught the glance of the barmaid. 'Can we get a flat white?'

She nodded and Jack returned his attention to the sullen, unshaven man. He realised Dan was older than he had first appeared in his jeans and red Docs.

'Is Kate okay?'

Dan shrugged. 'Angry is the best way to describe it. Don't say I haven't warned you.'

'Is she coming?'

'I told her where and when I was meeting you. She may come. I have no idea.'

'Listen, Dan —'

'What the hell is going on here?' said a familiar voice. Kate stormed up to them, a cold wind following her in to match her icy stare.

'Hi,' Jack said amiably. 'Why don't you sit down and we'll sort this out. Coffee?'

'Nothing, thank you,' she snarled, but it was at Dan that she directed her fury. She scraped a chair back to sit down. 'Dan, this is outrageous.'

'Kate, why don't you let him say what's on his mind.'

'Air our dirty linen in front of my boss? You must be joking! This isn't your business, DCI Hawksworth, and I'll be damned if I'll let him make it yours.'

Jack scratched at his stubbly face as the barmaid put Dan's coffee on the table. 'I don't want to interfere in a domestic, but Dan seems to have some skewed idea that our relationship isn't as platonic as it should be, and indeed is.'

Kate looked ready to hurl the steaming coffee into her boyfriend's face. 'You're a fucking idiot, Dan,' she snapped. 'How dare you.'

'Is it true?' Dan replied, ignoring her anger and staring at Jack.

'Is it true that your fiancee and I are involved in some relationship outside of work? No, Dan. It's pure fantasy — and she's not my type, either.' Neither man noticed how Kate's lips thinned at Jack's words. 'No disrespect, but I'm not interested in pursuing amorous affairs with any of my work colleagues.'

'That's not what I've heard,' Dan fired back.

Jack threw an injured glance towards Kate. She'd obviously shared the only skeleton that had been rattling in his cupboard. He watched her sit back and fix him with an embarrassed but hard stare he couldn't read. He composed himself and continued. 'As it happens, Dan, I'm seeing someone at present. She's new in my life, very lovely — no, she's better than that, she's incredibly gorgeous — and, if you must know, dominating my every waking thought outside of work hours.'

He saw Kate look away and out of the window. He hoped, with a pang of shock, that the glistening of her eyes was relief rather than what it looked like. He went on, keen to impress his innocence on Dan and help rescue this pair's foundering relationship. 'I met Sophie before Kate even started official work on this operation. She lives in my apartment building, and although the life of a detective is hardly conducive to an easy relationship — as you and Kate would know — it's ... well, it's rather intense right now, you could say.'

Kate looked back and Jack could see she was as uncomfortable as he felt. Her voice sounded strained. 'How was *Les Mis* last night?'

'Even better the second time.'

She gave him a sad smile. 'Shows are all well and good, but if you want to get close to this girl, you have to take her out dancing.' It was obvious Kate was reaching for levity but she fell hopelessly short.

He nodded. 'Well, it's lucky in a way that I'm such an atrocious dancer with two left feet, because Sophie's in a wheelchair. I suppose I could spin her around the floor.' His own sense of wit failed him just as miserably but his words certainly caught their attention.

'Oh,' Kate said, her surprise obvious. 'I, er, I'm sorry.'

'Don't be. It doesn't seem to affect us.'

'So, you know about this Sophie, do you?' Dan asked Kate.

'Yes,' she snapped. 'I told you this morning. You're being ridiculous and embarrassing.'

'It's alright, Kate, really,' Jack soothed.

'It's not, sir,' she said, her eyes watering now. 'Dan, I can't forgive you for humiliating me like this. How would you like it if I rang up your boss and accused you of bonking bloody Gail? How well would your sense of humour stand up then? And how *could* you have gone to Highgate?'

Dan shrugged with shame. 'It's alright for you to go there, I suppose.'

'Dan, I work with DCI Hawksworth. I had something I needed to talk to him about.'

It wasn't washing with Dan, and rightly so, she thought, hoping the warm feeling at her cheeks wasn't showing her to be the liar she was. Instead, her fiance tried for contrition.

'I wanted to confront you, Jack. I'm sorry.'

Kate closed her eyes and looked away. It was obvious Jack was going to be generous about this but her expression said she hated it all the same.

'It's forgotten,' Jack said. 'I'm not going to pry into how or why you made that leap to the wrong conclusion, Dan, but I'm glad we're all clear.' He put some brightness into his tone. 'And especially glad you didn't get access to my apartment to trash it.'

Dan gave a rueful grin. 'Yeah, you're lucky that strange German woman wouldn't let me use her keycard.'

'Mrs Becker?'

'I suppose. The angels are certainly smiling on you to give you two great-looking women in such a small block.'

Jack looked at Dan quizzically. 'What?'

'Well, you've made it clear that Sophie isn't ugly, and I'd certainly give Mrs Becker one if Mr Becker isn't doing his duty.'

'Dan!' Kate said.

Jack gave a burst of embarrassed laughter. 'Well, I wouldn't. I'm not into women over sixty.'

It was Dan's turn to frown. 'Over sixty? Are you kidding? Mrs Becker is hot. I just wish she'd hung around a bit longer but she was in a hurry to get away from me.'

'Who could blame her?' Kate murmured.

'Mrs Becker, who lives on the second floor for your information, is about sixty-seven,' Jack said.

'Then it wasn't Mrs Becker,' Dan said pointedly. 'This woman came down from the fourth floor. I was at the lift, watching.'

Jack cleared his throat. 'Um, fourth floor is Sophie.'

'And this wasn't Sophie either, then. This person wasn't in a wheelchair. She walked out of the lift and out through the fire exit.'

'No, that can't be Sophie. And she's not German either.'

'Well, I'm glad we got that sorted out,' Kate said, rolling her eyes. 'Okay, Dan, you've done the damage that you came to do. Why don't you —'

Jack was frowning as Kate spoke. He interrupted her. 'Wait. Dan, no one can access the accommodation levels without a keycard. I don't know who could have been coming down from Sophie's apartment.'

Again Dan shrugged. 'I know it was the top floor — I watched the numbers lighting as they came down.'

'She obviously had a visitor,' Kate said, picking up her bag and making ready to depart as Dan obviously wasn't.

'I don't think so.' Jack looked sheepish. 'I, er, only left her apartment a matter of hours ago.'

'Right. Ready, Dan?' Kate said, acidly, and Jack noticed how she wouldn't make eye contact with him.

'Pity, you could have done them both,' Dan said crassly.

Jack ignored the jibe. 'What did this woman look like?'

'Kate's age, no, a bit older, I suppose. Dressed casually in jeans, hooded top. Darkish blonde, dark eyes, lovely skin, great bod. What else can I tell you?'

The vague sense of unease that had been creeping up on Jack since his unsuccessful rendezvous with Sophie at Paddington washed over him again. Before he could ask Dan any more questions, his phone began to ring.

Jack answered and listened intently. 'Good work, Cam. Alright, I'm on my way up.' He nodded. 'Yes, she and Dan are here with me as a matter of fact.' He added after a pause, 'I don't know, I suppose she will. See you shortly.'

Kate frowned at him. 'What's happening?'

'I have to go. If you want to come into work, I think you should, because something's going down. I'll brief you on the way in the lifts. Otherwise, I'll call you later.'

'See you,' Kate said without hesitation to Dan. 'I'll phone you at home, shall I?'

'Will you be back this evening?' Dan said sadly.

Jack left them to it, embarrassed. He cleared security at the main staff entrance and walked slowly to the lifts.

Kate caught up with him. 'Sir, I'm really sorry —'

'Kate, please, enough apologising. I want to forget this as much as you.' He gestured for her to enter the lift before him. Mercifully, no one else followed them in. 'In fact, I'm sorry that Dan could ever think such a thing.'

She looked at him sideways, unable to hide how offended the comment obviously made her feel. 'Is it really so far-fetched? I can't be that unattractive.'

Jack heard alarms klaxoning in his head. He'd been here before. Liz had used almost the identical phrase to lure him into her arms and look where that had led. Martin Sharpe's warning sounded in his mind as he spoke seriously to Kate.

'Listen, you're a great girl and in another situation, another time zone, another life, perhaps things may have been different. But right now, I'm definitely the wrong guy.'

She tried to hide it but Jack saw the pain flicker in her eyes. He felt instantly mortified that he had read Kate so wrong, or, more to the point, that he'd misled her with his friendly manner. He now saw that Dan's suspicions weren't based on paranoia, and was reminded again of Sharpe's warning that Jack tended to allow his team to get too close and was much too vulnerable where women were concerned. *Keep a distance*, Sharpe had told him. *It's fine to be friendly and informal but draw a line around yourself and keep that personal space clear.* Jack had failed with Kate, obviously.

'What do you mean "another life"?' she asked, determined to make him squirm, it seemed.

'Just that. You and I are colleagues. We can't be anything more.'

'Out of interest … why? It's not in the Scotland Yard Rule Book for Detectives, is it?'

'It's dangerous, that's why.'

'Oh yeah, that's right, the last time you got romantically involved with a colleague, it led to a death.'

Jack hissed a pain-filled breath through gritted teeth, desperately wishing the lifts could whisk them faster to the top floor. The doors opened on the fourth floor and someone got in.

'Hey, Jack.'

'George, how are you?'

'I'm okay, mate,' the man said, pushing the button for the next floor. 'Any breaks on Danube?'

Jack nodded. 'Just this minute, actually. Wish us luck.'

George made a point of crossing his fingers in front of them and got out on the fifth, presumably to chase down some fingerprint information.

Jack punched the 'close doors' button and seared a glance at Kate. 'I'm going to allow that you're a bit emotional today and forget you just said what you did. But if you refer to anything connected with my private life again, Kate, you're off Danube and back at HAT Kingston.'

She looked back at him. 'What about my private life?' Her tone was tart.

'I didn't invite myself into it. You and Dan did.' Jack became businesslike. 'I'm not going to discuss this any further. I hope we both understand one another. Now, back to work. A phone call came in earlier today — Brodie took the call — from a guy called Phil Bowles. Apparently he was panicky, wanted to speak with me and wouldn't speak to anyone else and said he'd call back. He's hopefully on the line now.'

Much to Jack's relief, Kate clicked into professional mode as well. 'One of the four?'

'We don't know, but Brodie's taking the call seriously. He says his sixth sense tells him it's not one of the usual hoax calls and the guy seems to know there's four of them.'

Kate nodded. The doors opened on the twelfth floor and Jack strode out into the corridor, leaving Kate to follow in his wake.

Inside the Operation Danube office, the skeleton staff were subdued but Jack sensed a quiet undercurrent of tension. A red-eyed, clearly weary DC Brodie met him.

'Line two, sir. Hi, Kate.'

Jack pulled off his coat. 'Thanks, Cam. Get home, get some shut-eye.'

'No way. I'll go and take a shower, see if I can perk up a bit, but I'm not leaving, not now.'

Jack nodded, appreciative of the man's commitment, and moved quickly to his office. 'Kate?'

'Sir?' she said, strained.

'Listen in.'

Surprised, she nodded.

Jack picked up his phone and pressed line two. 'This is DCI Hawksworth, Mr Bowles. Thank you for calling back and for your patience.'

A nervous voice responded. 'Are you the person in charge of the serial killings?'

'I'm in charge of the murder investigation of the similar recent deaths in Lincoln and London. Are those the killings you refer to, Mr Bowles?'

'I . . . I think so. Mikey and Clive, right?'

Jack felt his pulse surge. 'Michael Sheriff and Clive Farrow were the victims, yes. Do you have some information that can help us?'

Bowles's voice turned panicky. 'You've got to give me some protection. I know I'm next.'

'Next?'

'Two of us are already dead.'

306

'Us? Mr Bowles ... may I call you Phil?'

'Yes.'

'Who are "us"?' Jack heard a long sigh and a silence followed. He waited through it until he realised nothing was forthcoming. 'I want to help you, Phil, but I need to know more. As you can imagine, we get a lot of —'

'He called us the Jesters Club,' Bowles blurted.

Jack held his breath and glanced over at Kate. He saw Brodie was still there. The detective turned a finger in the air to signal they were recording the conversation.

'The Jesters Club?' Jack repeated carefully.

'You know, like clowns.'

Jack felt his heart leap, and knew Kate and Brodie would be feeling the same. 'Why were you called that?' he said.

'He made us wear masks, probably because he did. It was pointless. I mean, she knew who we were. It was only his face that could be kept secret.'

Jack closed his eyes, felt the tingle of relief move through him. Kate's hunch had been on the mark, and his determination to follow it through looked like it was about to be justified.

'Phil, may I ask where you're calling from?'

'My home in Hove.'

'Alright, Phil, I'm going to organise for Sussex Police to come to your home. I can be in Hove myself in about ninety minutes. Is that okay?'

'Hurry, please.'

'Let me take your address.' He looked up and nodded for Kate to write it down. After Phil had stammered out his street address, Jack silently signalled to Brodie to get the Sussex squad car moving immediately. 'Okay, Phil, it's all in motion and I think it's best if we save the rest of this conversation for when I can see you face to face. Have you any family considerations?'

'What do you mean?'

'Wife or children that we need to help take care of?'

'Er, no. Just me. So you want me to wait here, right?'

'Right. Don't move. I'm on my way. A squad car will be parked right outside your door very shortly.'

'Thank you.'

'That's alright. Now let me give you my mobile number. You can call it any time between now and when we meet. Have you got a pen and paper handy?'

'Yes.'

Jack recited the number. 'Do you want to read that back to me, Phil?' The man did as asked. 'Okay, good. I'm leaving right now and I'll see you shortly.'

'Hurry. He's sure to have me on his list next.'

'He? Wait, Phil, you said "he"?'

'Yeah, Pierrot. He's obviously coming after us.'

Jack frowned. 'Who is Pierrot?'

'I never knew his real name. That's all we ever called him.'

'Pierrot is one of the oldest clowns in history. Was he one of your gang?'

'Our gang? We had no gang. We were just four dopey teenage losers who went along with his plan because we were too stupid to begin with and then we were in too deep to do anything but keep quiet. No, Pierrot wasn't one of us. He was the one who did all the harm.'

Jack wished he wasn't so far from Bowles at this point. 'And you think Pierrot is hunting you down?'

'Who else could it be?' Phil's voice rose with fresh panic. 'We know his dirty secret and so he's decided to kill us, one by one.'

'Okay, Phil. Hold tight.' He looked up and saw Brodie stick a thumb in the air. 'I'm on my way and the local police should be with you in a couple of minutes. Just stay put and don't answer the door, unless it's our people.'

He put the phone down. 'Brodie, feel like a run down to Brighton?'

The detective's tired eyes lit up. 'You're on. Have I got time to grab something at the cafeteria?'

'Make it quick. I'll buy you a proper slap-up breakfast somewhere afterwards. See you in the car park. Kate?'

'Sir?' she said, not looking up, her tone short.

'Will you hold the fort?'

'Of course.' She looked at him now and he could see her frustration but ignored it. She threw him a set of keys. 'Pool car. I'm assuming you didn't bring yours in.'

He caught them deftly and kept moving. 'Thanks. We have to find William Fletcher. Stay on it. Where's Sarah? She can help you. In fact, call in everyone you can. We need all hands on deck.'

27

Anne reversed the white transit van out of Mrs Shannon's garage and within half an hour was on the road to Brighton. She had plenty of time — Billy wasn't expecting to meet her until this evening — but she found his name in her mobile list. She pressed the call button, putting the earpiece in so she could speak hands-free. He answered after only a couple of rings. It seemed Billy went nowhere without his mobile at hand.

'Edward Fletcher.'

'Hello, it's Anne . . . Anne McEvoy.'

'Oh hi, Anne, I've been waiting for your call.'

'Sorry, didn't mean to make you sweat on it.'

'Are you still sure about this?'

'It's only dinner.'

'I know but —'

'But nothing. Do you want to have dinner with me tonight or not?' She kept her tone light, playful.

'Of course I do, but, Anne, I have to tell you that I still feel awkward, what with the history between us.'

'Listen, please, raking up the past will do me no good at all. I'm not saying it's water under the bridge — it happened, I can't undo it — but it was a long time ago.' She sensed his uncertainty and crafted a fresh lie. 'I rang my old therapist in London yesterday to tell her I'd met you.'

'And?'

'Well, I haven't seen her in years,' she lied, 'but she said meeting with you would be a huge step forward in my complete recovery.'

'I feel a bit odd about it all, Anne, I have to be honest. I mean, I didn't physically do anything to you, but I was there and too stupid and drunk to stop what happened.'

'Look, I don't mean to upset you, so why don't we leave it?' Anne said, holding her breath. When he didn't answer immediately she knew he was about to take the exit she was offering. She hurriedly added, 'Listen, I have an idea. If dinner's a bit too intimate, how about a drink? I've got some friends in town — we could hook up with them and you can stay for as little or as long as you like — no strings attached.' She heard the hesitation again. 'Come on, it'll be fun. We won't even discuss anything outside of school. Remember old Fanny Sexypants? She's still standing. I ran into her last year.' More lies.

'No!' he said, and she heard his curiosity. 'Did she ever marry Mr Mitchell?'

Anne gave a burst of laughter. 'I have all the dirt. And you'll be pleased to hear old Wallace got his comeuppance. How many times did he wallop your arse, Fletcher?'

'That bloody black plimsoll. I'd like to meet him now.'

'I even know what happened to Mr Pearce.'

'Good grief. I'd nearly forgotten him. How do you know all this?' he asked, clearly impressed. 'A drink does sound a lot easier.'

'Good. You'll like my friends too. One's in small hotels as well, so perhaps you'll have something in common,' she said, the lies coming easily to her as she reeled Billy in again.

'Alright, where?'

'Do you know the Citrus Wine Bar?'

'Um, no, where is it?'

'Just off Norfolk Gardens in Western Road. But they're kicking off at the Rotunda, which is at St Ann's Well Gardens. Is that familiar?'

'Vaguely. I mean, I know where the gardens are but I didn't know there was a bar there.'

'The bar opened only last year, I think. Bit cold, I'll grant you, but it's a beautiful spot and they light up the gardens with lanterns. I went there with a client once and was most impressed. Want to give it a go? The others are meeting early, around six-thirty.'

'Sounds terrific.'

'Okay, meet me at the Royce Street entrance. Better chance of parking there. I'll see you then.'

'Looking forward to it,' Billy said.

Anne smiled grimly as she hung up. 'So am I, Billy, so am I,' she murmured.

It was nearing two in the afternoon before Hawksworth and Brodie parked near the terraced house at Wilbury Road. Jack was relieved to see three police cars — one marked and two unmarked — strategically positioned.

Brodie immediately moved over to talk to their colleagues, thank them for the swift action, while Jack took the short flight of stairs and rang the bell. He saw a movement at the lace curtain in the bay window, raised a hand in a friendly gesture in order not to panic the already frightened Phillip Bowles.

'Is that Scotland Yard?' a muffled voice asked through the door.

'It's DCI Jack Hawksworth, from New Scotland Yard, Mr Bowles.'

The door opened slightly and Jack showed the short, round-faced man staring through the gap his warrant card. 'It's alright, you're safe with us, Phil.'

Bowles opened the door, stepping behind it as though expecting a bullet at any moment. Jack wanted to tell him that neither victim had died by gunfire but the man was clearly spooked enough already without the mention of knives or death.

'Thank you,' he said, entering the musty-smelling house.

'Thank you for coming,' the little man said, nervously closing and bolting the door. 'I've been so worried. Er, can I get you a drink?' he said, leading Jack into an old-fashioned sitting room.

'No, really, I'm fine.' Jack needed to calm the man's immediate fears. 'This is a nice house, Phil, quiet area.'

'My grandparents left it to me,' Bowles replied. 'I haven't changed much.'

Jack could see that. He also noticed the balding man was wringing his hands. There would be no calming down for now. Best to get on with it.

'I need to tape our conversation, okay?' Phil nodded, wide-eyed. Jack set up the digital recorder, saw Brodie coming up the stairs. 'I'll just let my colleague in, Phil. I won't be a moment.' He didn't wait for Bowles to answer.

Brodie followed Jack into the sitting room. 'Phil, this is Detective Inspector Cameron Brodie from our team at Scotland Yard. He's working very closely on this case with me.'

'Detective Brodie,' Phil said, raising himself from the dusty armchair to shake hands.

'Call me Cam,' Brodie replied, obviously sensing the anxiety in the man.

'If Kate or Sarah phone with Fletcher's whereabouts, get the details to the Super,' Jack said in a quiet aside. 'He'll put out a message via the media if he needs to flush him out.'

Cam nodded as Jack pulled off his coat and sat on the chair opposite Bowles, the recorder between them on the coffee table. Jack gave Phil an encouraging smile, depressed the button and gave the required formal introduction to advise the time, date, case, location and people present before saying: 'Mr Bowles has been advised that the interview is being taped and was asked if he wanted a legal representative or an independent witness present, which he declined.'

Jack sat back. 'Alright, Phil, I'm going to ask you some questions now relating to how you knew Michael Sheriff and Clive Farrow, when you last saw them or had contact with them, whether there was anything out of the ordinary that occurred last time you met with them, and whether there is anything — no matter how small or trivial it may seem — that you think might be able to assist us. Is that alright?'

'Yes,' Phil said softly.

'Don't be scared. And you'll need to speak up, Phil. So let's begin. Tell me about your relationship with Sheriff and Farrow.'

As Bowles began to speak, Brodie felt his phone vibrate. He stepped outside the room, not wishing to interrupt the little man's outpouring. 'Yeah, Kate?' he answered softly.

'Hi Cam — is Jack there? I can't reach him on his phone.'

'He's on silent. He's just this second begun the interview. He's recording — I don't want to interrupt him or this guy ... it sounds promising.'

'Okay, thanks.'

'Can I help?'

'No. Just tell him that we've finally got an address for William Fletcher. It's taken this long because we've only just discovered he changed his name by deed poll. Goes by Edward Fletcher these days.'

'I'll let the chief know. He did say if you came through with this that I'd have to let Superintendent Sharpe know. Apparently he'll put out the word to the media if needs be. Hopefully we can reach Fletcher before the killer marks him. Give me the address you have.' She recited it. 'Okay, can you get on to Lewes and have them dispatch a squad car to that address? Call me when you know anything.'

'Right,' Kate said, coldly.

Kate hung up on Brodie, annoyed. She didn't mind working alongside him but the tone in his voice suddenly sounded authoritarian. She had no intention of taking orders from her equal. She'd wanted to give her boss the news herself, earn back some brownie points, hear his voice congratulate her, give the next instructions. It wasn't going to be easy to earn back his trust but she needed to start somewhere. She couldn't blame Dan alone for the damage. He'd done plenty, but she hadn't helped herself at all by her unforgivable comment in the lift.

She forced herself to focus and dialled Sussex Police to follow through on Brodie's request. When it was done, she sent Brodie a text to say a squad car had been dispatched and they would call her as soon as they'd reached Fletcher's place.

She looked across at Sarah, who had already run all four boys through HOLMES but had drawn a blank. None had a previous record or conviction. Not satisfied, Sarah had also rung Lewes Police and double-checked there was nothing on file against any of them and again came up blank. Kate watched her now talking to the former Sergeant Moss, locking down every possible avenue for information on these boys. She wished she had something useful to do.

She wandered into Jack's office and made out she was reading a file, but really she was staring into space, not even seeing the mesmerising skyline of London city, lost in her thoughts about how spectacularly embarrassing this morning had been. She thought of Dan lurking around Hawksworth's apartment building and felt further shamed that they'd brought their problems so close to her boss's private life. Despite her best attempts to stop, she couldn't help but imagine the romantic night Hawksworth must have spent with Sophie — the woman he couldn't stop thinking about. She recalled how Jack had described her — incredibly gorgeous — and remembered how thick his voice had become when he talked about her. It made her feel ill. She also remembered how confused their chief had sounded when Dan had muddled the mansion's occupants; how persistent he'd been about the woman coming down from his girlfriend's floor.

Her gaze drifted back to his desk. His diary was open and she noticed the doodles at the top of the page. Hawksworth's doodles were well known amongst the senior police who had worked with him. If he was on the phone or listening to a conversation between people, he doodled. When she'd first seen him in action three years ago she'd done some research on the net to find out what it all might mean and had been surprised to learn that people's doodlings were apparently a portal into their very souls.

The stars and strong arrows Jack habitually drew, all linked with what looked like curling ribbon, were distinctive and surprisingly easily explained. She'd discovered that his star doodles revealed him to be optimistic but with a need to prove himself. The arrows suggested his amibitious nature and those ribbons — the almost feminine curves that she liked so much — were apparently indicative of his deeply sentimental nature.

But there were two new doodles here that she didn't remember from her last operation with Jack: a noughts and crosses motif, which meant nothing to her, and a tiny heart. She didn't need anyone to explain that symbol to her. Jack believed himself in love ... or was at least in an amorous state of mind. She grimaced again as the phone rang, hating Sophie even though she'd never met the woman.

'It's Hawk's line,' Sarah sang out.

'I'll get it,' Kate called back. She signed into the phone with her five-digit number. *Hawk?* she repeated in her mind. *Since when did Sarah get so familiar?* 'Operation Danube. Carter here.'

'I've got someone on the line looking for DCI Hawksworth,' the operator said. 'He hasn't signed in but I was wondering if he's around?'

'He's not. I can take a message if you want. Who is it?'

'Member of the public, I gather. Seems to know your boss, though. Thanks, luv. I'll put them through.'

Kate waited, heard the click. 'Operation Danube.'

'Hello. I'm looking for Jack Hawksworth if he's available.'

Kate recognised the voice. 'Is that you, Sophie?' she asked brightly, hating how two-faced she'd suddenly become. What had happened to her proud traits of directness, honesty? She reminded herself she had no right to be honest about her feelings for Hawksworth ... and certainly not with his present girlfriend. She stared at the heart doodle and was tempted to colour it green.

'Yes, it is. How do you know me?'

'It's DI Kate Carter here. I work closely with Jack. I answered the phone on Friday when he was running late to the theatre.'

'Oh, okay. Thanks for remembering me.'

'I hear he made it and the show was terrific.'

'It was the fourth time I'd seen it but don't tell Jack.'

Kate gave an artificial smile. 'I'll keep your secret, I promise.' Then decided she might as well dig around a bit, now that she was so deep in the shit already. 'He's actually a bit concerned that someone was coming down from your apartment level today,' she added.

'Oh?'

When Sophie didn't elaborate, Kate made a hasty retreat. 'I'm sorry, that's none of my business. We just happened to be talking this morning and it came up.'

'But what do you mean? Should I be worried?'

'No, truly, it's probably nothing.'

It seemed Sophie wasn't going to let it go. 'How on earth did my apartment come up in conversation?'

It was her own fault for mentioning it and now she'd have to come clean with the humiliating truth. Shame aside, however, Kate couldn't help but experience a helpless rush of *Schadenfreude* that her slip might upset Sophie's cosy attitude towards Hawksworth.

'This is a bit embarrassing,' she said, 'but my fiance was looking for me this morning, and because my mobile was off and I hadn't been home last night, he tried to find me through DCI Hawksworth.'

'Why would Jack know where you were?'

Kate wondered briefly whether she should start packing now for the Kingston office. 'Er, it's not what you think. I'm so sorry, I'm explaining this badly. I work very closely with Ja— DCI Hawksworth and I think Dan thought if anyone knew how to contact me, then my boss would.'

'Oh, I see. I wasn't inferring anything, Kate — just trying to understand. What has this to do with my apartment though?'

Kate thought Sophie was really being anal now. 'Dan came to see DCI Hawksworth and happened to run into a woman coming down in the lifts. He asked if he could borrow her keycard to get up to the third floor, but she was having none of it, that's all. Dan was telling us both about it.'

'Telling you and Jack,' Sophie qualified.

'Yes, that's right.' Kate frowned. 'Jack became concerned because the levels are meant to be secure.'

The atmosphere of the phone call felt suddenly tense and it had nothing to do with Kate's private envy of the woman she was speaking to. But then Sophie's manner shifted suddenly.

'Oh, I know what this is,' she said, laughing. 'That was Ava, a friend of mine. I lent her a keycard. She was picking up some stuff from my place this morning. Your fiance probably ran into her.'

'There you are. I told him there would be a simple explanation. He initially thought it was Mrs Becker.'

'Ah, yes, well, Ava's German.'

'And according to my fiance, extremely gorgeous. I won't repeat how he described your friend to my boss.'

The frigid atmosphere returned. 'Kate, I can't seem to reach Jack on his mobile — I thought you might know how I can speak with him.'

'Things are a bit chaotic just now.'

'Of course, I imagine it must be. I heard something on the radio a few moments ago. The police are asking for a Edward Fletcher to come forward regarding the two murders.'

'Okay, that's good to know it's already out. Yes, Jack's busy on the case right now. He's in Brighton and going to be hard to reach for a while.'

'In Brighton?'

Kate heard the shock in Sophie's voice.

'Yes, didn't he mention it?' She was deliberately goading Sophie now. Of course Jack wouldn't have mentioned it; he didn't know he was going himself until the call came through from Bowles.'

'Ah, that's right, he did.'

'Did he?' Kate said, unable to hide the riff of sarcasm that had crept into her tone. She was lightly retracing the lines of the arrows Jack had drawn on his diary page. 'I love Brighton, don't you?'

Sophie gave a small groan. 'Do you know, it's a place I've never been to. I was born in the south, but I'm embarrassed to say our family used to go to places like Portsmouth or Bournemouth for our family holidays, never Brighton. My father was a doctor, said the air was cleaner in Bournemouth.' She gave a soft, tinkling laugh.

'Really? I think our family spent every summer until 1979 on the Brighton and Hove beaches. Loved those piers.'

'Yes, we seemed to spend a lot of our summers on Bournemouth Pier. Of course, West Pier would have been closed for most of the years you holidayed in Brighton.'

'Oh? For someone who hasn't been there, you know the history well.'

Sophie laughed brightly. 'Not really. I love piers. Ask Jack — I even have photographs of them. A throwback to childhood. Anyway ...' Her tone said she wanted to wrap up the conversation.

'Yes, sorry, is there anything I can help with? Perhaps I can pass on a message.' Kate was staring at the phone's console, a pen poised over Jack's noughts and crosses now. She wanted to finish the game off for him but something was niggling at her.

'Thanks, but no need. I'll try him later or text him. If he calls, just let him know I reached Devon okay, the weather's damp and Mum's fine. And I'll definitely see him tomorrow evening as we planned.'

Kate bristled. 'Lucky you,' she said, hurriedly adding, 'I love Devon. I'll pass that on.'

'Thanks,' Sophie said. 'Bye then.'

Kate didn't wish Sophie goodbye, just let the sound of the dead line beep into her ear as she considered what was troubling her. Devon? She finally put the receiver down and stared at the console.

'What's up?' It was Sarah at Jack's doorway.

'Not sure,' Kate answered absently.

'I can't reach the boss.'

'None of us can, it seems.'

'Those names don't ring any bells with Moss. Can you tell the DCI if he rings in and I miss him?'

Kate nodded, still distracted. She coloured in one of Jack's arrowheads as she reached a decision. 'Sarah, do me a favour, will you?'

'Sure.'

'Get on to BT and double-check where that last call came from.'

'The one that came through to this office, you mean?'

'Yes.'

'Um ... is that wise. It was a call to Hawk's line, wasn't it?'

'Just do it, Sarah,' Kate said, reminding with her tone who was in charge today. 'And let me know as soon as you have the information. I want the number and the location of the phone.'

'O-kay,' Sarah said, clearly reluctant, but Kate was already picking up the receiver and dialling home.

'Hello?'

'Dan, it's me.'

'At last.'

'Listen, I don't have much time. I need to ask you something.'

'You never have time any more, Kate.'

'Don't start. This is important. Tell me everything you can about the woman you saw at Jack's apartment this morning.'

'Why? Are you jealous?'

'I'd have thought for someone who made a complete arse of himself this morning you'd have learned your lesson. I'm following something up for the case, if you must know.'

'Is that right? Perhaps you want to have a CCTV camera put into Hawksworth's flat so you can keep an even closer watch on him, since lurking around Highgate isn't enough.'

'You were the one lurking, Dan, not me. I was simply sitting in a park and clearing my thoughts. Are you going to grow up and help me, or not?'

'I already told you both what I saw.'

'Well, tell me again and this time I'll pay attention.'

'I can't see what this has to do —'

'Tell me again,' she demanded.

'She's pretty, okay? Perhaps a bit shorter than you. Blonde hair. Dressed real casual, slouchy cargo pants but can't hide a great arse or nice body. German accent. Great tits.'

'You didn't miss much, did you?'

'Can't blame me for looking, Kate. You give me nothing.'

'What colour was she wearing?'

'Cargo pants were olivey-grey, pockets on the leg. Those trendy trainers in a sort of khaki suede. Long-sleeved white T-shirt with the words "Bite Me" on them. She's lucky I didn't.' He heard Kate sigh down the phone. 'Dark grey hoodie tied around her waist.'

'Not exactly warm-weather clothes.'

'Don't ask me, I'm not the fashion victim.'

'See you, Dan,' she said, weary of his jibes.

'When?'

'Not sure.'

'Ever?'

'Not sure.'

The line went dead in her ear. She knew their conversation had been recorded but couldn't worry about that now. She closed Jack's diary and left his office.

'What?' she mouthed to Sarah, but the DS held her hand up to stop Kate saying anything more, then scribbled down some details. Kate heard her thank whomever she had been speaking with before she looked back up. 'The call came from a public phone at a pub called The Connaught.'

'And where is that located?' Kate held her breath, dreading that she already knew what Sarah was going to say.

28

Anne was sitting in the transit van, her recently purchased mobile, charged and ready with twenty pounds' credit, resting in her lap. She had been listening to the radio when breaking news was announced that progress was being made on the double murder case that some areas of the media were referring to as a serial killing. A snatch of an interview with Superintendent Sharpe told listeners that police were interested in talking to an Edward Fletcher of Hastings in connection with the case. They stressed that Fletcher was not a suspect but might be able to help them with their inquiries.

Anne slapped the dashboard with frustration. They were closing in far faster than she'd imagined. If Billy heard that radio report or watched a television between now and their meeting tonight, her mission of vengeance was over. The police were probably trying to phone him right now.

She made a decision, picked up the phone and keyed in a number.

Jack sat back, both disturbed and horribly fascinated by the macabre tale he'd just heard from Phillip Bowles. The man now sat sobbing in his chair, clutching a glass of water that Brodie had pushed into his hand.

'Phil, I need to ask some more questions,' Jack said. 'Are you okay to do this with me?'

The weeping man nodded.

'Why were you called the Jesters Club?'

'Because of the masks. He came up with the name. He said something about clowns being called jesters in the olden days or something.'

'He being this man who called himself Pierrot?'

'Yes. He met us one afternoon after school, must have followed us to Hangleton. Everyone but me lived there, but I used to go up after school to the Hangleton Library where my mum worked.'

'Is that where you first met him?'

Phil nodded.

'You need to answer for the tape, Phil,' Jack coached gently.

'Yes. He seemed to know Billy, but I don't think very well. He'd spoken to him once or twice, but this time he found us arsing about on the green next to Clarke Avenue. We got talking and he said he had a great idea and that we should meet him at Hove Park the next day after school. He said he'd have some smokes and sweets for us.'

'And you met him?'

'We did. There were four of us, so we weren't too bothered. I realise now he chose that spot because it was big and lonely enough. At Hangleton, everyone's watching each other, and the green, where all the kids met and played, was far too public.'

'So what happened at that first meeting?' Jack asked.

Phil shrugged. 'We talked a lot — about nothing really. Then Anne came up.'

'Did he bring her into the conversation?'

'I can't remember. I think he might have, yes.'

'And what was he saying about Anne?'

'Oh, he insulted her a lot and said we shouldn't put up with her high-handed attitude. Clive said she was too clever for their school, should be at the grammar and all that sort of thing.'

'And?'

'Pierrot kept encouraging him, kept saying we should teach her a lesson. He said we had to learn how to deal with women and not be dominated by them, and that he'd seen us teasing Anne and that we were pussies.'

'He used that word?'

'Yes. He taunted Billy and Clive with it. Said none of us knew what it was like to be with a girl; that we were fifteen and still virgins. Kept on about it.'

'Did you meet him again?'

'Yes, it became more regular over the next couple of weeks. He'd bring his car and take us for joyrides.'

'What about your parents?'

'Well, so long as I was at the library by five, my mum didn't know any better. I don't know what the others told their parents. I don't think Mikey's people cared much.'

It was time to get back to the night of the attack. 'So then what happened?'

'Well, we got used to Pierrot and the car, the smokes, the sweets. We were kids, thought nothing of it, although now I realise he was controlling us. On the evening that the thing happened with Anne I was supposed to be sleeping at Clive's place. Pierrot had this stupid mask — a plastic clown's mask — and he'd bought us all those Guy Fawkes masks. It was early November, so they were everywhere in the newsagents.' Jack nodded encouragingly. 'He'd obviously been following Anne to know that she'd be walking her pup where we found her.'

'Did Pierrot tell you what he was going to do?'

'No, Chief Inspector Hawksworth, he did not. And when he'd drugged Anne, we thought he was just going to ...' He trailed off, embarrassed.

'Go on, Phil, it's okay.'

He looked at his lap. 'Well, he'd been talking about giving us an education and I thought he was just going to strip her or something ...'

'So you could all see what a naked girl looked like?'

'Yes,' he murmured.

'And none of you boys involved yourselves, is that right?'

Phil shook his head vehemently. 'Like I said, I was holding her dog, but I know for a fact that none of us touched her. He grabbed her, he dragged her to that toilet block, he drugged her, he raped her and then he killed her dog. We were just there.' Phil's voice broke.

Jack wanted to ask why one or all of them didn't run to get help but it wasn't his place to judge. He kept his voice low and neutral. 'To your knowledge, did Pierrot set out to make Anne pregnant?'

'I can't answer that categorically but I'd say no. I'm guessing it was an accident, which would explain why he was so angry when he discovered it.'

'Did he encourage any of you to rape Anne as well?'

'Not to my knowledge. It was all so chaotic. One moment everyone was in the toilet block watching Anne fall asleep, and the next he'd undone his trousers, pulled down her knickers and raped her. I think it would be fair to say we were shocked. If he offered any of the others time with her, I wasn't aware of it, and I don't think anyone would have done anything about it. The only one amongst us interested in girls at that stage was Billy, and he told us he was sort of seeing someone, but Clive said he was lying, that no one would have the patience.'

'Because of his stammer, you mean?'

'Yes.'

'But you all stayed in touch afterwards?'

'Yeah, we kept in loose touch. We shared a secret, after all — not that any of us discussed it. We were too scared.'

'And Pierrot?'

'Pierrot kept bringing us sweets and chocolate — I think to keep an eye on us, buy our silence. Then he said it was time we learned to drink and so on.' He shrugged.

'Did you discuss the rape with him?'

'Never. I think we just wanted to forget it ever happened. I know I convinced myself that if I just didn't think about it, it would go away, because I wasn't part of it.'

Jack moved Phil ahead to the second attack. 'So why did you boys get involved in the abduction?'

'Because we were stupid. He said he'd found Anne and we were going to have a party and make it up to her. He knew just how to play us.'

'And you believed him?' Jack couldn't quite disguise the incredulity in his tone.

'I did, Chief Inspector. I wanted to believe we could set things right. But we were drunk, not thinking clearly. He said it had to be a surprise and we were going to blindfold her, take her onto the pier. That it was going to be fun and she would forgive us.'

'But it wasn't anything like that, was it, Phil?'

'No. Billy tried to stop it, so did I — even Clive said he was leaving — but Pierrot had more booze, more goodies. As I said, we were gullible, stupid. Before we knew it we were too pissed to care, but we left the pier as soon as Pierrot began hurting Anne. We went to the beach.' Phil began to cry.

There was no point in asking why they hadn't done anything to stop the attack. No going back and setting things right. Jack pressed on. 'Anne McEvoy's baby was born on the night the Jesters Club snatched her and took her to West Pier. Are you absolutely sure the baby was alive?'

'It looked dead, initially. I mean, if you'd seen what he did to Anne ...' Bowles sniffed, reached again for his large handkerchief. 'Pierrot flew into this huge rage and jumped on her. We all ran. Even drunk, it was too shocking for me.'

'But how do you know the child was alive? Did you hear it cry? See it move? What?'

'Both, but only for a second or two. We ran down onto the beach. I don't know what he was doing. I thought Anne was dead, and I was terrified he was going to kill the baby too — like he killed her dog — so I sneaked back.'

'And that's when you saw him bundling up the baby in his own clothes?'

Phil nodded, gulped some water.

'But you heard nothing more?' Jack asked.

'I heard it moan, I think, but it was like a contented moan.'

'And Anne didn't move after this?'

Phil shook his head sadly. 'I wasn't able to see much or for long, but she was dead still.'

'You said "most of us were smashed". What do you mean?'

'I don't understand.' He gulped some more water.

'Well, who wasn't smashed?'

'Oh, I see. Billy. He'd drunk as much as the rest of us, but he sobered real fast. He was the one who stopped us going to the police.'

'You were going to the police?'

'Mikey wanted to. I did too, but Billy said we'd be the ones who got into trouble. And Clive agreed. Billy said we were . . . um . . . I can't think of the word.'

'Accomplices?' Jack offered.

'That's right, that's the word he used. He said we'd been involved in her rape and the abduction and that we'd be considered criminals.'

'But you said only Pierrot raped Anne. That's right, isn't it?'

Phil nodded.

'Sorry, but I need you to answer for the tape.'

'Yes, only Pierrot raped her. We were kids. I don't think I would have known what to do.' He looked sheepish. 'Still don't. And anyway, I was looking after her dog.'

'What did the others do during the rape?'

'They were just watching.'

'Why didn't any of you do anything to stop him?'

'He said we were just going to tease her, frighten her a bit. We'd been doing that to Anne for months anyway — just a bit of fun. We were kids, you know.'

Jack kept his expression impassive, even though inside he was seething. He felt a surge of violence towards this man and his lowlife friends threatening to unleash itself. He fought it, ground his teeth hard to steady himself.

'Did you normally hurt her?' he asked.

'No,' Phil said firmly. 'We teased her, that's all. Pulled her hair, threw her schoolbag into the bin or the bushes. Anne was an easy target.'

'Because she never fought back, you mean?'

'Mmm.' He nodded. 'I'm ashamed.'

'You should be,' Cam piped up from where he was leaning in the doorway.

Jack should have reprimanded Brodie, but the detective was

echoing his own feelings. Instead, he allowed the admonishment to make Phillip Bowles squirm further.

'So after Pierrot drugged and raped Anne, he killed her dog,' Jack said. 'Why?'

'The rape was quick. He lasted only moments according to Billy. He was still very wired, you know, after he came out of the toilets. He seemed really angry. It was Clive who said we should leave her a happy birthday card. Clive was a bit slow. He thought it was funny to leave her the card. The rest of us didn't want to. But Pierrot let Clive write the note. It was a tragedy that her puppy died. He didn't have to. He was a lovely little chap. But he began to yap and cry. He was tired and frightened. I'd managed to keep him quiet but Pierrot kept slapping him to stay quiet and that made him worse and Pierrot thought it would bring people running so he held him down and stabbed him.'

'How many times?'

'Just once was enough. The dog died fairly soon after it and I was so pissed off I left them.'

'Where did Pierrot stab the dog?'

'In the park,' Phil answered, weariness taking over from his misery.

'I mean, did he stab him in the neck or —'

'The belly. Here.' Phil pointed to a spot on the left side of his abdomen.

Jack glanced at Cam, who nodded. Both made the connection to the stab wound to the already dead or dying victims. It seemed it was more to do with retribution than to speed their end. As the profiler had warned, the injuries were very personal to their killer.

'Phil, we're going to take you into custody.' Jack held up a hand as fresh panic gripped Bowles. 'I'm not detaining you. We are offering police protection at Sussex until we can sort out more thorough security for you here. We would also like to formalise this interview, take a proper statement — we will certainly have more questions.'

'He can't get me, can he?'

'Pierrot? Phil, I think you should know that our focus is on the five teenagers involved in this.'

Bowles eyed him. 'What, you think it's Billy? That Billy's killed the others and is now coming for me?' He stood up, agitated.

'No, no, we don't. Phil, listen to me. We think Billy Fletcher is under the same sort of threat that you are from the killer.'

'I don't understand.'

'We think the killer could be a woman. In fact, from what you've told me, we think the killer could well be Anne McEvoy.'

'Anne?' Phil whispered. 'But Anne's dead.'

Jack looked at him sadly. 'Anne survived the vicious attack you've just described. She was admitted to hospital in the early hours of the morning after the night of the abduction, having been found by one of the anglers who kept an eye on the pier.'

Phil was shaking his head. 'No, no way. Anne couldn't be doing this. Anne was timid. Anne's dead.'

'She lived, and we think she could be exacting her revenge now for all the terrible wrongs inflicted on her by the Jesters Club.'

Phil stared back, not seeing, not really understanding, Jack thought. He suspected that Mr Bowles, who lived alone and still seemed stuck in a time warp of childhood, needed professional medical help to deal with this shock. It would be best to get him into police custody immediately and get help from a doctor. He nodded at Brodie, who understood and left to tell the team outside what was happening.

'Phil?' Jack began gently. 'Can you give us any insight into who Pierrot might be? Any clue at all? Because, you see, he too is under threat from her — him most of all, in fact.'

'I can't really remember him so clearly. He was nothing special.'

'Well, tell me what you can. How tall was he?'

'Taller than I am, not as tall as you. He was thinnish, had freckly arms.'

'Alright, how about hair colour?'

'Nothing special, dark.'

'Curly, wavy, straight, long, short?' Jack reached for an easy example. 'Like Leo Sayer?'

'No, straight.'

'Okay. You didn't get his eye colour, did you?'

'Blue.'

'What sort of blue?'

Phil shrugged. 'Just blue.'

'Dark, light, mid-blue?'

'Yeah, the last one.'

Jack tried not to sigh. 'What about skin?'

'White.'

Jack couldn't hide the soft sneer. 'As in English?'

'No, I mean he was so pale you could see the veins in his arms. He was really white — and freckly, like I said before.'

Phil appeared to be drifting. His gaze had become distant.

'Was he hairy?'

Phil shook his head.

'What about his voice?'

'He spoke quietly. His voice had an accent — like Val Doonican, remember him? — but I don't know.' He shrugged an apology. 'What about the baby?' he added, as if in a trance.

Jack could tell he'd lost Bowles regarding any further clarification on Pierrot's appearance. He pressed on, moving with

Phil's thoughts. 'The child, yes, what do you think happened to it?'

'I don't know. I never saw or heard of Pierrot or any of the others again until I read in the newspapers that Mikey had died. I can't believe Anne's still alive,' he finished, looking terrified. 'She must have suffered so much. I don't think I can live with myself over this, not now that I know.'

Jack would have liked to ask Phil how he'd lived this long with such a terrible secret. Instead, he dictated the routine words to wrap up the recording, switched the contraption off and slipped it into his pocket.

'Shall we go? You'd better lock up the house, put on something warm. We can come back and pack a few things later.'

'We're leaving?'

'Yes. We're going to keep you safe.'

'I can't ever be safe from my memories, Detective Hawksworth.'

No, I don't suppose you can, Jack thought.

Phil stood. 'My dog. He can't be left alone. I locked him in one of the bedrooms. Do you mind if I get him?'

'He can come along. He's small, is he?'

'Tiny. Um, I also kept my mask from the Jesters Club. Do you want me to give that to the police?'

'Yes, Phil. Definitely bring anything that you think can help us to find Anne.'

Bowles excused himself. 'I shan't be long. I might visit the lavvy as well, if that's okay.'

'Of course,' Jack said, reaching for his phone as Phil left the room. There was a flood of missed calls: two from Sarah and three from Kate, including a text from Kate that said, *Ring me urgently*. He was still quietly angry with her about her behaviour and her comment in the lift. She could sweat on it, he thought, especially as next in line was a text from Sophie. He opened up the message.

Spoke 2 Kate. Said u worried about my viz. Don't be, she an old friend. Call ltr. Sxx

Jack felt a soft stir of fresh anger that Kate was meddling again in his private life. She had no business talking to Sophie about anything that he'd mentioned, and why were they talking anyway? His phone rang while he was still fuming.

'Hawksworth,' he snapped.

'Wow, Jack, what's up?'

'Sophie,' he said and sighed. 'Sorry, bad morning. I just got your message.'

'I haven't been able to reach you but was told you probably had your phone switched off. I thought I'd give it one more go.'

'I had it on silent. I was interviewing. Did you ring the Yard?'

'Yes, although I won't make a habit of it, don't worry. Your female colleague, Kate, sounded overly protective.'

Jack's jaw worked to keep his impatience at Kate in check. 'I guess when you work as a close team everyone tends to get protective.'

'She's probably in love with you,' Sophie teased.

'Whatever makes you say that?'

'Mmm, ribbing you clearly isn't a good idea this morning. Are things hotting up?'

Jack didn't want to argue with Sophie of all people. 'Yes. We finally have a witness.'

'To the killings?' she asked, incredulous.

'No, to that case all those years ago.'

'Oh, right. I hear the police are asking for someone to come forward regarding the two murders.'

'Yes, we're hoping to have him in custody later today.'

'Well, good luck with it all. I, meanwhile, need you to wish me luck with my mother. She's very cranky but I'll be taking her out to lunch and hope that will soothe her grumpy state.'

'There's a great pub in North Devon called The Half Moon. Real ales.'

'We'll probably just go to the George in South Molton. I've already booked it. She likes the roast of the day,' Sophie said with resignation.

'How's the weather?'

'Pouring.'

'So ...' Jack wanted to ask Sophie about the trains this morning but he had enough problems to juggle for today.

'What?'

'Looking forward to seeing you.'

'I'll let you go,' she said and he could hear the smile in her voice. 'Talk later.'

Brodie returned. 'Where's Bowles?' he asked Jack, who was dialling to check his voicemail.

'Bathroom and getting ready to leave.'

Brodie nodded. 'Kate's chasing you.'

'Yeah, so I hear from these messages.' He snapped his phone shut on Kate's voice urging him to call her.

'I've just checked with Sarah. Apparently no one home at the Fletcher household. They're tracking a mobile number now.'

'Okay. Maybe the media announcement will find him for us first.'

'Bowles has been a while.'

'Go check, Cam. I'd better call Kate.'

Brodie headed for the stairs, while Jack dialled the operations room.

'Operation Danube. DS Jones speaking.'

'Hi, Sarah, it's me.'

'Hello, sir. How's it going with Bowles?'

'He's given us a story to curl the hair. Kate was right — I think we can now say our killer is likely to be Anne McEvoy.'

'We'll get to work on it immediately, sir. Kate's desperate to speak with you.'

'So I gather. Switch me through.' Jack heard a muffled yell from upstairs.

'It's Kate, sir.'

'Hang on,' he said into the phone. 'Brodie?' he called.

'I need help!' Brodie yelled. There was no mistaking the panic in his voice.

'I'll call you back,' Jack said to Kate and began running up the stairs two at a time. 'Where?' he yelled.

'Here!'

Jack burst into the bathroom to find Brodie, his shirtfront drenched in blood, cradling a dying Phillip Bowles, the artery at the smaller man's wrist long finished pumping out the little life he had left in him. The blood was a mere trickle now, gurgling down the plughole and staining the feet of a tiny fox terrier who sat between his master's legs, whining.

'No-oo!' Jack bellowed, his fingers blindly dialling the emergency line.

'It's too late, Hawk,' Brodie groaned, his fingers at Bowles's throat. 'No pulse.'

The dog began to howl.

29

Jack leaned miserably against the front of the car, talking to the Super. He'd already outlined all that they'd learned from Bowles but now they were back on to his unexpected death, both still shocked.

'How could this happen?' Sharpe said.

'I'm so sorry, sir,' Jack answered, his misery evident in his tone. 'He didn't strike me as a risk. In fact, he desperately wanted our protection.'

'Then why?' Sharpe sounded angry now. 'He was our chance to break this case open.'

Jack paused, allowing the Super's understandable fury to dissipate into the silence. 'He'd just learned that Anne McEvoy survived the attack and is probably hunting him. I think that's what must have pushed him over the edge, sir. Until now, he'd believed her dead. Thirty years of guilt finally caught up with him.'

'Right,' the Super said with finality. 'Call in everyone from your team and anyone else you need. You find this Edward Fletcher, Jack, and find him fast. We have no idea who this Pierrot is, do we?'

'None, sir.'

'Then Fletcher is all we have. Don't let her get to him first. Keep me posted.'

'Yes, sir.'

The line went dead. Jack sighed, feeling done in. What a day. He dialled Operation Danube.

'Hi, Sarah. Can I speak with Kate, please?'

A moment later she clicked on. 'It's Kate. What happened, sir?'

'Bowles topped himself.'

'Oh my god!'

'It's such a fuck-up,' Jack said bitterly.

'Well ... how ... wh—'

'Slit his wrists while we waited for him downstairs. He said he was going up to get a few things. I was on the phone to you ...' He didn't finish; didn't mention that he'd also spoken to Sophie while Phil Bowles was bleeding to death.

'I'm sorry, sir.'

'Yes, that's just what I told the Super.'

'So Fletcher is everything now, I guess,' Kate said, already moving beyond Bowles, although the shock hadn't left her voice.

'Get the whole team in, Kate,' he said. 'Call in any extra staff you think we need. We have to find Fletcher. Get Sussex doorknocking the neighbours. Find out anything you can from his dentist, his doctor, anyone.'

'We'll find him, sir, I promise. So Anne McEvoy is our girl?'

'It seems so. Get Sarah hunting down everything she can on McEvoy; you stay on Fletcher.'

'Are you and Cam staying in Brighton?'

'I'll leave Brodie to sort everything here. I might get across to Hastings, see if I can help out there, although Fletcher could be anywhere,' Jack said miserably. Then added, 'It won't end with him, though.'

'What do you mean?'

'There was a fifth person, as we'd begun to suspect. An older man. The one who led the boys in the attacks. From what Bowles said, none of the lads laid a finger on Anne other than to help abduct her. It was this other fellow they called Pierrot who raped and then attacked her. They were the stooges.'

'Pierrot — after the clown?'

'Yes. Hence the masks — which reminds me, Bowles kept his.' Jack made a mental note to tell Brodie to find that mask. 'It may explain the blue paint.'

'How, sir?'

'Well, we know blue make-up is considered unlucky by clowns. Perhaps this was Anne McEvoy's way of reminding these clowns they'd had their last laugh.'

'Revolting. What about the other injuries?'

'Brodie and I think we've found the reason for the single stab wound. Apparently this Pierrot guy killed McEvoy's new puppy. Stabbed him in the belly, just the once. The pup's safety was how they coerced Anne into a toilet block in Hove Park.'

'Where they raped her,' Kate finished.

'They drugged her first, Bowles told us. Killed her dog, left a note wishing her a happy birthday apparently.'

'She's drugging each of them, too,' Kate said. 'It's not her being generous, sir. She's recreating the scene for them.'

Jack felt momentarily brighter as another piece of the puzzle slotted into place. 'I wonder if the odd places we found the bodies are also pointers to what they did to her. Farrow was found in a toilet block; Sheriff in an alley.'

'Where else is there? Did Bowles give you any other ideas?'

'No. I just let him talk. We were going to debrief him properly at Lewes. Fuck!'

'So we have nothing on this older guy?'

Jack shook his head in deep frustration. 'Nothing. We only know his nickname and that he obviously resided in Brighton or Hove at the time. According to Bowles, he has dark hair, blue eyes, freckles.'

'Well, terrific. That really narrows it down.'

He grunted. 'Bowles said he spoke with an accent — not very strong though.'

'What type of accent?'

'Bowles couldn't pinpoint it. Said he was like Val Doonican, so we're guessing Irish.'

'Right, well, that might lead somewhere. Something did occur to me last night, sir ... er, it was why I came over to Highgate this morning. I thought I'd share it after such a sleepless time of it.'

He ignored her awkward manner. 'Go on.'

'I was thinking about why a woman might wait thirty years — a lifetime, almost — to take revenge. This bloke we now know about aside, they were all kids when it occurred and it seemed to me that the passing years must have allowed her to heal and look at that time from a mature perspective — perhaps see it for the madness it was.'

'And?' He had to hand it to Kate. He liked the way her mind worked.

'Well, it got me thinking as to what might then prompt that same mature woman to go so suddenly beserk.'

'Have you come up with a scenario?'

'Well, sir, I know you don't like us to generalise but I believe there are a couple of major things that can cause a woman to turn violent: her passion for a man, and-or for her family.'

'What are you saying?'

'Perhaps Anne McEvoy had sudden relationship problems.'

'A woman scorned? And you think that's enough to send her on a psychotic killing rampage thirty years later?'

'No, sir, but I think it could be part of it. I think if her emotions were suddenly smashed around by the man in her life, it might have put her into a depressed state that took her back to that awful time.'

'Too thin, Kate.'

'Okay, hear me out. The other element is family. I don't know a mother alive who could stay calm if her child was threatened in any way.' The silence was deafening. 'Sir?'

'Your instincts do you credit, Kate.'

'Why? What do you know?'

'We learned from Bowles that Anne McEvoy's baby may have survived the attack.'

'Get out!'

'Bowles heard it cry, saw Pierrot wrap it in some old clothing. He doesn't know what happened after that.'

'That means the child could be nearing thirty. You think McEvoy's just found out?'

'It's still thin, Kate. If the child is alive, are we assuming she found out before or after she began her killing? If it's after, then something else triggered her revenge.'

'We're going around in circles on this, aren't we?'

'Yes; however, I think it all has merit. Get on to Tandy and give him all the information we have. Ask whether, in his professional opinion, someone who had suffered this sort of trauma in childhood, survived it, went on to live a seemingly normal life, could then lose the plot thirty years on because of some other trauma. And would such a person be capable of brutal murder?'

'I'll call him immediately,' Kate said.

'Okay ... here comes Brodie. The ambulance is here too. I'd better go. For now our priority is Fletcher.'

'Sir . . . er . . .'

'What?'

'There is something else.'

He could hear the hesitation in her voice, the reluctance to say what was on her mind. 'Go on.'

'Well, it's about Sophie, sir.'

Jack took an audible breath. 'Kate —'

'Sir, it's not my intention to meddle in your private life.'

'Then don't.'

'It's just that I spoke to her earlier.'

'I did too. I gather you weren't exactly friendly.'

'That's not true, sir. I —'

'She was trying to find me and you seemed reluctant to help.'

'Again, not true, sir. I did all I could to help, under the circumstances. Brodie had just got off the phone telling me that you were interviewing Bowles and couldn't be interrupted. I offered to take a message. In fact —'

'Good. What did she say?' He heard Kate suck back her irritation at being interrupted for the second time.

'She asked me to tell you that she'd reached Devon, it was cold and rainy and her mother is fine,' Kate said, her voice terse.

'Thank you. I already know all of this.'

'Except —'

'Except what, Kate?' Jack's voice suddenly had a dangerous edge.

He heard her take a breath. 'Except it's not raining in Devon today, sir. It's cold but there's also a perfectly serene blue sky and sunshine across the whole region. I checked.'

'You checked?' His voice had become icy.

'I — I don't mean to —'

'Kate, I have no idea where you think you're going with this. I shouldn't have to justify anything to you. Can we leave it that

Sophie is in Devon — no matter what the weather — and lunching with her mother at the George in South Molton. They're having roast of the day if you must know.'

'Jack, please, I —'

'You know, Kate, I don't think we can continue working together. It's certainly not healthy for you, and I'm finding your interest in my love life dismaying and uncomfortable. I'm really sorry to lose you but I think we should get you reassigned from next week. It will be easier for all of us.'

'That won't be nec—'

'Talk to you later,' he said, clicking off before Kate could say anything more. He'd had enough of her and her meddling for today. He dialled Martin Sharpe — in case Kate decided to call back.

In the operations room, Kate stared miserably at the phone. Jack was clearly pissed off with her now. His legendary tolerance and good humour was all spent.

'I assume that didn't go well,' Sarah said, coming over and perching herself on the corner of Kate's desk.

'He's reassigning me next week.'

'Oh, Kate.' Sarah paused, waited for Kate to say something, but when she didn't, she added, 'I'm so sorry it's got this far, but what did you expect? I told you not to say anything.'

'But the facts are there. Something's wrong, something's up. I don't trust her.'

'You don't even know her! Why should your boss's new girlfriend, someone who has never met you, work to gain your trust?' Sarah asked, incredulous.

Kate shook her head. 'She's lying, Sarah.'

'But what's it to you whether she's in Devon or not? That's DCI Hawksworth's business. I can't believe you'd involve yourself in his private life like this.'

Kate wasn't listening. 'Something isn't right here. Why is she lying?'

'Listen, has it occurred to you that she might be planning a surprise for him? Perhaps she's deliberately set this up to make him believe that she's out of town but she's really at home preparing him a fabulous surprise meal and getting herself gorgeous for a night of hot sex.'

'No, that's just it, she's not. She was guarded. She was too deliberate. I could hear it.'

'You're hearing what you want to, Kate. You hate her simply because she's with him.'

Kate fixed her colleague with a wintry stare. 'Sarah, you're not putting this together at all, are you? Jack admits that he only met Sophie very recently. Isn't that convenient?'

'For what? For whom?'

'For the case.'

'What? How about coincidental?'

'Alright. What about this? Dan saw a woman coming down from Sophie's apartment this morning. Even Jack was concerned because their apartments are all security controlled at the lifts.'

'She had a visitor.'

'Right, that's her claim too, but Jack said he left her only this morning, and Dan couldn't have been that far behind.'

'What does that prove?'

'Sophie said the woman was a German friend.'

'Well, there you are.'

Kate ignored her. 'She's lying. I asked her outright whether she'd ever been to Brighton or Hove and she denied it, yet she seemed to know a lot about one of its piers. And now the most damning part — she's phoning this office from a public phone box in Hove but pretending she's in Devon. If she's preparing some great surprise for Jack, then what the hell is she doing at the seaside?'

'Perhaps she's going to call him, ask him to spend the weekend there with her. Brighton's a renowned destination for lovers and affairs — perhaps she's married, who knows? Either way, none of this is your business.'

Kate gave a sound of exasperation. 'And none of your alarm bells are going off that Sophie's in the Brighton area, not that far from Hastings where we believe Fletcher, the next victim, is?'

Sarah looked back at Kate, totally shocked now. 'Wait,' she stammered, 'you aren't seriously trying to suggest that DCI Hawksworth's girlfriend is connected with our case, are you?'

She waited for Kate's denial. It didn't come.

'You are! That's truly what you're thinking?'

Kate thought of something, rapidly began dialling.

'Kate!' Sarah snapped.

'Brodie, it's Kate,' she said, staring angrily at Sarah. 'Yep, you obviously moved fast with the media. Is the call for Fletcher already out nationally?'

'The Super said he'd get the whole of the south-east moving immediately,' Brodie replied. 'The rest of the country would take a bit longer. Why?'

'Nothing important, just wondering. I heard what happened. I'm sorry.'

'Hawk's not taking it well.'

'He's headed back to London, right?'

'Yeah, I'm sticking around to oversee this mess.'

'I'll call you back, gotta go.' She put the phone down. 'Sarah, ring the main radio stations in the west, will you?'

'I don't like the sound of where this is headed.'

'Jack's always telling us to trust our instincts. Mine are screaming. I have to follow this through. It's just a few calls.'

Sarah's expression dissolved from opposition to acceptance. 'What am I asking?'

'Whether the bulletin from New Scotland Yard about Edward Fletcher has been aired yet.'

'This is so much worse than I thought. You think she's not just connected but that she's our killer.'

Kate refused to make eye contact but the set of her mouth told Sarah that she was unrepentant on her stance.

'You've gone mad, Kate. The DCI won't just reassign you — he'll burn your arse and it won't be to Kingston. It will be to the legislations office to provide permits for lorries to carry boats or mobile homes at odd hours! You'll need a promotion just to do traffic management.'

'Please, Sarah.'

'I'll think about it. Now tell me what our boss wants us to do.'

Kate sourly briefed Sarah, who began calling the most junior members of the team, dragging them away from their weekend.

Kate returned to their previous conversation. 'I know it sounds ridiculous and as though I'm speaking purely from jealousy, but I think Sophie is a liar.'

'Whatever, Kate. I've called everyone in. Let me know if you want me to get hold of any other staff as the DCI asked. And now I'm getting back to work. I suggest you do the same. You've got Fletcher to find.' Sarah left Kate to her dark thoughts.

Kate's phone call to John Tandy at his home revealed that it wasn't beyond the bounds of reality that some emotional trauma could have triggered Anne McEvoy's repressed memories, bringing them to the forefront of her mind again.

'What sort of trauma could do that, John?' she asked.

'How long is a piece of string?' he answered irritatingly. 'Loss of a loved one, death of a child — I could go on.'

'No, that's alright. So long as you can tell me that, in your professional opinion, it is feasible that some shock could motivate someone who is normally harmless into taking this sort of brutal revenge.'

'Those kinds of wounds never really heal — the victim just learns how to adjust and then cope with daily life around that wound. She's probably been with someone she loves and trusts for that time. Perhaps something's happened to that person. Perhaps they had children and she's lost a child again. That would certainly reopen the wound.'

'Could it send her on this killing rampage?'

'DI Carter, that's a sixty-four-million-dollar question. It may not provoke you or I to go on a killing spree, but it might motivate the next person to do just that. We're all wired differently. If it is this Anne McEvoy, then you have to look at her life as a whole. I'm presuming she's been a seriously depressed person for all of her life.'

'On medication?'

'Not necessarily. She's forty-four, you say?'

'Yes.'

'Then she was born in an era when antidepressants weren't prescribed as they are now. Mental health wasn't quite the same issue it is today,' he cautioned. 'No, if she's been on the edge all her life, then it's likely been sheer willpower that's kept her going through her teens. Perhaps medication in her twenties, who knows? It would have helped keep her moods even.'

Kate sighed. 'It's all so hypothetical.'

'It's what I do, DC Carter. I rarely have the luxury of dealing with all of the facts. I'll put out some feelers, see if any of my colleagues know of this Anne McEvoy. She may have been seeing a psychiatrist to cope with the past traumas.'

'Thanks, John. I'll let DCI Hawksworth know what you've said — and sorry again about interrupting your weekend.'

'No problem. Anything that helps.'

'Er, John, there is one more thing. Can I ask: do you think this sort of person could have a split personality?'

'What do you mean?'

Kate squirmed. 'Could she be this brutal serial killer while also living a thoroughly normal existence? Could she be in a loving relationship, for instance?'

'Yes, of course. I postulated from the outset that the killer was never out of control during the murders. She may be emotionally unbalanced in terms of what she's doing, but in her mind she's utterly calm and clear thinking. She is obviously highly intelligent. Why?'

'Oh, just a hunch. Thanks again, John. We'll let you know what's happening.'

'I appreciate that,' he said, and Kate hung up.

She stared at the phone, wondering whether or not to take the next step. It would certainly seal her fate with DCI Hawksworth. She keyed in some details at her computer and watched the screen. The information she wanted flashed up. Kate hesitated. This was it. What she chose to do next would commit her to a pathway she couldn't turn back from.

She dialled the number on the screen.

30

There was only one person who could be ringing her on this number. 'Finally,' Anne said into her mobile, pulling into a lay-by.

'Hello again. Yes, I noticed your calls. Sorry, my phone's been playing up. I've actually just had to go out and buy a new one, would you believe?'

She thanked her lucky stars for that. 'Listen, something's come up.'

'Oh, can't do tonight?' Billy asked.

'No, it's nothing to do with that. Bit of a strange request actually. I know you won't believe this but I've just taken a call from a client in Hastings.'

'No,' Billy said and laughed. 'What sort of client?'

'Well, apparently they've got a friend in London whose pied-à-terre I refurbished last year. They love it, want to try and achieve a similar feel for their mansion apartment at St Leonards,' she lied.

'Great. Are you taking the job?'

'That's just it. He wants me to supervise the whole project if I do. And that means I'm going to have to be on site for a while — certainly a couple of months or so — as I gather he wants to do some structural work as well.'

'And?'

'Well, I'm going to need somewhere to live during that time if I do accept the job. I don't want to use a hotel room — I'm not very good at living out of a suitcase and eating in commercial dining rooms.'

'Okay, I get it. You're thinking one of my B&Bs?'

'Exactly. Have you got anything that you'll rent out on a longer term?'

'Sure, several, in fact. Mainly in the old town but they're all lovely.'

'Sounds fine. I like being able to walk to restaurants, coffee shops and so on. A view isn't so important.'

'I can do all of that. In fact, I think I know which place will suit you best — there's a fabulous little two-bedroom cottage overlooking Alexandra Park but with fantastic views over the Channel, and it's in a really private close with just a couple of neighbours.'

'Sounds perfect. What sort of money?'

'We'll come to some arrangement, Anne, it won't break the bank.'

'Can I see it?'

'Of course. When?'

She laughed. 'Now.'

'What? You're kidding, right?'

Anne sighed. 'I'm not, unfortunately. This guy wants me to give a decision this week. I've extended further so that I can see his place tomorrow, but I want to have this accommodation sorted in my mind before I say yes. If I'm going to relocate for a couple of months and commute to London from Hastings, then I want to know what my temporary home is like.'

'I understand. Um ... well, perhaps I can get someone —'

'No, please. I won't need long. Just tell me where and I'll meet you there. I'll make up my mind on the spot and give you a cheque up front. It's how I work.'

He hesitated. 'Okay, look ... I've got a couple of things to do, and I was meeting someone in about half an hour so that will need rearranging. Um ...'

She pushed. 'Listen, I'm already on the outskirts of Hastings.' She laughed. 'I can be there in under fifteen minutes.'

'Alright.' He gave Anne the address. 'Just wait for me there — take a walk around the garden, enjoy the view. I might be a few minutes after that.'

'Thanks for this. I really appreciate it. See you soon.'

Anne felt the relief course through her. She couldn't deal with Billy Fletcher in Hastings. That would be too much of a risk. He was obviously going to let others know what he was doing, and the police were closing in on him. She had to hope he remained ignorant of them and vice versa for just another half-hour. And then she would need nimble fingers.

Jack had decided not to go to Hastings. His presence would likely irritate the local boys, especially in the mood he was in. Best he get back to the Yard and take command of the case from there, particularly with Kate spiralling off on a tangent he didn't understand or care for.

He left Brodie the pool car and grabbed a fast train from Hove. The train was pulling out of Haywards Heath when his phone vibrated.

'Hi, Sarah.'

'Sir. We can't find Fletcher on all the usual contacts, but we've had a break — we've found Fletcher's girlfriend. Her name is Lucy Baines.'

'Excellent. Does she know where he is?'

'Yes and no. Apparently Fletcher was supposed to be meeting her for a late lunch today. She was bringing it to his office. Lucy says he's been a bit odd the last two days.'

'What does she mean?'

'She couldn't really explain. Anyway, he rang her about twenty minutes ago and cancelled their get-together because he had to meet a client.'

'What does he do?'

'He runs a chain of bed and breakfast properties. She's totally pissed off and says this woman called him out of the blue and he couldn't ignore good business.'

'Woman?'

'Yes, sir.' He heard his own suspicions echoed in Sarah's voice. 'There's more.'

'Go on.'

'Well, Lucy said that yesterday morning Fletcher had gone to see his father at a nursing home in Hove. In her words, she and Edward had been talking on the phone, making arrangements for this evening, when she heard a woman say, "Billy Fletcher?".'

'Oh, god.'

'Sir, apparently he rang off from Lucy almost immediately. He called back later to cancel their meal out this evening and arranged this late lunch instead. Now that's gone bye-bye too.'

'It's her,' Jack breathed, his chest feeling tight.

'We can't be sure, sir.'

'I think we can. Did you get his phone number?'

'Yes. I figured you'd want to make that call, sir.'

'Give it to me.' Sarah rattled off a mobile number that Jack scribbled on the back of a leaflet he found on the seat next to him. 'Call Hastings Police. Did Lucy say where he was meeting this woman?'

'Yes. It's called the Dovecote.'

'Get them over there now. Tell them what they're dealing with. Detain her. I'm stuck on a train to Victoria — about thirty-five minutes. I'll call you when I get there. I have to make that call.'

'Okay, chief. Don't worry, I've already made the call to Hastings Police. Talk to you soon.'

Jack dialled the number on the leaflet, heard it ring once, twice, and then lost the signal when the train shot into a tunnel. He swore angrily under his breath, not caring that the person opposite glared at him. He sat out the interruption of the tunnel and furiously dialled again. This time he hit Fletcher's voicemail and knew he was too late.

Anne waved at Billy as he drew up in the driveway. She grinned through the window, her eyes flicking to the passenger seat where his mobile sat. 'Sorry again for all this,' she said as he got out.

'Don't be. This is a great spot, you'll love it.'

'I already do.'

'Good. Let me open it up for you.'

'You go ahead. I just have to pick up my voicemail. I think it was the same client ringing a moment ago.'

'How did you get here?' he asked, walking to the door of the cottage. 'No car?'

'Train and taxi today,' she lied. The van was parked at the local shopping centre car park where it blended in unnoticed. She pretended to dial up her voicemail and put the phone to her ear. 'Be with you in a sec,' she said.

As soon as Billy opened up the cottage and walked inside, Anne opened the passenger door of his car and grabbed his phone. It shocked her when it rang once but she hurriedly switched it off, looking up alarmed to check that Billy hadn't heard. She slipped his phone into her pocket and skipped quickly away from his car towards the cottage.

'Was it him?' he asked, meeting her on the porch.

'Yes,' she said with a sigh. 'He's pushing for an answer. That's what money does to you. You expect everything instantly.'

Billy grinned. 'Well, come in and have a look.'

She spoke as she followed him in. 'Er, listen, I hope I haven't put you to any inconvenience with this?'

He looked sheepish. 'Nothing I couldn't handle. I did have a meeting, as I said, but I've told them I couldn't pass up on business. So this is the kitchen and sitting room, living area.'

She smiled. 'Sounds personal.'

'Sort of. No problem though.'

'It's lovely. And you said two bedrooms?'

'Yes.'

'I don't need to see any more. This is perfect.'

He looked at her quizzically. 'Are you sure?'

'Absolutely. I knew from the outside it was ideal.'

He shook his head. 'Wish all women were as decisive as you, Anne.'

She laughed. 'I told you it wouldn't take long. Let's go sort out the details.'

'Don't want to do it here?'

Anne had already figured that if the police were closing in fast enough then they could find them here. 'No, let's get you going; you've been really good to do this for me. If you don't mind running me back to the station, I can write you out a cheque on the way.'

Fletcher nodded. 'Fine. Let's go.'

Jack had now dialled Fletcher's number four times — he could swear it rang the first time and then went dead. Each time since he'd hit the man's voicemail. Fresh dread claimed him. He rang the operations room and fortunately got Sarah immediately.

His voice was bleak. 'He's not answering.'

Sarah swore under her breath at his news. 'Hastings Police should be at the Dovecote any moment. What do you want me to do, sir? Er, may I put you on speaker so the team can hear your instructions?'

Jack hissed a breath, his mind racing. 'It's as though she knows our next step.'

'If she knows we're on to her, she'll go to ground,' Swamp said.

'It's too late for going into hiding,' Jack replied. 'She's found her quarry. She'll want to deal with him in the same way. She can't stop now.'

'We can't wait for a corpse, sir.' It was Kate.

'I'm not suggesting we do,' Jack snapped. 'I should hit London Victoria in just over quarter of an hour. Get Hastings Police to throw a cordon around the town as best they can and to hunt down any white transit van. It's the only clue we have to go on at present. I'll see you all shortly. In the meantime, Sarah, keep trying Fletcher's number.'

Jack rang off, feeling helpless. The train filled at East Croydon and then became more crowded at Battersea, at which point he left the carriage and impatiently waited in the corridor at the doors, eager to be gone from this prison. The train had barely sighed to its stop at the Victoria terminus when Jack burst from its belly and ran down the platform. He immediately picked out a familiar face waiting for him and his gut twisted. He wasn't in the mood for this now.

31

Anne handed the cheque to her companion. 'I really appreciate this.'

'The thanks are mine.' Billy beamed. 'A long rental at the tail of winter is fantastic, but I know it will suit your needs and I'm glad it worked out, Anne.'

They smiled at one another; a slightly difficult pause followed. 'What train are you taking?' Billy said.

She looked at her watch. 'Leaves in about fourteen minutes, plenty of time.'

'And I'll still see you this evening, okay?'

'I think you'll like these people. As I say, one's in hotels, I think you'll both get on really well. Who knows where it might lead?'

Billy nodded. 'Right, well . . .'

'Listen, have you got much on this afternoon?' He hesitated, shrugged. Anne didn't let him get much further. 'It's just ... why don't you hop on the train with me now?'

'Now?' He glanced at his watch.

'Come on, come now. We can travel into Brighton, grab a late lunch, roll into drinks and be leaving by eight-thirty.'

'Are you coming back to Hastings tonight?' he asked.

'That was my new plan. I thought I'd stay at the Dovecote. Don't worry, you don't have to set up any of the usual B&B gear in the fridge. So long as the sheets are clean and I have fresh towels and heating, I'm set to go. So, say yes, come now.'

Billy frowned. 'I did have someone I needed to see.'

Anne had no intention of letting this happen. 'Oh, come on, please. I'm going to see a marvellous mansion apartment on Brunswick Terrace. I haven't seen it for two months. The client has spent a cool fortune on its redesign and refurbishment, all to my specifications, I might add,' she said archly and noted Billy's frown lighten, turn to a grin. 'I promise you, you'll enjoy seeing it.'

'It must be fun spending other people's money,' he admitted. 'I'm always hampered by how far I can push my bank manager, how much overdraft I can play with. I so often want to do these places up better but I have to show restraint.'

'My sort of clients don't understand restraint when it comes to money,' Anne said gleefully. 'Great for business, of course.'

'Have you ever kitted out a place for someone famous?'

'Celebrity, you mean?' He nodded. 'At least a dozen I could run off the top of my head, probably closer to twenty.'

'Who's your most famous client?'

'A major movie star — I redecorated her magnificent mews in London while she was appearing in a West End production for two years.'

'Who? You have to tell me!'

'They make me sign papers never to share details, I'm afraid. It's a bit like a doctor-patient relationship.'

'Oh, rubbish — that just makes them feel important. I'm sure she sold the story instantly to *Hello* magazine.'

Anne turned a make-believe key at her lips and shook her head. Then grinned. 'I'll tell you if you come with me now.'

'Anne, I —'

'It'll be a lovely afternoon, I promise. You work so hard, surely you're allowed a half day off now and then? In fact, it's hardly even a half day. And the person you need to meet — well, you can see them tomorrow, I'm sure.'

Billy didn't look so certain. Anne guessed it had to be a woman.

'Come on, jump on the train and I'll drive us both back tonight. You can catch a cab from the fringe of town if you think it will set tongues wagging.'

Billy looked as though he was teetering on the edge. Anne pushed.

'Look, I have to go. I'd love you to come and see this place I've done up — no client, just us. I can show you through the whole apartment.'

She saw his shoulders relax and knew Billy's vanity had won through. No matter how the past nagged, he was flattered to have such a good-looking woman pestering for his company. If only he knew the truth.

'Oh, what the hell,' he said. 'But what about drinks? Am I dressed okay?'

'You look great,' she cooed. 'Love that jacket.'

Anne had changed in her van out of her mock catering clothes with a view to complementing how she expected Billy to be dressed in the middle of the day when he wasn't expecting company. She'd already noticed he was a sharp dresser, so she knew that even if he was in jeans they'd be smart, and she was right. In his designer jeans and suede jacket Billy had nothing to worry about, and her equally casual but smart attire assured him of this.

'I'm not changing,' she added.

'Okay,' he replied, resigned. He turned off the engine and locked the car. 'Let me just make a quick call.'

'No time,' Anne warned. 'I can see the train pulling into the platform. Let's just get on and you can call from there.'

He nodded and Anne touched the slim mobile in the pocket of her coat. Billy would never make another call during what little life he had left.

She grabbed his arm and hurried him towards the platform.

Jack strode towards a nervous-looking Kate. 'Why the welcoming party?'

'I need to talk to you, sir.'

'The Yard is just down the road.'

'In private.'

Jack sighed. 'Kate, we're in the middle of a major crime op—'

'It's about Operation Danube, sir.'

Jack stared at her, trying to guess what was coming at him. Could the day get worse? He suspected it might, going by Kate's fidgeting and worried expression.

'A quick coffee? What I need to say will only take a minute, sir, you don't even have to drink it.'

'Alright. But it'd better be good.'

Kate blinked, obviously unsure whether he meant the coffee. 'How about this place?' she offered, pointing towards yet another new cafe franchise.

He shrugged. 'Fine. Any sign of the van in Hastings?' he asked as he strode towards the coffee shop, Kate skipping to keep up.

'No, but they've found Fletcher's car. You grab a spot, sir. I'll get them. Strong latte, right?' He nodded. 'Won't be a sec.'

Jack moved unhappily to a tiny two-seater table in the corner of the equally tiny cafe and squeezed into one of the fake bentwood chairs. His long legs wouldn't fold comfortably into the sparse amount of space so he had to sit with his back to the window and stick them out beneath another table next to them.

Kate arrived balancing two glasses with paper napkins expertly tied around the top so the drinkers wouldn't scorch their fingers.

'Smells like a decent enough brew,' she began, trying hard, Jack noticed, to ease the tension between them.

He softened, feeling immediately sorry for her. He liked Kate very much and had meant what he had said earlier. In a different lifetime under different circumstances and in a different profession, they may well have become involved. He had lied when he'd said that Kate didn't fit his taste in women, but he could hardly admit to Dan that he was strongly attracted to his fiancee. He had learned a horrible but important lesson with DS Liz Drummond though, and he had no intention of repeating it. What he hadn't foreseen was Kate's fascination for him.

'Relax, Kate. This morning is behind us. I have far more catastrophic things on my mind,' he said.

As though she hadn't heard him, Kate launched into what sounded like a prepared speech.

'Firstly, I want to apologise properly about this morning. I'm embarrassed by Dan and I'm ashamed we put you through that. No, wait, let me finish,' she said as Jack opened his mouth to protest. 'The fact is, I have been harbouring an unhealthy admiration for you.' Jack looked into his coffee, uncomfortable. 'It's all been one way. You've done nothing wrong, sir. I think it's a lot to do with the fact that I have been feeling hesitant recently about Dan and making the whole marriage commitment. And then this position came up — I grabbed it with both hands, desperate to escape the boredom of Kingston but even more desperate to work alongside you again. I'd be lying to you if I didn't admit this. I can't help how my heart feels, sir. I can, however, control it and I'm begging you not to take me off this case, and I promise you that we won't have to speak of this again.'

She paused, began again wistfully. 'You and I, well, we couldn't work, I realise this now after all you've said, and I'm sorry for putting you in such a difficult position. I'm totally committed to this case, sir and I won't let you down.' She placed her hands emphatically on the table.

Jack sensed what it had cost Kate to reveal the truth. Her candidness was a quality that had drawn him to her originally and why he had chosen Kate Carter first when the Super asked him to select a team. He had named her third to Martin, of course, but that had been deliberately done to throw the old man off the scent of Jack's apparent 'fatal flaw'. It hadn't really worked. Martin suited his surname.

The silence stretched between them, the two lattes steaming untouched on the table.

'I too am sorry that you feel this way and I do appreciate your honesty,' he finally said.

'Do you always want my honesty, Jack?'

He looked up at her quizzically; calling him by name and the odd question surprised him. 'Absolutely! Why would you have to ask?'

'Because although my apology was necessary, it's not the reason I came to meet you from the train. There's something I need to share with you but I'm almost too frightened to say it.'

'Don't be ridiculous,' he said, his expression earnest but clouded now with confusion. 'You must never feel that way with me. We're a team, there must be candour at all times and if I'm making you scared to approach me —'

'I'm not scared of approaching you. I'm scared of how you'll react to what I have to say. I want to lay some facts before you and I want you to remove all your emotions so that you can look at these facts as you would any aspect of any case you work on.'

Jack sat back, shaking his head. 'Kate, I haven't got a clue what you're talking about. Why don't you just tell me what's on your mind? Time is ticking away.'

'Am I still working on Danube?'

He nodded. 'We need you. I need you,' and he saw the flash of relief and triumph in her eyes. 'But we can't work together so closely unless you can —'

'I can,' she interrupted, keen to assure him. 'I give you my word.'

'Then you can stay.'

'Thank you, sir.'

'Now tell me what's on your mind.'

Kate finally sipped from her coffee and Jack saw the previous agitation return to her expression.

He tried to make it easier. 'Alright, tell me about Fletcher's car.'

'His BMW was found parked at the Hastings train station.'

'Damn it!'

'The police are interviewing all the staff to see if anyone remembers Fletcher, or a couple with a man fitting his description.'

'He hasn't rung anyone?'

'Well, yes, he did call his mother after ringing his girlfriend, but before this meeting he spoke to her about. Nothing important was said, other than that he was due to meet someone and had to go. The most damning clue, I suppose, is that he'd already rearranged dinner tonight with his long-time girlfriend into a very late lunch, which she said was odd, but then he proceeded to stand her up. He never arrived as promised. She can't reach him via phone, either. He's on voicemail only and, in her words, "He never switches the damn thing off". She has no idea where he is or why he didn't turn up.'

'Nothing at the B&B?'

Kate shook her head. 'It was all locked up, nothing abnormal — fresh tyre tracks of a BMW. Fletcher had certainly been there today.'

'But the local boys are gaining entry, just in case, right?' She nodded. 'So, give me these facts you want me to hear,' he urged.

'Will you promise to hear me out totally before you explode?'

'Kate, for fuck's sake.'

'Okay, okay,' she said. 'I'm just warning that you're probably going to be angry, but I need you to hear it all.'

He nodded. 'Tell me.' It came out as an order.

Kate sucked in a breath, put down her coffee to one side. 'It's about Sophie. No, please! You promised.'

The sound of Jack's chair scraping on the floor still echoed as his jaw worked to control a fresh wave of anger. He remained silent at her plea.

'Thank you, sir — just let me say what I have to.' She took another breath, allowed a momentary pause before she began again. 'Sophie told you she was going to Devon today — that's right, isn't it?'

He nodded, fury barely repressed.

'She tried ringing you this afternoon, couldn't reach you, rang the Yard and got me. She left a message with me for you that she was fine, had arrived safely in Devon, it was raining and her mother was okay.' She was met by stony silence and Jack's glare made her look away. 'You applauded my honesty, sir, and I need to be utterly direct with you now. As I told you, it wasn't raining in Devon today. And before you say anything, I have friends in North Molton and I checked with them. They confirmed what the weather bureau told me. It was a splendid day in their region, glorious across all of Devon today, in fact, but especially in North Molton where it was cold but very sunny, not even drizzling.'

'Perhaps she was simply making conversation,' Jack said, his words icy.

'Perhaps she was, but she told you the same thing apparently and I can't imagine why the woman you're sleeping with, the woman — whom in your words — you hold in your thoughts for each waking moment, would need to make empty conversation with you ... sir.'

'Is that it? The sum total of why you needed this private, insulting discussion.'

Kate's fingers clenched and unclenched with anxiety. He could see how difficult this was for her. He no longer cared.

'No. I tried to ring the pub where you told me she was taking her mother to lunch.'

Jack closed his eyes with disbelief. 'You did what?'

'It's closed for renovations. Opening in the spring.'

'Is that conclusive, Kate? Could Sophie not have made an error? She doesn't live in Devon — perhaps it's been a while since her last visit.'

'It's been closed for almost a year, sir. They couldn't have taken a reservation. Did she say she'd made a booking?'

Jack refused to answer that, scowling his reply instead.

'As I thought. So she lied. Anyway, none of that matters, sir. What does is the fact that Sophie wasn't in Devon at all today, no matter what she told you.'

'Not in —? What are you talking about?'

'I happen to know that she was on the other side of the country today, sir.'

'Explain yourself, Kate, or I'm leaving now.'

She did so quickly. 'As you know, our phone consoles show where a call is coming from. When Sophie called, it wasn't the Devon prefix and she wasn't on a mobile.'

Jack felt the quiet flutters of alarm in his belly take full flight.

'And where was she calling from?' he said through near gritted teeth.

'Brighton,' Kate said, unable to look him in the eye.

The silence between them became heavy with insinuation.

She continued doggedly. 'I tracked the call to a pub in Hove actually. She used a public phone in its front bar.'

'Who else from Danube is involved in this?'

'Just me, sir. Sarah refused to help. She has distanced herself from all of it and is totally pissed off with me.'

Despite her admitting she was the only renegade, it gave him no satisfaction. 'So where does this lead?'

'There's more, sir.'

He watched her swallow hard beneath his gaze of contempt, but he said nothing and she continued.

'The media announcement that Sophie admitted hearing about Edward Fletcher had only been aired in the south-east by the time she heard it.'

'And of course you've corroborated this?' Jack asked, his tone dripping acid.

'Yes, sir. The radio stations out west will only be making their first announcements in this afternoon's bulletins. She didn't hear this news in Devon and could only have heard it somewhere in and around East Sussex. She was definitely in Brighton and Hove today.'

'So you —'

'Hear it all, sir,' she cut across his words. Jack pursed his lips, letting Kate continue her roll. 'Something Sophie said on the phone — I really can't remember what — prompted me to ask whether she'd ever been to Brighton. She denied it but explained about family holidays in Portsmouth and Bournemouth.'

'And why is that relevant?'

'Considering who I am to her, sir — which is no one — a simple "No" would suffice. And before you say it, she wasn't just

366

being polite. She was going to some trouble to give me information. Even as newbies at Hendon, we're taught to recognise when someone is colouring in far too much background, sir. And might I add that, for someone who has never been to Brighton, she seemed to know an awful lot about West Pier.'

The last two words made Jack sit forward. 'What do you mean?'

'She reminded me that although I had some fond memories of early childhood summers on West Pier, my memory was playing tricks — I couldn't have had that many summers because the pier was closed in 1975. She's right about that date — I checked — plus we know this from Sergeant Moss. A coincidence? Perhaps. But how about this? When I made the comment that I was surprised she knew so much about a place she'd never been to, she told me to ask you about some photographs on the wall of her apartment. Apparently they're of piers — that's how she explained away knowing about West Pier. But it sounded contrived, sir. I know I mustn't leap to a conclusion, but you insist we work on instinct as much as fact. Sophie used that as a throwaway line — in the same way that someone might close a phone call with "Give Jack my best wishes" — she really didn't expect me to mention the photos.'

Jack's eyes narrowed. Every inch of him was on full alarm now, his body flooding with adrenaline. 'They're not of piers.'

Kate's eyes narrowed, ready to challenge him. 'Well, she told me —'

'They're of one pier only,' he interrupted, not apologising. 'But I don't know which one.'

'Sir, she definitely implied plural. But you've seen them and I'd go out on a limb and suggest which one it is. If I saw them, I could confirm it. I can show you on the net what the ruin of West Pier looks like, or how it looked in its heyday.'

Jack looked dazed and Kate pressed her case. 'One more thing, sir. Sophie mentioned in passing that her father was a doctor — she used past tense, so presumably he's dead. Does that ring any bells with you?'

Nausea rose in Jack's throat. This couldn't be right. They were leaping to conclusions that surely weren't there. He played for time, tried to unscramble his own tangled thoughts.

'What are you drawing, or rather, hoping I will draw, from this cloak and dagger investigation into the woman I'm seeing?'

Kate finally looked up at him and Jack could tell it took courage to do so. 'I haven't met Sophie, sir, but she's blonde, very attractive, isn't she?'

'So are you attractive. So are thousands of women blonde. What's your point?'

'You met her almost immediately Operation Danube came into being.'

'Yes.' He frowned at her. 'So?'

Kate rubbed her face, clearly unsure whether to proceed, then she knitted her hands on the table as if to steady herself. Her voice wasn't so steady when she spoke, however. 'You told us this morning that Sophie uses a wheelchair. Are you sure she's dependent upon it?'

'I'm not going to dignify your curiosity with an answer. This conversation is over.' Jack left the cafe, with Kate in pursuit. She pulled at his arm, fighting back her despair. 'Wait, Jack!'

'No, this is vile, what you're doing to me. I deserve better. And you, Kate, can start looking for a new job — don't expect any reference from me.'

'Please, please, hear it all. I'm begging you, because I think you're in danger.'

'Danger?' Jack barked a harsh laugh. 'You're kidding, right? In

368

danger from a woman who can barely teeter a few steps unaided?'

'That's just it, sir. I don't think she's disabled at all. I think the woman that Dan saw this morning was Sophie — blonde, attractive and —'

'Kate! You've gone around the bend. You're so emotionally distressed or blinded by your misdirected feelings for me that you've become obssessed with Sophie. You're a liability for all of us. Don't even bother coming back to Operation Danube. I'll send your things to Kingston. You're off the case as of now.'

'Sir, if you won't listen to me I'm going to take this higher. I'll tell Superintendent Sharpe,' she warned, and Jack hoped bile was tingling through her throat at the undisguised threat to her direct superior.

She looked terrified when he turned on her and he allowed her to glimpse the depth of his wrath. 'You'll tell him what?' he said in a menacing tone, the words clearly filled with warning.

'I'll tell him my fear,' she murmured, clearly intimidated by Jack but not completely cowed, even though his face was close enough to hers that they could have kissed. 'I'll tell him that I think your Sophie could be Anne McEvoy.'

3 2

Anne pointed to the van parked at Hove Station.

'Very sporty,' Billy said, looking at her both amused and quizzical.

She laughed. 'I'm an interior designer, I have my tools of trade, you know. The van's great for moving around all my gear.'

'Blimey, no wonder you catch the train whenever you can,' he quipped, following her towards it.

'Don't be so rude,' she warned, feigning insult. She pressed the remote and the van answered, its doors unlocking. 'Hop in. It's very comfy.'

He grinned. 'I'm a BMW man. I'd never normally be seen dead in a transit van,' he joked.

'Is that so?' she said, reaching into a cool box behind the driver's seat. 'Mineral water, Billy?'

Jack stared at Kate. His reaction to her claim was beyond incredulity.

'What has got into you, Kate? Is this some sort of blackmail?'

'Oh, get real, Jack,' she snapped, her courage gathering. 'Do you really think I'd make such an outrageous claim unless I truly believed it? Blackmailing you? I'm trying to save your life! She's killed two men and now she has another man's blood on her hands. I have to say that I don't particularly blame her, considering what those bastards put her through, but my job is to help stop her. Now every fibre of my body is screaming at me that Sophie is our killer. Prove that she's not, Jack, by all means, and make me look as stupid as I must sound — ensure the only job I can ever do again is traffic police — but don't dismiss my instinct or this scenario. I've given you the facts that form my suspicions, and I agree a lot of it could be coincidence, and much of it is circumstantial, but what's in your gut now? Any doubts? Anything at all that leads you to think Sophie could have been lying to you?'

Jack felt his throat close.

'Answer me, Jack!'

His mind was whirring in every direction as he rapidly backtracked over the past couple of weeks and things began to jump out at him. Was that really how short a time he'd known Sophie? It felt like so much longer — as though he knew her so well. Did he, though? What did he really know about her?

'She told me she's in property?'

He could see the relief in Kate's eyes that he was cooperating. 'Sit down with me, sir, please.'

Jack allowed himself to be led to a seat. Kate risked taking his hand. 'Jack,' she began softly, 'can you think of anything that Sophie might have said that could incriminate her in any way?'

'No!' he replied automatically, his anger still burning.

She took a different approach. 'Take your time. Think — any clues at all that can totally refute this claim then?'

He saw the distress in her face, glanced down to see her hand gripping his, and accepted that Kate wasn't doing this to him out of any animosity. He thought of Sharpe and his warning of how vulnerable he believed Jack could be at times regarding women.

You've always been close to women, Jack, the Super had said. *You and your sister were inseparable as you grew up — and you've said it yourself: you were your mother's favourite and you lost her too early, in horrific circumstances. And who did you turn to for solace? Your grandmother became your greatest friend.*

And then he remembered Deegan from Ghost Squad, aiming to dig up the past and reopen old wounds connected with Liz Drummond. Women seemed to be his greatest asset, but Martin Sharpe was right: they were also his frailty.

'Jack,' Kate urged. 'We don't have much time.'

Everything that was so bright and shiny about Sophie suddenly felt blighted. He hated that Kate was doing this to him, sullying something that was so beautiful in his life. He answered robotically, 'I tried to see her off on the platform this morning at Paddington. She told me which train she was catching so I decided to surprise her with a farewell gift.'

'And?' she coaxed.

Jack shook his head once. 'She wasn't there. I rang, she said she'd caught an earlier train and that she was almost at Exeter.'

Kate waited but Jack said nothing. She pushed him. 'What happened next?'

Jack took a breath, sat up straighter. 'I checked with the platform attendant. He said there were no earlier Virgin trains, so then I checked more thoroughly at the ticket office and it was confirmed that not only were there no earlier trains from Paddington, but no Sophie Fenton was booked on any train from any station in Britain today.'

Kate held her breath, let it out slowly. 'So you already knew,' she said softly.

Jack looked down. 'I wanted to assume she paid cash.'

'Fair enough.'

'She told me that she was the daughter of a doctor as well. It was her way of letting me off the hook for keeping her waiting last Friday.'

'Anything else?'

'Yes', he said, frowning as all the odd comments that had jarred but not made more than a fleeting impact at the time, returned to fall into place like pieces in a jigsaw. 'She knew about my birthday shirt.'

'The striped one? So?'

'We hadn't met.'

'She probably saw you on TV like everyone else did. Perhaps she saw you leave the apartment building.'

He shook his head. 'Nope. When we first met she said she'd never seen me coming or going from the building. Anyway, I left very early that day of my birthday — it was dark and I was wearing a coat and scarf. Yes, she almost certainly did see me on TV at the press conference, but if she remembered my shirt so well — clearly enough to mention it — how come she played so dumb when I introduced myself to her? She made out she had no idea who I was or what I did for a living.'

'People look different in the flesh,' Kate offered, wondering why she was helping him to find excuses.

'Come with me,' he said, suddenly standing.

'Where are we going?'

'To Highgate.' And he strode away.

Kate grabbed her bag and hurried after him.

'What's wrong?' Anne asked, heading out of Hove and into Hangleton.

Billy twitched a confused smile, laid his head back against the headrest. 'I don't know. I don't feel very well.'

'Drink some more water, then.' Anne's voice was filled with mock concern.

'I've drunk more than half already. No, it's not that. I feel dizzy.'

'I'll stop the car soon. We're almost there.'

'Where, Brunswick? We don't seem to be heading into Brighton.'

He wasn't slurring yet Anne was pleased to hear, but it wouldn't be long before Billy was past the point of talking. She'd put a hefty dose of the drug in the mineral water, but she needed time to talk with him. She needed him to hold on, to fight the desire to sleep.

'No, we're not. I'm heading up to Devil's Dyke, a nice spot.'

'The Dyke? Why?'

'I want to show you something.'

'What?'

'Wait. It's a surprise.'

'What about the apartment in Brunswick?'

'Later.'

They drove in silence for a few more minutes as Anne took the van up Snakey Hill for only the second time in thirty years. Her last visit had been to choose the lonely place where she would end Billy's life.

Kate watched Jack as the underground stations snaked by them. They hadn't shared a word since he had told her they were going to Highgate. She had no idea what he had in mind, but going by the grim set of his mouth, he had some sort of plan.

'Phone the Yard. Tell them what we're doing,' he suddenly commanded.

'What shall I say?'

'Say I wanted to swing by my home first.'

'And what do I tell them about us being together?'

'The truth, Kate,' he said bitterly. 'Tell them you found out something, met me, told me.'

'Okay,' she said reluctantly. Although she wasn't prepared to let go of her theory, it felt suddenly dangerous to have Hawksworth on this mission, dragging him in her wake. What had she started? Kate began to imagine what would happen if she was wrong. She could never face Jack again, and with her private life in tatters it felt terrifying to think her career might also go the same way. He would never forgive her if her accusation was empty.

'Sir, um —'

'Do it, Kate. They'll be wondering where we are. And hurry up. You'll lose the signal any second.'

Anne switched off the engine and took a few moments to look out across the rolling South Downs and admire their beauty and peace. All she could see for miles was the colour green, cows and sheep. Birdsong was all they could hear. Billy would die in a serene place — he was lucky, she thought.

He looked to be sleeping and she knew she had to work fast now. Using strong duct tape, she swiftly bound his hands and then, with handcuffs, secured him to the van's door handle. Now he was helpless. She slapped his face gently, flicked it with fresh water.

Her quarry roused from his doze. 'Why are we here?' He looked at his hands, frowning as he tried to understand. 'What's happening?' he asked, surprisingly lucid.

'Billy, I brought you here to talk first.'

He gave a dopey grin. 'And afterwards?' he asked, his tone filled with innuendo.

'Afterwards you're going to die,' she said flatly.

Billy's gaze had been drifting slightly but now his eyes seemed to clear and focus. 'Die?'

'I'm going to kill you.'

'But what —'

'Let's not waste time, Billy. Let me explain. The water you drank was laced with Rohypnol. You will lose consciousness soon — it's why you're feeling so drowsy now. Do you remember the drug, Billy? It's the same one that Pierrot used on me thirty years ago.'

'You've drugged me?' he asked, disbelieving.

'Just think about how you feel, Billy — you know I'm not lying.'

He pulled himself straight in the seat. 'Anne ... why, what's this —'

'What's this about?' She smirked. 'It's about the theft of my life. Your gang raped me; you killed my dog; you gave me a sentence of pregnancy, ripping away any chance I had of making something of myself. And then,' Anne swallowed back what could have been a sob, 'then when I'd resigned myself to life as a young mother, decided I would make a go of it and be good at it, you attacked me again. I nearly died, Billy, and my baby did die. And now I'm making sure you die too. But first, I need some information — something Clive and Mikey couldn't tell me.'

'Mikey? What are you talking about?' He shook his head, confused.

'You've been away. You haven't caught up fully with the deaths, have you, Billy?' She watched him shake his head dully. 'I found Mikey Sheriff and I killed him, and I did the same to your old mate Clive. After you, I'll find Phil Bowles — actually, I already know roughly where he is. My early snooping tells me he never left Hove, the sad sod, so he won't be hard to track down.'

'Anne, stop this. It's not amusing at all.'

'It's not meant to be. I'm deadly serious. You *are* going to die. You are going to pay for your sins.'

'Wait! This is crazy. You told me it was all behind you.' His words were streaming together. Time was so short.

'Behind me? Do you really think a person can put that sort of trauma behind them? You were the brainy one of the Jesters Club — surely you can work it out. No, Billy, I never put it behind me. All I did was pretend it never happened. I had quite a nice life, to tell the truth, and that seemed to act like a bandage over the deep wound that so injured me. But we risked it; we risked it all on the chance of having a family. It was my fault and we failed and I lost everything — the man I loved, the happy home, the quiet life I was living. I was left with nothing but misery and my own memories. I can see the question in your eyes, Billy, so save your breath — you haven't got much left. Let me answer your question.

'When my husband abandoned me about a year ago, life turned very dark and I began to experience the same feelings that I remembered from three decades ago. Suddenly I was there again, in that toilet block, or caught in that alleyway. Suddenly I could feel all the pain and fear again and the loss of my child.'

Billy's eyes widened as he struggled to sit forward, but Anne held up a hand. 'I loved that baby so much, Billy. In spite of his manner of conception, I wanted to be a good mother and lavish my child with all the affection and joy that was lacking in my life. The worst part is, I still do. Can you imagine that, Billy? Thirty years of heartache. Thirty years of pretence. I've covered my yearning for Peter so well — I'm a brilliant actress. But all of the pain is back, Billy, and I'm taking revenge for the ruination of my life and all of its misery.'

'You're planning to kill us all?' His question came out as a croak.

'You'll be my third victim. Mikey and Clive are already worm food. Just two to go after you.'

'Anne, please,' he beseeched, his eyes unfocused. 'I don't ...'

'Don't beg, Billy, it's pointless, as you should remember from both of those occasions when I begged you to help me.'

'But I couldn't —'

'Yes, you could. There were four of you and one of him. All you had to do was say no. But you were either too weak, too dim, too cruel or too drunk to care enough that someone you knew was being hurt before your eyes.'

Billy shook his head, terror flooding his expression now. He began to scream.

She waited until his throat was raw from yelling and his energy was sapped. 'No one can hear you. Look around you. Take one last look at your world because you're about to leave it.'

'None of us touched you, Anne. I swear it!' he blathered, spittle sliding down his chin. 'He was the one who raped you.'

'Yes, I've worked that out too,' she said, her tone telling him she was unimpressed by his news. She became matter of fact. 'Now, you can make this go a little easier on yourself if you'll tell me what you know about Pierrot.'

'Easier?'

'I'll explain in a minute. Tell me what you know and things can be different.'

Billy sat up a bit straighter but Anne knew he couldn't tell just how slumped in his chair he was. The drug was taking over now — they had barely minutes.

'I've only seen him once since that night on the pier, Anne, I swear it, and that was by accident. He was walking with his wife and child on Hove seafront and I was there too with my girlfriend.'

'And?'

Billy's eyes began to droop. 'I knew it was him, although it took him a moment or two to realise who I was.'

'Hurry up, Billy, you're slurring so badly I can hardly make out your words. I need this information and you need to give it to me if you're going to save yourself.'

'He pretended in front of his wife that he'd met me fishing but didn't properly introduce me to her and I was about eighteen so I didn't have the balls to introduce myself. I can remember staring at the child in surprise and he glared at me and said, "This is our son, Peter". Then the wife said, "He's adopted" and I just knew it was your baby. That it must have lived and he'd stolen it from you.'

He was *alive*!

Anne felt her vision tunnelling and her chest began to pound. In fact she was sure she could hear the blood rushing through her ears. Another woman called herself mother to Peter. She got to cuddle him, kiss him, comfort him. That woman had watched him grow, taught him to walk, run, ride a bike. She had cooked for him and bandaged scraped knees and read to him and tucked him into bed at night. Anne felt a murderous rage of jealousy consuming her. Deep inside her a pain blossomed like a plume of bright red, exploding upwards and outwards throughout her body and her fury stoked the fire that was this agony.

Through a tensed jaw Anne forced herself to take a steadying breath. She finally said, 'I want Pierrot's name.'

'Garvan Flynn. The wife mentioned they lived at Rottingdean ...' He trailed off, his eyes closing.

'Thank you,' Anne said, reaching for the half-finished bottle of water. 'Let's get this done with then, Billy.'

His eyes flew open again. 'Anne, wait! You said I could save myself.'

'Save yourself a lot of pain. Not save your life. That, I'm afraid, is forfeit, Billy. Now drink this.'

'No.' He began to cry.

'Oh, Billy, drink it all and there will be no pain. You'll just go to sleep.'

'We were kids, Anne. I don't . . . What are you going to do?'

'You don't want to know. Drink it.'

He shook his head, pursed his lips as a child might to prevent any liquid going in. Tears streamed down his face. 'Don't, Anne,' he begged. 'I'm sorry. I'm so, so sorry.'

'I know you are. I think you were thirty years ago, Billy, but you just weren't brave enough. None of you were, so I had to suffer for your cowardice. But so much worse is that you kept the terrible secret — all of you. None of you told the police what had occurred, and I was so frightened and beaten up, and completely bewildered by losing my baby, I wasn't thinking straight either. And then it was too hard, too terrifying, to relive it. All I could do was run away. So drink this, Billy, and save yourself a lot of torment. You'll go to sleep and that will be that.'

'Why didn't you just kill yourself?' he wept, a last dash of anger surfacing.

'I should have, I suppose,' she said, her voice even, 'but then you'd all have got away with it. This way, my son and I get justice.' She looked at Billy's drooping body. 'Let me help you swallow this.'

'No!' He began to fight her, twisting his head.

'Billy, don't! I'm going to cut you, hurt you,' she warned. 'I'm happy for you to feel nothing. Drink enough of this and your heart will stop. Stay conscious and you'll regret it.'

His weeping turned to sobs and Anne ran out of patience. She could tell his last objection had claimed every final ounce of will and energy. Now he was as helpless as her own baby had been all those years ago. She forced open his mouth and tipped most of the contents of the water bottle down his throat, closing his jaw hard so he couldn't spit it out.

'There,' she said, almost tenderly, satisfied that she'd kept her half of the bargain. 'That should do it. Goodbye, Billy.'

While she waited for Billy Fletcher's heart to stop, Anne thought about her son. The name Peter had stuck — how incredible. He would be twenty-nine by now. He could be married, a parent himself. He could also be dead ... for all his mother knew. Her face twisted into a mask of pain. *No, dear heaven, no, not again. So many children lost, let this one live, please let him be alive.*

And this was when Anne decided she was going to find Peter come hell or high water, and the only way she would be able to do that was if she was able to hunt down Pierrot. She had a full name now — Garvan Flynn — and it was unusual enough that people would remember it. And she had a place to start looking.

33

Garvan Flynn stood in the damp back garden and sucked on the first cigarette he had smoked in thirty years. They tasted very different these days, but he didn't care. His hands shook and he felt dizzy as the nicotine coursed through him. He coughed, sipped again at the lukewarm, sweet coffee and closed his eyes.

Nearby, Peter sat on the short flight of stairs staring into the backyard, silent, his outward calm belying the alarm he'd felt since his father had told him that providing his birth certificate would not be possible.

Their discussion the previous night had been interrupted by the arrival of Pat's mother. Her tears and recriminations had told Peter that Pat had been true to their pact and told her parents of their decision not to wed. Sheila and his mother had wept and talked into the night until Peter could no longer stand it. He had left, frustrated, with a promise to return the next day to talk to his father. He'd arrived only minutes previous, scowling and confused.

'Dad?' he finally said. 'You've got to tell me what this is about.'

'I know.'

'Why the hell are you smoking?'

'You know, Peter, this is the first cigarette I've touched since the night you were born.' Garvan sighed.

'That doesn't explain why you're smoking now. Mum will kill you!'

His father smiled privately, said nothing.

'Okay, Dad, I want to know what's going on. Last night, before Aunty Sheila arrived, you said something about not being able to give me a birth certificate — why not? I told you, I can't win this contract without it. I can't get a passport either, I've just realised. You know, Dad, this has never come up before because I've never needed a passport. Can you imagine it? I'm nearly thirty and I've never been anywhere, not even on school trips. I know Mum never trusted the school to keep me safe, but why was I more precious than any other child? I mean everyone else got to go on that Swiss ski trip, except me. I know you always tried to give me a big summer holiday in England, but I have to admit I always felt like the nerdy, over-protected kid.'

'You never said anything,' his father replied.

'Well, because it caused a row and I also knew we didn't have the money.'

The older man shrugged. 'You never chose to travel when you were old enough.'

'Dad, Mum and Aunty Sheila have been controlling my life. I've been partnered off with Pat since I was twenty-one. Remember how Mum used to carry on with my early girlfiends? Everyone was either a tart or too posh. There was always a problem. She was never going to let me see anyone but Pat, so me going off to Paris for the weekend or something was not going to happen because she would have imagined it was for an orgy. Anyway, I never had the money to go abroad. Every penny I earned you made me save for the flat.'

'And do you criticise us for ensuring your future? Look at you. You're sitting on a goldmine with that place.'

'Dad, I know. I'm not criticising you. I know it was a great investment, but I had to sacrifice the sort of fun that other people in their early 20's enjoy. Now I have to be more responsible, but it's time for me to travel and see a bit of the world. I am going to take holidays and enjoy my earnings. Plus I need the passport for work — they're talking about sending me to —'

'I can't give you your birth certificate, Peter, because I don't have one for you.'

'Okay, so I order a copy through Births, Deaths and Marriages. Where's the great problem?'

The older man grimaced.

'What does that look mean?' Peter said, exasperated, standing up and stomping into the garden. 'Dad, look at me. Tell me what's happening.'

His father's gaze seared him and the normally gentle voice sounded hard, cruel. Peter had never heard this tone before. 'There is no certificate for you. There never was. Your birth didn't happen, Peter.' Then he softened back to his normal tone and turned away. 'I'm sorry, son. I prayed it wouldn't come to this. I thought after all these years we'd got through it.'

'You're not making any sense! Dad, tell me it all. Whatever this is, just give me the truth and stop talking around it. Why don't I have papers? How could I have got to this age without a birth certificate?'

'You've never needed a passport, that's why. The rest was easy enough. When you began school we gave your date of birth, which we did know. Schools never check those things.' He shrugged. 'A record is born. From there on, the schools knew you and could verify who you were for your national insurance number. Your Saturday job at the petrol station was another tick. Our family doctor has known us since the day we moved into Rottingdean — he had no reason to question when you were born or even that you were adopted. He vouched for you, as did your teachers, when you went for your driving licence and university entrance.'

Peter looked stunned. 'You're right, I've never needed a birth certificate,' he said with amazement.

His father flicked his cigarette butt away into the compost heap. 'It's all about building a record. So long as that's squeaky clean, no one troubles you.'

'But, Dad,' Peter implored, 'I need a passport and I need a birth certificate for this job. Tell me why I don't have one.'

An eruption of anger drove his father's vicious response. 'Because, officially, you weren't born! Alright?'

'I wasn't born?' Peter murmured. He looked around at the neighbours' gardens, suddenly fearful of this odd conversation being heard.

'Don't worry, they've all gone away ... together. We've lived here for three decades, but we just get asked to keep an eye on the houses,' his father said bitterly.

'You need to explain what you mean, Dad. You said that you and Mum adopted me — there has to be paperwork attached to that.'

'There are no papers attached to you at all, Peter. You weren't born in a hospital or at home with attending medical people to witness your birth. As far as the authorities go, you weren't born at all.'

'That's ridiculous,' Peter scoffed. 'Here I am!'

'But no one knows who you truly are.'

'Dad, this is pissing me —'

'Except myself,' his father finished.

Peter rubbed his eyes beneath his glasses. He preferred to wear contact lenses but his eyes were too tired today. This was going to make it worse and he could feel a headache forming. 'Tell me,' he said.

'I bought you,' his father began, lighting another cigarette. 'No, don't interrupt me,' he said to his son who had turned angrily on him. 'Let me finish this, okay?'

Peter nodded, a mixture of disbelief and fear etched on his face.

'I bought you from a man I met in a pub. Your mother wanted a child so badly and . . .' His voice wavered.

'Dad.'

'And it seemed I was to blame, according to the doctors. The look on your mother's face when we found out broke my heart. I had let her down, but I had especially let her folks down. We're both only children. Our parents only had us to produce their precious grandchildren. The pressure . . . well, you can't possibly imagine. But her mother, your nanna, was such a bitch about it. You don't know what it's like to feel so controlled, so manipulated, by parents.'

'I think I do,' Peter said, more sourly than he'd intended.

'No, you and Pat not marrying is nothing compared to us not giving her mother a grandchild. Trust me on this! We're modern parents to you by comparison. You simply make a decision, inform us, weather the initial storm and then it's over. No, son, we had to pay our penance every day — Elsie questioning us constantly, and relatives and then friends, and then friends of friends, winking at each other, raising their eyebrows at the family gatherings. Your nanna couldn't bear it that her sister had a truckload of grandchildren and so she punished us. It was awful.

'Your mother — I can't blame her — finally broke down and admitted it was me. I was the reason we couldn't have children.

So she was let off the hook, you could say, and all the attention swung entirely to my shortcomings. And that only made it worse. Not only did I have a low sperm count, but their constant fuss and attention meant I could no longer even get it up. I just got angrier and angrier. It was a terrible time in our life and I considered leaving your mother so that she could find someone new, start again, have her family. I even thought about running away completely — going to Ireland or even overseas.'

'I can't believe I'm hearing this.'

'We've never told you this but we did separate for a while in 1974. It was the beginning of autumn. I remember the leaves on the ground in all the parks, but it was a short separation — we were together again by Christmas. It was a terrible time of rage and bitterness for me, but through it all I loved your mother and we couldn't bear to be apart. So we reunited and thought about adoption. But finding an English child was impossible — it seemed we were never going to be considered for anything other than Asian children, and your nanna would have howled each full moon if we'd gone down that path. We spent months looking into it, being constantly disappointed — you see, in the early 1970s young women were encouraged to keep their children. The government did everything to make it easy for them. And then this golden opportunity presented itself. A man offered to get me a child for five hundred pounds, no questions asked. It was all of our savings but we paid it gladly, and all I asked was that the child had dark hair, so that he or she could pass as our own.'

'You negotiated a deal for me?' Peter asked, incredulous.

'It was a mad time, son, you can't know what torment we were going through. Your mother wanted a child so badly that it warped us into taking such risks.'

'And Granny and Grandad were okay about this?'

'We didn't tell them. They went on that coach trip around America for ten weeks. By the time they came back, we just pretended you'd been adopted properly. They were so blinded by joy they didn't ask any more.'

'But what about Nanna and Pop? Surely they didn't go along with this?'

His father shrugged. 'Elsie did, and your pop did what he was told anyway. They weren't happy about it but they couldn't bear watching their daughter disintegrate. I thought your mother might lose her mind at one point, then you came along and suddenly our world righted itself. The madness had passed. Your mother's parents, especially Elsie, were practical people — when they heard about your background, they stopped fretting over it. They knew we could offer you a better life. It was Nanna who gave us the money to move to Rottingdean and start afresh, so no questions would be asked. We cut ourselves off from all the people we'd known before so we could have a year with you and then pass you off as our own, as though we'd got lucky and been blessed by Mother Nature.'

'So tell me about my parents,' Peter demanded.

Garvan shook his head. 'The father is unknown. The mother was a slut, I was told. She apparently slept around and you were one of many bastards. She took her money and ran. But we got you, Peter, and we gave you a life that you could never have known with her.'

'That's all irrelevant. It's the deceit, Dad, the fact that I've been led along all these years thinking I was adopted.'

'You were,' his father said, his tone beseeching.

'I wasn't adopted! I was stolen and that's the truth of it. How could you trust this bloke? Who is he?'

His father shrugged. 'Went by the nickname of Pierrot.'

'He didn't even give you a name?' Peter all but yelled. 'How could you trust that what he was telling you wasn't simply a pack of lies?'

'I told you, we were desperate. We would have believed anything. You had to live it to know what we were going through.'

'But, Dad, my blood parents could be decent people. How could you have known? Their son could have been stolen!'

'Impossible. Why wasn't there a hue and cry? Why weren't the local papers full of a kidnapping if a beloved son was stolen? There was nothing. If your biological mother cared, she had a strange way of showing it. No, Peter, your true mother is upstairs crying her eyes out, the same way she did on the day I walked in carrying you.'

On the last word, his father's voice, which had been threatening to break, did. Peter shook his head sadly, unsure of what to say next. He waited but his father said nothing. When he finally spoke again his voice was laden with sorrow.

'Dad, how did you do it? How did you pull this off?'

'It wasn't hard. We lived in Hove, and the week you came into our life we moved to Rottingdean, started again in a new neighbourhood, found new jobs, changed everything.'

'But what did the family think?'

'What did they think? They were told we'd been successful in finding a baby boy to adopt. No one was any the wiser. The only people who knew the truth were myself, your mother and her parents. As I told you, they gave us the money to move here. They loved you. With us you had a future. You were loved from the instant we all set eyes on you.'

'And Sheila and her family?'

'Sheila sewed your christening outfit! She doesn't know the secret we've kept for almost thirty years.'

'Thirty years ... seems a lot happened back then, Dad.'

Garvan looked startled. He swung around to Peter, his eyes narrowing. 'What do you mean?'

'Well, only last night you were glued to the telly. That bloke, the victim of that killer — you said you knew him thirty years ago.'

'Oh, that.'

'Yeah. You were — what? About twenty-seven?'

'Something like that. Anyway, that's irrelevant, we're talking about how your mother and I came to have you, Peter. Yes, I was twenty-seven, hot-headed, humiliated by my impotency, angry, desperate to please our families like any good son.'

'Dad, what you did was illegal.'

'But —'

'Actually, it's worse. What you did was criminal. You took someone else's child. The last time I checked, human trade was punishable by law.'

'We adopted you,' his father said firmly. 'It was just done a little differently.'

'A little differently?' Peter echoed, aghast. 'You paid someone to steal me from my parents!'

'And he paid the fat pig who gave birth to you and happily turned her back on you.'

'Until you can prove that, be careful, Dad. If I find out that my mother did not give me up willingly ...' Peter didn't finish. He didn't need to. The alarm in his father's face was enough to stop him making any further threat.

'What are you going to do?' Garvan asked.

'Find her!'

'Peter, no! It will kill your mother.'

'Listen to me. Last night I was the happiest person alive. Today, I'm shattered. I can't think straight. Last night I didn't care who had given birth to me — I knew only two parents and

390

loved them blindly. Today I must know who carried me in her belly. I must!'

'Why?' his father begged.

'To set things straight. To be sure that she gave me away willingly and didn't have me stolen from her.'

'I beseech you, son.' Garvan reached for the boy he had loved since that day he'd handed the infant Peter to the woman now staring out of the upstairs window at them, weeping uncontrollably. 'Don't open this box that has been sealed shut for all these years. Please.'

Although it pained him to do so, Peter pushed his father's hands aside. 'I have to, Dad. I couldn't live with myself otherwise. And, frankly, I don't know how you and Mum have done so for my whole life.'

34

Kate leaned against the wall next to where Jack was crouched before a door, staring at its lock.

'Sir, this is illegal!'

'Have you ordered the warrant?'

She let out an angry breath. 'Yes, while you fetched your gear.' She glanced down at the roll of miniature tools Jack had unfurled minutes earlier.

'Then you'll know that on a weekend we're hours away at best from having a legal search warrant.'

'But —'

'Sssh!' he ordered, trying to concentrate. Then he stopped, looked back at her. 'You set this in motion. Now, either you're right and congratulations, or you're wrong and you'll never be able to look me in the eye again, let alone feel comfortable at the Yard.'

'Threats aren't going to help —'

'I'm not threatening you, Kate, I'm simply telling you how it is. You've gone too far now with this theory to back off. You've meddled in my life and you've presented a scenario that you believed in enough half an hour ago to blackmail me over. So don't baulk now that I'm taking it seriously.'

'Blackmail?'

'What else do you call it when you threaten to go to the Super unless I explore this crazy notion fully?'

'I wouldn't call it blackmail,' she shot back. 'I'd call it good policing.'

'Then trust your hunch, Kate. I have to, but then I have no choice, do I?'

Nothing was said for a few moments as Jack worked.

'Where did you learn to do this?' Kate asked eventually. 'Not cadet school, I'm guessing.'

'I know a couple of guys on the Ghost Squad.'

'You look like a pro.'

He gave a humourless smile. 'This is my first time for real.'

Again, a silence fell between them until Jack gripped the doorknob, twisted and it clicked open. He looked up at Kate and she could see the loathing in his eyes for what he had just done.

'Wait!' she said.

He paused while she gathered her thoughts, then said, 'Well, Sherlock?'

'I just don't think you'd do this if you thought it was as crazy as you're making out.'

'Are you sure about that?'

She nodded. 'Listen, before we both break the law, can I just say something?'

He wrapped up his tools, put the roll in his pocket and straightened. He gave her a hard, unblinking stare. Kate swallowed, realising suddenly how tight and dry her throat was.

'Jack, I just want you to know how sorry I am that you're in this position and I'm still hoping I'm wrong. If I am, I'll resign immediately and you can reassign me to parking attendant, but unless I've never read you right, then I think you also have some doubts. Tell me you do.'

Jack's hand gripped the doorknob. 'Let's go in.'

'No, please, tell me first that you are harbouring some sort of suspicion.'

He sighed and a bleak pause reigned in the corridor before he finally answered her. 'Apart from the fact that Sophie claimed she was on a train to Exeter this morning that I now know never existed, something's been nagging at me.'

'What is it?'

Jack shrugged. 'She's much too toned, her body's too heavy with muscle to be wheelchair-ridden. Her limbs should be more wasted. She hides her arms. And now that I really think on it, I reckon she's wearing coloured lenses. I've always thought her eyes to be curiously dark. Perhaps beneath they are blue ... intense blue, as Moss once described.'

He lowered his head and Kate felt a strong urge to step forward and put her arms around him. Instead she said, 'Go on.'

'Well, I'm guessing that if Sophie is Anne then she must have found out I was going to be heading up Operation Danube before I did. Sharpe appointed me on my birthday but she'd moved into this apartment a couple of months earlier.'

'So what does that mean?' Kate frowned.

Jack's mind irrationally leapt to DCI Deegan as the villain, but he dismissed the thought as quickly as it arrived. 'Well, probably that she's infiltrated the Met.'

'Oh, my god,' Kate breathed.

'Come on,' he said. 'Let's do this.'

They stepped inside the apartment and moved into the living area. His arrival into somewhere so recently familiar prompted a bittersweet sensation in Jack: memories of lovemaking and laughter were suddenly tarnished by doubts and dark thoughts of murder.

Kate broke the difficult silence. 'She's got great style.'

'Mmm,' he muttered. 'When she's not out murdering people, she's an interior designer and property developer.'

'Sorry, Jack, I —'

'Don't,' he warned, his jaw working to keep his emotions in check. 'Right, you do a search of the apartment. I'm going to fire up her computer.'

'What are you going to look for?'

'The history mainly. I'll see what she's been hunting on the net, check her email, perhaps see if she's kept any files that might point to the victims. I'm no expert — we can take the computer in if we need the techno wizards to find out more.'

'Unlikely that she'd be silly enough to leave that information so accessible.'

'Unlikely also that her home would be broken into by her lover who is now under the impression that she's a serial murder. But here I am.'

Jack watched Kate suck in a breath and whatever retort was coming back at him. He wanted to hold on to the anger and Kate was the easiest of targets because she was the cause of this pain. Although the worst part of this disturbing sitution was the vicious certainty that his colleague was right.

Anne looked at her watch. It was nearing five and the day was darkening swiftly. She didn't want the headlights of the van to be noticed by any potential witnesses so had planned to leave the South Downs before darkness fell fully. That would mean she could leave Billy's body at St Ann's Well Gardens during the night. The location had a crisp symmetry for Anne. So far she'd dumped bodies in a public toilet and an alleyway, both symbolic of her own memories of her childhood trauma. It was fitting that she leave at least one corpse in a park. Hove Park would have been the ideal choice, but since the great storm of

1987 her childhood playground had lost virtually all of its woodland and was now a huge, open expanse with houses on all sides. The chance of someone seeing her there was too high. And so the pretty gardens at quiet St Ann's Well would do instead. Her own name aside, it was still a park in Hove and also in very close proximity to the home of the policeman who had tried so hard to help her when she was in that hospital bed, still shaking from the birth and loss of her baby. She could remember Sergeant Moss as clearly as if it was yesterday — his eyes filled with regret and his kindly voice, the smell of tobacco that clung to him and the outrage she sensed he felt on her behalf. She had wanted to tell him everything and yet something prevented her. Whatever it was, it kept her throat closed and her voice silent. She had been in a deep state of shock and disbelief then, had built a shell around herself that she permitted no one to break through. Although she'd taken the time to hunt down where he lived these days, she held no grudge against Moss. In fact, Billy was her gift to him. A response to all those questions she'd been unable to answer so many years ago.

Anne looked at Billy. She'd forced enough of the drugged water down his throat to kill him she was sure. She hoped so. Leaning across, she felt at his warm neck for a pulse, her fingertips scratching on the stubble of his chin and neck. Billy had borne out his promise of good looks. The lines of age added depth and interest to what had once been just boyishly handsome. Stray strands of his dark hair rested against her hand and Anne could imagine how today's William Edward Fletcher could likely win almost any woman who caught his attention and was open to his charm. She wondered about his former wife and the present girlfriend and whether Billy could ever sustain a long-term, honest relationship after what she imagined was probably years of philandering. She herself had found it easy enough to lure him, which suggested that Edward the man wasn't really so different from Billy the boy — easily led. She decided that was being harsh and she should give him the benefit of the doubt. Poor Billy. He really had sounded so remorseful. She believed he had genuinely wished he could turn back time and change the course of their individual histories. Perhaps what had happened to her had been eating away at him for years, which might explain why, against his instincts, he'd agreed to spend time with her. Perhaps Billy had been trying to atone for his sins.

'Only one way to do that,' she murmured softly, caressing his dead face. 'Rest now, Billy, and I'll take my own recompense.' She was glad that the man's heart had finally stopped beating and his struggles were over.

Jack could hear Kate behind him moving systematically through the kitchen. Both of them had donned gloves, which he'd grabbed from his own apartment, and they worked in silence. Kate tiptoed around, even though Jack had assured her that no one could hear anything, especially as his was the apartment below this one. There was something niggling at him about Sophie's living room but he hadn't had time to think it through, needing to focus his attention on her computer, which was surely the best indication of his lover's interaction with the outside world.

Sophie's most recent internet history showed only ten hits — mainly train timetables, which was reassuring, and the telephone directory, which was also feasible for any wheelchair-bound person. It wasn't enough to exonerate her though, and Jack knew it. He dug deeper, looking back over histories from previous days, and his dread deepened when he saw she had visited the

Brighton and Hove Council sites. That in itself wasn't damning considering her occupation, but she'd also visited other Hove sites, including a variety of bed and breakfast spots, some restaurants and, curiously, a park called St Ann's Well Gardens.

Kate came up behind him. 'Anything?'

'She's certainly interested in Hove.' He took her through the various sites Sophie had visited.

'Well,' Kate began and then shrugged. 'Sounds to me like she was planning a hot weekend for you both.'

He grimaced. 'Yes, except this St Catherine's Lodge, which she seems to have hit several times, doesn't sound at all logical considering she's in a wheelchair and they make no mention of whether there's invalid access. It sounds like an old place with lots of stairs.'

'Lifts, surely?'

'Yes, but no mention of any sort of ease of wheelchair use. Knowing Sophie as I do, she's too practical to risk not being as independent as possible. She'd want wheelchair ramps and a lift at the very least.'

'Well, perhaps she called to check. What are you saying anyway?'

Jack opened his palms. 'I don't know ... simply that she's been dwelling on sites in Hove, which possibly supports your theory.'

'What about West Pier?'

Jack closed his eyes with realisation and swung around to where the photographs had been. 'Ah,' he said, a sigh in his tone, 'they're gone.'

'Gone?' She followed his line of sight.

'The photos — they were over there. They looked brilliant, very haunting.'

'Is that a clue to Sophie?'

'Just more damning but inconclusive information to support your theory.'

'Do you want to do the bedrooms with me?' Kate asked.

'Don't want to intrude, eh?' Jack said, an edge of bitterness in his tone.

'Please don't make this harder than it is.'

He sighed again. 'Okay, let's do it. I've never seen the bedroom myself.'

Surprised at the comment, Kate followed him silently towards the two rooms still left to search.

Anne unshackled her prey and stripped away his bindings, then released the lock on his seat until it reclined as far as possible. Entering the van from the back, she hauled his body into the main empty space of the vehicle. And then she waited, allowing his body to do what it must as its organs registered death. While she waited, she watched the sky lose most of its blue, becoming a fiery pink. 'Shepherd's delight,' she whispered as she finally turned back to her gruesome task.

She pulled on the stocking mask and worked fast now, easing Billy from his trousers and shirt. A single stab wound punctured his trim, lightly muscled abdomen. It was seeping blood but very little. Anne's early patience meant the blood pressure in Billy's body had dropped sufficiently to prevent copious amounts of blood spurting forth during her work on the fresh corpse. Still, the van had plenty of blood traces to incriminate her. As careful as she was, and despite all the cleaning, Anne knew that if the van were found and traced to her it would reveal forensic evidence of Michael Sheriff, Clive Farrow, William Fletcher and herself, of course.

The police were closing in fast. She wondered, as she turned her knife to Billy's crotch, whether Jack had begun to doubt her.

She couldn't imagine how he would connect Sophie with the serial killer he was hunting, but Jack was sharp and he surrounded himself with equally clever people. She'd made one mistake she knew of — mentioning the shirt. He hadn't said anything, so she was hoping it might have gone over his head, especially as it sounded as though plenty of people had teased him that day. Perhaps her comment had blended in with the rest. She couldn't count on that, however. Then there was that Kate woman who had been decidedly aggressive towards her. She couldn't imagine why at first, then she'd heard the tension in Jack's voice when she'd quipped that Kate was probably in love with him.

She delicately placed Billy's genitals into his hand. 'That's for the rape, Billy,' she murmured before going to work on his lips.

Perhaps her remark had inadvertently awakened memories of an old office fling between Jack and Kate? There was no telling. But getting to know Hawksworth had surprised her. What had begun as a purely strategic move on her part had very quickly turned into a genuine romance. She hadn't been ready to like him — despite his good looks and charm — and she certainly hadn't been prepared for love again. She was sure Jack could have any woman he wanted and yet he hadn't appeared to be involved with anyone when she came on the scene. If there ever had been a situation with Kate, that was behind him. And now that Anne knew him better, she could appreciate that Jack was the real deal.

In her early planning, she had simply hoped to use Jack to get close to the case and find out how much the police knew. She'd got herself into New Scotland Yard by pretending to be a mature student enrolled in a forensic psychology degree. It was easy enough to gain entry to the admin unit, and from there to ingratiate herself with key members of staff. One in particular, Elaine, PA to the head of the operations planning division, had been most helpful in explaining how the bigger cases were assigned. DCI Hawksworth's name had come up as one of the Yard's rising stars and Elaine had been unable to help herself when Anne had probed as to whether there were any juicy cases about to be assigned. It seemed Jack was a favourite across the board and Elaine couldn't resist speculating that the dishy DCI would probably head up the investigation into a suspected serial killer case that was about to break.

It had been trickier finding out where DCI Hawksworth lived, but Anne had managed to track him home to the mansion apartment building one evening, and from there it had been relatively simple to enter his life. She hadn't imagined for a moment that her intention of using him for information would be replaced by genuine pleasure in his company. What had seemed so easy and tactical had become dangerous and highly impractical to her cause. Jack was now a liability to her mission, and she realised with a deep sadness that they would not have another night together. Again she was reminded what a curse she was and how everyone she loved ultimately deserted her. Jack would be no different. She could already imagine how his expressive face would contort into despair and disbelief once the truth came out — and it would, she knew that now.

She shook her head free of thoughts about Jack — there was no more time to dwell on what might have been. She piled the mess that had been Billy's lips on top of the quivering flesh in his hand. 'And now you have a permanent smile, Billy. You don't need your clown mask any more. Although I'm sorry that it's changed your looks so dramatically,' she said, wiping the blade on his trousers.

There was just one more task. She reached for a small can.

'I would have preferred you to do this, of course,' she said to Billy's now ruined face. 'I made Mikey and Clive smear the paint on their faces themselves while I explained what it meant. But we ran out of time for you. The police already know you were my next target, which means I have to get rid of you fast, so I'm going to do the paintwork for you and then we're going on a short journey — your last journey, Billy — so I can lay you to rest at St Ann's Well Gardens. It's not Hove Park, but that's not for anyone else to know, is it? This is between us alone, Billy. You and me and the rest of the Jesters Club. All of us know what this is about.'

She smoothed back his hair from his forehead and, using a screwdriver, eased the lid from the sample pot of paint. She dipped two gloved fingers into the bright blue liquid and carefully daubed it on Billy's cheeks.

'You see, Billy, real clowns refuse to wear blue in any of their make-up. They're highly suspicious of the colour. Strange, isn't it? I love the colour myself. It's the colour of the ocean and the sky, of glaciers — the very essence of nature. It's also the colour of Rohypnol, I suppose, and the pale hue of death. I thought it fitting that all of you clowns should be painted with the unlucky blue of your profession. Your luck ran out when I found you, Billy ... or should I call you Coco? I haven't forgotten those names. I know who Pierrot is now, and I think Bozo was Clive, Mikey was Blinko, and that leaves Coco and Cooky. Phil was always so enamoured of food I think we'll leave Cooky to him. I'll look forward to calling him by his jester name. Now, you of course, are dark and tasty like chocolate. Yes, I think Coco suits you, in spite of the spelling.'

Anne wiped her hands clean and sat back to admire her gruesome handiwork. Treacherous thoughts of Jack returned to taunt her. Did he doubt her? Kate was unfriendly — did she suspect Sophie of lying? The conversation with the nosey female detective had been fraught with danger: talk of the weather in

Devon, the mention of West Pier — both were stupid, damaging slips. Everyone makes mistakes, she wasn't perfect, but she shouldn't have been drawn on it, even though she knew all there was to know about West Pier, the location of her personal tragedy. But surely neither of them would piece anything together yet, although her lie about the train might undo her. If Jack didn't believe her and checked the schedule, he'd soon discover there was no earlier train. Why would he doubt her though, unless nosey Kate started stirring trouble? Jack had no reason to mistrust her. As far as he was concerned, she'd be home tomorrow and he'd cook her dinner. She'd have to keep that pretence going. 'But it will never be the same,' she whispered to herself. 'That's why I took down the photographs.'

Was it insurance against immediate discovery ... or was it some kind of subconscious attempt to lead him to her? Anne wasn't sure, couldn't answer her own question.

'We'll just have to wait and see, won't we?' she said to herself as she leapt lightly from the van's back doors. She returned to the driving seat and gunned the engine.

35

Jack stood on the threshold of the second bedroom, unable to move. Kate was looking at him with a mixture of alarm and sympathy. His face had lost its expression of disbelief. Now he just looked shocked.

'Perhaps there's a reasonable explanation,' she tried.

'Rehabilitation, you think?' he replied darkly.

Kate nodded, embarrassed. She felt as though her breathing had become constricted such was the tension swirling around them.

'I somehow don't think a person in Sophie's condition is capable of using most of this training equipment,' he went on, 'but thanks again for trying, Kate.'

'Sir ...' She reached out to lay a hand on his arm but Jack stepped back as if burned.

'Don't touch anything else. Ring the Yard, get that warrant and a full forensics team into this place. Let's get out of here,' he ordered.

'Right,' she said, feeling more bleak than she'd thought possible. She moved past him, intending to leave him to his misery for a few moments, but then paused. 'I'm so sorry.'

All he did was nod, and she left him to his thoughts while she made the call, returning with the news that the warrant was ready.

Jack stalked away from the bedroom that had revealed Sophie's secret. 'Good, have it served. You and Brodie handle it. In the meantime, get the word out that we're looking for a woman who goes by two names. I can provide a detailed description, although I suspect she's employing various disguises.' His voice was leaden.

'Yes, sir. I'll just turn off the computer.' She did so, feeling the tension in the room rise behind her. When the computer had sighed into silence she turned back. 'Shall we go?'

'I'm going to call her.'

'Is that wise?'

'It would be normal. I don't want her to think we're on to her.'

'I'll be outside then.'

'Get Sarah to coordinate a small team to trace passports for Anne McEvoy or Sophie Fenton.'

'She could be using an alias.'

'I realise that. But, for now, let's get those names into Immigration's security checks and across to Interpol. I want a full ports warning sent out immediately.'

As Kate was turning to leave, Sophie's home phone rang. They both froze.

'What shall we do?' Kate looked spooked.

'Leave it, she has an answering machine. It may divert to her mobile, of course.'

They waited for five rings and the answering machine picked up the call. Jack heard Sophie's gentle voice apologising for not being available and asking the caller to leave a message.

Kate spoke over Sophie's voice. 'I could pretend to be her,' she offered tentatively.

'No warrant covers that,' he replied. 'Let's just listen.'

A shaky voice, an old woman it sounded like, spoke through the machine's receiver. 'Sally? Are you there? Oh dear. Look, it's Mrs Shannon here, luv. I don't want to sound ungrateful about our arrangement but the news reports are asking about a white van that this murderer has been using. It's in the papers and on the telly — I'm sure you haven't missed it, luv. Now, I do like the money, and you've never given me a moment of bother, but I'm a bit nervous that the police are going to come poking around when they hear I store your van in my garage. And it's white, dear, you get my meaning. I know it's silly but I don't want the police knocking on my door, what with me telling fibs to Social Security. Don't bring your van back here, luv. I hope you understand and don't think too badly —' The answering machine beeped loudly, cutting the old girl off before she could finish what she was saying.

'Oh my god, Jack, it's definitely her,' Kate whispered, her hands flying to cover her mouth.

Jack stared at the answering machine, ashen. All hope was gone. 'Get someone to trace that call. We have to find that woman in case she knows where Sophie is.'

He simply couldn't bring himself to call her Anne . . . not yet.

Operation Danube was thrumming with excitement. It was nearing seven and although everyone had worked a long day when they hadn't expected to, and most had gone without anything more nourishing than tea or instant coffee and stale biscuits, no one had any plans to go home.

Jack had just retreated to his office to call the Superintendent, having closed a meeting with the team. Each had their jobs to do and every scrap of information on Anne McEvoy and Sophie Fenton was being collated now. He listened to the phone ring at his boss's house. Although he felt sick at heart, he knew honesty was the only way to deal with Sharpe.

'Hello?'

'Cathie, it's Jack.'

'Hello, dear, how's everything?'

'A bit frantic, actually, I won't lie.'

'It always is, Jack. Martin said you might call over, although apparently we can't twist your arm to stay for a meal.'

'That's right and now it's all gone pear-shaped, Cathie, I'm so sorry. It's why I'm calling. Something's broken on the case.'

Her voice changed instantly from sweet and welcoming to brisk and professional. Cathie had been a senior policeman's wife for too many years not to recognise the tone of her caller's voice and that he needed her husband swiftly. 'I'll get Martin.'

'Thanks,' Jack said into the vacuum as Cathie put him on hold.

Barely a minute passed before Sharpe's voice growled into his ear. 'Tell me we've got a good lead, Jack.'

'Yes, sir, we have. We believe we know who our killer is.'

'Hell's bells! Wait, I'm going to take this in my office. Hold a sec, Jack.' The line went dead again and Jack closed his eyes, wondering how Martin was going to react to the news. 'Tell me,' Sharpe said eagerly, returning to Jack.

'Her name is Anne McEvoy,' he began, and told his boss everything he knew about Anne's trauma-ridden childhood and brought him up to date.

'She's held a grudge for thirty years?' Sharpe asked incredulously.

'We've spoken to Tandy. He seems to feel it's plausible that some fresh emotional disturbance in her life could have reopened the old wounds that she thought had healed, or at least had managed to push away for all of this time.'

'So where are we with this? How close to putting her in custody?'

'We believe she's in the Brighton and Hove area again, sir. We fear that she might already have Fletcher captive, although that's still open to question.'

'What's your gut tell you, Jack?'

'I think she has him, sir. I think unless something happens very fast to enable us to find this van of hers, then we'll be looking at another corpse.'

His Super gave a sound of deep disgust. 'How could she know what we were doing? From what you told me this morning, the Hastings boys were all but on top of Fletcher.'

'It's not that she knows what we're doing, sir, I think it's more that we've been playing catch-up and she sensed we were getting close and most likely sped up her own activities.'

Jack stared at his diary, noted that someone's red pen had left giveaway dots near the heart he'd doodled a few days ago. It had to be Kate and he felt his gut twist. Today he had been accused of sleeping with one of his DIs, and he hadn't thought it could get worse until he'd worked out that, despite all the heated denials to her fiancé, she was in fact carrying a torch for him. Now, as if life was deliberately kicking him while he was down, he had discovered the woman he was sleeping with was the serial killer Britain was hunting. He imagined what kind of headlines it would make in the press if word of this got out. He closed his eyes in shame as the Super ranted.

'... and now we've lost Phillip Bowles. That's all four of them she's effectively killed.'

'I don't think it would be fair to blame her for Bowles, sir.'

'Not in legal terms, no, but you know what I mean, Jack.'

'Yes, sir, I do.'

'So where do we go from here?'

'I've got Swamp heading over to St Albans where this Mrs Shannon has apparently been garaging Anne McEvoy's van. We traced her call to Anne's answering machine, and although I doubt she knows very much, there could be something.'

'What else?'

'The housekeeper from the Castle Hotel has been located. She's been on a trek of some sort — no telephone contact. She verifies that a woman claiming to be an old friend of Michael Sheriff ran into him on the evening he disappeared.' He heard his Super let out an angry breath. 'I won't go into the details, sir, but we suspect this was Anne McEvoy, as also the hoax call from the hospital.'

'Right,' Sharpe said. 'Any more good news?'

'Brodie's found the roadster that she picked Clive Farrow up in outside the fish and chip shop. She hired it in Manchester apparently and drove it south, returning it two days later.'

'Why has it taken us this long to find that bloody car?'

Jack took a steadying breath. Martin Sharpe hadn't yet heard the worst, and he wasn't going to take it at all well if the roadster was forcing his blood pressure up. 'Sir, it was a small boutique rental place — she chose cleverly. The guy who owns it has been in the Caribbean for the last two and half weeks and has only just seen the call to action. He came up with the details pretty swiftly on his return, but that explains the hold-up on that piece of the puzzle.'

'Okay, so how does this help us now?' the Super said, somewhat wearily. 'Do we have an address we trust?'

'Yes, sir.' He swallowed. 'It's in Highgate.'

'Highgate, London?'

'I'm afraid so, sir.'

'Good grief!' Sharpe exclaimed.

No turning back now. 'It's worse than that, sir, far worse,' Jack said, lowering his voice. 'Any chance we can meet?'

'What's up, Jack? I don't like the sound of this.'

'And won't, sir, when you hear it all, but I can't tell you over the phone.'

Sharpe understood. His protégé needed to speak off the record where no conversations were monitored. 'Where?'

'Fancy a pint?'

'I'll see you at the Star in half an hour.'

'Thank you, sir.'

Jack put the phone down, grim-faced, and looked up to catch a soft glance of concern from Kate. She was at her desk, listening to someone on the phone. He gestured for her to come in when she was free. She arrived moments later.

'That was news from Fletcher's mother. Seems he did say something to her about meeting an old schoolfriend.'

Jack sighed. It was already too late for Billy, he suspected. 'I told the Super. Well, that's not true. I haven't told him everything yet, but he's meeting me shortly to hear it all. He knows there's something unpleasant coming at him.'

Kate nodded.

'I want to tell the team,' Jack went on.

'Are you sure?'

'I have to. I'd expect any one of you to come clean with me.'

'Yes, you're right. But only the core members need to know.'

'Get them together, will you. I'd order cakes for a coffee break but I'm not in a party mood.'

'They aren't either. We're all holding our breath and waiting for news of another body. I told them as much as I could . . .' She trailed off, uncomfortable to say more.

He nodded glumly. 'I have to find out how Sophie learned about me being appointed to the case. She moved much too fast not to have inside information.'

'I agree. Want me to look into it?'

'You don't have time.'

'I'll make time,' she insisted, adding more gently, 'I want to.'

'Okay, see what you can dig up. The commissioner would have sent out the directive, but I know Commander Drewe was on the SMT that set up Operation Danube as soon as Farrow's body was discovered. But I know how these things work. When Sheriff's body was discovered, the mutilations would have alerted the decision-makers that this killing had the potential to be repeated. They'd have taken steps on the off-chance that another similar murder occurred. I know Superintendent Sharpe recommended me to head up the case if required, but I don't think anyone from Sharpe upwards would have said anything to anyone about me until it was formally announced at the media conference. It was coincidence that the apartment in my building was free, but irrelevant really. She could have moved in anywhere close by and achieved the same result.'

'Accidentally on purpose bumping into you?' Kate offered.

'Any number of scenarios leap to mind. A pretty blonde and me single. How could I resist? That said, Sophie had to have had at least four or five weeks' notice to get set up in the apartment before I met her.'

'So, admin staff, right?' Kate asked, frowning. Jack nodded, pleased as usual with the DI's fast-moving mind. 'Why don't I begin with the Super's secretary.'

'Helen, yes, good idea. She's much too wily to be bandying around information, but she will know who the gossips are, where the leak might have occurred, and will certainly point you in the right direction.'

'Do I tell her why I'm asking?'

'Hell, yes. She'll learn soon enough anyway.'

'I'm on to it. See you in a minute then.'

Jack waited for her to go and then finally found the courage to dial the number he'd wanted to for the past couple of hours.

She answered almost instantly. 'Jack, hi, I've been longing to hear from you.'

'How was lunch? How's Mrs Fenton?' he asked as casually as he could.

'Lunch was sufficiently terrific that Mrs Fenton's sleeping it off.'

He'd got what he wanted from her. She was pursuing the lie.

'You sound out of breath,' he commented, doodling hard on his pad to keep his mind empty of the anger.

'Yeah, I hurried — if you can call it hurrying at my speed — to pick up the phone,' she said, taking a furtive glance behind her at Billy's corpse.

'Are you outside?' he asked.

'I'm in a hire car now,' she said, slamming the van door and putting the phone on loudspeaker. She quickly started the engine.

'I didn't know you drove. You're okay to talk?'

'I'm not a complete cripple, Jack. Of course I can drive. And, yes, I can even talk at the same time, but forgive me if I'm a little distracted while I'm managing things in the car.' She laughed but he didn't. 'Jack, are you alright?'

'Just a big day. I'm still at the office.'

'How's it going?'

'Not great.'

'No progress?'

'Yes, actually. But the deeper you get into these operations, the uglier it always is.'

'So what have you turned up? Anything that will help you get this killer?'

He hesitated, wondering whether to bait Sophie. He opted not to at this stage. She'd tricked him with such ease that she was obviously far too smart to be deceived, especially when she was on the alert for hints of discovery.

'I don't really want to talk about the killer,' he said. 'I'd hoped you could cheer me up.'

'I will tomorrow.'

'So you're definitely coming home tomorrow evening?'

'Absolutely. I can't wait to get away from Devon, to be honest.'

'Well, that's great. I'll be waiting for you.'

'You sound really odd, you know.'

'Sorry. Guess I miss you.'

'Ah, that's more like it. Thank you. I've been thinking about you all day.'

'Me too,' he said truthfully. 'I've got to go, Sophie. I'll see you tomorrow.' He ended the call, unable to keep the bile down a moment longer. He dialled Sarah's extension. It was a pointless, last-ditch effort to understand.

'DS Jones,' she said, sounding distracted.

'It's Jack, sorry to disturb you.'

'No problem, sir. I was just closing down some computer files — apparently there's a meeting in a minute.'

'There is. Can I ask you to look into something for me?'

'Sure.'

'Can you hunt down a Mrs Fenton who lives at North Molton in Devon? I'm pretty sure it's a small enough place that not having her Christian name shouldn't pose a problem.' He gave her the address.

'What am I tracking her for, sir? Is there anything specific to look for?'

'Her existence,' he said abruptly.

★ ★ ★

As the van idled at the lights, Anne allowed her thoughts to wander sadly back to Jack and the fact that there could never be a future for them. Everything about Sophie was fabricated: the bright gold of her hair, the cosmetic enhancements on her perfect teeth, the coloured contact lenses. Only the body was Anne's, sculpted over years of hard training and careful eating, but even that had been disguised in the wheelchair. Sophie was simply a vehicle for Anne: a tool to get her close to the source, close to the one person she knew could get in the way of her full revenge. It was unplanned that she'd develop such genuine feelings for Jack, but, she told herself again, it was a relationship based on lies and misdirection and was always going to end. Had the end just arrived? Jack had sounded strained, remote. Granted, he had plenty on his mind, but he usually found some warmth for her, no matter what was happening at work. Had the bitchfaced sidekick set off warnings in his mind?

Anne tracked back through the day. The first bell that could have sounded the death knell of their relationship was almost certainly Jack not finding her on the train platform at Paddington. She thought she'd sidetracked him adroitly but perhaps not. Jack was a police officer after all, and he didn't get to the position of DCI without some genuine talent, no matter who was pushing his barrow. So perhaps he did some checking up on the timetable and discovered there were no earlier trains. It was the only trick she could pull out of the hat when he had put her on the spot and she'd known as she said it that she was laying herself bare to scrutiny. Nevertheless, more must have occurred for him to become suspicious enough to take it further. But Anne's internal radar was giving off signals of dread; she was convinced Jack was on to her. Whether he had made the final connection she had no idea, but his edgy tone suggested something was amiss between them and, unless he had stumbled upon something, there was no reason for it ... not even work stress. No, it had to be his nosey colleague, that Kate woman. And then daylight switched on in her mind as she realised the crucial error she'd made.

Cars honked with irritation that the van hadn't lurched forward immediately the lights had turned green. She apologised, holding a hand to her rear-view mirror, and quickly pulled off the road into a parking spot to consider this new development.

How could she be so stupid! She'd become familiar with the phone system at Scotland Yard when she'd posed as a research student there: *Every phone call recorded. Every phone number flashing up on the consoles.* Now she understood how she'd given herself away to Kate.

'Bitchface was smart enough to register I wasn't calling from Devon,' she murmured. 'And she's told Jack.'

That was it. It had to be. Kate's jealousy, or whatever was driving that bitter tone in her voice when they'd spoken earlier today, had prompted the police officer to bring Sophie's lie into the open. Kate could have left it alone, or she might never have noticed the number, but neither of those scenarios had occurred. Not only had Kate noticed the Brighton number — damn her — but she had decided she'd tell Jack to boot. And assuming he had checked the train timetables, this news would have set off a much bigger explosion in his mind.

Anne shook her head to clear her thoughts and tried to reassure herself that Jack couldn't possibly have connected Sophie Fenton with the serial killer just yet, no matter how suspicious he might be about his new girlfriend telling fibs. But doubts persisted.

She rang Mrs Becker. 'Hello, Traute, it's Sophie here. How are you?'

'Ah, Miss Fenton, I'm alright, thank you. I —'

Anne didn't give the older woman the chance to get into one of her long conversations. 'I was just wondering, have you seen Mr Hawksworth today?' The older woman hesitated and Anne decided to help her along. 'I'm not sure if you know this, Mrs Becker, but Jack and I are seeing each other. We blame you for bringing us together, actually,' and she gave a soft laugh.

'I can put two and two together,' Mrs Becker replied in her thick accent.

Anne laughed again, began crafting the lie. 'I figured you would. Anyway, I'm trying to reach him but I can't find him at work or home and I'd promised him I'd call him this evening. I don't know what to do. I thought you might have seen him,' she prompted.

'Well, that's what I'm telling you, Miss Fenton. His people are here. They're in your apartment.'

Anne froze. She felt as though she couldn't breathe. 'Pardon?' she finally croaked.

'Ja, your apartment has loads of police people walking in and out of it.'

'Mrs Becker, what's happening?' Anne said, already guessing but needing to have it confirmed by someone else.

'Mr Hawksworth came to the apartments with a woman — his colleague, he told me later — but I didn't speak to them at first, just saw them out of the window. I'm on the first floor after all, with a very good view of the street, and you know I miss nothing.' Anne wanted to reach down the phone and throttle the old busybody. 'Anyway, he came banging on my door not very long later and told me not to be alarmed but a team of investigators — ja, that's the word he used — investigators would be coming to enter your apartment.'

'What time was this?'

'About, ah, let me see, I spoke to him just after four perhaps and they were here from six-ish or so. I can't be sure. What is going on?'

'I have no idea but I will be finding out. I have to go,' Anne said firmly. Jack had put all the sums together, it seemed, and come up with the right answer.

'Do you want me to take the phone up to them?' Mrs Becker asked and Anne could hear the greed in her voice, the desire for any excuse to get into that apartment and see exactly what all this excitement was about.

'No, don't worry yourself, Mrs Becker, but thank you. And don't mention I called. I'll find Jack and sort this out.'

'I don't want to be involved, Miss Fenton. I am simply telling you what I know,' the woman replied, obviously offended that she might be considered overly curious.

Anne hung up, her breathing ragged. Jack wasn't just suspicious, he was on to her.

She dialled the St Albans number. 'Mrs Shannon?'

'Oh, I'm glad you've called. Now, you won't be bringing that van back, will you, luv? I don't want any trouble with the police.'

Anne's stomach did a flip. She was too late. 'What's happened?'

'Nothing yet, but I've been seeing those reports as I told you on that machine and I know they're going to come snooping around my house. I can't be caught breaking the law, luv. I hope you won't take this the wrong way.'

'No, no, I won't, but what do you mean about the machine?'

'Oh, I left a message on that answering contraption of yours. I thought that's why you're calling.'

'No, I haven't been home yet, Mrs Shannon,' Anne answered, her mind dull with rage.

'Well, great minds then, luv. I'm sorry we can't continue — I liked the cash, but I can't have Social Security cutting me off and all that. I know you understand. Just post back the key, there's a luv.'

Anne shook her head. It was all falling part and she was so close . . . just so close to her nemesis. She couldn't believe he was going to elude her again.

'Will do. Keep mum, Mrs Shannon — don't tell them anything if they ask any questions.'

'Why would they?' the old girl demanded, freshly anxious.

'I mean just in case any neighbours say they've seen a white van and all that. You have nothing to be afraid of.'

'I'll say it was my niece's or something.'

Anne couldn't care less any more. 'Whatever. Goodbye, Mrs Shannon.'

She hung up, her mind already racing ahead. She couldn't go back to Highgate, and she had to get rid of this van. But the truth was, she no longer had many choices. Fortunately, she'd packed cleverly — she had all she needed in her backpack and small luggage case. Again she counted her blessings at removing the most incriminating evidence from the apartment — the note from the Jesters Club — but they'd have worked out within minutes that the occupant of the fourth floor was no invalid and they would have decided that Sophie Fenton was the alter ego of serial killer Anne McEvoy.

Time was no longer on her side. She had to find the last pair of clowns and kill them in less than forty-eight hours. And in that same period, she had some important arrangements to make.

She gunned the engine again and suddenly her mind felt cleared. Jack was already in the past and all she could think of now was killing the final two and somehow finding Peter. If she could only look at him once, that would be enough, she assured herself.

36

Jack's team stared at him in utter disbelief, but he kept his head high. There was nothing he had to hide from, other than his own shame of being gullible — and it could have happened to any one of them.

'We know it's definitely her, do we?' Brodie asked, his expression stunned.

Jack let out his breath. 'Her second bedroom served as a personal gym, Cam. This was a serious set-up with professional equipment. According to Sophie, she has no siblings, an ageing mother in Devon, few friends and no flatmate. Who do you think was using the barbells, the treadmill, the cross-trainer, the rowing machine? And if we believe that she is Anne McEvoy's alter ego, then the gym makes sense. Confined to a wheelchair in public, she could hardly stay fit in all the normal ways. She used this equipment to train keep herself strong.'

'She'd have to be strong to move the bodies around,' Swamp followed up.

'That's right,' Jack agreed. 'The truth is, I haven't known her long . . .' He cleared his throat, keen to be honest with everyone but feeling hopelessly humiliated. 'And, well, I've never seen her arms naked. Now that I think about it, I believe Sophie deliberately kept her physique as disguised as she could. She has a very straight bearing, not necessarily common to invalids.'

He noticed everyone was looking down or away. Only Kate had the courage to look him in the eye but her expression was filled with sympathy. He pressed on. This was no time for self-pity or self-recrimination.

'Anne McEvoy is drugging these guys. Now that I know who she is, what she looks like, how likeable she is, I can see that's probably relatively simple for her. I fell for it, why not other blokes?' This time everyone shifted uncomfortably. He ignored it, continued. 'So she charms them, lures them into her car or van on the pretext of a lift or whatever, drugs them, waits for them to become unconscious. Then she does what she does, dumps the body, returns to her alter ego and waits for the news to break.'

'So, for the killing of the first two victims, she didn't need her disguise as such,' Sarah said, thinking aloud. 'Although she had dark hair for the London job.'

'We probably have to presume that she used the Sophie alias only as a means of getting close to me so she could keep an eye on the police.'

Kate responded swiftly to this and Jack knew she chose her words carefully to protect him. 'But you didn't tell her anything about the case, did you, sir?'

'No,' Jack admitted wearily. 'We discussed it only in the same sort of casual way that any of us might talk about a big case at home with our folks. I told her it had been a long day, that we may have found someone with some information on a cold case that might help.' He shrugged. 'All very general. To my knowledge, I never once revealed anything about the case itself that the public hadn't already learned, other than perhaps the mention of the blue paint — and, curiously, Sophie supported what Sarah had already discovered. I might add that I never discussed my colleagues either. The only reason she came into contact with you, Kate, is because you've happened to answer my extension on the two occasions that Sophie called me at the Yard.'

Kate nodded. 'I'm glad I did now, sir.'

'Me too,' he said and meant it, although a difficult silence followed. 'Look,' he said, 'I know this is tricky and you're all feeling a bit ill at ease about my involvement — perfectly understandable — but we have to move forward and do so fast. I've told you everything, and you can see for yourselves that I was set up by an extremely calculating and clever woman, who could have chosen to befriend any one of us in whichever manner she wanted. I'm meeting with Superintendent Sharpe in about ten minutes and I'll be telling him everything. If he chooses to take me off the case, you all know what you've got to do, and I'll be appointing DI Carter to run the operation, most likely with the Super's more close supervision.'

He let that sink in. To their credit, Brodie didn't baulk and Kate looked anything but triumphant.

He continued, 'If he wants me to remain at Operation Danube, then I want you all to stop feeling so uncomfortable around me. I couldn't know who Sophie was and, believe me, I hold enough despair about the hoax for all of us. You lot don't need to beat yourselves up over it because none of us could have known. She is a smart woman and she's obviously able to plan meticulously and quickly, adapting as needs be. We're dealing with a talented criminal here.'

'Chief, I have to admit here, just between us, that I don't really blame her.'

Jack could have hugged Brodie for saying aloud what he had felt, and Kate too, when the identity of Anne had first broken, but he was surprised when most of the others in the ops room began to murmur their agreement.

'So you all feel like this?'

Heads nodded. Sarah looked around and spoke, it seemed, on behalf of the younger members of the team. 'Sir, ever since Sergeant Moss told us about Anne McEvoy, I think a lot of us are working against our own inclination, which is to feel sympathy for her.'

'I understand, and I'd be lying if I said I felt any differently. What these men subjected her to is unthinkable for most of us, and, yes, it might have been three decades ago, but they weren't so young that they didn't know exactly what was happening. They could have prevented the rape. But they were obviously gullible and easily persuaded by this faceless, nameless guy. He's the true villain of the piece, and if he's still alive by the end of this and we find him, I intend to nail him for serious sexual assault, abduction, kidnap, attempted murder and child abduction, as well as anything else I can get on him, including murder of the infant if we can learn more.

'All of that said, it doesn't escape the fact that Anne McEvoy is a ruthless murderer, and even though I will struggle for years to match her MO with the Sophie Fenton that I've come to know and like so much, our job is to put her behind bars.' He didn't know when this had turned into a mini-lecture, but it needed to be said, especially to the younger officers. 'We are police officers and we are not appointed to make judgements. We are appointed to apprehend and make available for prosecution anyone who breaks the law.' He eyeballed the younger policemen and women as he spoke. None of the senior officers needed to be reminded of their duty, not even Brodie who'd expressed his regret. 'Let me stress that none of you have to worry about whether or not I'm as anxious as the next person to do that.'

He felt rather than saw the collective relief amongst his senior team at what he'd just said.

'Can I ask what we know about this last of the jesters?' Sarah asked.

'Absolutely zilch,' Hawksworth admitted, 'but I want us to go over the old files with a magnifying glass. There has to be a clue in there somewhere.'

'What about Fletcher?' Brodie asked.

'The Sussex unit is doing everything it can.' Jack sighed. 'I've got an awful feeling it's going to end badly for him. But we don't give up yet. Roll your sleeves up, settle down to the long night. We trawl the facts over and over until something breaks. If I'm not mistaken, McEvoy is leaving clues with her every move. In fact, the murders themselves are clues to the past wrongs — we can see that now.'

'Do you think she wants to be caught?' Kate asked.

He shook his head. 'I can't say. But she's no psychopath. She's got a very deliberate range of targets and —' He stopped abruptly, caught in a thought.

'Sir?' Kate coaxed, meeting the quiet glances from the other senior officers. 'Chief?'

Jack refocused. 'Swamp, tell everyone the Phillip Bowles suicide is to be kept inhouse for the time being.'

'Sure,' he said, frowning. 'I'll get on to it now.'

'Cam, fancy a trip back to Hove?'

Kate looked between Hawksworth and Brodie and knew exactly where this was headed. 'Oh, come on, you've just told us how smart she is, sir.'

Jack gave his DI a wry look. 'Not so smart that she can guess how the voice of a teenager might have changed in thirty years — if she can even remember Bowles's voice that clearly. Presumably she has no idea of his death at this point.'

'It's a good idea,' Cam said. 'How do we handle it?'

'A sting. Nothing elaborate, she's too clever. We simply lure her to the house with the bait she's planning to prey on anyway.'

Kate shook her head. 'She's been too careful. She'll know we're watching.'

'There'll be no police presence in the street. Kate, you and Swamp can run the stakeout. Cam and I'll be inside the house long before she arrives. We know Bowles is likely to be the next target.'

Kate wasn't convinced. 'What if she already knows about his death?'

'How? And if she has already staked out the place and watched today's events, then although we're no closer, we're also no further from her.'

'But she'll know we're on to her,' Kate insisted.

'We have to do something that entices her closer to us. The public, the media, our superiors — they'll all be demanding it.'

'It's worth trying,' Cam said. 'When?'

'Tomorrow, but get on to Sussex now and get them to clear away all signs of a police presence at the house. I imagine Anne McEvoy's a little preoccupied with Fletcher right now. She won't turn her attention to Bowles until tomorrow.'

'You hope,' Kate warned. 'Sir, you'd better get off to your meeting.'

Jack stood, nodded his thanks. 'Okay, Cam, get everything set up. Swamp, Kate, get organised to be in Hove — we'll leave in the early hours of tomorrow. The rest of you, please trawl the files for clues. We need the fifth person — we need to know what we've missed.'

He glanced Sarah's way and both of them understood that he anticipated her expertise at detail would deliver them the break they so badly needed.

Everyone murmured their assent and Jack hurried away for what he knew was going to be an unpleasant meeting with his boss.

It was past eight-thirty and Anne had to think about where to dump the van. Without it, she'd have to risk killing Phil Bowles at his home, or worse, out in the open. Would she risk it? She began to feel it was too dangerous. Her main target was Pierrot. Perhaps Phil's luck was in. He had been kind to Beano all those years ago, before the little dog's brutal demise.

Nevertheless, Phil was as much to blame as the rest of them. He shouldn't be given a reprieve because of a rare act of kindness that didn't save Beano anyway. No, Phil should die too.

She sighed. Tomorrow was almost upon her and she was exhausted, but the van could undo her faster than anything; she needed to rid herself of it. She toyed with the idea of finding a lock-up to rent and hiding the van in there. There were plenty of options sandwiched amongst the terraced streets past the London Road Station just north of Brighton. But the chances of finding someone to open up a garage late on a Saturday night and then forget her and it seemed relatively slim. Her next idea was to simply dump the van in the wilder region of Stanmer Park and hope it wouldn't be found for at least three days, which should give her the time she needed. But she discarded this option because in winter Stanmer Park's undergrowth wasn't lush enough to conceal the van adequately. So, despite her fatigue, she sped off towards Gatwick Airport. She would leave the van in the long-term car park and hope it was a week or so before it was discovered. She could hire a car at the airport using cash.

Now that Scotland Yard was on to her, all pretence of being Sophie Fenton would have to fall away. Her new alter ego — the one she had taken the precaution of setting up several months previous — would be the last incarnation for Anne McEvoy. And it would have to come into effect immediately.

Superintendent Martin Sharpe eyed his protégé balefully, his pint of Ruddles sitting untouched on the table between them.

'How did she mark you?' he asked.

'We're trying to establish the leak. I'm certain she knew of my appointment before I did because she was already in the apartment on the day of our first press conference when the story of the serial killing broke publicly.'

'Helen wouldn't have —'

'No, sir, I'm not suggesting she would,' Jack hurried to assure the older man. 'In fact, I'm hoping Helen may give us some insight as to who or where amongst the administration staff the information could have been accessed. All McEvoy needed was my full name and which part of London I lived in. The rest would be easy enough to hunt down. All she had to do really was follow me home from work one night. Who was privy to the info on the appointment anyway?'

Sharpe shrugged. 'There were two commanders in on the decision and of course the Commissioner of Police. I don't think you have to concern yourself with any of those officers. Far more likely is that the clerical staff have been blabbing to each other. You're not exactly our most inconspicuous DCI. There are probably more private emails, texts and coffee room conversations about you than any other officer in the Yard.'

'I'm getting very tired of that tag,' Jack said with irritation. He flung down the cardboard coaster that he'd been fiddling with.

'I don't doubt it, Jack, but until some good-looking young gun roars up the chain of command, you remain the most eligible of our senior officers and the grapevine will continue to feed off you. What we need to focus on now is how to limit the potential damage of your relationship with the most wanted criminal in Britain.'

Jack flinched at his superior's words. 'I can't see how we do that,' he replied glumly.

'By finding her, Jack! She's in Brighton, she's probably killing a man as we speak, and in her mind she's got two more to go. Your sting is the right option, considering we have so little to go on, but there's potential for that to go nowhere as well. So you've got to get to this Pierrot guy first.'

'Whoever he is,' Jack qualified.

'Yes, whoever he is. That's our job. That's police work. Somewhere, someone has a clue as to who he is. Find that clue and it will lead us to this killer.'

Jack stifled a yawn of intense fatigue. 'We're on it.'

'So, you're heading up to Hove, is that right?'

'Yes. Everyone's working around the clock at the moment. I'll let DIs Brodie, Marsh and Carter get a few hours' shut-eye and then we'll head up while it's still dark.'

'Good. Listen, Jack, I don't want to make your life any more difficult than it is right now, but I've been contacted by DCI Deegan.'

Jack groaned.

'Just before I came out actually. He's not wasting any time. He wants a meeting.'

'And?'

'I have to give him one. I don't have a choice.'

'I understand.'

'Is there something you want to tell me?'

Jack shrugged. 'I have no idea what card he's about to play. All I know is that it has something to do with with former DS Liz Drummond.'

'Oh god, not this again. And if he finds out about Anne McEvoy —' He bit back whatever he was going to say.

Jack gave him a pained look. 'I don't deliberately set out to have affairs that are awkward for the Yard. Romances happen. I've explained this. Liz and I were thrust together undercover. You'll recall how dangerous that operation was. We were all we had to keep each other safe and what's more, it was the Yard's idea that we play the part of lovers, not ours. We had to make it real, sir — you can't go undercover and leave any room for doubt. You know that. They would have killed us.'

Sharpe did know. 'So what's Deegan doing dragging this up again?'

Jack rubbed his face. 'Liz is the only time I've had a relationship inside the Met. It didn't last long, but it was meaningful under the circumstances. But I've learned my lesson.'

'An officer died during that operation, Jack. Is there anything else I need to know?'

'No. The inquiry exonerated all staff. What happened to Paul Conway was an accident. Deegan was a DS then — not at the Yard — and I hardly knew him, other than to dislike his manner. He hasn't improved with maturity.'

'What's he got on you?'

'I honestly don't know.'

'Well, sounds like we're going to find out.' Sharpe picked up his flat ale and put it down again in frustration. 'And by the sounds of things, I'd better start preparing a statement for the press about a third corpse!'

'We're doing all we can, Martin.'

'Do more, Jack. Do more!'

3 7

Anne handed over the crisp series of twenty-pound notes.

'I'll just get your change,' the pretty service assistant at the Gatwick car rental counter said, handing Anne an envelope with all the details for the small blue car she'd just hired. 'So you'll drop it back to our Manchester office, yeah?' the girl asked.

'At the airport,' Anne reminded.

'That's fine. Thank you.' The girl handed her some coins and turned on a bright red lipsticked smile.

Anne wondered how she looked that chirpy so late at night and under the harsh airport lights. She headed out to find her car, glad now to be rid of the van and Sophie Fenton with it. She found the hatchback rental, threw in her bag that now contained her new life and headed for the first family-style hotel she could find en route back to Brighton. But first, a cafe of some sort.

Back on the top floor, with London stretching out around them in a glittering sprawl, Jack dragged his gaze away from the blue-lit capsules of the London Eye. He'd already told Kate and Cam to head off, get some sleep and to meet him back here in five hours. Kate looked reluctant to go home but although Jack felt for her, he couldn't be worried about her relationship woes now.

'Sir?'

He swung around, his eyes tired and stinging. 'Yeah, hi, Sarah, what have you got?'

'Firstly, I can confirm there is no Mrs Fenton in North Molton. She doesn't exist according to everyone I could reach on a Saturday night, including the local police station. I'll keep trying for —'

'No, don't bother. I think we now assume that Sophie Fenton and everything she told me about her background was a ruse. But thank you. What else?' he said firmly, determined to show his team that he was already past any hurt over Sophie's lies.

Before Sarah could speak, one of the younger police constables appeared at the door. Jack beckoned. 'Come in, Con. What have you got?'

'Sir, we've found the owner of the garage that housed the white transit van. Neighbours called police. Turns out she's the woman who spoke on the answering machine at Sophie Fenton's apartment.'

'Good work. Tell me.'

'The garage belongs to a Mrs Betty Shannon. She's seventy-six and lives in St Albans. She's pretty scared and said that she's worried anything she tells us might ruin her Social Security payments, sir.'

'I hope you assured her otherwise?'

'Yes, of course, but that's why it took so long to find out anything. She was very reluctant but we sent around a female officer from the local branch and she has given us this information, sir, that Mrs Shannon was approached almost six months ago by a woman who called herself Sally Hartley, who's in catering. She needed somewhere to garage her work van and has paid Mrs Shannon in cash.'

The young man held his hand up to preempt the obvious next question and Jack was impressed by his composure. It seemed his ambition was conquering his nerves, as Jack had suspected it would, given the right circumstances.

'She's only met Sally Hartley once and her recollection is vague. She believes she was blonde but can't remember much else, other than to say she "wasn't a real youngster but definitely a looker" — her words, sir.'

Jack glanced at Sarah, who didn't return it. Other than Kate, they were all embarrassed still, it seemed. 'Do we have a licence plate?' he asked.

'Yes, it's right here.' He read it out.

'Okay, give this to Swamp, ask him to circulate it. He'll know what to do. Thanks, Con, good job.'

The police constable found a shy smile and left to continue his shift.

'Go on, Sarah.'

'Yes, sir. It's a vague thread but can I run it by you?'

'I'll take anything you've got.'

Kate appeared. 'Okay, Cam's leaving now and I'm heading off. See you back here at 0300.'

'You will.' She turned to leave. 'Kate?'

'Sir?'

'Good work today. Thank you for your persistence and the risks you took.'

She gave him a sad smile that left her mouth almost as quickly as it arrived. 'You need some sleep too, sir.'

'Good luck,' he said as she turned to go and knew that Kate understood what he meant. She didn't look back. He returned his attention to Sarah, who was wearing a suddenly sheepish expression. 'What?'

'No, nothing.' She squirmed under his tired blue gaze. 'Well, I'm just feeling bad that I didn't help Kate very much today. She needed assistance, but she had to order me to give it. I ... well, er, I felt she was prying into your life under the wrong pretext. I felt angry to be put in that position and now I don't know what to say to her.'

Jack stared out of the window, his gaze falling on Big Ben. 'DI Carter can be tough when she's got a feeling in her water. It's one of the reasons she's on this case and why she's good at what she does. She really does have excellent instincts. But I don't think she'd be one to hold a grudge. Tell her the truth. You owe her that much considering what she risked to tell me. She knew it might cost her career to make the accusation, especially if it were wrong. I have to admire her courage, and especially her tenacity, because she was right.'

Sarah nodded. 'I'm sorry it turned out so badly for you, sir.'

Jack didn't want to do this but he had to accept that every one of his staff would be feeling the need to say something that locked away the business of Sophie. He shrugged. 'I'll survive. So tell me what's niggling at you.'

Sarah opened a file and pointed. Jack recognised it as the cold case file that Moss had given them.

'What am I looking at?' he said, scanning where she was pointing.

'Sir, it's only just occurred to me that when Anne McEvoy was found that night on West Pier in Brighton, the alarm was raised by a Mr John "Whitey" Rowe — he was one of the anglers that doubled as a sort of loose security team for the pier during the early seventies.'

'Okay. I imagine he was interviewed by Moss's team in '74.'

'Yes, that's right, Rowe was, but it doesn't say anywhere that anyone else from that group was interviewed.'

Jack straightened. He took a moment to glance out again across London while he thought it through. 'So they did shifts?'

'I imagine so. There was nothing formal about the arrangement. The anglers all liked to fish from the pier at the dead of night and it was — in Moss's words — a you-scratch-my-back-and-I'll-scratch-yours set-up. They had access to the pier but no one else did, and the Pier Trust benefited from them keeping an eye on the place, preventing squatters and so on.'

'But more than one person might have access on any one night.'

'Well, that's what I'm now thinking. Rowe might have discovered Anne McEvoy and raised the alarm, but someone had already done the rounds on the earlier shift. There's nothing at all in the file, and although I'll speak to Moss again, I imagine not much was done about the guy who was there before Rowe came on at whatever time he did.'

'You're going to try and contact Rowe then?'

'Yes, sir, if that's alright.'

'Alright?' he said archly. 'Sarah, this is exactly what I needed to hear. There are always layers of facts and we missed this on the first few passes. Whether it yields anything or not, seriously well done. But find me something. Promise me you will.'

She grinned. 'I promise,' she said, thrilled by how much she'd pleased him. 'But you'll definitely owe us those French cakes.'

Anne entered the hotel room, exhausted. In the end, she hadn't had the strength to sit down for a meal and had opted for a drive-in takeaway. The burger was soggy and tasteless but her grinding belly recognised it as food and immediately set to dealing with it, and the effects of the greasy chips were almost instantaneous, making her feel drowsy enough not to be terribly picky about the accommodation. The spotty-faced young woman with the surly manner who checked her in at the tired hotel hardly made eye contact, which suited Anne, who had hidden her hair beneath a beanie, just in case any alerts were out.

Louise Parker could look however she wanted her to in the morning.

Tomorrow she would probably cut and certainly dye her golden hair back to auburn, and remove the coloured lenses that she wore around Jack — in fact, around anyone who wasn't one of her victims. It was only the Jesters Club who were allowed to see Anne. She would also call Phillip Bowles and contrive a way to meet him, but with time running against her there could be no elaborate plan — she was going to have to trust her luck and persuasive powers.

But, right now, she would wash away the stench of blood from her nostrils and block out the cries for mercy ... and she would sleep and try very hard not to mourn the loss of Jack Hawksworth.

Jack told himself he couldn't be bothered to go all the way back to Highgate tonight, but the truth was, he couldn't face the apartment building ... not yet. Was it only this morning that he had felt that glorious sense of wellbeing lying in a tangle of limbs with Sophie Fenton? No, that wound was still too raw to look at. Instead, he found the spare overnight bag he kept at the ready and booked into a room at the St Ermin's Hotel, close to the Houses of Parliament and just a short walk from the Yard. He grabbed the least offensive-looking sandwich at one of Victoria Station's night kiosks, ate it on the run before checking in, showering and collapsing into bed. He set his alarm to give himself three and a half hours' sleep. He snuggled beneath the sheets, praying that the time would pass in a dreamless state. He didn't want to think about Sophie. He wanted to dwell purely on

Anne McEvoy ... and what he would say to her when they trapped her tomorrow.

As Jack and Anne were drifting off to sleep in their respective hotels, a youngish couple whose six-month-old teething infant refused to settle for his evening sleep and, worse, refused to stop howling, decided that a long walk may wear him out and give them the chance of a few hours' peace. Their one-year-old dalmatian, off the lead, scampered ahead and, against their firm calls, ran into the park they were circling.

'Where's George gone now?' the woman said, rolling her eyes. She fiddled with her son's blanket, tucking it closely around him.

'He's in the park,' her husband said, yawning, rubbing at his day-old stubble. 'I'll get him.'

The wife yawned too. She was desperate to hit her own pillow, knowing her son would be looking for a feed in a few short hours. 'He's so naughty — all that money at obedience classes for nothing,' she scolded but without any heat. 'Hurry up, I don't want to be out here much longer.'

The man didn't dare yell out the dog's name. It was almost midnight and the area was silent, the houses asleep. He peered through the park gate. 'George,' he called softly.

The dog answered with a low growl.

The man stepped in further and saw the dalmation sniffing around a park bench.

'Belinda?' He waited a few moments before calling again. 'Belinda!'

'What?' she whispered, arriving at the gate. 'Ssh, Howard, you'll wake the whole bloody neighbourhood and Matthew. He's just gone off.'

'Look,' Howard said, pointing.

She stared, thought about it and looked back to her husband. 'A tramp?'

'I don't know. I'd better get George though, or he's going to get a kick for his trouble.'

'Be careful and hurry.'

He tiptoed to where a man was slumped on the bench. It was too dark to see much, and the streetlight had been broken, so the only illumination was the eerie wash of yellow from other streetlights that were spaced far apart in this area.

'Hey, mate,' Howard said, shaking the man. 'You'll catch your death out here.'

The man didn't move. He imagined the fellow must be dead drunk, although there was no smell of alcohol and not even a flicker of movement. He frowned, put George on the lead, wondering at the dark sticky patch below the man where the dog was sniffing.

'Did you bring the torch?' he whispered back to Belinda.

'Only a tiny one — that pen light on the keyring.'

'Bring it over.'

'No, I don't want to come any closer. He may wake and scare Matthew. What are you going to do anyway? Invite him home?'

Howard rolled his eyes. 'Throw the keys here,' he said, approaching her, but looking over his shoulder. The man hadn't stirred. 'We have to check he's okay. He could die of hypothermia.'

He caught the keys, switched on the tiny beam of light and trained it on the man, pulling him around. As he did so, the man's jacket fell open. Howard staggered backwards.

'Call the police!' he yelled, no longer bothered by how much noise he made.

38

Jack woke blearily to the sound of his mobile screaming into his ear. Couldn't they leave him alone for just a few hours? He squinted at the clock. It was twenty past one in the morning. He'd barely slept. He sighed and answered.

'Hawksworth.'

'Sir, it's DS Jones. I'm sorry to disturb you.'

'It's okay, I was getting up around now,' he lied.

'I figured you'd want to know that Fletcher's turned up,' Sarah said flatly.

'Dead?' He held his breath, fully awake now.

'I'm afraid so, sir. I'm sorry.'

Jack groaned softly. 'Brighton?'

'Hove, a park called St Ann's Well Gardens. I was there only days ago with Sergeant Moss. He virtually lives in it.'

Jack swung his legs out of bed, scratched his head glumly. 'I wonder if that's another of her messages.'

'Possibly, sir.'

'What do we know?'

'Fletcher was found by a young couple just after midnight — they were walking their baby and dog around the neighbourhood.

Apparently the baby's teething and couldn't get to sleep. It was all very quiet, as you could imagine — it's quite a nice area populated with relatively well-heeled people.'

'How long has Fletcher been dead?'

'We're waiting on pathology but they're rushing it through for us. Early indications suggest about five hours, but that's just a rough estimation, sir. Ken is doing core temperature, etcetera, back at the lab to give us a more accurate time of death, but given that Fletcher was still in Hastings this afternoon, we know it had to have happened sometime after four but before seven.'

'Agreed. Have his family and girlfriend been informed?'

'Someone's on their way over to his father's nursing home in Brighton and we've contacted Hastings. They're going to send a car to his girlfriend's and mother's places now.'

'So the father doesn't live with the mother?'

'Estranged for years apparently. He's much older than she is.'

'What about the van? Anything?'

'No. Until this couple, Belinda and Howard Evans, found Fletcher, no one in the neighbourhood who has been contacted by police had heard or seen anything connected with the van. Hove branch is planning a doorknock, but I think they want to wait until the morning.'

'She's either very lucky, or she's planned everything to such a finite degree that this whole mission must have been in motion months before she even began her killing spree,' Jack said.

'I know you don't want to hear this, sir, but I can't help but admire her.'

'You're right, I don't want to hear it.'

Sarah persisted. 'Ex-Sergeant Moss felt it, too. He said the police let Anne McEvoy down all those years ago. For whatever reason, she turned vigilante, and I imagine a lot of the members of the public are going to quietly applaud her once they realise that they and their families aren't potential targets of a random killer.'

'I couldn't agree more, but I reiterate that we mustn't lose sight of what we're charged to do.'

'No, sir, I have no intention of doing that. I want to find McEvoy, but between you and me, if I ever met her in a soundproofed room, I'd tell her that I understand her actions completely.'

'I think we all would,' Jack said quietly, rubbing the remnants of sleep from his eyes. He wished it were as easy to rub away the sudden vision he had of Sophie. 'Right, I'll be at the office in about forty minutes. Can you handle things until then?'

'Of course. I've tracked down Whitey Rowe. I'll be calling him as soon as is feasible on a Sunday morning, sir.'

'Don't hold off, Sarah. He has to understand that this is a major murder investigation, after all.'

'Will do. See you soon.'

Jack hung up and spent a moment in silence, sifting through his thoughts, mourning Fletcher's death and their failure to prevent it. He vowed to himself that she wouldn't find the fifth man — Pierrot, as he was known. Jack intended to find Pierrot first and save him Anne's butchery, but not because he wanted to help the man. No, Jack's determination to get to him first was so he could put him behind bars for the maximum sentence any court could impose. Life in a British jail might be considered by some as a soft option, but Jack knew better. He knew this guy would suffer at the hands of his inmates and would likely end up yearning for the numbing effect of Anne's drugs and the near painless death she offered.

Anne woke to the early morning local news that the body of a man had been discovered in St Ann's Well Gardens in Hove by a couple. She watched the woman being interviewed by a reporter hungry for the theatre that surrounded a suspicious death, who was rewarded by Belinda Evans breaking down in tears. Anne regretted the young woman's distress and tried to assure herself that she'd soon forget the trauma of the grisly discovery and hopefully dine out on the story in years to come.

She took herself and her overnight bag into the bathroom and eventually emerged a brunette — no more wigs, she'd decided. She'd twisted her hair back into a clip and was quite pleased with the result.

By eleven she was dressed in jeans, her Docs and a short but baggy cardigan over a warm, long-sleeved T-shirt. Her waterproof jacket was in the car. It was all normal daywear in neutral colouring and instantly forgettable, which was her intention. She kept her face devoid of make-up and returned to her eyes the lenses that made them an intriguing dark brown.

In Patcham, she found a phone box and dug out her notebook and the section on Phil Bowles, which gave her his phone number and street address. Phil hadn't been hard to find. He'd never left the area and a search through directory enquiries online had soon yielded his number.

She dialled it now and held her breath.

They'd been sitting there for hours, both so tired but trying to keep each other alert with mindless conversation about favourite films, favourite pubs, hottest dates and maddest moments — anything to keep themselves from silence and the opportunity to drift into a doze. Kate and Swamp joined in on their walkie-talkies, determined to stay awake in their respective cars where they were watching for any sighting of Anne McEvoy.

Hawksworth and Brodie jumped at the sound of the ringing phone. This was the third call to Bowles's home; the first two from men. Brodie had pretended to be a friend of Phil's and said that Phil had just gone to the corner shop. Neither man had left a message. Now Jack alerted his colleagues outside to another call.

'Do I use the same line if it's her?' Cam said.

'Absolutely. Play it safe, just stick to the story. She'll decide when to let you know that it's her.'

Cam picked up the phone. 'Hello?'

'Is that Phil Bowles?'

Even though Jack wanted it to be her, it still gave him a shock that she'd come into their web with such ease. He stuck his thumb in the air at Cam. No one could know how hearing that voice made him feel weak with despair inside.

'Yes. Who is this?'

'Phil, I hope you're going to remember me. It's Anne McEvoy here.'

Cam had rehearsed his response to this situation over and over again. And now he replayed it precisely how he and Jack had practised. First he hesitated, then he repeated the name, remembering the quiet way in which Bowles spoke and how he tended to lick his lips when he was thinking. 'Anne McEvoy?'

'Yes, Anne . . . from Russell Secondary School.'

Now he deliberately fell silent but breathed a little more loudly.

'Phil? Phil, are you there?'

'I'm here,' he said softly. 'Why . . . why are you calling me?'

'Phil, you sound scared. Don't be.'

Cam remained silent and forced Anne to talk. Meanwhile, Jack had set in motion the check through British Telecom, using a secure line via the Met, as to where this call was coming from. The operater told him it would take a couple of minutes.

He returned his attention to the landline Cam was talking to Anne on and realised it had gone dead. They looked at each other, shocked.

'She can't be on to us,' Cam said.

'Fuck!' Jack slammed down his mobile. He quickly dialled the Yard again, apologised, reorganised a secure line.

'What happened?' It was Kate, crackling over the walkie-talkie.

Jack grabbed the handset. 'It was her but the line — hang on.' The phone had begun ringing again. He pressed the button on the walkie-talkie. 'She's back. Hold the silence.' Once again he asked the operator to contact BT to trace the call.

Cam answered again. 'Hello?'

'Sorry, Phil, this is a dodgy phone, I don't know what happened there.'

'Where are you calling from?'

'Hove.'

'No, I mean why a phone box?' He was trying to keep her on the line as long as possible so Jack could trace her.

'I'm having some work done at home, so there's nothing but hammering and men talking, and to make matters worse I've mislaid my mobile. Murphy's law, right?'

'Yeah,' Cam said, remembering to lower his voice and speak a little more haltingly. 'Why are you calling out of the blue? You're not collecting money for some cause, are you?'

She laughed and Jack was again struck by despair that this was Sophie on the other end of the line. He simply couldn't put it together that she was also the ruthless serial killer that had the whole of Britain talking.

'No, no, I'm not collecting money. I'm actually ringing because I have something you may want.'

'Oh?'

'Do you still collect Biggles books?'

Cam looked to Jack for guidance. His boss nodded.

'Yeah, of course. Once a Biggles fan, always one.'

'I'm glad to hear it. Now, I know this must feel strange to suddenly hear from me but as I say, I'm having a lot of work done at my place and I'm clearing out a pile of stuff. I came across this box of my dad's books and there are about fourteen Biggles novels. They're in such amazingly perfect condition that I didn't have the heart to take them to the charity shop. And then, a blast from the past, I suddenly remembered how much you loved reading this stuff. I know it sounds crazy but I thought I'd try and find you — I think also for old times' sake. I must admit I didn't imagine it would be so easy.'

Cam paused, rather too dramatically, Jack thought. He'd heard from the BT operation that this was a phone box in Patcham — he had the number and street it was on. He knew there was no point in dispatching a car — he didn't anticipate that she would be on the line long enough — but at least he knew now that she was definitely in the Brighton area and accessible. He listened to Cam.

'But, Anne, why after all these years would you remember me?'

'I can hardly forget you, Phil.' Her voice took on a slightly harder edge and Cam sensibly waited for the silence to feel awkward.

'I don't really want to talk about that time,' he said.

'Neither do I. I was just trying to do something kind. Don't you find yourself reminiscing now that you're in your forties? I know I do. I've been thinking a great deal about all those people we went to school with. But look, if you don't want these books ...'

'I do, really,' Cam spluttered, breathing heavily. 'But this is so strange, you must admit.'

'Yes, it is.'

Cam continued as if she hadn't spoken. 'I mean, what with the deaths of Mikey and Clive, I'm just a little shak—'

'What are you talking about?'

'Haven't you heard about them?'

'Who?'

'Michael Sheriff and Clive Farrow. They're dead.'

Cam and Jack listened to the long silence that followed before their caller said softly, 'Dead?' She made a sound of regret. 'I . . . no, I've been living overseas, I haven't heard anything. How can they both be dead?'

'Not just dead, Anne, but murdered.'

The woman Jack had so recently thought he could fall in love with inhaled sharply, as if slapped. 'Murdered?' she whispered. Then conveniently made the connection: 'Not Pierrot?'

Cam was ready. 'Who else?' he said. 'I'm scared, I have to tell you. I only heard about them myself a week ago. I'm changing my phone numbers and having a new alarm fitted and fresh security around all the windows. Then I'm going away for a while, I think, until the police catch him.'

'Wow, what a shock,' Anne said. 'I don't know what to say.'

Cam gave Jack a wry glance.

'Anne, I have to tell you I'm not terribly comfortable about you calling. But at the same time, I've longed to talk to you for years and tell you how sorry I am about what happened.'

Both men waited. They heard a sigh.

'Phil, I think I knew that if you'd had a choice, you wouldn't have gone along with what happened. I used to be really angry about it, but although I won't say I'm over it, I have put it firmly in my past. I can't fix what happened, or bring my son back. I thought at least a million times about killing myself but never had the courage, so I've worked hard to make the best of my life.

I never blamed you, Phil, but I do blame that bastard Pierrot, or whatever his real name is. I never went to the police because I didn't know who he was, and after it all happened I was totally spaced out, you know . . . so completely confused. I just ran away. And then it was too late to start making accusations — I was too young to know what to do, who to turn to. I let it be. As I say, I wasn't going to get my life back, no matter what I did. I honestly don't think about 1974 very much at all.'

'Don't you? I think about it all the time. And I'm deeply, deeply sorry on behalf of all of us. You know that none of us boys ever touched you, Anne, don't you? It was him. He did all the bad stuff. I wish I could make amends but I know I can't.'

'No, you can't, Phil. Perhaps I should just leave these books somewhere for you? I'm happy to drop them on your doorstep.'

'Oh, that wouldn't be fair. Let's at least say hello, no matter how awkward it is for both of us.'

'Well, that's nice. Seems you've certainly changed from the Phil Bowles I recall.'

'Really?'

'Definitely,' she said. 'Do you still live in your grandparents' place?'

'How do you know that?' Cam asked, unsure of how to play this now.

'You've forgotten that we were once friends in primary school, Phil. I came to your birthday party — those were the days when you used to like pretending to be a dog. Odd but funny.'

Cam wheezed a laugh.

'Do you remember that?' she prompted.

'I do actually. How embarrassing.'

'No, it was sweet. Like my dog — you liked him, didn't you?'

'Sure. He was cute.'

'Do you remember his name, Phil?'

Cam looked wildly at Jack, who shook his head. 'I don't think I can, Anne. It was so long ago.'

'Oh, come on, you loved him.'

'That's right, I did. Tell me his name again, Anne, or it will bug me all day.'

'It was Buster,' she said.

'Buster! Of course. He was such a lovely fellow.'

Anne hung up.

Cam looked over at Jack, said the obvious. 'She's gone.'

Jack had no expletives left in his arsenal of curses. He banged his fist down on the table instead. His phone began to ring and he assumed it was Kate. He didn't even look at the screen.

'Yes!' he barked.

'You should give me more credit, Jack.'

The shock hit him like a punch. 'Sophie. I —'

'What were you planning to do? Did you imagine I'd be oblivious to how smart a detective you are? I knew you were on to me, Jack, I just didn't know how close you were. Now I do.'

'I suppose I should call you Anne,' he said coldly, fighting the urge to ask her all the questions that were burning between them.

'I suppose you should, although I'll always treasure my time with you as Sophie,' she said, and he hated to hear that softness in her voice and feel how her words could generate such empathy within him. He was not over Sophie, but he had to fight her.

'Meet me, Anne. We'll talk, no other police, I promise.'

'Meet? Talk? What about? The body count maybe? Or perhaps you want to get more deep and meaningful, understand why I've killed. No, Jack. There's nothing else to say. I've done my talking through my actions. Where's Phil Bowles?'

There was no point in hiding it now. 'He's dead. He killed himself yesterday when he learned you were alive.'

'Ah, I see. Well, Phil saved himself an uglier end. Clever move, Jack. You nearly had me. Who was I speaking to?'

'DI Cam Brodie.'

Brodie shook his head. He picked up the walkie-talkie and stepped out of the room so he could let Kate and Swamp know the sting had failed.

'Well, tell Cam from me he did a good job with replicating Phil's manner, but he has a far nicer voice than Phil ever did and, try though he might, he can't fully cover that Scottish accent. I heard it peep through towards the end.'

'We'll watch that next time,' Jack said evenly. 'Bowles suicided and it was through remorse, not fear.'

'It doesn't matter. He's dead and I can't say I'll mourn him.'

'What now, Anne?'

'Time to go. I'm sure you've traced the call. Have you sent a car?'

'No.'

'Not sure I can trust you.'

'I've never lied to you.'

'That's probably true but there's always a first time. I must head off now.'

'After Pierrot, you mean?' He heard the hesitation. 'Is he next?'

'Goodbye, Jack. For what it's worth, for all my anger, all my ruthlessness, the cynical way I entered your life, all the lies and deception, you should know that everything that happened between us was real. I think you'll have guessed already that I prepared meticulously to rid the world of these criminals, but I wasn't prepared for you, Jack. You were meant to be something to use and cast aside. I wasn't ready for you to be so special, so easy to be with ... such a good fit. In another lifetime, who knows what could have been ...'

As she trailed off, Jack was reminded of his conversation with Kate, when he'd offered her a similar platitude.

'Is that meant to comfort me?'

'No. It's simply my way of letting you know that although I didn't think I could ever respond to another living soul after all that's happened, I was surprised by you. And it was a delicious surprise. Perhaps if we'd met before I set all this in motion, I might never have gone down this path.'

'Then stop, Sophie!' He hadn't meant to call her that again.

He could sense her smile of regret. 'I can't. The worst of them is yet to meet his fate.'

'When I find him, I intend to put him behind bars for life. I promise you, he will never see the light of day.'

'I can promise you the same but it will be infinitely more final.' She gave a sad laugh. 'No, I think I'll go out swinging, Jack. Festering in a jail isn't for me and you can't protect me from that. And I want Pierrot to pay. He's really the person responsible for the deaths of all these men, and certainly for the ruination of my life. Justice won't be served unless I mete it.'

'Please let me —'

'Take care of yourself, Jack. All of my stuff is yours — it will look lovely in your apartment, I'm sure. You could even sell up and move into mine! By the way, I've mailed you the address where you can pick up the photographic series you liked so much, in case the Yard won't let you keep my things. I have no one else to give them to. Think of me when you look at them.'

'Sophie!'

The line went dead in his ear. Jack yelled and hurled his mobile phone across the musty-smelling sitting room.

39

Superintendent Martin Sharpe glared at his visitor as he reluctantly welcomed him into the office. He had already asked Helen not to offer coffee.

'So, this sounded pretty urgent, DCI Deegan. How can I help you?'

'Straight to the point, as I like it, sir,' Deegan began.

'We are balanced rather precariously on the edge of a major operation here. Holding meetings about my staff is not my highest priority right now. We need to make this brief.'

'I understand completely, sir, I'll take no more of your time than I have to. I've called this meeting about DCI Jack Hawksworth because I'm recommending a formal internal investigation surrounding Operation Blackbird during 1997.'

'I presume this is connected with the death of DS Paul Conway?'

'It is, sir, yes.'

'My understanding is that all staff involved in that operation were interviewed and no case was brought to bear on anyone. Conway's death was pronounced an accident.'

'Yes, but there is now more information coming to light.'

'What new information?' Sharpe demanded, angry now.

'Well, sir, it seems that the information DCI Hawksworth originally gave about where he was on the evening in question may not be accurate. I'd like to reopen the inquiry and make it a formal internal investigation.'

Sharpe took a breath. He depressed a button on his intercom. 'Helen?'

'Yes, sir?'

'Hold all calls,' he requested, knowing this would cancel his original instructions to Helen to interrupt him if this meeting stretched beyond ten minutes. 'Now, Deegan, start from the beginning, please.'

'Thank you, sir.' Deegan oozed sincerity. 'I'll keep it brief.'

Anne sat in her rental car feeling sick. Hearing Jack's voice had unnerved her, made her feel distracted and sad when she needed to find the anger again. Garvan Flynn was still out there, probably smiling to himself that he'd got away with all that he had while she'd dealt with those who might point the finger at him. They were all gone now — Billy, Clive, Mikey and Phil. Only she was left. Her voice alone could accuse him of a range of crimes that any judge would happily put him behind bars for. She couldn't walk away, not now. She was a serial killer. She would be hunted down. What would one more death by her hand mean … life in prison was life in prison. You couldn't serve it over and over.

No. Garvan needed to pay — with his blood.

She had no more time to think on this. Jack and his team were close enough to smell her perfume. And if Phil Bowles had given them Pierrot's name before he died then all was lost. Anne suspected this hadn't happened though, because Jack would have already got to Flynn if he knew who or where he was. He wouldn't have wasted time on the ruse at Bowles's house with the remaining target still in a position to be saved.

She shook her head. Scotland Yard had no idea who Pierrot was. They were waiting for her to lead them there.

She needed to throw away her mobile and leave Patcham quickly, she decided, turning the key in the ignition. She had to buy a new phone, and there were some important arrangements still to make if she was going to pull off what she hoped.

She stared at the number in her notepad. She would wait until she was at Rottingdean a few miles out of Brighton proper, before she rang. First, she had to get to the seafront.

Kate and Brodie sat in the pub silently, uncomfortably, watching Jack as he stared forlornly at his battered phone. Swamp had left to make some calls. Around them, people were enjoying leisurely post-Sunday-lunch drinks. Their own table held the debris of their lunches, waiting to be cleared. They had no more leads to follow, and no one was sure whether to head back to London or stick around in Brighton. Jack didn't seem to be in any hurry to leave and it was getting close to three.

'Did she give you any clues?' Kate said finally, knowing Brodie wasn't prepared to trample into Jack's space just yet.

'No. Except I don't think we should imagine for a moment that this is over. She's got nothing more to lose. She'll go after whomever this Pierrot is, and we have to presume that she knows his identity.'

'You think she got the information from Fletcher?' Brodie said, sliding into the conversation now that Jack had stopped brooding.

'Yes, I think we can hazard that guess.'

'What do you want us to do now, Hawk?' Brodie went on. 'Swamp's just checking in with Sussex. He said he'd call the ops room as well.'

451

Jack sighed. 'Let the forensics boys back into Bowles's house — we have no further need for it. Although I'd like you to nip back and hunt down that clown mask Bowles spoke of.'

Brodie nodded, glad to have something specific to get on with. 'I'll do it now.'

Jack's phone rang. It was Sarah. 'How come you're still there?' he asked as he answered. 'The occupational health and safety stalkers will have my guts.'

'I did get a couple of hours' shut-eye but their rules don't apply to us,' she said archly. 'Especially when I have some good news.'

Jack felt his heart lurch. 'Tell me.'

'I spoke with Rowe, the angler who discovered Anne McEvoy on the pier.'

'And?'

'To cut a long story short, there could have been a person on the graveyard shift that night — a guy called Garvan Flynn. According to Rowe, no one was fishing that night because of the storms that were threatening. He said Flynn had cut his own key for emergencies and had offered to keep an eye on the place during the winter months.'

'No one followed it up?'

'Remember the crash at Chanctonbury Ring? That grabbed a whole load of police time and some of the details of Anne McEvoy's case got lost amongst the drama. Colin Moss did try to follow up but this Flynn guy disappeared and then Moss had a heart problem, retired early. Anne McEvoy was forgotten. As I said, there was nothing formal about this security arrangement, sir, it was more like an understanding between the Pier Trust and the anglers. So there aren't records to consult — we're dealing with people's recollections.'

'Okay, I understand. So what do we know about this Flynn?'

'This is the good bit, sir. Rowe says he's of Irish descent.

Didn't Bowles mention something about Pierrot sounding like Val Doonican?'

'Bloody hell,' Jack breathed. 'What else?'

'Rowe reckons in 1974 Flynn was around twenty-seven, perhaps twenty-eight, so that fits the profile. I asked if he smoked and Rowe said he seemed to remember that Flynn rolled his own.'

'The tobacco tin,' Jack murmured.

'That was my thought,' Sarah said, unable to keep her own excitement in check. 'Rowe thought he was married but had no kids.'

'Is that it?'

'No, sir, the best is yet to come.'

'You're killing me, Sarah.'

'I heard it's been a bad day.'

'I've had better. Go on.'

'After Rowe found Anne McEvoy early on that morning, not only did no one from the Brighton angling gang, who were quite a close-set mob, see Flynn again, they heard on the grapevine that he'd resigned from his clerical job and moved house. He was effectively gone from their lives within a week or so of that event. No one put two and two together at the time, but the clues are in the detail and you only have to step back a short way to see the picture coming together.'

Jack could barely believe what he was hearing. 'The timing's so neat.'

'Definitely too much of a coincidence to ignore, whether Rowe's memory is dodgy or not. We have to go after this Flynn guy.'

Jack wanted to blow a huge kiss down the phone and hear Sarah laugh, but he daren't, not with Sharpe on his back. Instead, he asked her to listen while he put his mobile onto loudspeaker. Then he drummed the table and made cheering and whistling sounds. It was the first time any of them had had anything to grin about in a long time. He picked up his phone, flicked it back to its original setting. 'Find me an address for Flynn,' he said. 'And, Sarah ...' He waited, knowing she was probably blushing from the drumroll and catcalls.

'Yes?'

'I'm very proud of you. That's a great morning's work.'

'Thank you, sir.'

'Keep us in the loop, okay? Cam's heading over to Bowles's place, and Swamp — well, I think he's still with us but sorting out a few things with the Sussex boys.'

'Back soon, sir.'

Jack flicked the phone closed. 'A break,' he said and quickly filled Kate in.

'Brilliant.' She was relieved just to see Jack on top again. She knew his guilt was weighing heavily on him. 'I'd have Sarah on any team of mine,' she added, knowing it was the right thing to say.

Jack eyed her as he drained his glass. 'Then reassure her that there's no hard feelings.' When Kate frowned, he added, 'She's feeling awkward about mistrusting your judgement earlier.'

'Really? What did you say?'

'That I know you're not the kind of person to hold grudges and that I'd count you amongst the best detectives I've worked with.'

Kate flushed. 'You said that?'

'I'm not lying. How's Dan?'

She looked down. 'We haven't talked.'

'Don't write him off.'

'I haven't, but until we close this case I can't focus on anything else.'

'Come on. Fancy some fresh air? We've got to kill some time until Sarah calls back.'

40

Anne had worked fast. It was nearing four-thirty and she felt ready. Nothing could be too meticulously planned, but she had learned from her previous experiences that she needed to be flexible in her approach. Flynn might not behave the way she anticipated, although she felt confident he would if he'd been keeping close watch on the news reports.

Billy Fletcher's death was hitting all the main radio and TV services — Flynn could hardly fail to acknowledge that the members of his Jesters Club were being systematically picked off. What she needed to do was frighten him sufficiently into following her instructions. And whatever the personal risk to her, this was the best chance she would ever have to settle the score.

Anne checked the time again and decided to wait until she was near the house before she made the call. She turned the ignition, pulled out into the seafront traffic and headed for the address in Rottingdean.

Jack and Kate strolled along the Brighton seafront. The afternoon had turned grey and cold but at least it was dry. A sharp wind whipped across their faces, numbing their ears, but both were glad to have it blow away the blurriness that came with too little sleep and too much work pressure.

Kate paused to lean against the promenade's green Victorian railing and stared out at the choppy waves lashing the ruin that was West Pier in the distance.

'Did you ever go on it?' she said.

Jack, who was looking the other way, seemed to grasp her cryptic question instantly. He matched his gaze to hers as she continued, obviously not requiring his answer.

'I was fascinated by everything about it, from the twisted serpents on its lampposts to the iron benches that made you feel like your arse was hanging out to sea.'

Jack smiled. 'I've only been on it once when I was very young. I remember those serpents but very little else except the candy floss and that helter-skelter. It's why I didn't realise what those photos were in Sophie's apartment. I knew they were of the ruins of a pier, but not which one. You know, it's arguably the finest example of Victorian seaside architecture in the country. She was obviously a very graceful old girl in her time. It's such a pity it's been allowed to get to this state.'

'Makes a nice home for the starlings though,' Kate said. 'If you weren't at the Yard, I'm sure you'd have made a very good stuffy old history academic.' She looked again at the ailing pier. 'But it's going to be renovated, isn't it?'

'I gather. It's going to be amazing, I imagine, when it's finished.'

'And all of its secrets, good and bad, will be cleaned away,' Kate said.

'We'll make sure one never gets forgotten,' Jack replied, his voice passionate. 'Whatever kind of monster Anne McEvoy has become, the monster was likely shaped by her experience on that pier in 1975. I glimpsed what Anne might have been through knowing Sophie,' he added. 'It's heartbreaking to think those two people existed alongside one another.'

'Sophie wasn't real, Jack.'

'She was to me.'

Kate decided to change tack. 'Fancy a coffee? I'm buying.'

Jack allowed his mood to lighten. 'How about tea? There's a great spot further down called the Mock Turtle Tea Shop that has been around forever. Great cakes.'

'Cake? In that case, lead the way.'

Jack offered his arm in a theatrical manner. 'Come on then. I need somewhere quiet anyway to take Sarah's call when it comes.'

It wasn't Sarah calling when Jack's phone gave a strangled rendition of what sounded like the 'Mexican Hat Dance'. It was the only ringtone it would play since he'd hurled it across Phil Bowles's lounge room.

'It's Martin, Jack. I've just got rid of Deegan.'

'What's it about, sir?'

'Apparently the Paul Conway death isn't over. Deegan seems to think he has something incriminating on you. He's pushing for a formal investigation.'

'That's bullshit, sir!' Jack said, winning the attention of two older ladies in the tea shop. He added hurriedly, 'Pardon my French.'

'I hope so, Jack. He doesn't seem to think so.' Sharpe took a few moments to fill his DCI in on what precisely Deegan was following up. He finished with a sigh. 'Look, there's nothing you can do. I'll keep stonewalling him, but I can only hold him off for so long. The Ghost Squad has a lot of clout. If he persuades the right people that a formal investigation needs to be set in motion then you know even I won't be able to prevent them from stopping you in your tracks. I don't want the operation stalling because of some past indiscretion, Jack, so be very sure there are no skeletons rattling in your cupboard.'

'There aren't.'

'Alright,' Sharpe said, happy to accept Jack's word. 'So, tell me what's happening.'

Jack spent the next few minutes bringing his Superintendent up to date with the morning's events. It did nothing to improve Sharpe's humour.

'What a bloody mess,' he said when Jack had finished. 'So we're no closer to McEvoy?'

'Well, that's not true, sir. The fact is, she's made contact. It was her call, not mine. We know where she is and we know she's remaining in Brighton. I'm waiting for an urgent call from the ops room. Fingers crossed, we may have an address for Garvan Flynn. I know she's going after him.'

'Get there first, Jack. I don't need to tell you how it will work in your favour and against Deegan's crusade if you can apprehend the nation's most wanted killer. Not to mention saving her final victim so he can face the music he should have faced decades ago.'

'Yes, sir.' The appeal of the carrot cake sitting on the table in front of him had suddenly soured.

Kate nibbled at her brownie. 'What was that all about?'

Jack told her and admired her ability to hide whatever she was thinking.

'So that's why Dan's accusation scared you,' she said, referring back to Jack's reaction to her quip in the lift. 'The case may re-open.'

'I won't make the same mistake, Kate. My liaison with Liz is still haunting me.'

'Obviously I knew about the Drummond thing but I was under the impression you were exonerated. Are you worried?'

'I *was* exonerated. I've got nothing to hide. I don't know what Deegan's got on me.'

'I know Deegan, worked with him briefly. He's a creep.'

'Tell me something I don't know,' Jack said and groaned.

'Well, not many people know this. He's gay but hides it well. The Met's not homophobic outwardly but ...' She trailed off.

'I know what you mean.'

'It really wasn't an issue. I'm only mentioning it now because we're talking about him. No one else seemed to register it, but I realised he never joined in the blokey stuff easily and he certainly didn't flirt with the women, as far as I could tell. Not with me, ever.' She shrugged. 'I'm far too good for him,' she added loftily and Jack grinned. 'The only reason I know for sure he's gay is because I saw something I wasn't supposed to. I've never said anything to anyone until now.'

Jack didn't press for more information. 'I can't imagine why he's targeting me,' he said.

'A grudge, presumably. Somewhere, somehow, you've trodden on his toes and either not apologised, or worse, not noticed.'

Jack's face took on a pained expression. 'How could I have? I've never had anything to do with him. I've run across him, but only in passing or via other people.'

'He hasn't too many friends around the Yard from what I remember.'

'Then Ghost Squad's probably the best place for him. Finish your brownie.'

'Bit dry. Can I eat your carrot cake instead ... as you're not touching it?'

'Sure.' As he pushed the plate towards her his phone rang. It was Sarah again.

'Got it, sir,' she said breathlessly and began reciting the Rottingdean address.

41

Peter hadn't been able to face his parents. He'd left the family home on Saturday afternoon and refused to take their calls while he brooded. He'd told Ally he was going to be caught up in work for a couple of days, and that got him off the hook of having to explain his foul mood to the person he least wanted to offend. He promised to see her on Monday evening.

But now it was Sunday afternoon and he'd dwelled long enough on his next move. He was determined to find his mother, to reassure himself that she was either dead, or, as his father claimed, a drug addict who didn't regret giving him up as a baby and wanted nothing to do with him now. Either of those scenarios would make it easy for him to forget this situation had ever presented itself.

Peter didn't want to upset his parents any further. It was obvious they had never planned to tell him unless it was forced out of them, and he certainly didn't want a new mother in his life, but something wouldn't permit him to let the shock pass or the moment disappear without him doing something about it. Perhaps it was because he was ready to settle down, marry and start a family of his own? Family was important to him. He would never forgive himself if — now he knew the truth — he didn't try to find out more about his birth mother. Besides, there was too much at stake. Apart from Ally, this new government contract meant everything to him. It was the step up in status and income he'd been yearning for, and would undoubtedly mean travelling overseas. He couldn't do any of that without knowing exactly who he was, and getting a birth certificate to prove it. He needed to get to the bottom of this, which was why he'd steeled himself to face his parents. He couldn't imagine they were having a terribly happy Sunday afternoon anyway.

He pulled up outside the house and let himself in as usual. He waited for the inevitable greeting, expecting it to be awkward. No one came.

'Dad?' he yelled.

Perhaps his mother was out and his father in the shed? But the back door was locked, so no one was outside. Peter checked the time. It was almost four-thirty. He couldn't imagine where they'd be at this time, other than his Aunt Sheila's. He had to assume they'd sought the comfort of their nearest and dearest.

Outside of the usual gripes and groans in any family, Peter had never had a falling out with his parents. Even their disappointment over the business with Ally replacing Pat in his heart had quickly turned into a diplomatic response. His parents weren't argumentative people and he was a good son; they didn't need reminding of that and treated him as respectfully as he did them. But the revelation of his birth had rocked the household and Peter felt as though he was navigating an unknown course right now. Just knowing what to say to them, how to put into words the cascade of strange feelings he was experiencing, would be hard enough.

He put on the kettle and went through the motions of making a pot of tea while he thought about how to approach the situation without inflaming it further. He had no intention of changing his mind but he needed to find a way to convince his parents that tracking down this woman was important to him.

He'd just put the tea cosy on the pot when the phone rang.

Anne heard a man answer.

'Hello?'

'Er, hi,' she said. 'I'm looking for a Mr Garvan Flynn.'

'He's not here right now. Can I take a message?'

'Oh, so I do have the right number for him?'

'Yes. Who is this, please?'

'Um, I'm an old friend.'

'Shall I leave your name, perhaps a number where he can call you back?'

'No, look, I might try again later. Are you expecting him back today?'

'I imagine so.'

'Okay. Who am I speaking to?'

'This is his son.'

Anne couldn't speak. The silence stretched.

'Hello?' the man said.

'I'm here,' Anne said, her voice suddenly thin and shaky. 'Sorry, er ... what's your name?'

'Peter.'

Again the choking sensation in her throat, her chest.

'Okay, well, feel free to call back tonight perhaps,' he offered.

'No, wait,' she said. It came out as a plea. 'Peter, you said?'

'That's right. Who am I talking to?'

'My name's Anne McEvoy. I ... knew you as a baby ...' Her voice shook again and trailed off.

'Are you alright?'

'No, not really.' A soft sob escaped.

462

Peter clearly had no idea what to say. An awkward silence hung between them as she sniffed, gathered herself. 'I'm sorry,' she said again. 'This is rather difficult to explain. Is your mother there?' She nearly choked on the word.

'No, she's probably with Dad.'

Anne felt a thrill pass through her. She couldn't let this opportunity pass by. She gathered her wits, swallowed back all the emotion of hearing his voice for the first time in her life and pinched herself to steady her voice.

'I see. This is going to sound very forward of me, but can I ask whether your parents have told you anything about when you were born?'

It was as though someone had slapped him hard. Peter rocked back from the phone, staring at it dully. He couldn't believe this stranger had called out of the blue and zeroed in on the very topic that had dominated his thoughts these past two days.

'What do you know about my birth?' he demanded.

'I know all about it. It's why I'm phoning.'

'I don't understand. What do you mean, you know all about it? How can you?'

'I can, darling Peter, because, you see, I'm your mother.'

Hawksworth scribbled the street name Sarah dictated onto a small pad. 'You're sure about this?'

'Yes,' she said. 'Garvan Flynn has been registered as being at that address for the past twenty-nine years. His phone and other utilities are all current. In fact, I've just checked with BT. The phone's in use as we speak.'

'I owe you.'

'The debt's mounting up,' she quipped. 'What can I do to help, sir?'

'Nothing for now. Just stand by. Kate and I are on our way.'

'Shall I send a squad car?'

'Not yet. Let me take stock of the situation first. I don't want to alert him to the police. I have a feeling our quarry will run.'

'Okay. Keep us posted. Good luck, sir.'

Jack looked at Kate. 'We might have him.'

'Let's go,' she said, making for the cafe's exit, glad they'd paid when they'd ordered. 'Shall I drive?' She sounded exhilarated.

'No, I hate being driven,' he said with a grin, the excitement of being so close to their prey infectious.

Anne had steadied her clamouring emotions. Tears still streamed down her face but her voice was steady and her resolve had become granite. She stared across at the modest house in Rottingdean, knowing now that her son was inside, holding the phone to his ear and not believing what he was hearing. She imagined he felt as dizzy as she did.

'What did you say?' he croaked.

'I'm your mother, Peter,' Anne repeated firmly, sniffing. 'You were stolen from me in 1975.'

She didn't need to see him to know that this revelation would send his mind spinning out of control.

'What?' He gave a series of unintelligible groans but each spoke of grief. 'Have you been searching for me ever since?'

'No. I was told you were dead. But certain recent events revealed that you were very much alive and I've done nothing since but try and find you.'

'What events?' he breathed.

'I'll tell you all about them if you'll agree to meet with me.'

Anne could barely believe the gift that had just been given to her. An angel must be guarding and guiding her through this time; she had no other explanation for the stroke of luck. She had Peter within her grasp, and this changed everything.

'When?'

'Now.'

'Where are you?'

'Opposite your house. Just look outside the front door for the light blue car. That's me.'

She heard him pause, heard the rustle of his movements as he obviously moved to the front door. She spotted his outline behind the glass on one side of the door.

'I can see you, Peter.' She lifted her hand in hesitant greeting but he moved away.

'What do you want?'

'I should think that's obvious.' Anne spoke softly, not wanting to frighten him. 'Forgive me the shock I've caused you, but I want to look at my son now that I've heard his beautiful voice. I want to listen to his story, learn about his life — the things I've been denied these last thirty years.'

'This is too much,' he moaned. 'I only found out a day or so ago that I wasn't formally adopted.'

'I can imagine the state of shock you're in — believe me, I'm only just coming to terms with you being alive myself — and I'm sure that having me turn up on your doorstep is unnerving. I'm sorry.'

'I don't know what to say.'

'Just don't be scared of me. I have grieved for you for twenty-nine years, Peter, and now I've been given the gift of your life. Will you at least let me meet you?'

She waited through the difficult silence as her son made up his mind.

'Okay, I'll be out in a minute,' he said finally.

42

Kate flicked through the Brighton directory, looking for the Rottingdean address. Jack guided the car through the 'Sunday driver' traffic, cursing as he went, heading for the historic coastal village that was more conservative than its big cousin, Brighton.

'Want to put the siren on?' she asked.

His mouth twisted as he thought. 'No, we'll only alarm him more. Best to arrive quietly.'

'What if she's already got to him?'

He shrugged. 'She'll have left a trail, I hope. This sort of villagey community would likely have nosey neighbours everywhere. Someone will have seen something, but I don't even want to think about the fact that she may beat us to him.'

Kate held her peace. The way Anne McEvoy had outsmarted them thus far left no doubt in her mind that she would almost certainly get to Flynn before they did.

Finally they pulled up not far away from number thirty-two.

'Go round the back if you can, Kate. I'll do my utmost not to spook him, but you never know.'

She nodded, stepped over the low fence and looked for a lane or gate that might lead her around to the rear of the house. Jack took the stone stairs two at a time and rang the doorbell as he searched for his warrant card. Nothing happened, so he rang again. A woman's voice called back that she was coming.

The door opened and a small woman in her late fifties, he guessed, with a round, kindly face, answered the door. She was wiping her hands on her apron. 'Yes?'

'Mrs Flynn?'

'Yes.'

'I'm Detective Chief Inspector Jack Hawksworth. Is your husband home?'

'No, he's not,' she said, frowning. Disappointment knifed through Jack at her words. 'What's this about?' she added, reaching for a pair of glasses that hung at her neck so she could read his card.

'I need to speak with Garvan Flynn urgently. Do you know where he is?'

Kate appeared, shrugging, unable to get around to the back of the house. Jack shook his head slightly to tell her they were unlucky.

'This is Detective Inspector Kate Carter, Mrs Flynn.'

The woman nodded at Kate. 'My husband's with our family in Hove. I've just come from there, although I think he was going out.'

'Do you know where?'

'Yes, to our son's house. Look, I'm not answering any more questions about my family until you tell me what this is about.'

Jack sighed. 'May we come in, Mrs Flynn?'

Peter sat stiffly alongside Anne in her rented hatchback. Even small talk seemed too difficult for either of them.

Despite the enormous surge of helpless emotion that engulfed her when her son approached the car, Anne was determined not to spook him by bombarding him with questions, or worse, hysterical tears. She swallowed them back ruthlessly. Touching him, as she wanted to, felt impossible even though he sat so close in the cramped space.

He was tall and a bit raffish, like his namesake, her father. She had to assume his symmetrical features were more like his own father's, the man she had never seen clearly. The blue eyes were hers, though. She hadn't seen Peter smile yet, just that self-conscious twitch of the mouth when he opened the car door. Nonetheless that small, shy gesture had reminded her so much of herself from childhood.

'What do you want?' he finally said when the apprehension of what was ahead and the pressure of silence became overwhelming.

'Just to talk with you,' she answered carefully. She was in love with his voice, with him, already. 'How about a walk on the seafront,' she offered. 'We can talk privately there, and there's also something I want to show you.'

'What?'

'You'll see. It will speak more clearly to you than anything I can explain.'

Anne was readjusting her plan as she spoke, her mind racing ahead as to how to make the most of this unexpected gift of Peter alone with her. She didn't want to hurt him, but he was also her key to finding Flynn. It was a struggle to balance the love for him and the hate for his father.

'Okay,' he replied, uncertain. 'But first, tell me my birthday.'

She nodded, glad that, despite all the trauma and emotional upheaval, he was sharp enough to make her earn this. 'That's easy, Peter. You were born on a stormy night in August 1975, in Brighton.' She gave him the exact date.

His mobile phone rang. He looked at it. 'It's home.'

'Leave it for a few minutes, will you? Hear me out and then you can tell them whatever you want.'

He nodded, pressed the button that told the caller his phone was busy.

Jack listened to Clare Flynn talking to her relatives. He could tell from her side of the conversation that her husband had already left.

'I know you said he'd gone. I just hoped he might have come back for some reason ... Yes, I've tried Peter's mobile. It's busy and then it went to that recorded message thing. I'll have to keep trying, I suppose.' A pause. 'I'm telling you, I don't know. They could have missed each other because Peter was here. I can see he's made a pot of tea, although it's untouched ... Look, I'll call you when I hear something. Let me get off the phone now, I don't want to keep these people waiting any longer. Bye.' She turned to the detectives. 'Shall I try his mobile again?'

'Yes,' Kate said. 'In fact, can you give us your husband's and son's mobile numbers, please?'

'My husband doesn't carry a mobile, says he doesn't want to be that contactable,' Clare said, before reciting Peter's number.

Anne had just parked when Peter's phone sounded again. 'Home again, I presume?' she said.

He nodded, having glanced at the screen. 'My mother can be relentless. I'll send the busy signal again, but you'd better start talking. I'll give you one hour.'

'Fine,' Anne replied. She would need far less if her rudimentary plan worked. 'Walk with me.'

'What's in the urn?' he asked, nodding at the vessel in her hand.

'Trust me. This is for appearances only. You'll see.'

Peter shrugged. This whole experience was weird; what was one more strange element? 'Why West Pier?' he asked.

Although she found it hard to, Anne smiled. 'I know you think you've never set foot on it in your life, but believe me, this place is as intrinsic to your history as it is to mine.'

He frowned. 'We can't go on there. It's completely closed off. It's been declared unsafe.'

'It's only closed to those without a key,' she said and held one up in her fingers. Earlier that day, Anne had spun a poignant tale to the woman who owned The Rock Shop at the start of the pier on the promenade. Anne's story about the husband who had died far too early and her need to cast his ashes from the pier where they had first met as childhood sweethearts had touched the shopkeeper's romantic nerve and she'd agreed to give Anne her key, on the proviso Anne would deny it if ever asked.

Anne slid the key into the gate's padlock and turned it. 'Come on,' she said, pushing the gate open and waving her son inside.

Jack's sixth sense was sending him all manner of alarming messages. 'Has he turned his mobile off, Mrs Flynn?'

'No, it rings and then just goes to his voicemail,' she said. 'I don't understand all this new-fangled technology.'

'He's pressing the busy signal, sir,' Kate warned.

Jack knew she was right. Peter was deliberately not answering his mother's calls. 'And you think he's with his father?' he said to the worried woman.

'He has to be. Where else could they both be? Perhaps they went for a pint together. I told you, there's been some bad feeling in the house but my son hasn't done anything wrong.'

'Mrs Flynn, we haven't told you everything. We want to assure you that we're not here for Peter.'

'Then tell me. Why are the police in my house?'

Jack began the story of what they knew. His listener sat silent, tears streaming down her face, as he spoke. Kate moved to sit alongside her and took Clare's hand when Jack got to the most difficult part of his story about a heavily pregnant woman being abducted and attacked, the baby all but stomped from her body as it laboured to be born.

'I'm so sorry you had to learn this from us,' Jack finished.

Clare Flynn wept. 'This is not my Garvan you speak of.'

'Mrs Flynn, again I'm so sorry,' Jack said earnestly, 'but we suspect your husband to be the ringleader of this gang who abducted and raped Anne McEvoy when she was fourteen in 1974, then abducted her again when she was heavily pregnant and forced her to deliver the child.'

The woman wept harder.

'Clare, the baby was a son and we believe he was stolen by Garvan Flynn. Your son is called Peter, isn't he?' She didn't answer, didn't need to. 'He's not your son, is he? He's adopted. And he's twenty-nine? The timeline fits.'

'He told me he bought him,' she whispered, her lips almost white, her complexion suddenly colourless. 'I wanted a child so badly. I couldn't get pregnant. It was Garvan, he had a low sperm count we were told. But it was lots of things, I'm sure. Pressure from my parents, them wanting a grandchild, a grandson! He told me a man got Peter for us from a woman who had plenty of kids she didn't want. This was just one more she didn't care about. We gave him a loving home ... a good life ...' She was sobbing.

'We understand your position, Clare,' Kate assured. 'You couldn't have known the truth.' She decided it was best not to mention that Clare and Garvan Flynn had deliberately and knowingly broken the law in taking a child that was not theirs.

'But I believed him!' Clare cried. 'I had no reason to doubt him. He said a man in the pub told him he could get a baby. It was an unwanted pregnancy to a drug addict mother. She'd already had four kids to different fathers. According to this man, she didn't even know who Peter's father was.'

'Well, a paternity test will probably prove that Garvan is Peter's biological father,' Jack said. 'The likeness is there in these photos you have around the room.'

'I always thought so, although I tried to tell myself that Peter was too tall, that his smile was nothing like Garvan's, that his personality was much brighter and outward-going. I convinced myself he was someone else's child, ignored the similarities in colouring and features.' She began sobbing again, gasping as she spoke haltingly. 'Garvan is a gentle man. He couldn't have done these things you speak of.'

'It was many years ago. He's not the same person now, I'm sure. He was the same age then that Peter is now. Was he an angry younger man?'

She nodded. 'He got very frustrated that I couldn't fall pregnant. He'd go out drinking. He was very angry for a while and we even separated for a short time in 1974.'

Both Jack and Kate straightened. 'When in 1974, Mrs Flynn, can you recall?' Kate asked.

'Oh yes, it's the only time we were ever apart. It was winter — all of October and November. We got back together by early December . . . you know,' she shrugged, 'in time for Christmas.'

'And now?' Kate asked.

'He doesn't drink, he doesn't smoke, he doesn't do anything wrong. He's a wonderful father — has been since day one. He loves his family. We love him.'

'Did he smoke thirty years ago, Clare?' Jack asked. 'Did he roll his own cigarettes using tobacco from a tin?'

'Yes,' she stammered. 'He did.'

Jack glanced at Kate. 'Clare, have you received any odd phone calls from a woman calling herself Anne McEvoy, Sophie Fenton, or any woman you didn't know but seemed to know your husband?'

Clare shook her head. 'No, nothing.'

'But you think Peter was here this afternoon, while you and your husband were with your relatives?'

'I know he was. He has his own key. I can tell he was here because he always leaves the used teabags in the sink. His father and I break them open and use them on the garden. It's our routine. Peter just tips the pot out and leaves them. Besides, I can smell his aftershave.'

'I smelt that too. I think it's Fahrenheit,' Kate said, trying to keep Clare Flynn chatting.

'That's right, the deep orange bottle. His father used to use Brut 33 a long time ago. He said it was strong enough to cover the smell of the fish he handled — he was a great angler, my husband — but I hated the smell of it. He doesn't wear aftershave now. Hasn't worn it since then. Doesn't go fishing much, either.'

'"Then" being when he came home with Peter?' Jack prompted.

She nodded. 'Garvan seemed to change overnight from the moment we had Peter. We left Hove, moved into this house. My parents helped us to buy it. All our old folks are dead now but they went to their graves knowing they had that precious grandson. And Peter knew them, loved them.'

'They knew how he came to you?'

She nodded. 'My parents did. It's not that they didn't care how he came to us, but they knew how desperate we were and that this baby had a terrible home. If he'd stayed with his no-good mother — not that she wanted him — he'd have been lucky to get through school and not turn out a yob or a tramp.' She looked at them, apology and beseechment in her expression.

Jack kept his face deliberately impassive, but inside he was thinking about Sophie Fenton and how the actions not just of Garvan Flynn but of his extended and very selfish family had shaped a serial killer.

Clare sniffed again. 'He left his job, he stopped fishing, gave up smoking and drinking. He stopped being an angry man. Everything changed. We were happy again.' She looked up, her red weepy eyes defiant. 'He is not a bad man. He has been nothing but an attentive and loving father, a good husband.'

'That may be, Mrs Flynn, but we believe your husband was also responsible for serious criminal offences during his late twenties, and his actions then might have prompted what is occurring now with the serial killer we're hunting.'

She shook her head vehemently. 'I can't believe that, Mr Hawksworth. I can't.'

Jack sat forward. He was worried that Clare Flynn, already pale and trembling, might collapse if he pushed her too hard, but time had run out for them. He covered her hand with his. 'Think, Mrs Flynn, please. Where could Garvan be now?'

The house phone rang.

43

As Jack was questioning Mrs Flynn, her adopted son was looking with wonder around the ruin that was the West Pier concert hall.

Anne noted his interest. 'This used to be like a fairytale palace in its heyday. During the 1920s, amazing musicals and events were held here, including open-air dancing.'

'It's so sad to see it in such a state,' Peter agreed, 'but why have you brought me here?'

Anne sat down on a rickety old workbench and unscrewed the top of a bottle of spring water she'd pulled from her backpack. 'Drink, Peter?' She watched him hesitate. 'It's okay, I brought another one for myself,' she said, drinking thirstily from the other bottle she'd carefully marked. 'Sit down, I'll tell you everything,' she said, passing him the water.

'Thanks,' he said and lowered himself gingerly to avoid dirtying his pants too much. He took a long draught from the bottle.

Anne sighed. It had begun.

★ ★ ★

Garvan Flynn banged again on the door of Peter's flat, an empty gesture born of frustration. He knew his son wasn't hiding from him or ignoring him — he simply wasn't there.

He pulled out the mobile phone Clare didn't know he owned and reluctantly dialled home. His wife answered, her voice shaky, as if she'd been crying.

'It's me, what's wrong?' he said and was bombarded by a torrent of weepy information. He could barely make out her words but understood enough to know that his past had finally caught up with him.

A man's voice suddenly spoke. 'Garvan Flynn?'

Flynn remained silent, frozen to the spot.

'Mr Flynn, this is DCI Jack Hawksworth from Scotland Yard. We need to speak with you in connection with —'

Garvan clicked off without thinking, terror flooding his veins. They couldn't trace him, surely. And his wife didn't know his number, didn't even know he had this phone. He leaned against Peter's door, his heart pounding so hard in his chest he was sure he could hear it.

Peter. He had to talk to Peter.

His son's was the only number he kept in the address book of his phone. He found it and hit the automatic dial button, desperate to get to his boy before anyone else told Peter anything about the past. If Peter's phone was on, he'd answer. He would never ignore his father calling from his rarely used mobile.

'Hello, Pierrot,' a woman's voice said. Garvan's shock was complete. He slid down the door to the ground, his legs buckling with fright.

'Who is this?' he said in a hissed whisper, his eyes wide with fear. His mind had already computed that only one female in the whole world knew to call him by that name.

'I'm offended you don't remember the mother of your son. And he's such a handsome fellow — much taller and gentler than you.'

Garvan's eyes widened further. 'You've seen him?' he croaked.

'Seen him?' She laughed, a cruel sound. 'I'm with him.'

'With him?' Garvan nearly choked on the words.

'He's not feeling terribly well, Pierrot, but then you only have yourself to blame for that.'

Rage of the kind Flynn hadn't felt in almost thirty years coursed through him. 'Don't you dare touch a hair on his head,' he began, his voice laced with menace.

Anne matched him. 'Or what? You know what I've already done to your precious Jesters Club. They're all dead, Pierrot — every one of them except you. They all died weeping, begging for forgiveness, as is right. If you want to save your son, Pierrot, you know where to find me. Just think back to where his life began.'

The line went dead in his ear and Flynn screamed with impotent fury.

Clare Flynn was no longer making sense. She'd disintegrated into a wailing heap and Jack realised there would be little information from her in the foreseeable future. He left Kate to organise a family member to come and sit with her, and to contact the local police. He stepped outside to drag in some fresh air and to calm himself.

His gut was screaming at him that not only had Clare Flynn been right about her son being here this morning, but that Anne McEvoy had got to the house before they had and persuaded Peter Flynn to accompany her.

He sat on the stoop and tried to clear his mind and allow his thoughts to organise themselves into a logical pattern. Anne was obviously making her play for Garvan Flynn, her final target, but he couldn't second-guess her plan. He could understand her need to see her son, but entangling him at this stage didn't make sense. Unless, of course, Peter was the lure. She had been helpless with Peter as a baby, but now he was an adult and she was the aggressor, baiting a loving father to come and rescue his son. She would have Pierrot in her trap, could make him bargain his own life for his son's. Yes, that had symmetry and meaning. But where was she?

His phone rang. It was Sharpe and there were no salutations. 'Deegan wants to launch the investigation tomorrow morning. I don't have to tell you what that's going to mean.'

Jack closed his eyes. 'We're so close, sir. You have to stall him. You can't shut me down. If they pull me off now, the investigation goes to hell. I'm the only one who's seen Anne McEvoy.'

It was a desperate pitch; a very thin premise for the Ghost Squad to cut him any slack.

'I'll do what I can,' Sharpe said wearily. 'Deegan's not telling me what he's got on you, Jack, but I sure hope he's rattling a chain that's not attached to anything.'

'I presume he's going to try and blame me for Paul Conway's death somehow, sir.'

'My thoughts exactly.'

'I've got nothing to hide, sir. I only wish I knew why Conway's death means so much to Deegan that he'd chase it so hard after all these years.'

He heard his Super sigh. 'I agree. I'll hold them off, but I don't think we'll have more than twenty-four hours, Jack. You know how Ghost Squad works.' Sharpe sounded suddenly older. 'So tell me some good news.'

Jack told him everything that had happened this afternoon.

'You spoke to him?' Sharpe repeated, incredulous.

'Kate's having the call traced but we already know it was Flynn. Wherever he was when he called home, he won't be calling from there again. Tracing that location is pointless.'

'Find that woman, Jack. This time tomorrow you're likely to be suspended.'

Jack didn't even bother to say goodbye. There was nothing more to be said. He rang the ops room and was promptly put through to Sarah, who had more news.

'The van's been found at Gatwick Airport, sir.'

'Have you checked if she's rented a car?'

'Yes, but no Anne McEvoy or Sophie Fenton on the records. However, the girl who was on early this morning is being contacted at home. We're hoping she may remember a woman from the early hours. Perhaps another name was used.'

'Good,' he said, happy that Sarah was such a stickler for detail.

'In the meantime, we're going through the motions of checking rail, bus and so on. But she seems to be cashed up, so tracing her via credit card doesn't strike me as an option.'

'She could have hitched a ride back to Brighton, for all we know,' Jack said helplessly. 'How are you holding up?'

'I'm fine, sir. What else can I do to help? I spoke to Kate about ten minutes ago and she's briefed me on where you're at down there.'

'Nothing. Just back up Kate with whatever she needs and keep Swamp and Brodie appraised.'

'What about you, chief? What are you going to do now?'

'Rack my brains to think where Anne McEvoy might be luring her prey to.'

'If she stays true to her previous MO, sir, it'll be another location that's meaningful to her past.'

'But we know she killed her victims somewhere safe before dumping the bodies in that meaningful place. She could be anywhere in Brighton or Hove.'

'She had the van to do her gruesome work before,' Sarah mused. 'She doesn't have it any more. And she knows we're close now. Perhaps she'll risk it. If she's using their son as her bargaining power, perhaps she'll force Flynn to meet her.'

'Maybe,' Jack said, frowning. 'I need some time to think. Get on to Tandy, see if he has any ideas. Try the others and get back to me if anyone has any inspiration.'

Jack rubbed his face, trying to clear his mind. Kate opened the door and came out onto the step.

'She's in the bathroom trying to get herself together,' she said.

'Don't trust her. I made that mistake with Phil Bowles.'

Kate nodded. 'Her cousin, Sheila, is on her way over. Should be here very soon, but I think we should call a doctor.'

Jack quickly brought Kate up to speed on Sarah's news.

'She won't hurt her son,' Kate reassured. 'It's his father she wants.'

'I'll try the boy's phone again,' Jack said, standing. 'Perhaps he'll answer this time. Keep an eye on Mrs Flynn.'

44

Anne looked down at Peter's face. In repose it reminded her strongly of her father's and she felt an intense love for this young man she'd been denied access to. And, in equal measure, she felt fury towards the rapist who had sired and then stolen him.

The drug had worked quickly on Peter and he was now asleep, bound, his mouth gagged with duct tape. She hated to do this to him but she had no choice. It was crucial that Pierrot believed she would hurt their son in her madness if she chose to.

She smiled sadly. Hurt Peter? All she wanted to do was hug him. But she wasn't even going to get that pleasure. She'd felt only despair when she saw him realise he'd been drugged, saw him lose control of his movements and heard his voice slurring. She watched the disbelief and fear register in his eyes as she gave him a potted history of his conception and his birth.

How sad that it had come to this. But he was her precious ace, the card that had turned up at just the right time in the deck. It was despicable to use Peter in this manner, but Pierrot had to pay.

Flynn would be here soon — she was sure of it. And he wouldn't call the police and he wouldn't tell the boy's stepmother.

He would be trying to cover his tracks, still vainly hoping that no one ever need know of his sins of the past. She had news for him.

Anne stroked Peter's hair, then pulled her hand away as the emotion released by this simple act threatened to undo her. She briefly flirted with the notion that she could convince Peter to come away with her. There was still time. They'd be starting their relationship twenty-nine years later, but it was better than nothing, surely?

The lone voice that offered up this utopian notion was howled down by all the demons in her mind. She was definitely deluded if she believed Peter would want to set eyes on her again after she'd done this to him. And he didn't need another mother. He had one. One he loved. Anne was a complication he'd prefer not to know about. They were strangers. He wasn't going to run away with her. No, she'd had her precious moments with her son and they would have to be enough to sustain her for however long she had left on this earth.

Ensuring Pierrot's punishment was a far more realistic option than hoping she might be permitted some new and wonderful relationship with her son. She needed to be strong now. Facing Pierrot again wasn't going to be easy.

Casting a final soft glance towards her sleeping son, Anne walked carefully around the ruin of the concert hall, ensuring everything was set, then headed out onto the decaying boards of the pier. She checked for the final time that what she needed was there, wondering whether her luck would hold for this last part of her revenge.

Peter's phone erupted into song and she saw *Home* flash up on the screen. She wondered whether Flynn had gone back to the house in Rottingdean and was trying Peter once again from the landline. She decided to risk it, knowing she could hang up before Jack's team could trace their location.

'Why are you at home, Garvan, and not here bargaining for the life of your son?'

The silence at the other end instantly told her this wasn't Flynn. Perhaps it was the woman who had happily accepted the stolen child and raised it as her own. What she didn't expect was the voice that did speak.

'It's me.'

She tripped and fell against the wall of the concert hall, upsetting the roosting starlings who took off as one into the darkening sky. Anne staggered back inside, her knee momentarily numbed.

'Jack, what a surprise. I'm impressed you've made it this far, but you really must leave well alone now.'

'There's nothing to be gained by this,' he urged. 'I have enough on Garvan Flynn to put him away for the rest of his life. Please, don't do whatever it is you have in mind.'

'Why? Are you trying to save me? It's pointless. I've killed three men, Jack. What's one more?'

'Where are you?' he begged and she could hear the desperation in his voice. 'Let me come there.'

'You still see Sophie, don't you? Let me be, Jack. I'm Anne now, and she has unfinished business with Garvan Flynn.'

She hung up and went outdoors again, tossed Peter's mobile phone into the churning sea below. The water had turned charcoal, matching the sky. It was freezing but Anne didn't care. She wanted the dark to wrap itself fully around her.

'We didn't get a trace,' Kate said, obviously preferring to deliver the bad news without any sweetening.

'She's too clever for that,' Jack said, running his fingers through his hair, his expression one of deep frustration. 'How much longer for the cousin to arrive?'

'She said fifteen minutes, so she must be almost here,' Kate replied, glancing at her watch. 'Clare's taken two tablets. She should be asleep soon.'

'Did you tape the conversation?'

Kate nodded. 'Here, I'll play it back.'

They both listened intently as Anne McEvoy's voice warned Jack to leave her be.

'She was outside,' Kate said. 'You can hear the seagulls in the background.'

Jack's eyes had been closed as he listened, praying for a clue. Now they flew open, his mouth agape.

'What?' Kate said, startled.

He shook his head, looked for the car keys. 'I know where she is. Oh god, I've known all along. We all have!' He was babbling. 'Where are the fucking keys?'

'Here,' Kate said, digging them from her pocket and throwing them over. 'What do you mean, you knew all along?'

Jack gave a short, harsh laugh. 'She even told me,' he said, his voice distressed. 'She said to think of her when I looked at her photographs.'

'I don't understand.'

'The missing photos in her flat — that's why she took them. She didn't want us to work it out too soon. They were all of the same place!'

'Where, Jack?'

'The starlings, Kate. Didn't you hear them suddenly above the seagulls? There's only one place in Brighton I know of where starlings roost in those numbers. It's famous for them. I remember now my grandparents telling me about them when I was about four. She's at the West Pier!'

Kate opened her mouth but nothing came out. Jack was already running, calling behind him. 'Get a squad car down there immediately! They are not to move in, I repeat, *not* to move in without my signal. Tell them to wait until they hear from me. If Brodie's still around, tell him to meet me at West Pier. I'm putting my phone on silent. Let ops know.'

He was in the car now.

'Let me come with you,' she said, looking around desperately for the car that would bring Clare's cousin.

'You can't, you have to wait here until help arrives.'

He gunned the engine and gave her a final glance of sympathy. He knew she resented it, but there was no time to worry about hurting people's feelings. He had to get to the pier before this whole sorry mess unfolded.

45

Flynn arrived alone, as she'd known he would. She could hear him coming along the temporary walkway. Anne had already called The Rock Shop, explained to the woman there that she and her son were just watching night come in and that they'd called a friend to pick them up because they were too upset to drive home.

'I'm locking up now. You'll have to hurry,' the woman had said, a note of exasperation creeping into her voice.

'Can I slide the key under the door?' Anne had offered, 'along with my thanks for your trouble?'

'What do you mean?' the woman had asked.

'My son and I would like to leave you a gift. We've put two hundred pounds in an envelope and we're going to return the key in that envelope too, if it's okay with you?'

'I didn't ask for payment,' the woman said, but Anne heard the change in tone from irritation to sheepishness.

'No, you didn't, but we're so grateful to you for giving us this precious time and this chance to fulfil my husband's dream,' she'd lied. 'We want to thank you properly.'

'Alright,' the woman said, melting. 'Thank you — just put the key under the door when you leave. That's fine.'

With the kiosk owner maintaining the secret of their presence on the pier, no one would bother them now. She watched the slightly stooped figure approaching up the makeshift ladder in the murky light and steeled her will to do this right.

Jack had put the flashing light on top of the car but refrained from using the police siren. He needed other motorists to move out of his path as he sped towards West Pier, but he didn't want to alert Anne to his arrival.

He had no idea what he was going to do but hoped his mere presence would derail whatever plan she had in mind for Flynn. He agreed with Kate that Anne McEvoy wouldn't harm the son she had borne near on thirty years ago, but her intentions towards Garvan Flynn were far from peaceful. And he wanted Flynn alive and in a position to face the justice he was long overdue.

Anne had dragged her sleeping son gently to the back of the concert hall, leaving a wide space between him and Garvan's arrival at the northern entrance.

'Stop there!' she ordered. Flynn blinked into the powerful torchlight she trained on his face as he stepped fully into the hall. 'Welcome back, Pierrot.'

She looked at the paunchy, middle-aged man who had once terrified the daylights out of her. His hair was cropped close to his head these days and she imagined it was white now. She had never seen his face clearly before and realised now how nonedescript and plain it was. Peter's good looks obviously derived from her genes then, and her son simply echoed some of his father's features. She felt nothing for Garvan other than revulsion. Power rushed through her as she realised she was no longer scared by him.

'Where's my son?' he demanded, the reedy voice filled with anxiety.

'Right here,' she said, switching off the torch and lighting the single candle she had prepared nearby. She held her ugly blade close to Peter's throat, thanking her lucky stars that he would never know she had done this.

Flynn sank to his knees, fear overwhelming him. 'Don't hurt him, I beg you.'

'You beg me?' she taunted. 'You have the nerve to beg anything of me!'

'Please, I'll do whatever you want. Give you anything,' he blubbered. 'Just don't hurt my son.'

She nodded, her smile cynical. '*Your* son. What about *our* son, Pierrot? Tell me why you called him Peter.'

Peter began to stir, his eyes flickering open. She snapped the blade away.

'What?' Flynn said, confused.

'You heard. Wake up, Peter, listen to your father.'

Peter's eyes opened fully. He struggled against his bonds, made angry sounds behind his gag.

'Be still!' she ordered.

'I ... I think you murmured it after ...' Flynn's voice trailed off.

'After you'd finished jumping on my belly and punching me, all the time knowing I was in labour, trying to deliver my son. Do you hear that, Peter? Tell him, Garvan. Tell him what you did to me, or so help me, I'll do what you fear most. Don't push me. You know how many have already died by my hand. Tell him!'

And Garvan Flynn did, in halting, weeping tones. He confessed to his son what he had inflicted on teenage Anne McEvoy when he began stalking her from school. He told his son of his impotence, his inability to impregnate his wife, and the unimaginable pressure his mother-in-law in particular had visited upon him. How she had ridiculed him and made him feel worthless in their family. He told his son of the separation from Clare during the winter of 1974, when everything had boiled over and his world had turned dark. How he had befriended the boys and brought them under his spell and finally gone ahead with his hideous plan to rape Anne and prove that he could sustain an erection. He told of his shock upon realising that Anne McEvoy had become pregnant.

'I doubted myself so much. By the time your mother and I separated, son, I couldn't even get it up. I don't know half of what your grandmother was whispering to her, but she was poisoning her against me and all because she was the only one in the family without grandchildren.' He gave a helpless sound of disgust. 'I hated her.'

'Tell him everything,' Anne said coldly.

'I knew I was the father,' he wept, 'because none of the others had raped her. Only me. I wanted to kill her when I saw her huge belly and your mother so grief-stricken.' The old anger slowly emerged through his tears. 'I wanted this woman dead. I couldn't believe she was going to have my baby, the child I couldn't give your mother. I couldn't let your mother know, son. I couldn't disgrace her any further than I already had. I tried to hide behind the teenagers — I thought things might escalate if I got them drunk. I hoped they might do something stupid, but they didn't. Fools. I had to do it.'

'Tell Peter that you planned to kill him too,' Anne said. 'Let him hear it from your lips.'

Flynn's voice was ragged now. 'I didn't know what was going to happen. I just felt such rage that this woman was pregnant by me, and the one who should be remained barren. I was hoping you'd both die somehow. Until you arrived, that is. You were so perfect, so beautiful, so helpless. And suddenly it hit me that you were mine. I wanted to keep you. I saw how it could be if I took you home and gave you to your mother, how happy everyone would be.'

Peter shook his head in despair and loathing at what he was hearing.

'I told this woman that you were dead,' Flynn went on. 'She was near enough dead herself, and I figured she wouldn't last through the night as she was bleeding heavily. I knew to wait for the afterbirth, and once I'd tossed that in the sea I let you have a few minutes at her breast, and then I took you. I was already in love with you.' He shook his head helplessly. 'By the time I picked you up, I thought she was dead and I was relieved.'

'Tell him about his name!' Anne screamed. The blade cut into her palm, she held it so tightly. Blood dripped to the ground.

'Peter was her chosen name for you. She murmured it, and I thought she died with that as her last breath. It seemed right to call you by that name.'

'And you're too stupid to know that the hideous clown name you chose when you attacked me — the French "Pierrot" you were so proud of — translates to Peter in English,' Anne said. 'The stench of your crime has followed your son throughout his whole life.'

Garvan broke into deep sobs. 'It was nearly thirty years ago. I was a different person then. I'm an old man, Anne. The anger has gone. I've been a good father to your son — our son. I've raised him well. I want to say I'm sorry, but I can see it won't be enough. I want to make amends but I don't know what to do. What do you want me to do?' he begged.

Anne gathered her composure. Night had fallen. It was time.

'I want you to do the honourable thing. It's the only way to make amends to me. Do you see that can next to you?'

Flynn looked, nodded dumbly.

'Tip the contents over yourself.'

Peter began to panic, shaking his head, screaming behind the duct tape.

'Hurry, Garvan, or I will slash his throat. I should tell you that I feel nothing for Peter,' she lied. 'I hate him as much as I hate you.'

As she said those terrible words, she felt something die inside her. She couldn't care less what happened now to her, but she intended to see Garvan pay with his blood.

'Do it!' she screamed at the haggard man who suddenly looked a century old.

He reached for the can and splashed a sizeable portion of the petrol over himself, the potent-smelling fumes filling the concert hall.

Anne picked up a lighter and a glass bottle. Petrol sloshed around inside it and a dampened cloth formed a wick to help fashion a rudimentary bomb.

'And now we'll cleanse your father of his sins,' she said softly to Peter, who was whimpering on the floor, helpless.

'Any last words for your son?' she taunted Flynn. 'At least I have the grace to grant you that, which is more than you offered me.'

46

Jack finally reached the seafront. He drove the car up onto the pavement outside the kiosk and switched off the police light. He hit the stairs by The Rock Shop at a full run and was on the beach in moments, searching for the temporary ladder and walkway that would give him access to whatever was waiting for him on West Pier.

He could hear pigeons cooing in their roosts beneath the decking as he climbed and the odd haunting squawk of a gull. The starlings were all mercifully silent for the night beneath the damaged roof of the concert hall. He prayed that their earlier cries had given him sufficient warning to stop the insanity that was surely unfolding inside. He tiptoed across the old and precarious timber strutting that, on other piers, he remembered gazing between when he was a small child, marvelling at the sea below. There was no wonderment now, only fear for what was taking place in the concert hall where he could now see the thin guttering light from what he presumed was a candle.

Jack thought of the array of haunting photos that Sophie had framed and put up in her apartment. He recalled how he had admired them and she had admitted that they were her favourite artworks amongst what even a layman could see was a quality line-up of art on her walls. Jack remembered how sad her voice had sounded when she had agreed with him that, West Pier's pedigree and loneliness aside, it was beautiful because of its strength — battling against the elements, still standing after all these years. He realised now that she saw herself reflected in West Pier. Her connection to it was obvious because of the abduction, the horrific attack and her son being born and, she thought, killed here. But it was more than that. Bittersweet, he thought. She sees herself as wrecked and battered like the pier, but still standing, still being strong.

He turned off his pen light and continued his stealthy approach in darkness, praying he didn't step into a gaping hole or on rotten wood that gave way beneath him. He could hear a voice. It was Sophie, he thought sadly.

'At least I have the grace to grant you that much, which is more than you offered me.'

And now he could smell petrol. Jack's mind made the instant connection and he forgot about being silent and barged through the concert hall doors, taking in the scene of a man on his knees and two people at the end of the once grand Victorian concert hall. The starlings once again took flight.

'Ah, Jack, they gave me away the first time, didn't they?' she said in welcome.

Jack nodded, saddened to see her golden hair dyed a deep brown. The petrol fumes were overwhelming. 'Your lovely art and the sound of birds,' he said, moving forward slowly. 'Two beautiful things connected with such ugliness.' He arrived by the side of the kneeling Flynn. 'Look at him. He's a pathetic little man, he's not worth it. Don't do this.'

'Darling Jack. You can't save me and the world,' she said sadly. 'This is my son, Peter, by the way. He was ripped from my body and stolen from me.' She turned to Peter. 'I'm sorry you've only known me like this. DCI Hawksworth here can give you a different picture of me. I would have been a great mum to you, and you should know that I loved you and wanted you with all my heart, even though you were conceived in such pain and brutality.'

She pushed him away, expertly slashing at the bonds that tied his legs and hands.

Then she stood up, brandishing the lighter and the Molotov cocktail. 'Step away, Jack. This isn't your fight.'

'It is! I'm going to convict this man. I'm going to ensure justice is done. Not your way, Anne, but the right way.'

'This is the right way! He deserves nothing less.'

She flicked on the lighter's flame. Peter, who was leaning groggily against the wall, gave a yell and fell to his knees as he tried to get back to Anne to stop her.

'Peter, wait!' It was Garvan Flynn. 'Let it be, son. This is my lot.'

'Oh, very gallant,' Anne mocked. She glanced at her watch. 'Peter, can I suggest you run, because we're out of time. Please don't try and do anything heroic because I can smash this bottle and toss this lighter quicker than you can reach me and we'll all go up. The thing is, I don't care about living but you've got a reason to live, Peter, okay? You probably have many reasons. Someone you love, perhaps?'

She saw that she'd said the right thing, noticed the fear for someone register in his eyes.

'Go, Peter, that's right,' she said, watching him edge away along the wall. 'Run, my son, run away from all of this. Go to the person you call Mother and tell her what happened and that it is good riddance. Your father is bad, Peter, don't mourn him too hard.' She could see Peter was in shock, and confused too, the drug still affecting him, but he was moving and in the right direction, away from her.

'I won't warn you again,' she said, turning to Jack. 'Step away from him and get my son away from here.'

The sound of men shouting came out of the darkness and torches flickered in the near distance. Jack recognised Brodie's voice. There was nothing else for it; he grabbed the petrol can and tipped the contents over himself.

'What are you doing?' Anne shrieked.

'Brodie?' Jack yelled, for once glad that his team had disobeyed his orders.

Cam arrived, another two policemen behind him, all crowding through the small doorway. 'Hawk!'

'Get Peter Flynn out of here and then back off.' Cam began to say something. 'That's an order!' Jack barked. He leaned down and grabbed Flynn's arm. 'Stand up, Mr Flynn.'

'Jack!' Anne said, her eyes wide with fear at last. 'Don't do this. Don't make me sacrifice you.' She watched a plainclothes officer pull a struggling Peter Flynn away. 'Get him away from here,' she screamed. 'We're going up, I warn you. Everything you see around you has been doused with petrol.'

'You'll have my death on your conscience as well,' Jack said, his eyes stinging from the petrol. 'I don't think you want that.'

She shook her head ruefully. 'You still think I'm Sophie and that I have a conscience. Goodbye, Jack.'

Jack watched in horror as she lit the soaked bundle of rag that acted as a makeshift wick. It ignited instantly and as she pulled her arm back, he saw the despair etched on her face.

'Sophie!' he screamed, before he grabbed Flynn and blindly ran, just seeing out of the corner of his eye that Anne McEvoy had hurled the bottle in their direction. Jack heard the glass shatter and the dull explosion, but he was running, dragging a terrified Garvan Flynn alongside him. He chanced a glance over his shoulder as flames erupted all around the concert hall and then, without allowing himself to wonder if it was possible, he ran them both straight at the larger French windows on the south-eastern side of the hall.

His prayers were answered as the windows splintered on impact. He and Flynn were through, the flames arcing after their petrol-soaked bodies. It was four long strides to the edge of the pier. Jack had barely a moment to notice the serpent-entwined lamppost before he hit the rotten railing.

Flynn hesitated.

'Jump or burn,' Jack yelled into the terrified man's face and suddenly they were falling, the roar of burning timber and exploding glass surrounding them.

The two bodies fell the six or so metres towards the churning seawater in a tangle of limbs and yells. Jack had a second to notice that Flynn's head was on fire but didn't register his own left arm was also ablaze.

They hit the water hard, their shapes backlit by the burning concert hall, as if they were two spent fireworks descending into oblivion. Jack felt something give and thought it was in his leg but couldn't be sure, and then mercifully everything went dark.

47

He heard whispering voices from far away long before he realised he had regained consciousness. His throat was parched and yet he could taste saltwater, smell burning timber and flesh, hear the roar of flames over the whispering. Jack opened his eyes to slits but was assaulted by the painfully bright light that greeted him and instantly shut them again. He groaned as a new sensation of agony, sharp and deep, emanated from somewhere he couldn't pinpoint — his foot perhaps?

'He's awake. Can you tell them, please,' someone said softly nearby and he was aware of a door opening, the whirr of a machine around him and then footsteps.

A cool hand touched his own lightly and he turned his head gingerly towards that small comfort. His neck ached.

'Jack,' the person whispered and he risked opening his eyes again.

'Kate?'

'Hello, you.' He could see her eyes were watering. 'It's good to have you back.' She tried to smile away the tears. 'The gang's all here.'

'Chief,' Swamp said, flicking his finger in a salute.

'Hey, Hawk — that was some leap but I don't think our Olympic dive team want you,' Brodie said, grinning wryly.

'Hi, Sarah,' Jack said for her. She looked too anxious to give any salutation. He glanced around at them all. 'I am alive, aren't I? You all look so worried.'

Everyone gave less awkward smiles now.

'You've been unconscious since Brodie hauled you from the sea on Sunday night, Hawk,' Swamp said. 'It's Tuesday, midday.'

'You've smashed an ankle and done a fairly decent job of burning your left hand,' Kate explained.

'You have a great bedside manner,' he croaked. 'You'd make a good nurse.'

'The uniforms itch,' she replied archly. 'You've cracked a rib or two as well, so no dancing for you for a while.'

'Or diving,' Brodie quipped.

Jack took his hand from beneath Kate's and flipped Brodie the bird. That got everyone laughing, but only Kate realised that he slipped his hand back to its same comfy spot under hers.

A nurse bustled in, all starched and crisp efficiency. 'How are you feeling, Mr Hawksworth?'

'Shitty,' he replied.

'Excellent, marginally better than dead then,' she replied crisply. She offered him a drink through a straw. 'I can't sit you up just yet, with your ribs all beaten up. We'll get to all of that when your visitors have gone, but they've been waiting a long time so I'll let them have a few moments.'

Jack mumbled his thanks.

'Five minutes,' she said, giving them all a look that said not a moment longer.

'Blimey, you've cracked Nurse Ratchet,' Brodie said. 'What happened to sweet, young, well-endowed girls in tiny white uniforms?'

'They're in your sad fantasies only, Cam,' Kate said tiredly but not without some amusement.

Jack found his voice now that his throat had been sluiced with weak cordial that tasted of Tupperware. 'Flynn?'

'We got him,' Brodie said. 'He's not well but he'll live and face trial.'

Kate explained. 'He got burned. Apparently he was even more soaked with petrol than you were. His head and face were the worst affected but fortunately for us, although he looks like a freak, it's all relatively superficial according to first reports. But then hospitals are used to serious burns so their idea of superficial probably just means you don't need years of skin grafts. The fact that one side of his face has melted and he has no hair isn't considered their problem.'

'Tell someone who cares,' Jack said, relieved. 'And the son?'

'We got him out before it all went up,' Brodie said. 'He's pretty messed up emotionally, but he's given us a statement based on everything his father confessed in front of him. Garvan Flynn can't escape justice this time.'

A freshly awkward silence stole around the bed. Jack decided to make it easy on them.

'Is Anne McEvoy dead?'

'We don't know,' Kate admitted. 'By all rights she should be, considering the concert hall went up like a tinderbox.'

'I presume that was a Molotov cocktail she set it all ablaze with?' Brodie said.

Jack nodded, shards of pain arcing through his body as he moved his neck in a direction it didn't want to go. 'I didn't think she'd throw it.'

'You'd soaked yourself in petrol. It could have been much worse if she'd really aimed it at you,' Kate said, and he was grateful to her for trying to make him feel easier about his lover's actions.

'When will we know?'

'The SOCO team is crawling all over the place now.'

'Is anything left of the pier?'

Kate squeezed his uninjured hand. 'No, Jack. They're going to salvage what they can, I imagine. A lot of the ironwork can be saved but the pier itself is a burnt skeleton. What is left, the weather will finish off. I'm sorry.'

'All those starlings have lost their home,' he said, his mind wandering.

A knock at the door revealed that Superintendent Martin Sharpe had also travelled down to the Brighton General Hospital to check on his DCI.

'Morning, sir,' everyone said at once, standing to attention.

'Please,' he said, 'relax, and well done to all of you.'

Swamp nudged Brodie and Sarah nodded.

'Excuse us, sir. Nurse Ratchet has put us on a deadline anyway. Be warned,' Brodie said. 'Coming, Kate?'

'Yeah,' she said, glancing at Jack. 'I might stick around in Brighton today. I don't feel like doing the Dan scene just yet. Need some time to think.' She smiled sadly. 'See you later?'

'That would be nice,' Jack said and a look passed between them. 'Thanks.'

Kate left with the others as Sharpe took up position at the end of the bed and made a show of looking over Jack's charts.

'So, you got your man.'

'At a cost, but yes, sir, I'm very glad he's in custody.'

'They tell me you tipped petrol over yourself to save Flynn before you pulled off some sort of extraordinary leaping stunt. That was pretty heroic, Jack.'

'All very selfish, sir. I wanted to put him behind bars and claim lots of glory for Operation Danube. I figured I'd make Superintendent a lot quicker.'

Sharpe nodded at the dry comment. 'Nevertheless, well above and beyond the call ... and all that.'

Jack wanted to shrug but was too cowardly. He knew the pain was just waiting for him to make a move. 'It all happened so fast,' he admitted. 'I wasn't thinking. I just reacted.'

'Well, that reaction has earned you lots of nods from above.' He sat down. 'We don't know about McEvoy yet. SOCO is hunting for her remains now.' He didn't see Jack wince, or chose not to. 'But either way, you did a good job.'

'Thank you, sir. We all did.'

'I'm told you're pretty beaten up. Why don't you take some time off? Perhaps go on that Australian holiday when you get out of here.'

'I was thinking just the same thing myself.'

'Good, that's settled.'

'What about Deegan?'

Sharpe grinned. 'He's off your back for now, but not out of your life, I suspect.'

'Off my back? How?'

'Your colleague, DI Carter. I presume you told her what was going on?'

'Just a rough outline. She heard us talking on Sunday afternoon. I had to explain after my outburst.'

'Well, good job you did. I gather Kate Carter did some private sleuthing. She knows a bit about DCI Deegan's personal life. Let's just say she put her Monday, while waiting for you to wake up, to good use.' Sharpe winked.

'You have to tell me.'

'Well,' Sharpe began, enjoying the build-up, 'it seems that Deegan and Conway were lovers. He was heartbroken when Conway was killed and, like most of us in that situation, he needed someone to blame.'

'So he blamed me? He took his time.'

'I think your fast rise at the Yard helped him dislike you more, but yes, he knew there was some question over whether you ignored the call from Conway.'

'I was exonerated —' Jack winced in pain from trying to sit up and make his point.

'I know, Jack, I know. But he wanted to dig around and make more of it. Felt there was a case to answer, although heaven knows what triggered it so long after the event. That's what I mean — he's off your back for now but don't get too comfy. I doubt this will go away completely yet.'

'But it's over, is that what you're saying?'

Sharpe nodded. 'Professionally, yes. Kate had a word to him, let him know that she knew he was building a case based on a grudge, that she knew about the affair — and I gather a few other things that she refused to share with me. Anyway, Deegan knows it won't withstand the scrutiny now that his secret's out.'

Jack's frown deepened. 'What do you mean professionally? Why not personally as well?'

'Ah, well, I think you need to catch up with Liz Drummond for the personal bit.' He gave Jack a searching look. 'But not yet, son. You need to get well, get out of here and take that holiday.'

Before Jack could press him, the nurse bustled in. 'Still here?'

'Just leaving,' Sharpe said.

'I should think so,' she said and made shooing gestures.

Sharpe gave Jack a look of helplessness. 'Talk tomorrow, eh?' He winked and nodded towards the nurse and her obvious plans for a bedbath before smiling with sympathy. 'Enjoy.'

Jack felt suddenly too weary to protest. He fell back on his pillow as his boss left him to the nurse's ministrations.

'Oh,' she said, 'this came for you. I said I'd bring it in. Someone loves you,' she beamed, handing him a handwritten envelope. 'Right, I'm just going to get a couple more things and I'll be back for a nice wash down, okay?'

She left him to undo the card awkwardly on his chest with one hand.

It showed a picture of West Pier with a flock of starlings lifting from its roof. Inside was a dried and pressed pale pink tulip — he was sure it was one of the twelve he'd paid through the nose for in Chinatown. The words on the card read:

I hear you made it safely out of the murky Brighton waters. Be well, Jack. Love Sophie x

And, despite all the pain, he smiled.

48

Penelope Baudrier smiled sweetly at the immigration officer when he handed back her passport and then joined the queue to step aboard the ferry from Newhaven in East Sussex to Dieppe in France. From there her plans were sketchy — a few days in Paris to rest, shop, set up a fresh bank account, but it seemed Santorini in Greece called to her.

Why not? she thought. *I've always wanted to see it.*

She pulled on her sunglasses and headed for the outside deck, hoping the wind would blow away the memories of this past month and the smell of smoke that clung to her.

ACKNOWLEDGMENTS

The West Pier, which seemed to be the boundary between the Hove seafront — where I lived on Brunswick Terrace as a child — and Brighton proper, is very much part of my earliest memories. I can remember glorious summer days with our granny taking us onto the pier for special treats. It cost sixpence to enter and every inch of it was a magical land so separate from the humdrum of everyday life. On the pier there was vibrant colour, exotic sights, wild sounds, the incredible experience of fairy floss that has never tasted the same in adulthood, and the red striped helter-skelter that made us scream. There was magic and mystery; it was both sinister and enthralling. One-armed bandits — or fruit machines as we knew them — were the latest hi-tech invention and much of the pleasure of the pier was that sense of leaving behind reality, walking out above the sea and into a land of fantasy.

And so it seemed fitting when I decided to tackle a crime novel, to return to the familiar stomping ground of Brighton, particularly as today the West Pier is such a sad skeleton of its former magnificence. Its brooding, sorrowful presence gave me a perfect setting. To this day, no one has been held accountable for the terrible fire in March 2003 that destroyed it. The mystery surrounding its destruction and the suspicion of arson suited this tale perfectly. I wish the hardworking members of the West Pier Trust every success with their plans to rebuild the grand old lady and I cherished the opportunity, in May 2006, to walk amongst the salvaged items of the pier. They prompted a host of memories — my favourite being to see those lampposts again after thirty-five years, with their entwined, scary serpents.

I've taken lots of liberties in this novel for the sake of story — such as having the 2003 West Pier fire at night, rather than just before 10 a.m.

My sincere thanks to Professor Fred Gray, Dean of the Sussex Institute at Sussex University, member of the West Pier Trust and historian-author on seaside architecture. Our paths crossed by chance and he was a godsend for the early part of this project.

Another stroke of luck — or was it destiny? — brought Anthony Berry into my life. Tony became my partner for every step of the journey through this tale and I couldn't have crafted it without his regular, often daily input of facts and advice, particularly in regard to police procedure.

Thanks also to Dr Michael McEvoy, Dominic Broadwith, Mark Hibbert and Arthur Hazeldine for their help with various aspects of the story at just the right time, and to Samantha Rich and Judy Downs for their early insights into the draft. I'm most grateful to Linda Funnell for her constant guidance, to my editor Nicola O'Shea and to my agent, Chris Lotts. Everyone at HarperCollins has been so enthusiastic about this project — thanks to all for believing in it.

Love and thanks to Sandra and Giles Stone in Hove. Together with their beautiful boys, Jack and George, they helped me to rediscover Hove Park, Western Road, The Lanes, Brighton seafront and various other childhood haunts.

As usual, I'm indebted to the patient understanding of my trio at home, who managed to pretend it's thoroughly normal to be discussing the modus operandi of a serial killer over a pot of tea. — LC